The
Midwife's
Revolt

THE
MIDWIFE'S
REVOLT

JODI DAYNARD

Text copyright © 2015 Jodi Daynard

Published by Lake Union Publishing, Seattle

www.apub.com

Amazon, the Amazon logo, and Lake Union Publishing are trademarks of Amazon.com, Inc., or its affiliates.

ISBN-13: 9781477828007
ISBN-10: 1477828001

Cover design by Elsie Lyons

Library of Congress Control Number: 2014953297

Printed in the United States of America

I desire you would Remember the Ladies, and be more generous and favourable to them than your ancestors. Do not put such unlimited power into the hands of the Husbands. Remember all Men would be tyrants if they could.

—Abigail Adams to John Adams
March 31, 1776

1

OCTOBER 18, 1818. MY FATHER ONCE TOLD me I had the mind of a man. He meant to say I was a freak of nature, as was—so he suspected—my mother. But I feel no such mind within me now. Now I am soft and tired and feel like weeping, though I cannot bring forth any tears.

In death, Abigail rests peacefully. The fever that had her body trembling for near two weeks is gone. The fluid no longer rattles in her poor chest. And the telltale rash of the typhus has begun to fade on her belly.

She lies in the master chamber at Peacefield, her beloved home in Braintree. But Abigail is no longer. They say that in her youth she looked like Venus: fair and so harmonious in all her parts that men grew awkward around her. But John was never awkward in her presence. A fiery Humpty Dumpty to the laughing world, around his Portia he grew tall and handsome.

He called her Portia after faithful Brutus's wife, but she is no Portia now. Her body, at seventy-two, has wasted to skin and bone. The assaults she bore—the deaths of Charles and poor Nabby, her eldest, who died in agony in this very room of a cancer in the breast—lie upon her as defeated folds of flesh. Calluses mark her fingers from days and years of sewing, husking, weaving, and gathering. And there are faded burn marks, too—on her arms, elbows, and palms, scorched often through the years while her mind was on other things. She hardly felt them but wondered afterward from whence they had come. And all those years away from John—those marks are there, as well, around the eyes I have shut, in lines that tell the pain of loss. I will anoint them with precious rose oil. I will put balm on her lips and hands and rub it in gently with the love I still feel and have felt for her for more than forty years.

I look out the window at Abigail's gardens. The roses and hollyhocks are gone to sleep for the winter, but violet asters and pink sedum still line the paths. The maples have rained their gold, red, and orange leaves upon the ground. The wind has scattered them about; no one has thought to rake them. Her last sojourn into the garden had been with John, to pick apples for a pie. But in these two weeks, John has halted all work, except to feed the animals.

One day last week, she seemed to revive. And when she looked out her window across the grounds to where the orchards lay, she was appalled that the apples, bursting with ripeness, had not been picked.

"John!" she called, although Dr. Holbrook had forbidden her to speak. "Fetch John, Louisa."

Louisa Smith is her niece, the daughter of Abigail's brother, William Smith; she stays here in the guest room. A bright and obliging woman of youthful middle age, Louisa ran to fetch John, who, believing his wife to be out of danger, had gone to work in his study down the hall.

He came running, panic on his face.

"John"—she turned upon hearing his footsteps—"why are the apples not picked? They will rot."

"My love, I told the boys to put off their farm work while you were ill. I didn't want the noise to disturb you."

"Nonsense," Abigail replied. I thought I saw her smile faintly. "They must carry on, or it shall all go to waste. I couldn't bear that."

She glanced at me then, and I knew we were both recalling the summer of the terrible drought in 1778, when mine were the only apples to survive, thanks to the ingenious watering invention of a certain Mr. Cleverly.

．　　　．　　　．

The next day, Abigail's fever returned, and I knew it would not spare her. She lay close to death all weekend, conscious but perfectly still. On Monday, I packed to go home, as my husband had sent a messenger with news of a sick grandchild, but she stopped me. She must have heard a change in my footsteps, because she called weakly, "Lizzie, don't leave."

I went into her room, sat on the bed, and took her hand. John was on the other side, and a more stricken man I have never seen, though I have seen many stricken men in my day.

"I feel I am dying," Abigail said, "and I'm ready to go to my Maker. Except that I hate to leave him." She looked at her husband. "It is parting from you I cannot bear."

I turned away to hide my tears.

John kept a brave face, even managing a smile for his Portia. "We shan't be parted for long, my love. Rest now."

She seemed to fall into a doze. I gently took my hand from hers and went downstairs to speak with the family. Louisa sat in the large parlor next to Tommy, Abigail and John's youngest son, now in his late forties. His head was tipped back; his eyes were closed. Also present were Dr. Holbrook, asleep in a chair by the fire, and Abigail's good neighbor, Harriet Welsh. Upon hearing my footsteps, Dr. Holbrook woke from his doze. They all turned to me inquiringly, but I merely shook my head.

Louisa began to sob; Tommy stood up and took me by the shoulders, begging to know what had happened. In another moment, he disengaged from me as his father, barely able to stay on his feet, entered the room.

John passed a trembling hand over his head.

"I can't bear it. Can't bear to see her this way. I wish . . ." We all held our breaths, wondering what this remarkable man, our great patriot and second president, wished for as his wife of fifty-four years lay dying. "I wish to lie down and die with her."

Tom went to his father and embraced him. Moments later, they sent for a messenger. John Quincy had to be notified that his mother was dying.

•   •   •

I waited upon Abigail, but she never spoke again. We all took turns spending time in her room so she was never alone. I recalled vividly our many days and years together—before she left for Europe, then afterward, when she returned much changed on the outside, though not at all within. I recalled those first hard years of our friendship, when I was a new widow and she was a widow to the Cause, with four children and not a morsel of bread for many months. Our men were dead or gone, and we had but ourselves to rely upon. It was death that first drew us together: first my husband, Jeb, in June of '75, then her dear mother in October of the same year, of the bloody flux. We call that the dysentery now. Her mother lingered for two weeks. The children had also been ill, and John was far away, as he often was at that time.

I made her mother a dish of willow bark tea, which relieved her suffering but could not save her. And when I washed the body and dressed it—slowly and carefully, the way I had learned to do from my own mother—Abigail looked on in fascination. Then she smiled, although her eyes remained grave.

"Dear friend," I said to her gently, "what makes you smile at a time like this?"

She turned to me and replied, "When my turn comes, I want you to wash my body like that."

"Oh," I said, shrugging off her comment, "I am sure to go to my Maker long before you. You are made of flint."

But she would not be put off. "Promise me," she said.

And by her mother's eyes, which I then closed, I promised her. Soon I will fulfill that promise. But first let me tell you of those early days, when we were young, and the Troubles were upon us, and I first learned what a woman could be. Otherwise, as Abigail might say, a perfectly good story will go to waste.

2

MAY 1775. IT WAS A BRIGHT SPRING morning in the North Parish. I had been fighting tears since waking with the dawn. I milked and fed our cows, then fed my husband, Jeb, to whom I had been married but eight months. Then I prepared his sack, and Thaxter, our field hand, brought our horse around to the front of the house. Jeb was busy gathering his things and so did not notice, as a young man set upon battle will not, that I could not look at him for fear of breaking down.

He was heading to Cambridge, where he would join Colonel Prescott's regiment. The bloody events of Concord and Lexington were fresh in our minds, but we didn't speak of them. I kept my face turned to my tasks: filling his flask with cider, cutting a goodly morsel of dried beef, measuring out the preserves.

"Lizzie, have you seen my cap?" he called from our pokey little chamber upstairs.

I espied the cap upon the kitchen chair before me, but said nothing right away. The sooner he was ready, the sooner he would leave me with only the roaring sea for my companion.

•　　•　　•

We had come to housekeeping on this parcel of land given to Jeb by Josiah Quincy in September of 1774. Jeb's father was a cousin of Colonel Quincy; he had given us the farm as a wedding gift. Josiah Quincy was also Abigail Adams's uncle. And so, in a sense, I was related to that illustrious lady.

We arrived to discover the splendor of our situation: our parcel had been carved out of a three-hundred-acre estate called Mount Wollaston, upon which Colonel Quincy had newly built a large home. This beautiful, rolling land stretched all the way from the road to the sea. Our parcel, closer to the shore than the colonel's house and slightly to the east of it, contained wooded acres, hay fields, and pasture. We had to clear the land surrounding the cottage-garden plots. Close by our cottage stood several sheds and a barn, all in great need of repair.

Winter in Braintree had made me and Jeb intimate by its very harshness. We had not enough wood, despite Jeb's efforts, and he was obliged to wade through shoulder-high drifts of snow up the hill to the colonel's house. The old colonel had suggested Jeb take what he needed without coming inside to ask.

But Jeb did not like to make free use of others' labor. Only in the direst circumstances did we ever impose upon that connection, although Ann, the colonel's wife, often left parcels on our stoop, for which we felt gratitude and shame in equal measure.

And so, borrowing as little as we could, we slept by the fire in our kitchen. We had a window there, and, oh, what a view we had! How many hours did we spend lying together, looking out that window across the dunes and toward the sea? On days when the wind blew from the northeast, the pungent aroma of the colonel's stables wafted over us. The stench always made us laugh.

In the parlor—a grand word for what it was—we had placed a settle by the fireplace. Its thick plank top folded down for ironing. We lit the fire in this room only for company. Parson Wibird stopped in every week after meeting to see how we were getting on, which was kind of him. We were still adjusting to our new church. The parson was a gentle but—Lord, forgive me!—somewhat ridiculous man. He had a stooped and wiry frame, and when he listened to us, his toothless mouth hung open so long we thought he would drool. We often saw him riding bumpily down the lanes in his rusted curricle. Oh, he was a gentle, kindly soul, but in our youthful eyes that made him all the more laughable. He is gone to his Maker now.

I was happy to lie close to my Jeb in the darkness. From time to time, we heard the drunken groan or whistle of Thaxter, our field hand, making his way to the necessary behind the corn shed. Though we would have been sleeping one moment earlier, upon hearing Mr. Thaxter smack blindly into the necessary, missing the step and cursing, Jeb and I would burst out laughing.

Thaxter, a man of perhaps thirty-five, was an odd fellow content to spend his days alone, especially if he had a good bottle of rum and a pouch of tobacco. He was willing enough to work if you asked—much like an old ox reluctant to take a step without a whip. On loan from the colonel, Thaxter was meant to be a temporary fixture in our young married lives. But, finding himself quite content in the little shed behind the necessary, he stayed for several years and soon blended into the landscape like the opossums and groundhogs that crept about by night.

Jeb touched my face by the firelight and teased me that I'd be quite fat by spring, so frequently did we obey the holy command to go forth and multiply. And all around us was silence, save for the crackling embers, the ocean's roar, and the mournful howling of the wind.

· · ·

Now, as he readied to leave, I hoped and prayed I was with child. I was naive enough to believe that the Lord would not take a father from his unborn child.

Jeb descended the stairs and espied his cap upon the chair. "Here it is." He sighed with exasperation and looked at me. "Oh, Lizzie." He smiled and came to embrace me, but I rejected his touch. I had no wish to fall apart then. I wished to give him all my strength. Feeling me reject him, Jeb merely laughed and said, "Oh, you'll miss me, all right. I know you better than you think." With a tender smirk, he hoisted his musket and gear over his shoulder and strode out of doors, where Thaxter had readied our beautiful horse, Star, a sprightly Narragansett pacer. He had been a wedding gift from the Boylstons.

Jeb hoisted himself up, and I handed up his sack. I had filled it with everything I could: cheese, oatcakes, bilberry preserve, good dried meat, and a leg of chicken left over from the night before. Looking up at him, I had to shield my eyes from the sun.

"You are tan," he remarked, looking down at my arms. "May you be a good little farmer while I'm gone. Watch Thaxter doesn't drink all our rum." He smiled. Everything he said to me in those days had an ironical tone, for we were both quite new at this farming business and still felt ourselves to be playacting at it. Jeb and I had grown up in staunch British families surrounded by city comforts, right on Cambridge's Tory Row.

He looked back at me thoughtfully and tenderly as he turned Star toward the path to the road. "You're a strong woman. Oh, how I love you, Lizzie Boylston!" And with that, he blew me a kiss. Star began to trot quickly down the path.

What? Was there to be no tender embrace? Did he think I was made of stone? Did he think I could bear it without at least a final kiss? Why should he think so? Because I hauled bushels of corn? Because I delivered healthy babes in the dead of night, with no help save from ignorant servant-girls? Because, bored and shut in as a girl, I had read my father's library? Shakespeare, Dante, Ovid, Saint Augustine—of what use were they to me now? I wanted to cry out that I was soft inside and could not bear it.

"But I'm not! Jeb, I'm not strong!" I cried after him.

Sensing my agony at last, Jeb slowed. He turned Star around, leapt off him, and came running into my arms. He kissed me then. I reached up and with my fingers touched his soft face, barely yet shaven, and his soft curls, which I had pulled back with a piece of my finest homespun linen.

"Oh, be careful, my love," I said.

"I will," he whispered. "Indeed, I have no *wish* to leave you." He lingered about my neck, kissing it tenderly. I felt his fingers move toward my bosom.

I might be soft, but he could not afford to be. I pushed him away. "Up you go, soldier."

He tore himself from me, mounted Star, and gave me a salute. "Yes, sir." Then he nudged Star with his knees and disappeared up the coast road toward Boston.

•   •   •

When he was truly gone and I could no longer hear Star's hooves upon the ground, I sat myself in the open doorway of the kitchen garden. The chickens, thinking I had something for them, came pecking at my feet. But I had nothing for them except tears.

Within moments, the enormity of my solitude wrapped itself around me, and I felt quite done in. I had no one in the world now. No one save his family, whom I ardently disliked. My own mother had died of the throat distemper in 1769. And my father, who had been a judge in His Majesty's court, had fled to England at the start of the Troubles. A man of great secret sympathy for the Cause, he had intended to return once the Rebels had been "put down," but he caught pneumonia and died within a week of landing there.

Finally, there was my brother, Harry, who had joined a privateer ship that fall, just after Jeb and I moved to Braintree. I knew not whether he lived. I missed them all unspeakably now and felt heartily sorry for myself.

To shake off my gloom, I stood and wandered about my too-silent house. I entered the dairy, a small room to the right of the kitchen, to gaze upon my medicines, which lined the wall shelves. "Witch's potions," Jeb called them. I ran my fingertips over the jars and vials of powder, potions, and poultices. Senna, manna, Glauber's salt, snakeweed. *Here's rosemary. That's for memory.* Of what use were they to me now? None could bring back my Jeb.

He wrote me every day from Cambridge, and I wrote him back. I nearly borrowed a horse and rode out to him. But Jeb would not have liked that. Conditions, while they were to get much worse, were already bad. The water was putrid, and our soldiers, who were drinking cider all day, were dirty and unruly. Many were sick, he wrote. The fearsome canker rash was everywhere, and some also had the bloody flux. No, I could not ride to Cambridge. It would have pleased me to do so, but not him. I was just learning to be a woman—to give pleasure freely and to take it when offered. But I was also learning to defer. To defer was the lot of womankind.

Then, in the second week of June, I received a message that made me shiver: rumor had it that Jeb's regiment would soon be marching to Charlestown. The Regulars were poised to fire from Copp's Hill, and they must be held back.

I can tell you no more at present. But know that you are dearer to me than anything in the world. I will write from our new camp.

I heard nothing further. I wrote once more, but I knew not whether my letter had reached him. All the while, I had hoped and prayed I was with child. Then I began to bleed and suffered terrible cramps.

I lay in bed feeling ill all that hot June day, and did not realize that I had fallen asleep until a loud noise woke me.

3

JUNE 17, 1775. AT FOUR IN THE morning, our entire parish was awakened by what sounded like a terrible explosion north of town. I bolted up in the darkness. I felt the blood that had pooled between my legs during the night. I lifted my chin to force the tears back into my eyes. No time for tears. *He has no heir*, I thought. I changed my pad of cotton, wishing desperately to steady my shaking body by a cup of lady's mantle tea, but was driven abroad by the thunderous noise.

It was a long mile's walk to the base of Penn's Hill from Mount Wollaston, but that was where everyone was headed, as it afforded the best view of Boston. I recall figures passing me in the darkness— vague, shadowy figures, some still in bedclothes and others with torches. The tanner and Parson Wibird, Brackett the innkeeper, and the Cranches—and me, a young wife among many, though some had babes beneath their shawls. We all headed through town to climb the hill.

And, oh, how I prayed it *was* Boston under siege, not Cambridge or Charlestown. At last I found myself atop the hill where many others stood watching in awe and terror, whispering or quietly sobbing. I did neither that I recall; I merely stood there in the hellish torchlight, feeling the rumble and watching the flames shoot up higher and brighter. There was a rumble of fear upon that hill, too, mixed with that of the cannons. Occasionally, a cry pierced the darkness. Young children clung to their parents' legs while the older ones ran about, excited by the commotion. I didn't speak but only watched the smoke form above Charlestown, gray against the black sky. I knew Jeb was there.

As the sky lightened, I noticed a woman standing by my side with her arm around a small boy of about seven or eight. She, too, said nothing, spoke to no one, but merely watched in horror, clutching her child.

Someone with a torch passed by, and in that momentary flicker of light I saw that it was Abigail Adams, wife of our delegate John Adams, with her eldest boy, John Quincy. When our eyes met briefly, her face softened in recognition, but still I saw she could not quite place me.

"Jeb Boylston's wife," I offered. "Elizabeth. Lizzie."

"Oh," she said, surprised. "Of course. We met several months ago, I believe, at meeting. We are related. I'm Abigail, and this is Johnny." Johnny looked up at me from under his mother's arm. "Is Jeb not here?" She looked around.

"No, he is *there*"—I nodded in the direction of the smoke— "with Colonel Prescott."

Suddenly, there was a terrible *crack*. It sounded close, like lightning hitting a tree. I could feel my knees buckle beneath me.

"Are you hurt?" Abigail fell at once to her knees, searching my person. "Where? Where is the wound?"

"No, no." I shook my head, endeavored to stand. "I feel—I have this feeling . . ." I sobbed into my shawl, unable to voice what I felt. What I *knew*. I struggled up. "I must go," I said.

"Go? Where do you plan to go at this hour?" she asked, thinking reason had left me, as indeed it had. All around was darkness, save for the hectic torches blurring swaths of firelight.

"I must go to him."

"*There?*" She nodded toward the smoke over Charlestown. "You know that's impossible." She placed her arm around me. "Oh, dearest, I know what it is like to be separated from your beloved. But you must bear it. There is nothing else to be done. Tomorrow . . ." She sighed. "Tomorrow we'll know more, perhaps."

"But I will *not* bear it," I rudely replied. "I must go, and go now. I will borrow a horse of Colonel Quincy."

I moved away, certain she now thought me a most unpleasant woman. I began to walk down the hill toward home but soon felt a hand press against my forearm.

"If you really *must* go, then take John's mare," Abigail said. I shall never forget the way she said *must*. There was no irony in her tone but rather a kind of acknowledgment, even resignation. "Tell Isaac to accompany you. It will be faster that way and far safer. Go to Cambridge. They will have news there, if anyone has."

I hugged her to me, grateful to have made a friend in this darkest hour.

4

A SHIMMER OF DAWN WAS JUST RISING to the east, casting faint light across the village, when I found myself knocking at the shack door of Isaac Copeland, who lived behind the small barn on the Adams property. He seemed to have slept through everything. Only my frantic rapping woke him, and when I finally stated my business, the young, dirty lad rubbed the sleep from his eyes with black knuckles.

Isaac shook his head. "We have no lady's saddle, ma'am. The missus always rides in the chaise."

"It is of little import to me, so long as you have a saddle of some kind and a horse to go beneath it."

He glanced at me briefly, then went to the barn, which had but three walls and a sorry thatched excuse for a roof, and brought out a sweet little mare to greet me. She came right up to me and pressed her forehead against my side. I took consolation in her warm breath and soft muzzle. Isaac offered his dirty hands to my grimy boot and up I went, sitting astraddle just like a man. Isaac then handed me a tattered blanket, which I placed across my lap. It was the first time I had ever sat in that fashion, but I was heedless of any discomfort.

The dawn grew brighter on my right flank as Isaac and I made our way up the coast road toward Boston. With the rising light, my strength rallied and my fear calmed.

Many were awake and running about Milton when we arrived in that town; it was Sabbath morning, but there would be no Sabbath that day. Not even the most fervent pastors could draw the people off their hills as the pummeling of Charlestown by British cannons continued, accompanied by a thunderous din and choking black smoke.

People stared rudely as I passed through the center of town. A woman upon a man's saddle had never been seen in those parts before. Despite the blanket, my legs were exposed from my knees to the tops of my boots. I hardly cared; it seemed a trifle given the burning of Charlestown.

The closer we came to Cambridge, my birthplace, the more fearful I grew. Isaac looked drawn and jittery, but said nothing. At Roxbury, we came across a camp of ragtag militia. A band of boys with bayonets, giving themselves the airs of soldiers, was stopping all those headed west toward Cambridge. Across the street stood a large and bustling tavern. Isaac said he wished to water and rest Mr. Adams's little mare, and I longed for a dish of tea and a biscuit.

I took my refreshment, and when I exited the tavern, a young soldier approached me.

"They say the fighting intensifies at Charlestown."

"My husband is there with Colonel Prescott," I answered simply, and moved to cross the street, where Isaac and his charge waited.

The boy let me pass, but at the last moment called after me. "Colonel Prescott is already upon Breed's Hill. You can't reach him. It's a foolish effort! Everyone seeks to leave Cambridge, not enter it!"

With Isaac's silent help, I hopped upon the little mare and urged her west toward Cambridge and the Great Bridge. On the road through Brookline, we saw many fleeing in the other direction: families with all their worldly possessions heaped onto carts, crying children, dogs darting wildly about, and young men on horseback with the guilty expressions of deserters. They stared at me as if I were a madwoman, but I pressed on.

At last, we arrived at the bridge. The late-morning air had grown hot and, in that moment, I was able to enjoy the grandeur of God's earth. Here the Charles River was beautifully winding and tranquil, and the trees were all in bloom. Two months earlier, the planks upon which I stood had been removed to prevent the British from crossing over. The ruse had failed: the troops found the planks and put them back.

I glanced at Isaac. He looked as if he might actually faint. His mouth hung open, and his eyes had a wild and desperate look.

"Isaac, go no farther. Please return to Mrs. Adams. I'm certain she needs you."

Once Isaac had gone, I felt freer. My flagging strength rallied from the tea and biscuit. As I entered Cambridge, I could almost feel my Jeb's presence. Prescott's regiment would have spent the night on the Common, or perhaps upon Prospect Hill farther east. I would soon have news of them, if nothing else.

At the Cambridge Common, a strange scene awaited me. Across the yard lay scattered the vast detritus of a recently abandoned camp: heaps of ash and coal, iron cauldrons too heavy to carry, the stench of urine and feces and horse dung, the tents of men too ill to have moved east with the others. I heard groans and the cries of illness. I shrank before it all, everything made worse by the unnatural summer heat.

On the southernmost edge of the Common, Parson Boardman was in the midst of a sermon. Though his lecture was clearly meant for the soldiers, not half a dozen men of fighting age sat in the audience. Women and old men listened with half an ear. The parson was a large man in a thick wig; perspiration rained down upon his black habit on this hottest of days. He decried human frailty just as officers and servants scrambled to gather their tents and munitions and head east. I stopped one dirty boy as he raced off with an armful of muskets and inquired as to the whereabouts of Colonel Prescott's regiment.

"There." He turned and nodded toward Charlestown. "They passed the night on Breed's Hill. Some of us are bringing aid."

Aid indeed. I studied the boy and his pile of bad muskets that I doubted could kill a crow at a rod's distance.

"Well, God spare you," I said.

It was, in all, a journey toward death. You must not suppose me fool enough to believe otherwise. And yet I hoped. In my mind I saw Jeb, dirty yet whole, running toward me. I saw him stumble toward Mr. Adams's little mare and press his weary head upon the creature's warm flank. Oh, I saw many a ghost of things that might have been in those hours before I saw what truly was.

I looked back to the parson and felt only a mounting anger. Of what earthly use were his words about human frailty? Let him take up a rotten musket like my Jeb and risk his own mortal skin upon Breed's Hill!

By now the sun was quite high in the sky. The clock in Christ Church told the time: past one. To the east, I could hear cannon fire, which seemed to intensify. And still the parson droned on. Though hot and faint with exhaustion, I could not bear it on the Common a moment longer and made the decision to move down the road to Charlestown. Unlike in Roxbury, no one stopped me. I met with no orderly rows of soldiers, no organization of any kind, only chaos. Frightened boys—some bloodied, others looking at me wildly—fled past me.

At the base of Prospect Hill, I found evidence of a recent encampment and a few horses. No sign of Star. I pressed on and within ten minutes came at last to our "army"—a bedlam of sick and dirty men and boys. There was blood and gore such as I dare not describe. I had arrived at the ninth circle of hell, but even the great Italian poet could not have imagined the scene. The clear, still air was pierced by unceasing and wild cries of the wounded and dying, to whom there were not women enough to tend. All around, the suffering of our boys was extreme—some were black with burns; others had multiple bayonet wounds and leaked like stuck sausages. A hasty surgery had been set up in one tent, and it was from this tent that the most terrible sounds arose. At one point, I had the misfortune not to have averted my eyes in time and saw an arm unceremoniously tossed into a pile of white and bloodless limbs at the back of the tent. Oh, Lord, what misery!

I tied the mare to a post where several other horses stood. Looking about me, I saw a boy with a bucket and stopped him, asking would he kindly water my horse. He nodded and went off, I hoped, to get water. I then approached a woman who, though bent with fatigue, I recognized as a Cambridge lady. She was streaked with blood and dirt, but her face was pale and fine. I asked if I could help her, and without a word she nodded to a boy lying on a pallet of straw some ten yards off. He was blue-white in color, and his lips were drawn back across his teeth in suffering. He could not have been more than sixteen.

"Hold his hand," she replied. "It can't be long."

I went to his side and took his hand. "I'm here," I said. "I won't leave you."

His eyes rolled to the side, catching me in their enlarged pupils. He grasped my hand, and when I looked down I saw that half his chest had been torn away.

"Marmy," he said. "I would like my Marmy." His eyes leaked tears; he knew his "Marmy" was very far away.

"I won't leave you, brave soldier," I murmured. Those two words seemed to give him some faint comfort, and he soon shut his eyes. His face relaxed. In a few minutes, he was gone.

Oh, the suffering of this world!

•   •   •

Around five in the afternoon, when for the better part of an hour we had ceased to hear any sounds of war, I saw a young man lying facedown beside another dead boy, upon a rustic cart. He wore a fine linen ribbon in his hair.

It was the ribbon I recognized first. I ran to him and turned him over. I may have cried out but was not sensible of doing so. I knew at once he was dead. And may the Lord forgive me if I say that this understanding was a great, selfish relief. Had there been time for a parting scene with him, I surely would have gone mad.

"This is my husband," I told the gentlewoman I had been helping all that day. She looked at me with astonishment; my calm must have surprised her. "Would you like me to wash him?" she asked. "It is more than a wife should have to bear."

"No, I want to. You are kind to offer." I did not say that I wished to *feel* something; I had grown cold and numb.

I will leave my reader to imagine that final caress: the young, healthy man and his single, fatal wound, which I gently felt around. I marveled at how so small, so insignificant a thing as a bayonet tip could bring down my Jeb's strong spirit. I gently untied the linen with which I had gathered his hair the morning he'd left and placed it around my neck.

After I had washed his body, I began to shake and sat myself upon the ground to keep from falling. The blanket I had brought from Isaac's shack was upon the mare, but I had no energy to fetch it. I was in a quandary. I knew I could not make it back to Braintree. After a long and anxious wait, I finally saw the boy who had brought water to Mr. Adams's mare. He was a welcome sight, and I called to him.

I had a message for the Boylstons, I told him. They would give him a shilling for the news that their son was dead and their daughter-in-law requested help. I could not bear for soldiers to bury Jeb on this filthy hill, and I would not leave him. The boy offered to take John's mare, still tied forlornly to that post, but I said no. That far, I wouldn't trust him.

It was night before I was delivered of my agony among those dead and dying. At first, I kept glancing at Jeb, fearful lest I fall asleep and he disappear. Or perhaps I sought a glimmer of movement. It never came. At some point I must have dozed, though, for the first thing I recall after being lifted from that field is the voice of someone saying, "Gently, gently! Lift her gently!"

I could hear no horses' hooves and at first knew not where I was. I then perceived that we were before the Boylston house, and I asked, agitated, "Star, where is Star? Did you find him? And have you Mr. Adams's little mare?"

"Yes, ma'am. They're in our stables, rest you easy."

I was greatly relieved to know the animals were safe. I was led to bed upstairs. Someone came in to bathe and change me, for I was quite, quite filthy. Within the Boylston home, with its thick walls and dark, north-facing chambers, it was cool. A soft feather bolster caressed me. It was blissfully dark. A prayer escaped my lips for the Lord to take me as I slept.

5

IT IS NOT A CHRISTIAN SENTIMENT TO wish for death. But I was twenty-one and knew not how to suffer. My sleep that night was dark and restless, invaded by images from waking life. I kept dreaming of our parting scene, of Jeb's kiss good-bye the morning he rode off to Cambridge.

With this memory, and the closer one of walking up Penn's Hill, the mantle of sleep lightened. I rose up through my uneasy dreams to find one of the Boylston servants standing over me with a dish of tea.

The maidservant, a plump woman wearing a starched white pinafore, had the morally superior manner of someone who has been up for many hours. Handing me my tea, she said, "Whenever you're ready, ma'am, the mister and missus wish to see you."

"What time is it?" I asked.

"Past eleven," she replied.

I had only yesterday been at a field hospital near the battle at Charlestown. I now found myself amid the fading luxury of those to whom time had been kind. Their home, on its third generation, bespoke a sense of ease and permanence. Only the large wooden crates placed here and there suggested that change was imminent.

Facing the Charles River, the Boylston house presented eight large, glitteringly clean glass windows to the world. Behind the house lay vast gardens and stables. On this day, cotton-tree blossoms had fallen to make a gauzy white carpet in the front garden.

But within moved a family in crisis. In the unreal brightness and brokenness of that morning, it took me some time to realize that the Boylstons were packing, readying, no doubt, to flee as soon as Jeb was buried. Where they planned to go, I knew not.

I rose and dressed. My limbs refused to move without constant command. While I was dressing, Eliza Boylston, Jeb's older sister, entered my chamber without knocking. She looked as tall and haughty as I remembered her. Tears stained her red face, and she wiped them with the ruffled silk sleeve of her French gown.

"I see you're awake," she said.

"Yes, I hadn't slept since early Saturday morning. I was overcome . . ." Upon saying the word *overcome,* I was indeed overcome and could not utter another word. There is nothing so humiliating as a show of grief before someone whose heart is unmoved.

"Indeed, none of us has slept. You have slept fourteen hours together. Mama despairs of your *ever* getting up. Shall I tell her you are coming? Papa is waiting, too."

"I wish to see my husband," I said. "Where is he?"

"He lies in his chamber across the hall. You may go there," she said.

As if I needed her permission!

"Indeed, I shall. I must finish dressing." As I stared at her, signaling her to leave, a smile played across her thin lips.

"Your skirts and bodice are being cleaned. You will find some of my things in that closet. Something will no doubt be suitable." She nodded to the deep closet across the room—a real sign of the Boylston wealth. Jeb and I had not a single such closet. Each room in our house looked like a workshop of some kind: tannery, spinning shop, butcher's, or bakery.

Eliza moved toward the door, cast me a look, and then departed. I hastily finished dressing, then peeked into the hallway. My heart beat quickly, though no one was there. Twice I nearly turned away, losing courage. But I told myself that some things are more important than one's own grief. I had to say good-bye. I had to do him that honor.

He lay in an unfamiliar blue vest and jacket and clean breeches, his hair neatly brushed and pulled behind his ears. Scented candles surrounded him, casting a torpid yellow glow upon his once-handsome face. In the very neatness of his dress, he had already ceased to look like Jeb. In life he had been far too impulsive, too quick, to be tidy. But someone had tidied him, probably one of the maids. I gazed at his mouth; it, too, was still, set in a painfully grim expression. And in this stillness and grimness I knew Jeb was gone.

His arms lay at his sides. I touched one just below his shirt-sleeve. It was quite cold. Then I kissed his cold cheek and turned away. I cried a moment—out of grief for him, pity for myself. I knew my womanhood had died with Jeb. Who would lay his tender hands upon me now? Who would kiss me in the dark of night, with the sea crashing upon the shore behind us?

Annoyed at my self-pity, I stopped crying and looked about me. His articles—such small, pathetic things!—stood on the dresser. Some were still in the sack he'd worn over his shoulder when we said good-bye. Other items, like his ring and billfold, lay alone. I took them all up in my arms and brought them to my room to go over with great care later. For now, I had to hurry to the parlor.

I found only Mr. Boylston. He sat in a wing chair by an unlit fire. His hands rested on his knees, as if to steady him. The haughty, self-satisfied air I recalled was gone.

"Sit, Elizabeth," he said, nodding toward the sofa across from himself. "Would you like tea? Cassie can bring us some." He turned to a small Negro woman who stood in silence by the parlor door. "Some tea for us, Cassie. And cakes."

Far from appearing grief-stricken, Mr. Boylston appeared agitated, almost angry. I dared not tell him I'd already had my tea.

"The—the funeral will take place on Wednesday. At King's Chapel," he informed me.

"In Boston?" I asked, surprised.

"We have little choice in the matter."

I then recalled that the church by the Common had been closed for regular service for many months now. Here again, I dared not suggest that Jeb would have preferred to be buried on our own land in Braintree, or even where he fell on Breed's Hill, rather than in King's Chapel.

Suddenly, Mr. Boylston slammed his fist on the parlor table and blurted out, "Deuced troublemakers!"

I bounced up from my seat with the sudden noise of his explosion.

"Deuced so-called patriots! He was smitten by the Devil! He was no more one of them than *you* are!"

I kept my eyes down, my heart mute. I feared that, were I to open my mouth, a wind the likes of Aeolus' sack upon Odysseus' ship might blow Mr. Boylston back to England. I recalled the grief that Mr. Boylston had given Jeb for not wanting to be a merchant like himself. When Jeb had told him he would enlist, Mr. Boylston had bellowed, "As useless and foolhardy a pursuit as ever I've heard! It'll as soon get you killed as win you glory."

Well, he had been right about that.

"After the funeral, we will send a man to return Mr. Adams's mare and to pack your things."

"What mean you, sir?" "That naturally you shall come with us. We would not think of leaving you alone."

"Come with you! In exile?" I cried. Many things had occurred to me since first standing on Penn's Hill and realizing that Jeb might not live through the day, but one plan had never entered my thoughts: to join his family.

"Mr. Boylston," I said, "I thank you for your kindness. But I cannot possibly come with you."

"Of course you'll come with us. Where else could you go? We can't in good conscience send you back to that hell pit of a North Parish, what with the Adamses and Hancocks getting people killed every day. We can't possibly abandon you, a gentlewoman and the wife of our son, to tend a farm alone. What would people say?"

"It's my home, and I will return to it."

Mr. Boylston turned red in the face and muttered, "Obstinate creature!"

"Mr. Boylston," I entreated more gently, "the women need me there. They have no midwives such as myself. And soon there will be no men, either. There are many animals in need of tending and a rather large garden."

I recalled my promise to Jeb to be a good farmer in his absence, and my resolve hardened within me. "I hardly need mention that we could not see more differently upon the subject of the current conflict, and that I consider certain members of the North Parish to be the best of people and my friends."

"Yes," he grumbled. "How that happened, and you with a father so respectable, I cannot guess."

To this, I had no reply.

What I had said about my prospects in Braintree was not entirely true. While the women needed me, they still called upon me only in the direst extremity. The truth was, they did not yet trust me. The entire parish knew that my father had been a royal judge and had fled the country. Rumors abounded, as well, about my mother and myself: that she had been practiced in the alchemical arts, and that I myself grew strange plants in my garden and made powerful potions and poisons. This last fact was partly true. I grew deadly nightshade, whose derivative, belladonna, served me well for stubborn cervixes. I enjoyed delicious tomatoes as well, the seeds of which a friend of my mother's sent her from Europe. But some believed the rumors about alchemy and poisonous potions and shunned me.

Jeb's father grasped my hand hard, and a cry caught in his throat. "It is unsafe, woman."

Here, the old man's entreating look made me feel that perhaps Mr. Boylston did have some feelings for me after all.

"Come now," I replied, grasping his arm, "there is nothing unsafe about the North Parish."

He shrugged off my grasp. "I can't reason with you now. We'll discuss it by and by. Rest assured, I shan't leave you in Braintree alone. You *shall* come with us."

I stood, curtsied, and left just as the maid was bringing us tea.

Back in my chamber, I bolted my door and let out an exasperated groan. I took Jeb's sack and musket. I could smell the powder and knew he had fired it. I pressed the sack to my face, smelling for traces of him. Then, carefully opening it, I removed its contents: the oatmeal biscuits I'd given him, now but two broken ones remaining; a bladder that had once contained water, but now had neither cork nor liquid. My heart flooded. Had he reached for it, parched with thirst, at the last? A small piece of dried beef. A lock of my hair tied with string. Then, tucked far at the bottom, my last letter to him. I unfolded it and read:

Dearest Jeb,

I am grieved to hear you move closer to danger. But what can I, a mere woman, do to steer the course of generals, colonels, and the world? I steer my shuttle to fashion you a shirt, and the plough to make a straight line for the corn. You see I keep my promise to be your good little farmer while you are gone. Come back, and I'll be your better wife.

Your ever loving Elizabeth.

Overcome, I lay back in my bed clutching the sack and willed myself into unconsciousness until dinner, when one of the servants woke me.

The funeral, a solemn affair, took place two days later, and we were alone neither in the church nor at the cemetery. Several other families surrounded us, including some quite prominent ones. They looked as flushed and harried as the Boylstons, as if at war within themselves. The choice was acute: leave Boston immediately or grieve their dead.

It was another hot day. Women in black skirts fanned themselves and looked upon the point of fainting as they listened to an unfamiliar parson and wept.

It was a group service and burial, and we mourned as one. Perhaps because of this, I felt somewhat buffered from my own pain. I looked about me and felt mostly a welling pride for all those boys whose families had discouraged them, boys who had nothing to give in going off to Breed's Hill except their mortal selves.

As the parson finished his business and moved to condole with each family, Jeb's family and I walked slowly away, heading toward our carriage to return to Cambridge. It was then that I saw an officer emerge from the crowd and approach me.

He was quite tall, over six feet, and bore himself like a man of some rank. His hair, parted in the middle, was braided in the back, revealing a high forehead and brilliant blue eyes. His grim face betrayed a compassion that threatened to undo me. As he approached, I saw that he was holding something in his gloved hand. Then I knew who this man was.

"Madam Boylston?"

"Yes?"

"Colonel William Prescott." He bowed to me and kissed my gloved hand. "I'm so very sorry. Would you allow me to give you this?"

He handed me a folded paper.

I took it from him without breathing. Then I swayed, as if a strong wind had tipped me to one side.

"Ma'am," he said. "Let us sit. I have important things to share."

He took me by the arm and led me toward a stone bench. I looked back at the Boylstons, who were speaking to the parson and making their way slowly toward us. Colonel Prescott sat by my side and spoke quickly, rightly sensing that his time alone with me was short.

"Your husband was among the few who did not desert me when the fighting began. He fought right by my side. I have rarely seen anything like it. But we were far outnumbered, and easy targets. Still, he refused to hide himself behind a barricade, but stood tall. I've never seen a braver man."

"He was a fool!" I cried, then felt instantly ashamed. For, to this brave and noble man who did not know my heart, I must have sounded just like my father-in-law.

I stood up. The colonel stood as well.

"You will be anxious, no doubt, to read that. He gave it to me the morning of the battle. Why he believed I would make it out alive, I know not. I was as close by his side in the battle as we are now. It was only blind chance that the Regular's bayonet ran him through and not me. He was but a boy himself, perhaps sixteen. I killed him."

I shut my eyes at the horror of Colonel Prescott's narrative, yet was glad he did not spare me.

"But what's done cannot be undone," he concluded. "If you need anything, anything at all . . ." He grasped my hand.

"Thank you. You are very kind. I did not mean to say Jeb was a fool. I am very much for the Cause. I meant—"

The colonel looked me in the eye. "I know what you meant. Perhaps we *are* fools, Mrs. Boylston. You are an honest woman, and Jebediah was a lucky man."

He bowed and left, and I was alone with my letter. I had to read quickly; the parson was just bowing and taking his leave of the Boylstons. Soon they would be upon me. Carefully, I broke the seal and read:

Dearest Lizzie,

 I pray you never have to read this Letter, for I of all people know the great Joy and the great Suffering of which your fine soul is capable. I know you would not distract yourself from the grief of my death, and this alone gives me pain now.

 I am glad to hear you carve a straight row for the corn. You are a good farmer, and all the wife I should ever want. Now, though it shall give you pain, I must say this. Resist the Attempts of my family to o'ertake your life. You should remarry, if at all possible given your unsightly intelligence. Tho you can't keep a fellow from hoping that he will never be quite so handsome or so gallant as your First, Yours Always—Jeb.

 P.S. Cherish my Star, if he survives. I love him second only to you.

"What's that you read?"

Eliza was standing over me, her black parasol casting a sudden shadow.

I was awash in tears but hastily folded the letter and put it in the pocket of my skirt. "Something Jeb left me."

"Oh, I'm sorry to intrude," she said, adding, "but we must hurry. Dinner is set for two o'clock, and our guests will be there before us."

I felt neither hungry nor inclined to society, especially not the society of those Tories who might have secretly rejoiced at the British victory. But I resolved to bear it as best I could, for I had plans.

I arrived back in Cambridge quite exhausted. Still, I pushed forth with my plan. I engaged a servant boy to take two messages home for me. The first was to Abigail Adams. I apologized for having detained Mr. Adams's mare and let her know that she would be returned the following day. The second message was to Thaxter, asking him to borrow a horse and chaise of Colonel Quincy and to fetch the horse as soon as may be.

At the reception, Mrs. Boylston smiled at her guests but spoke to no one. Jeb was the Boylstons' second loss. A younger daughter, Maria, had died of the throat distemper. It seemed to me that the loss of her children one upon the other had closed her heart forever.

She was still beautiful, however: white skin; thin, grim mouth; graying brown hair mounded high above her crown. There was no question of my condoling with her, even had I been so inclined. While she had never approved of me for Jeb's wife, she now ignored me entirely. She had not the courage for pain. My suffering—so obvious, so overt—was odious to her.

My messages sent, I rested easier, and while the small gathering was still politely eating baked meats, I watched Eliza making conversation with the guests, some of whom I knew to be her jilted suitors. It was said she had already turned down half a dozen eligible men. But Eliza was not content merely to foil her suitors' plans. She, like her mother, had tried to talk her brother out of marrying me. For this I had not forgiven her. True, my father had left me little in the way of money, but he had been a man of excellent learning and solid background. My mother, on the other hand, was a true aristocrat, far above the merchant-monied Boylstons. Indeed, my mother once told me she could trace her ancestry back to Queen Margaret, wife of Henry VI. That knowledge, though, gave me little solace now.

I turned away from Eliza and made my way out of the parlor. Once in my room, I fell onto the bed in my hot black mourning gown and there lay as if dead.

But I had yet one more letter to write. I knew it to be a great rudeness to shirk my leave-taking, so I thanked Mr. and Mrs. Boylston for their kindness and condoled with them. I wished them a safe journey. I left the note on my desk and, after gathering my and Jeb's things, slipped out to the stables.

The stable boy seemed surprised to see me.

"I hadn'a any message to ready the carriage," he apologized with a pained expression.

"Oh, a carriage won't be necessary. If you could saddle Star, that will be sufficient."

He looked at me as if I were mad, but I stood there quite resolutely until at last Star was saddled and his girth tightened. The boy made a step with his hands for me to mount, and I rode Star into the darkening afternoon, down Brattle Street, across the Common, across the Great Bridge, and east toward home. I felt the saddle warm against me and felt the aura, one last time, of my husband's thighs on mine.

6

THE MORNING AFTER MY RETURN FROM CAMBRIDGE, I wandered my house like a newly blind person, brushing my fingers across the once-familiar objects. I touched the old pewter tankard Jeb had liked to take his cider in after milking the cows. I grazed my fingertips across his soft, but dusty, pillow lying next to mine on the bed. I lay my cheek against his farming breeches—grass-stained and smelling of hay and sweat—which were cast heedlessly where he had last left them across a chair in the corner of our chamber. Oh, how his smells lingered! I smelled them once every hour, ever fearful that this act might rob them, little by little, of their perfume.

I listened for the sound of a carriage. In those first days and weeks after I returned from Cambridge, I expected the Boylstons to come and wrest me from my home at any moment. I resolved to run to the sea and let the cold darkness take me rather than go with them.

I wandered slowly into the dairy. Within, the numerous tools of my trade lay neatly arranged or hung by hooks: a brass kettle, a sieve, a gourd, a pair of tongs, several galley pots, a cork, pewter spoons, two strainers, a small cauldron, an iron mortar and pestle, a small tin funnel, a pair of shears, a press, and many vials in a wooden box. A neat and clean slate sink stood in readiness for either cheese- or medicine-making, depending upon the day and hour.

Without, the air was mild; the sun shone as if the world took no notice of my Jeb's death. I milked the cows, fed the chickens, watered the tender young plants, saw that Thaxter was at his chores, and hauled water from the well. It still had not rained, and while I was tempted to let everything on the farm die with Jeb, I had made him a promise. I thus suffered through the risings and settings, the waterings and feedings of life, though I neither ate, nor slept, nor drank much myself.

While I had not the energy to walk the near two miles to the Adams's farm, I did send a message to Abigail inquiring about the safe return of John's little mare.

I received a reply the next day. Not by means of a letter, but by Abigail herself, a neat and dainty little woman who walked with great determination down the path from the road. She lifted her skirts to avoid the dust and dune grass. From my window, I saw her turn her head left and right to admire my fledgling plantings: yellow lilies, pink roses, lavender, and medicinal herbs.

I reached the door before she could knock. As I looked down upon her, I saw that she carried something in her arms covered by a cloth.

She was ready to condole, but when she looked up at me, her expression changed from sorrowful compassion to one of alarm. I reached a hand to my hair, realizing that I had not brushed it in . . . well, I could not remember when.

"You look like something I could stick in my cornfield."

I smiled at that. Such tart and simple honesty from the mouth of such a dainty little thing! Smelling the pie, I tried but could not recall when I had last eaten a meal, and I bade her enter. My voice, unheard by me for many days, sounded strange to my ears.

I moved into the kitchen and set the parcel on the table. Then I asked, "Would you like a dish of tea?"

Her bright, pale-gray eyes widened at the question. "*Real* tea?" she inquired.

"Yes. Quite real. My father left me a great quantity of it. Though I do realize I should dump it in the bay."

"Oh, no," she said, "don't do that. I'd sell the shoes off my feet for some right now."

And with that, this remarkable woman sat down. Together, we had tea and pie, like the real ladies we might have been in another time and place.

•   •   •

Abigail had come bearing not just a wonderful pie but heartening news as well: General Washington had reached Cambridge and taken command of the army. I watched her twirl her wedding band nervously around her finger as she spoke. No doubt she was thinking of John, who had been in Philadelphia since April and had been the first to suggest Washington for commander of the Continental Army.

"Do you truly think he can make the difference? Our men seem neither very willing nor very able."

"He will make them able," she said with conviction. "Certainly my husband believes so." And then she smiled at her own words, as if *husband* were too grand a word for the ethereal memory that was John Adams.

I was gladdened by the news of Washington's arrival for secret reasons as well: surely the great Continental Army must need such homes as that owned by the Boylstons. Surely the family would have removed to Halifax or some such place by now, and I had but a distant regret.

"You look to be very suddenly quite delighted by something, Lizzie," mused Abigail, while staring over at me quizzically.

"Oh." I smiled. "I was just thinking an un-Christian thought. It doesn't bear sharing with a virtuous woman such as yourself."

"Lizzie, *please*. Tell me. I will soon go mad with virtue. I am dying to hear something unrelated to children or farming."

"All right, then." I smiled. "I shall tell you. I have lived these weeks in daily fear that my in-laws should come and fetch me away and force me to live with them. But with Washington's arrival, I have reason to hope that they have already departed Cambridge."

"Know you where they might have gone?"

I shook my head uncertainly. "They spoke of going to Portsmouth."

"England, preferably," she offered. "I should like to send all the Tories back to England."

I glanced at my new friend to see if Abigail spoke in earnest. Upon seeing my questioning stare, a little corner of her mouth tightened against a smile. Then we both began to laugh. Oh, it felt good to laugh!

After recovering ourselves, we spoke a little about Mr. Adams and his doings in Philadelphia. I had seen only glimpses of our illustrious citizen since my arrival that past fall. I had watched him descend from his carriage at meetings on Sundays. I recalled how he'd stood beneath the carriage to take Abigail's arm, and I'd watched him lift his three young boys and set them safely down beside the carriage. Johnny was eight; Charles, six; and little Thomas but two. Young Nabby had climbed down last, shy of society.

The boys were a rambunctious lot, and only Abigail's harsh stares kept them from dispersing down the road in hot pursuit of a lone turkey or groundhog instead of going into the meetinghouse. The day I recalled, the boys went chasing an opossum, and Abigail called to them to return at once.

"Oh, just let them go," Mr. Adams said, waving his arms in the air. "They have all day to suffer through the good parson's sermons."

"John!" Abigail had remonstrated, looking about to see who might have overheard.

This memory brought a smile to my face.

"What makes you smile, dearest?" asked Abigail, who had been speaking about George Washington and the likely first step of the Continental Army: Would they attack the British and, if so, when would they attack? My smile, no doubt, seemed incongruous.

"Oh, I was just remembering when I first laid eyes upon your John. He was helping his children from the carriage, and I noticed how fond he was of them. I was thinking how he looked to spoil them horribly. For while his voice was loud, there was nothing stern in his entire countenance."

"You are observant," she said. "He's like that with his family, if not the rest of the world. With the world he is a lion; with us, a tabby cat. He sees his children so rarely these days, he hasn't the heart to discipline them. That falls to me."

I grasped my new friend's hand in silent sympathy.

Soon, Abigail stood and made to leave when she noticed the door to my dairy. "What is all this?" she asked, glancing back at me.

My medicines, my most precious commodities, sat in glass jars, alphabetized. I kept a list of them in chalk on the inside of the door, carefully marking each remaining amount:

Article	Amount	Use
Senna	~~1 ph.~~ ~~1/2 ph.~~ 1/4 ph.	The punk
Manna		Etc.
Glauber's Salt	~~1 sm. bottle~~ ~~3/4 b.~~ 2/3 b.	Etc.
Ipecac	~~1 lg. bottle~~ ~~3/4 b.~~ 1/2 b.	Etc.
Powdered Rhubarb		
Butterfly Weed		
Wormwood Oil	~~small jar.~~ ~~3/4 jar.~~ 1/2 jar.	
Gum Armoniacum	Asthma	
Willowbark		Fever
Indian Physick		Bloody Flux
Queen Anne's Lace		No Babies
Carolina Pinkroot		Worms
Witch Hazel	lg. jar	
	Rashes Broom Snakeweed	
	Speeds Delivery	
Belladonna - POISON		Softens Cervix

After studying this list for some time, she moved closer to peruse my many vials and jars of powders and the odd tools that hung from various hooks.

"Know you how to use these medical tools?" she asked.

"I do."

"And grow you these medicines yourself?"

"On the whole. Some I have been obliged to order."

"And know you how to use them?"

I smiled, for she seemed truly astonished. "I do."

"You must indeed have a real gift." She gazed admiringly at me then, as if my dairy—and the story it told— had placed me in an entirely new light.

"Perhaps," I admitted. "Though I hardly have the strength for work, even should any woman of the parish decide to trust me."

It was her turn to comfort me. "You will use them again, Lizzie, for there are no men left with time for tending mothers. And you shall find the strength, just as I have. For what choice have we?"

I looked at her earnest little face, knowing she was right but not quite believing it.

Suddenly, she started and made for the door. "My children are alone—I must go."

"Oh, yes."

She turned back to me. "By the way," she said after a moment, "would you like a dog? Our bitch just had five pups. We could gladly spare one."

"A dog? Heavens, no. What for?"

She looked through the kitchen window at the dunes and the dark sea. "It's far too quiet here, too desolate. If a carriage should come for you, he would bark."

This latter idea did hold my interest for a moment. But then I said, "No, I shouldn't know what to do with a dog. It is just something else to care for."

Abigail narrowed her eyes but said nothing. It was as if she could see right through me. I dearly loved animals, but a dog was just another thing to love and lose.

7

ABIGAIL'S WORDS TURNED OUT TO BE QUITE prescient, for the very next day, at around seven in the evening, I was called upon by a frantic servant of the Brown household.

The boy who stood at my door panted for breath. His freckled little face looked imploringly up at me. Susanna Brown, he announced, was "very sick."

I told him to wait and excused myself to get my shawl and sack. I was sewing a sheet of linen I had woven to make Jeb a new shirt; now, I sewed myself a petticoat instead. I set the work aside and moved quickly to find my medical sack. I checked its contents to be certain all was there: razor, stitching quill, twine, clean rags, ties, clouts, a jar of soft soap, scissors, and several packets of medicinal tea. It was a goodly weight.

As we left, I asked, "Is this Mrs. Brown's first child?"

"Oh, no, ma'am, her third. It was Dr. Crosby delivered the others, but he has gone to join the army."

"Her third? Then we must hurry."

I set off with great haste up through the dunes, the heavy bag knocking against my shoulder. But the boy called me back.

"Miss Boylston! Miss Boylston! This a' way!" He pointed in the opposite direction.

"What can you mean, pointing there?" I ran back to him with my cumbersome load.

"She's not at home. She's on Grape Island. We must go on horseback to the launch at Hough's Neck."

"Grape Island? What on earth is she doing there?"

Grape Island had been the scene of a recent skirmish in which one of our boys had been killed.

"She received word that her husband was there and wished to see him, but when she arrived, he had already joined his regiment."

"It's a long way off." I sighed. "And it grows dark."

I looked about me. The sun had descended in the sky; it nearly touched the sea. The water looked black, foreboding. I had never liked boats. I liked nothing about the irregular rocking feeling, or the wind, or the salt on my clothes. No crisis would have induced me to go with this boy, save a woman alone and in travail. Neither had I any great desire to witness a woman and her babe just then. My own grief was too close, too pressing. I feared breaking down. But if I neglected to save this woman, how long might I be welcome in this town? Long enough to pack my things and join the Boylstons.

"All right," I finally said.

He helped me onto his horse, and together we set off to Hough's Neck, where a little boat, hardly more than a dinghy, awaited us. The wind was strong; my hair was swept out of its pins. The beach was empty save for a pair of young lovers who'd escaped the eyes of their relations. They pressed against each other, oblivious to the wind. When they heard us, the man disengaged himself; they then strode hand in hand down the beach in the other direction.

The boy got down first, then helped me off his horse. He steadied the boat, which rocked to and fro in the water. I set my sack in first, then lifted my skirts and stepped in. The boy took a running push and jumped in after me, soaking his poorly shod feet. Off we went through rough waves toward Grape Island. I thought I might faint, and I did something I don't often do: I prayed.

The boy, small though he was, was a skillful rower. We arrived only slightly the worse for wear about forty minutes later. By then it was dark, and the boy had brought no torches, so we had to grope our way toward a shack in the moonlight. We heard faint moans. Within, we found Mrs. Brown and a Negro servant-girl alone in the gloom.

"Is there no fire?" I called to the girl.

"I've had no time to tend it, ma'am," she said, tears in her voice. "Her illness came on so sudden."

"Well, then, go now. Take—"

"Peter," the boy offered, for in my distraction I had entirely forgotten to ask him his name.

"Yes, well, go. Fetch wood. Anything dry will do."

They left the shack in haste. I heard the wind scream as they opened the door. The island felt abandoned. During the skirmish between our troops, a munitions building had been set afire, and one could still pick up blackened bits of wood. Now we were all alone with naught but screaming wind and crashing waves. What desolate music to accompany a birth!

I approached my patient. Her waters had broken and her sickness was full upon her. She lay on a bed of straw by a cold fire. No anxious husband paced the hall; no women sat chatting.

I bent down and took Mrs. Brown's hand. "It shall be brighter in here presently," I said.

"I care little about the ambience," she replied.

I merely smiled at her foul mood. I was inured to foul moods in laboring women.

"Well, you may not, but I do. I can hardly be expected to work in the dark."

The door banged open, and Peter entered with an armful of branches. When the fire was going again, I handed the girl a pouch of snakeweed and bade her make some tea of it. My mother had learned about the herb from an Indian woman of her acquaintance.

Turning back to the mother, I asked gently, "How long have you been having pains?"

"Near three hours, but they have not been regular. They don't feel right to me. I don't suppose you'll be much use, light or no. They say you're a witch. I'm like to die here with my babe."

Here another pain came upon her. She cried out, and I shooed Peter out of the shack.

"I am not a witch. I'm a midwife," I said smartly. "Allow me to touch you. It will relieve you to know how long you have to bear this suffering. It cannot be long now."

I placed a cloth beneath her and felt. A moment later, I drew back with fright.

This babe was breech. I looked up into the darkness in silent entreaty. Oh, Lord, why didst thou seek to test me so?

Endeavoring to sound calm, I said, "The babe is breech. We must find a way to turn him about."

I had never delivered a breech baby, but had seen my mother do so several times. She had spoken to me about it. But what had she said? I strained to recall that conversation now.

"Peter!" I called. "Peter!"

The boy reentered the shack at a run, his hands full of wood.

"Roll up this pallet and find a second. Quickly, please."

To Mrs. Brown, I said, "We must use gravity to let this baby fall. I shall guide it as best I am able. Now, if you would stand over here." I pointed to the foot of the bed.

•　　•　　•

At last, with the pallets rolled, I had the mother straddle them in a sort of crouching stand. I was obliged to kneel down on the floor at her feet. I knew that once I saw the umbilicus, I had but little time to get the baby out, as it would be pressing upon the cord and could die within moments. The mother wept silently, and when she looked down at me, it was not suspicion or anger I saw but genuine fear.

"Have you children?" she asked me suddenly, but her pains came too quickly for me to form a reply. Then, all at once, I saw the babe's bottom. "Now, push!" I said, and with a heroic cry from the mother, the babe came into this world.

I rose from my kneeling position with the babe, a tiny girl with a mass of dark red hair. I cleared her mouth and blew on her chest gently. She took a gulp of Grape Island air and let out another loud cry. I tied and cut the cord, then quickly cleaned her, head to little writhing toes—all present and accounted for—with my soft soap and a little butter. I applied a belly-band across the umbilicus and bundled the babe. Then I placed her directly into Mrs. Brown's arms.

"A beautiful girl she is," I said, willing back tears.

At the sight of her daughter seemingly alive and well, Susanna Brown burst into tears. She reached for me and touched my arm. Her eyes glistened.

"Where did she get her beautiful hair?" I asked.

"Her father has red hair. He is with Prescott's regiment in Cambridge."

I merely nodded.

"He's a good man." I saw her smile at her babe, who had found her mother's breast as I waited for the placenta. I called for the servant, whose name was Janie, to bring me a dish of pennyroyal tea, and I gave it to my patient. Soon she delivered the placenta quite whole. I made her comfortable and sent Janie to find Peter, who was no doubt just beyond the door, attempting to clear his senses of the bloody scene of birthing.

Mrs. Brown suddenly realized she had not introduced herself. "I'm Susanna, by the way." She smiled. "I'm not always so awfully rude. I'm sorry. I was so frightened—"

"It's all right," I assured her.

"No, please. Allow me to apologize. I'm sincerely sorry. Forgive me."

She took my hand and I nodded silently. Then she gazed at the babe sleeping upon her breast. "She has the look of vigorous life about her. I'll name her Anna, for my husband's mother."

I nodded my agreement. Often, parents held off naming their children—for days or even, sometimes, months—for fear of growing too attached to them.

"And you are Mrs. Boylston?" she asked shyly.

"Elizabeth. But you can call me Lizzie."

"People say you're related to our Mrs. Adams. Is it true?"

"Only distantly," I said, "through my husband."

"And is your husband in Braintree or has he gone off like all the others?"

"He has—" I began but struggled to continue. "He is dead. On Breed's Hill. Three weeks ago."

"Oh." Her wan face looked stricken. "I have been doubly cruel, then."

"You may rest easy for your man," I said. "Washington is there now." I smiled as reassuringly as I could, willing the tears to stay at bay a little longer. But grief has a will of its own, and the tears came. I sobbed, a hand over my face.

"Dear girl," she said, placing her hand on my back. "Rest yourself. You must be exhausted, too."

"I'm sorry."

"Please, sit yourself down. We shall both rest."

Indeed, there was no question of leaving my patient so soon, and in any case my strength had left me. When Peter returned and had tended the fire, I bade him fetch some straw to make us pallets.

We—Peter, Janie, and I—slept in the shack alongside mother and babe. There were no more blankets, though Susanna offered me one of hers, which I refused. I was cold all night and slept very ill.

I awoke the next morning to find Susanna up and around, the baby in her arms. She was not a new mother and was accustomed to getting on her feet after the birth of a child. I would have preferred she remain in bed, but she seemed eager to be active.

When she saw I was awake, she smiled warmly and said, "Here. Have something. Do."

I thanked her and took a morsel of biscuit and a dish of tea.

"Who minds your household?" I asked.

"My mother. She will be in a panic by now, I'm sure."

"Oh, you are right," I said. "We shall tell her directly."

"I admit it would ease my mind greatly, though I have no great desire for you to leave, Elizabeth."

Oh, the way she looked at me then—it was worth every moment of my previous terror!

·　　·　　·

Susanna would have liked to leave with us, but I told her she should heal another day before endeavoring to travel. I would send Peter back with the boat to fetch her. In bidding her good-bye, I let her go no farther than the shack door, as there was a fierce wind. But she embraced me tenderly; her reserve and suspicion had vanished. Her precious child dozed in her arms. I gently touched Anna's cheek, which was soft as corn silk.

"I will pray for your husband," I said. "I'm sure he cannot be long from you. And I will visit you at home in two days' time."

"Oh, do. Please." She grasped my hand. Her gray eyes looked at me with earnest entreaty. "I should love to see you, Lizzie. And you shall meet my other children. They're spirited, but not wholly bad."

"I'm sure they're not." I smiled.

"And you shall meet some neighbors, too. It is high time. Our women are busy, but not cold. Rough, but not heartless. I imagine they shall even invite you to quilt with them."

Here Susanna rolled her eyes, telling me she shared my dread of quilting and the hours of vicious gossip such parties often entailed. Then she burst into giggles, showing two missing teeth, which in part explained why she had not smiled previously.

I walked down to the shore, where Peter held the little boat for me in the strong wind. I threw my sack in first, then lifted my dirty petticoats and stepped in. I felt damp and chilled, but my spirit was light as I nestled myself in my shawl. I had done some good in the world and felt myself no longer quite so entirely alone.

8

NEWS OF MY HAVING WORKED SOME "WITCHERY" out at Grape
Island spread quickly in our small parish. Colonel Quincy and his
wife mentioned it the very next day, when they had me to dine at
the great house.

I have not, I realize, mentioned the Quincys or their extreme
kindness to me during my period of mourning, and I would be
remiss if I did not.

Colonel Quincy was a blustery man of about fifty with a growing paunch and a large red nose. His wife, Ann, was far more genteel, younger than her husband, and nearly a head taller.

For the first two weeks after Jeb's death, the Quincys thought
it prudent to leave me be. Ann sent a servant with baskets of provisions to set at my door. I greatly appreciated these gifts, though I
hardly touched them—dried apricots, preserves of various kinds,
and an assortment of breads. But by the third week, the Quincys
clearly felt I might be ready for company, and thus I found myself
invited to their great house upon the hill the day after Susanna's
delivery.

As I approached through the dunes, I came upon a family walking up the circular path toward the front door. At once
I felt ashamed of making my way like a vagabond, emerging as I

did through the tall grass. But upon seeing me, the couple came quickly toward me with smiles.

"Elizabeth Boylston?" asked the man, warmly shaking my hand. Suddenly I realized I knew these people: they were the Cranches, Richard and Mary. Mary was Abigail's older sister.

"Yes. It is I." I smiled. "I live just there, in a cottage. That's why—"

"Of course." Mr. Cranch forestalled my apology. "You need no carriage to make your way a stone's throw through the dunes."

"And I'm Mary. We've seen you at meeting, though not for some time now."

"No," I replied.

"We are most sorry for your loss," Mr. Cranch said as we approached the door.

"Yes, most sorry," Mary agreed, and by her pained face, I knew her to be in earnest.

Two children, a tall boy and his little sister, came running round the bend, out of breath.

"Children!" Mary scolded. "Stop running at once!"

"But Mommy!" the little boy, Will, objected. "We saw a porcupine!"

"Will poked it with a stick!" cried the girl.

"You foolish boy," Mary admonished. "Come here." She hugged him tightly.

I smiled. A normal family with normal children. Gazing upon them, I doubly mourned my loss.

Twice before I had been in the great house, when Jeb and I had first moved to our cottage. It had been autumn and the leaves had all gone from the trees, making the large house feel forlorn. But it was mid-summer now, and it seemed that Mrs. Quincy had ordered more furniture or taken some out of storage, because I felt within a warmth of color and texture I had not noticed previously.

We sat in the north parlor, and a servant brought us some refreshment. Sherry, I believe it was. I admired the imported tiles surrounding the fireplace and at first did not join the conversation between Colonel Quincy and the Cranches. Mr. Cranch, a judge, spoke of a new case. I nearly offered the information that my father had been a judge but then thought better of it. I knew the Cranches to be ardent patriots, and my father had been a loyal servant of the Crown. In his last year, however, he had begun to have doubts . . .

There was a sudden knock on the door, and when the butler opened it, I saw Abigail Adams and her children. Oh, was I glad of it! For while the Cranches were amiable, I found I could not speak of trivialities in the usual way and so sat there quite silent, unable to contribute.

Seeing me, Abigail grinned and came up at once to embrace me. Her children were ushered off to another part of the house, perhaps to the kitchen. Her lively presence changed the course of the evening for the better, for she seemed to sense that I could speak but little, and she took up the lion's share of that task, unconsciously leaving her hand in mine the entire time. I loved her greatly at that moment!

We were soon called for dinner, which was delicate and delicious and consisted of five courses beginning with aspic of fish. Over dinner, I found something to talk about with Richard Cranch, and Mary's warm looks in my direction made me feel safe in my grief. Her glance seemed to say, *You need not pretend for our sakes.*

And so I did not. But, as one must eat at a dinner party and have at least some conversation, Mary began by asking whether I needed anything for my home.

"Yes, indeed," Mr. Cranch added gladly. "I would be happy to loan you my Shakespeare collection."

Mary frowned at her husband. "Shakespeare? I had in mind some chickens or a flax loom." She sounded so serious that suddenly Colonel Quincy guffawed, and everyone laughed.

"But Mr. Cranch," I cut in, "how could you know that I love Shakespeare? Indeed, I have a volume of Tragedies from my father's collection, which is very precious to me."

"Then allow me to loan you the Comedies."

At this solecism Mary nudged her husband with her foot. I know because it was my foot she nudged beneath the table. Richard Cranch meant no harm. I thanked him and said, "At some point, I shall love to borrow them."

"Then let us agree," he said, to close the conversation on Shakespeare, "that we shall discuss one of his plays on another occasion."

"Oh, yes, let's," Abigail joined in. "I am heartily tired of farming and chores and long for ten minutes of intelligent conversation."

"Mrs. Adams, you shall have it." Mr. Cranch smiled. "For it seems that such conversation might prove medicinal. I shall leave you to choose the subject. Shakespeare, Virgil, or perhaps Pliny—"

"Oh, no government," Abigail quickly objected. "Please, no government."

The dinner passed pleasantly after that. Just as we were about to take to our separate parlors, the colonel raised his glass and announced, "I would like to congratulate our esteemed lodger on certain patriotic activities of her own yesterday."

Ann looked at her husband as if he were mad. She was used to his loud, unreserved ways and was clearly anxious lest this should be some new faux pas.

Mary inquired, "Lizzie, what activity might that have been?"

I felt my face grow hot. "Oh, it is hardly worth mentioning, but I was called to the side of a woman in travail. She was safe delivered of a little girl."

"Balderdash!" bellowed the colonel. "The woman would have died without you. It is said the baby was breech, and the poor foolish mother was stranded on Grape Island, all alone."

I glanced quickly at the colonel, amazed by the fact that a man of such great stature should so enjoy the gossip of servants.

"Grape Island?" asked Richard, looking at me with new interest.

"Dear, do you think this is really the time and place . . . ?" Ann began.

But the colonel would not be gainsaid. He told the entire story as he had heard it from a servant, who apparently had heard it from a friend of the Brown family.

"After all," he concluded, "we must have babes to populate our new country, mustn't we?"

"Josiah!" Ann finally put her foot down. "You are mortifying this poor woman. Can you not see?"

Indeed, I must have looked beet red, for Ann quickly asked a servant to bring me a glass of water.

Abigail came to my rescue. "Lizzie is indeed to be commended, but I suggest we save our praise of her for others' ears."

"Well, Lizzie," said Mary kindly, "if news spreads as quickly as I think it does around this parish, you shall soon be run quite off your feet."

Abigail closed the discussion by adding, "Yes, and I truly believe she will need help if she is to stay with us."

"Stay?" Ann asked. "Is there even a question of that?"

"Indeed there is," Abigail replied. "Her in-laws, staunch Tories, mean to remove her from our midst."

"Well, that won't do," said the colonel. He sat erect in his chair and leaned across the table to Abigail, bellowing, "She needs a servant, you mean?"

"A servant or an apprentice. Yes, that is exactly what I mean, Colonel Quincy," Abigail answered.

"Oh, no, no," I began to object.

"Well, then, you shall have one as soon as may be."

With that, the master of the house bade us leave the table for our separate parlors.

9

THE PROSPECT OF HAVING A SERVANT IN my house was not a welcome one. It would take a frightening event, which would befall me later that autumn, before I would accept not only the idea of a servant but also the servant herself. Still, as I fell asleep later that night, I felt it had done my wounded soul good to dine with caring friends. I had liked the Cranches at once, and Abigail had shown great tact in suggesting they all spread the word about my midwifery. The colonel, too, had proved a loving father in his readiness to help me.

I had little time to congratulate myself, however, for the very next morning I was awakened by a knock at the door. It was Abigail, come to tell me that old Deacon Williams had fallen ill with the bloody flux, and two others besides.

"I'm terrified, Lizzie," she said, grasping my arm. "This must be some new calamity the Lord has seen fit to try us with."

"Nonsense." I moved to dress myself. I never could believe our Maker would force us to suffer on purpose. "It's those filthy soldiers marching to and from town. They bring sickness on their clothing, on their boots."

I asked her did the deacon wish me to attend him, but she said no. She had only stopped in to warn me of things to come.

"Well, I hope you won't hesitate to send for me, Abigail, if I am needed." Then I blushed. I was, after all, but twenty years old, and she was a worldly thirty.

"Never fear, Dr. Boylston. I shall call upon you at the slightest sign of a sniffle."

I shall always remember Abigail's ironic tone. From nearly our first meeting, she evinced an almost uncanny ability to see all my flaws. She remarked upon my tendency to self-pity; she laughed at my occasional grandiosity; and she could always put me in my place with a well-timed joke. But always, always, her prods were blunted by the tender restraint of love.

As July went on, the air grew even hotter, and more people sickened and died. Disease acquired a lusty taste for us. So many men were gone that women were left to suffer alone with only ignorant child-servants to help. The youngest and oldest died first. In August, our own Parson Wibird fell gravely ill, and as a result there was no meeting on the Sabbath during August or September.

God had abandoned us, it seemed. From our homes, rivers of blood and feces ran such that no one dared step anywhere. Houses, hot and filthy, stank. I shrank from going inside them, and yet I did. Though people will say I was brave to do so, I will say it was the path I took back to life, for nothing eases one's own pain more than to ease that of others.

This same month I delivered my second newborn, having been called to the bedside of the tanner's wife, Hannah Baxter. And on the eleventh, I was called in the middle of the night to tend a young farmer, Elisha Niles, who seemed to be expiring. When I arrived, he was conscious but very low. His skin was hot to the touch and dry. I cooled him down as best I could, but I knew he was near his end. There was nothing I could do but hold his hand. At dawn, he shut his eyes and departed this life without struggle.

I stayed to wash his body and, with a servant's help, got poor Elisha into his burial clothes. After I had finished my work, the sun was just rising above the sea. It had never cooled during the night; the air was still warm. Greatly fatigued, I hurried home and went to bed after stripping down to my skin, so close and hot was it in the house. I left all the doors wide open for the breeze. An Indian or a king's soldier could have entered quite easily, and yet I slept without fear.

I should have been afraid. Indians lurked about the perimeter of our parish. British soldiers trawled the coast road, looking for women. Bears, wolves, and thieves roamed the land, taking advantage of our chaos. And wayward sailors, whom I could see beyond my kitchen window, stared at the shore, longing for one night in a warm bed. I should have been afraid, but I was not. Not of strangers, anyway. Only of the Boylstons, for to live with them would have been a living death.

•   •   •

August of the year of our Lord 1775 wore on, with no abatement of disease. Indeed, it seemed to grow worse. I did what I could, glad to be too busy to think of myself. Abigail fell ill, followed by Tommy, and I gave them every comfort I could, though medicine was in short supply. By now, word had spread that I was a goodly midwife, and the women of the North Parish began to call upon me to tend their sick children, which I did to the best of my abilities.

By the middle of September, the bloody flux had seized the neighboring village of Weymouth. Every last household contained the sick and dying. Abigail's mother fell ill with it. After several days, it seemed as if the crisis had passed. But then, on September 30, she had a relapse and fell unconscious.

I knew that Abigail had removed to Weymouth to be with her mother, but did not know how gravely ill the elder woman was until I received a panicked boy at my door. He spoke so quickly that I could hardly understand him. He asked could I come quickly to the parsonage in Weymouth—but as for the rest, I could not make it out. Abigail's mother had either expired or was thought to be expiring.

"Well, which is it, child?" I asked with ill-concealed impatience. The poor flustered boy could not say. The first indeed required haste; the other, none at all.

For Abigail I would summon my energy. I had Thaxter saddle Star, and once again, I set off astride him. I resolved to gaze neither left nor right as I passed through town, imagining that if I did not see them, the people of the parish could not see me. This time riding Star, the thought occurred to me how much easier it would be if I were a man. I'd heard of women dressing up to go to battle as recently as in our war with the French and the Indians. Such thoughts fled when I arrived in Weymouth, however, and Abigail espied me from the dooryard of her father's parsonage.

She came flying out of the ancestral home perched on its pretty knoll as I dismounted and tied Star. She hugged me close, whispering, "Thank God. Lizzie, I am despairing."

I asked her for water for my horse as it was a very warm day, and I had not stopped once for him. When Isaac had been called for that purpose, I walked up the knoll, for which effort I was awarded a fine view of the broad white beach, the dark-blue bay, and Boston beyond. The leaves of the maple trees had just begun to turn, and to my left, Weymouth village was awash in warm reds and golds. How indifferent Nature can seem, at times, to our suffering!

There was no such heartening view within. I found Abigail's mother alive but very gravely ill. I touched the woman's arm. She turned and groaned. Even a slight touch upon her skin tortured her. She was shut in and bundled against her chill, even on this warm day. I took it upon myself to open a window and remove the bolster.

"Could you fetch me some cool water in a bowl, please?" I asked one of the Smiths' servants. The girl nodded and returned with a bowl of water. Very gently, I proceeded to cool Mrs. Smith, pressing the wet cloth to her arms and legs and neck.

At one point she opened her eyes and saw me—a total stranger—and appeared frightened.

"Do not be alarmed." I smiled. "I'm Lizzie Boylston, a friend of your daughter's." Abigail had been dozing in a chair by the bed, but upon hearing my words she sat up.

"She is an angel," added Abigail, touching her small hand upon my shoulder.

"I thought my eyes played tricks," the mother murmured. She seemed to fall asleep then, but awoke in the middle of the night unable to breathe. Parson Smith entered with Dr. Tufts. Together we watched her final struggle. There was nothing at all to be done for her. When there is a struggle for life, the end is always much worse, and so, while I didn't know if she would hear me, I bent over and whispered, "You may go to your Maker knowing you did good on this earth. You created one of the finest women alive."

My words seemed to calm her; her breaths became easier, but also farther apart. Soon they ceased. She was gone.

Abigail wept inconsolably. I made her a good strong tea, which she took, and when she was able, she turned to me and asked, "What did you say to her? She seemed to rest easier after that."

"I told her she could be proud of you," I said simply.

She thanked me, then wept again. "Oh, my poor mother. My poor, dear mother."

It was near dawn when she had calmed herself somewhat, and I asked her if she would like me to wash the body or if they had a servant, for I did not wish to intrude upon this sacred task.

She said her father had no particular person in mind. And so I did it. I can still see Abigail staring in mute awe as I washed her mother's body.

"When my turn comes, I want you to wash my body like that."

I hesitated. "Oh, I am sure to go to my Maker long before you. You are made of flint."

"Promise me," Abigail replied most gravely. At dawn on October 1, 1775, I promised her.

10

IT WAS FROM MY MOTHER THAT I learned my medical arts. She was practiced in healing, and the women of our neighborhood relied upon her. She first learned them from a family slave, with whom she snuck off in the dead of night to watch slave children enter an unfair world.

Soon my mother was taking calls at all hours—to deliver a baby or nurse the sick or dying. I often went with her, although she never asked me to. Once you see a patient's eyes shine with gratitude—well, if your heart does not break or your blood cringe, you are called for life.

I loved to bundle myself in cloaks and mitts and launch myself into the cold outdoors and the world of men. My father always grumbled from his room, "The whole town will think you're a pair of witches! Heaven knows I do sometimes myself."

I found my father fearsome, but clearly my mother did not. A true noblewoman, she had an innate sense of worthiness. Usually she just laughed at him.

But her flesh, oh, my Maker! Her flesh was mortal. It was on such an excursion as I have described that my mother herself first caught a devilish malady. Mrs. Whitcomb—wife of our local blacksmith—was in travail, and her throat was much inflamed.

The baby, a healthy boy, lived, but his mother, burning with fever, died two days later. Laying her out, Mama grimaced and pushed me away. I was hurt, not comprehending.

Several days later I understood. She took to her bed burning with fever, her throat so raw she could not swallow. When I brought her tea, she would not let me touch her. My mother pointed to her bedside table. "Leave the tea there."

A second day passed, and she was no better. I sent for my father, who was in New Hampshire at a trial.

When I came into her room after giving the letter to a servant, she was lying very still, her eyes wide and fixed on the ceiling. Oh, it frightened me! I reached out to her, but she drew her hand away.

"Send for the doctors," she said. "I feel I am dying."

I ran. No servant could run faster than I, certainly not Bessie, my mother's maid, or Giles, my father's manservant and a former slave, whom he had freed upon my grandfather's death.

I was before the residence of Dr. Bullfinch by the Common within eight minutes' time. He was at home and looked quite astonished at my sweaty face. He walked toward our house with maddening slowness, not wanting to call for the chaise.

"Can you not walk a bit faster?" I urged him.

At long last we arrived. My mother was alive but breathing shallowly. Her skin looked dried, yellow, and parched. She glanced at me wildly and reached out her hand, whether to repulse or draw me near I could not tell. In any case, Dr. Bullfinch shut the door on me. I knew he would draw out her blood.

Later that afternoon she was resting easier, and my brother, Harry, finally returned from his hiding place. I flung myself upon him like a wildcat. I loved my brother, but where had he been? At gaming and drinking, no doubt. He was fifteen and headed for nothing but ruin, our father said. He had recently refused a place at Harvard College, finding books "awfully dull."

Harry wasn't a bad boy, but his mind needed action, not books. In a few years, he would get his action: the Revolution and a privateer ship, upon which he sailed gaily out of Boston Harbor in search of treasure. At that time, he cared nothing for the Cause.

I beat at his chest, but he held me to him and tenderly stroked my hair.

"Lizzie, Lizzie, I'm sorry," he said. "She'll recover, I'm sure. She's made of stone."

These gay young men always think strong women are made of stone!

But she did not recover. The next morning, with Dr. Bullfinch asleep in a chair by her bed and my father galloping down Brattle Street toward our door, she expired this life.

I was new at loss then, not a master as I am now. I didn't know how I should live without my mother. I spent hours locked in my chamber, refusing to speak to my father or brother. I was angry with both of them—for their belated presence at her death, and because rage was far more tolerable than grief.

I lived in near seclusion with my father for the next five years. He was often abroad, and in that time I read much of his library. When not reading, I spent my time chatting with Bessie.

Bored and alone a great deal of the time, I begged my father to procure me a tutor. Seeing no great harm in it, and with only the warning that I should not learn to speak in tongues, he agreed. The man came thrice weekly thereafter, in the mornings. He was an old, sickly-looking fellow named Mr. Trask. He had a balding pate and gray nose hairs. Yet I was delighted with him; he was kindly and expected no great genius from a girl. But with relatively little effort I learned to read Greek and Latin just like a boy. Upon hearing Mr. Trask's report, my father said, "Well, it seems you've the mind of a man, Lizzie." I knew this to be a very great compliment from him. But from that moment I also began to count myself a sort of freak of nature. *Of what use,* I asked myself, *could a man find the mind of a woman?*

One Sunday in the summer of 1774, when I was but nineteen, I espied a new family in our meetinghouse. They sat two pews in front of ours and looked quite put out. I didn't know at that time that their own church had closed. A decade earlier, my mother had prevailed upon my father to switch to the Congregational church, finding her own—and its perpetual prayers for the king—"dreadfully tedious." My father, being only as religious as he needed to be, consented willingly enough.

This new family consisted of a rather pompous-looking man, a rigid but beautiful older girl with blonde upswept hair, and a restless boy who kept shifting his position beside his sister. Mrs. Boylston was not at meeting that day, and I later learned that she refused to go to the meetinghouse once her church had closed.

I heard the boy laugh at one point and turned 'round. This time, I saw him clearly: his face was bemused, his eye sharp, his fair hair pulled into a neat plait. He raised his eyebrows at me mischievously, and we both began to laugh so uncontrollably that we had to excuse ourselves.

That was Jeb.

The next day, he paid me a formal visit. I think I must have already loved him because I allowed him to stay quite a long time. My father kept coughing in his study, and Bessie, his spy, kept trudging noisily in and out of the parlor. But we chatted amiably away, paying them no heed, lost in our own happy meeting. Above all, Jeb had an ironic sense of humor and was delighted to discover someone who shared it. That I was a girl at first seemed a secondary consideration. But only at first.

We were soon engaged, and the Boylstons bestowed upon us the gift of our beautiful, yet green, Narragansett Pacer, Star.

When the actual fighting began the following April, my father found himself on the wrong side. Not in his heart, perhaps, but, as he was in the service of the Crown, he could not abandon his position without also abandoning his livelihood. He made the decision to return to England, and he wanted me to go with him. But I was engaged and in love and refused to leave.

"You must come, Lizzie," he urged in most passionate tones. "There shall soon be nothing left here. What will I do without you?"

Indeed, our house was in disarray. He had packed as much as he could take on board ship, sold off some furniture, and let all but two of the servants go.

Though I loved my father, I was of an age to love a man more. Jeb and I were soon to be married, and I would not leave him. Nor did I wish to leave my patients, for by then I had a goodly number—the same women who had called upon my mother to deliver them of their babes and more. They trusted and needed me. Although young, I was already renowned for being able to remove a stubborn babe.

I had seen my mother many times reach into a womb and turn a babe or lift the head off the *os pubis*, where these little ones can lodge themselves like seals beneath a sea shelf. Reaching in and turning them caused mothers terrible pain. My mother hated to do it. Sometimes the womb cramped around her hand so firmly she had to withdraw and try again several times before she succeeded.

But the mothers survived, and, in the end, they were grateful to her. None of them wanted Dr. Bullfinch to attend them, what with his frowns, his hems and haws, and his big metal forceps that looked more apt to crush the skull of the babe than draw it out safely.

Between pain and harm, my mother taught me, lay a vast moral divide. Sometimes one must cause pain to avoid harm. This lesson was my mother's great gift to me. After her death, I took a vow never to cause harm, if I could help it. I now reasoned that while I would cause my father pain, it would cause the women actual harm for me to leave them. My father and I reconciled ourselves to a parting that we believed would be of a few years' duration, at most. If the Rebels won—an unlikely event, my father believed—those judges who knew British constitutional law might prove useful. If they did not—well, he would have done nothing wrong in the eyes of the Crown. In all, he was a fence-sitter hoping to climb down successfully on the winning side.

But Providence had other ideas. My father left for England, caught pneumonia on board, and died soon after his arrival. I hardly had time to mourn him. His death, so far away, seemed unreal to me. For days after I received word of it, I wandered the upturned house, marveling at the spirit I continued to feel there. His books were still on the shelves—I had taken but two, a single volume from his eight-volume set of Shakespeare and my mother's beloved edition of the Sonnets. His desk still held his papers. A portrait of my fair mother, which he dared not take aboard a ship, still stood above the parlor mantel. For a while, I even allowed myself to believe that my father had not in fact died, that he was alive and well and that the message had been written in error.

•   •   •

Less than one month after Jeb and I moved to Braintree, my brother joined a privateer ship bound for the West Indies. He sent me a hasty word by messenger along with a curricle, and I bumped my way all night in that old chair to Boston Harbor, arriving at dawn.

I pleaded with my brother to the last. "Why not come live with us?" I begged. "There's plenty to do right in Braintree."

"Me, a farmer?" He laughed with a toss of his fair head. "I'd as soon be a midwife."

I smacked him, and he laughed some more. Then I nestled my face in his breast. "I'm afraid. I'm so afraid I'll never see you again."

"Oh, you'll see me, all right. I'll be tan and hale, a stranger bearing gifts."

"The Greeks taught us to beware strangers bearing gifts," I replied tartly.

"Oh, Lizzie." He sighed, casting a brotherly arm about me. "You really must try to be less intelligent. A handsome fellow has little use for a brainy woman."

But before I could reply, it was time for him to board the vessel. I waved until I could see him no longer. I thought it probable that I would never see my brother again and wept my fill before arriving back at the farm.

11

NEAR THE ANNIVERSARY OF MY BROTHER'S DEPARTURE, I was
seized with cramps and a dizzy headache that made me puke. I
could not go far from the necessary. Without, it was cold. Autumn
leaves swirled about as if a storm were brewing. I was gathering the
last of the pompions and gourds when I had to drop them upon
the ground and curl up in pain. I called weakly for Thaxter, who, as
usual during a crisis, was nowhere to be seen. Finally, with a break
in the cramps I knew would be quite mercilessly short, I ran to the
fields and found him having a smoke by our back fence.

"Take Star and go to the Adamses at once. Tell Abigail I'm ill
and need help."

I never liked to ask for help, but I knew my illness would soon
grow worse. Indeed, I did not know how I would make it back to
my house without soiling my dress. Arriving in my kitchen, I had
just enough strength left to throw a pallet by the fire and collapse
onto it. There, I lost consciousness. At some point later in time, I
know not exactly when, I heard Abigail enter and call out to me.

"Lizzie?"

"I'm here," I replied weakly from my bed in the kitchen.

I heard her approach, then stop. No doubt she was taking in
the mess. Tasks I had started lay unfinished where I had begun

them. My loom stood undressed in the second parlor. Baskets of tow, apples, and corn were strewn about, rotting and gathering dust.

Abigail came at last to the kitchen entrance and peered in. I lay by a fire that had gone out long ago. I felt her stare at me for a moment, then heard her say, "You are quite unwell. Rest. All shall be well."

I fell into a delirium that lasted a full week. At one point, Abigail told me, I sat upright in horror, for to me Abigail had become the living image of my dead mother.

I was not aware of her comings and goings, but I was later to learn that Abigail visited twice a day until the dire nature of my illness made her come one morning with her trunk and stay for several days. It seems she had sent the children off to her sister's so she could nurse me.

I certainly owe my life to her. But, upon my waking after a time of grave illness, there was no tender scene, no expression of love and devotion. Instead, my first sight was of her tiny face peering down at me with an expression of disgust.

"Abigail? Dearest, is that you? How long have you been here?"

She ignored my question. "Truly, Lizzie, I am quite put off."

I merely lay there, thinking she meant the stench of my sick-room.

"Let there be no mistake. It is not the dangerous state of your house that annoys me. I can forgive you that. It is your pigheadedness I cannot abide. You are getting a servant this week, and that's that."

Without waiting for a response from me—I was too weak to proffer one in any case—she set about removing my chamber pot, opening my windows, and scrubbing the kitchen floor. Indeed, she shrank from nothing, stopping only now and again to scold me—me, still sick and in my bed!—for having no help, and mine a bigger farm even than her own.

At one point in her cleaning, she reached over my limp body to remove a pot from the hearth. As my voice was not yet strong, I whispered to her, "You don't frighten me, you know!"

And bending down with a fierce, hawk-like face, she said, "Well, I *should.*"

Greatly cheered, I attempted a laugh, for had I been expiring, she would not have abused me thus.

12

I WAS ABLE TO RISE FROM MY bed in a week's time. I began to attack the tasks I had sorely neglected during my illness and was just hanging herbs to dry when, from the parlor window, I saw a beautiful carriage drive down my bumpy lane. Its painted swaths of French blue and gilt wavered through the glass. Two very fine horses stood impatiently before my door. None of us had such carriages then in Braintree, except for Colonel Quincy, and even his was not so fine.

Fearful, and with the basket of herbs over my arm, I made my way outside. Just as I stepped forth, a gust of autumn wind rose off the sea and blew a huge pile of leaves in my direction. The wind tugged my hair violently out of its pins. When the leaves settled and I had plucked my hair off my face, I saw Eliza Boylston step down from the carriage, helped by her coachman. I gripped my basket to me and braced myself to run.

"I am not going anywhere," I said to Eliza.

But Eliza merely smiled indulgently, as if speaking to a child. "I agree—you're not. But might we come in? We are tired after our journey, and my driver needs refreshment as well."

Suddenly a skinny girl, her face obscured by a large black bonnet, descended from the carriage, and I felt a swift shame that my bad manners had been perceived by a stranger. "Excuse me. I have only recently recovered from a dire illness."

"I'm sorry to hear it," said Eliza, backing away as if perhaps she would reconsider entering my cottage.

I led them inside, took their cloaks and bonnets and mitts, and bade them warm themselves by the fire. The driver, an old Negro by the name of Jupiter, unhitched the horses and led them to my barn. He then disappeared, presumably to find the necessary, and did not reappear. The girl had not yet looked up, and Eliza had not yet introduced her. I put the kettle on to boil, then inquired, "And this is Miss—"

"Oh, forgive me. Miss Martha Miller, Mrs. Jebediah Boylston."

"How do you do, Martha," I said.

"Well, thank you, Mrs. Boylston." She looked up just long enough to catch my eyes, then looked away. I guessed her to be about fifteen years of age.

"Poor Martha has had a terrible time of it," Eliza began. "She has lost her mother and father both. She has but one brother in all the world, but he has lodgings at Rowe's Wharf. Not at all suitable for a young girl."

This was indeed a sad story, but as yet I had no thought of its having anything to do with me. I gave them both good hot dishes of tea with milk and biscuits. While I was unable to add sugar to the meal, I had some honey stored for special occasions. I went and fetched it in the cellar. I took a small dollop from the jar, placed it in a china cup, and served it. Going even that far exhausted me, however, and I sat myself down.

"It's nice honey. From the bees I—we kept."

"Martha"—Eliza turned to the girl as if she hadn't heard my comment—"if you've finished your tea, fetch Jupiter and have him ready the carriage. I plan to depart in fifteen minutes. Tell him he may ready Star as well."

"Ready Star?" I stood, knocking my dish off its saucer and spilling tea onto the table. "What for?"

"Papa wishes to have him back. Surely, having no carriage you can have no need of a horse."

"But I *do* need him—I am very often abroad helping the women of this parish. And other parishes as well."

"Oh, that," she said distastefully. "I had forgotten."

"He was Jeb's. I won't give him up. You may tell your father that."

"If you recall, Star was a particular gift to Jeb upon his marriage."

"Yes, and now that he's gone, his few things are mine," I said, turning so that she could not see my involuntary tears. I then took a deep breath and exclaimed, "Why is it you have shown me no love or kindness since the day you met me, when every day I was prepared to love you? Why is your heart so cold?"

"My heart is my affair," she said stiffly, reaching for her cloak and bonnet.

"And no doubt it shall remain so!"

Eliza merely threw her cloak about her and said, "You don't know me. Or my heart. Martha"—Eliza turned, her long neck stretched to its full swan-like length, her color high with pique—"tell Jupiter we're going."

"Yes, ma'am."

Martha nodded and, hat and cloak hastily donned, headed for the tiny cabin behind my house where Thaxter lived.

I realized then that Eliza's errand was not to kidnap me. No, it was to kidnap Star. Needing food and clothing, I would be a burden to a family in reduced circumstances. On the other hand, Star was worth a good hundred pounds. Selling him would make them comfortable for many months. I stood at once and moved to the side door.

"Thaxter!" I called.

Hearing two people calling him, my field hand did not at first know whom he should approach. I opened the door. Seeing me, Thaxter nodded. Though I was not very close to him, I smelled rum.

"Thaxter, please tell the driver that Miss Boylston and her maid wish to leave. Then ride Star over to the Adamses. You can walk back."

It appeared as if he would ask me a question, but my peremptory look cut him off.

"Yes, ma'am," he said. Before two minutes had passed, I heard him gallop off upon Star. Triumph!

"Well," said Eliza, "we shall leave aside the discussion of Star for the moment."

"Think that if you like," I replied bitterly. "You shall never have him. And never again shall I discuss it. Now go."

"*I* am going," she said. But the way she said it, I suddenly felt as if I had been lingering under a misapprehension. "But before I do, I must tell you about Martha. Her presence here is not our doing, but is entirely due to the goodness of Colonel Quincy—"

"Colonel Quincy?" I cried. I had not a clue Martha was meant to stay with me.

"Colonel Quincy sent word to us that you were ill and in need of help. He suggested Martha. She is the daughter of former friends of my parents. Good, loyal subjects, neighbors of the colonel at his Boston house. Poor Martha's parents succumbed to illness on their way to Halifax. They say the conditions were pestilential."

"Oh, no." My heart suddenly understood the girl's mute, desolate countenance.

"Well, as I was saying," she continued, "it was soon arranged for the girl to come here. She could help you and meanwhile learn a useful . . . trade."

"I see." At last, I finally did see. Abigail and the colonel had finally made good on their promise to procure me a servant. "Well,

I will take her because it is the Christian thing to do. Clearly she has nowhere else to go. To stay with you would be a fate worse than death. Surely you cannot believe you will be allowed to return to Cambridge anytime soon."

"You may be right about our having to remain in Portsmouth," she allowed. "We are resigned to it."

I was going to say, "I am pleased to hear it," but my father always told me that sarcasm was for second-rate minds. I therefore said nothing.

Eliza took her leave then. I did not curtsy. The clatter of hooves and rattling of the wheels were already growing distant as the November sky grew dark. Immediately, my thoughts turned toward this orphan who had quite literally landed on my doorstep, and who, no doubt, wanted to be there as little as I desired her to be.

Martha said not a word after Eliza had gone.

I was used to silence. In the months since Jeb had died, I had built up a great deal of silence around me. Apart from Abigail's visits, or my midwifery, or "Thaxter, have you chopped the wood yet?" I often went for days on end without uttering a single word.

However, I now needed to say something; it would be ill-mannered not to.

"Well," I began, taking her one small bag and heading toward the stairs, "let me show you your room." I could have set her in the tiny dairy by the kitchen, but I was always in the kitchen and didn't want her upon me every waking moment.

I gave her the second-best bedroom, the one I had thought to populate with children one day. It had a small bed and chest, and I left her to look about while I fetched the only other linens I had besides my own—some fine ones I had brought to housekeeping from my family and never used. She helped me tighten the ropes and beat the bed, then spread the fine linen upon it without my having to ask her.

"I will weave you a rug by and by, and see if perhaps Abigail—that is Mrs. John Adams—has a chair she can loan," I said.

"Thank you," she replied.

I looked at her downcast head.

"You must be tired."

"Yes, a little," she said. Though only three words, I noted in them a fine, clear Boston accent.

"Well, there is a chamber pot here." I pointed to the corner, where a rather elegant Staffordshire blue-and-white chamber pot sat, another heirloom of my mother's. "And just behind the house, to the left of Thaxter's cabin, is the necessary. Oh—but you'll need a candle."

Though exhausted, I made to descend the stairs, but her hand on my shoulder stopped me.

"I have no urgent need of it," she said. "I can fetch it later, when I go down—"

At once I knew she felt she had misspoken and would say, "for supper," to which I had not invited her.

"You are no guest here, Martha. You are free to eat when you choose, or you may take your meals with me. Indeed, it would be easier that way. Nothing fancy, mind you. I rise before dawn, generally, and have my breakfast as the sun rises after I have milked Mildred and Bertha and fed the other animals. Dinner is at one, except on the Sabbath, when we eat at noon."

I heard my words: they sounded ridiculous. Indeed, I had not made an actual meal in many months. But I was driven to present my life to this stranger as if it were full and orderly instead of hectic and lonely. Now, locked into this false tack, it appeared I could not stop. "One does not want to be digesting during Parson Wibird's sermon. He has no sense of humor, I assure you. For supper, I generally have some cheese and bread before falling unconscious upon my bed."

At this, Martha gave me a tiny curl of her lip, and I was heartened. For though I knew her to be in mourning, there was nothing I abhorred so much as a soul with no leavening of humor about it.

I had the opportunity to observe Martha's appearance then: she was quite small, about the height of Abigail Adams, but thinner. Her hair was a shiny sable brown, fashioned in a simple knot above her head. Her eyes were of a quite beautiful amber color. Had there been some life in them, they would have shone like the sun. Her brow was dark and thick, redeemed from commonness by a tall, fine forehead. Her mouth was full and charming, but I would know more when I saw her smile. All in all, she seemed as plain and shy as a fawn. And yet . . .

"Well, I'll bid you good-night. I am not quite well yet and so shall retire early. Perhaps I said that already? Oh, but of course you knew that anyway. That's why you are here. Or part of the reason why—well, good night." I cut myself abruptly short, as my words had begun to make little sense. "Let me know if you need anything. I'm just across the hall." I pointed to my chamber, but five feet away from hers. "There's a great deal to do on a farm. I think I can safely say you will not be bored. As for books, I myself find precious little time to read, and I have but six books, though they serve me well. Make free to read them. And now," I inhaled, almost comically, for indeed I had long since exceeded my supply of breath, "good night."

I was just shutting her door when she called to me in a soft voice, "Mrs. Boylston?"

The name sounded strange to my ears. "Yes, Martha?"

The girl frowned, and I thought she would tell me that she wished to return to Cambridge at first light.

"I suppose if I am to be shipped downriver like a slave, I am glad to have a grieving madwoman for my mistress and not that tedious snob." Her words, clearly articulated, bespoke the finest upbringing. Their content, on the other hand, could not have been more surprising. It made me burst into relieved laughter, in which she soon joined me.

13

I AWOKE BEFORE DAWN TO MILK THE cows and feed the animals. Halfway out the door, I realized that I had a servant now. I returned to her chamber to rouse her. Martha was sleeping soundly, and I hated to wake her. But she rose without complaint and followed me out of doors in the dawning light, watching as I scattered seed for the chickens, poured grain into the pigs' trough, and added fresh water to their drinking pool. I then demonstrated how to milk a cow.

We sat in Mildred's stall—or, rather, we took turns sitting on a three-legged stool Jeb had made—and I showed her how to pull down on the teats. Pressing my face into Mildred's warm flank, I grasped two teats in my fists and yanked. Out came the milk into the tin pail. Suddenly, I heard Star whinny.

"Ah." I smiled. "There's the object of my dispute with Miss Eliza yesterday. You may visit him if you like. He loves carrots or apples." My voice quavered at the memory of how I used to scold Jeb for stealing my pie apples to give to Star.

With a deftness not lost on me, Martha returned us to the subject of milking Mildred. "Let me try," she said.

She took up the stool in my place and grasped Mildred's teats too gently. When no milk was forthcoming, I said, "That will do well for a woman's teats, not a cow's."

"What's that you say?"

"To bring on stronger travail, if it has slowed or ceased," I explained.

Martha turned red in the face and shrank down until she was nearly beneath my cow.

"Come now, Martha." I smiled. "I am sometimes called to do far ruder things. As you soon will be. It will help greatly when you learn to think only of the safety of the mother and her babe, not the means by which we sometimes achieve that end."

She nodded. Summoning all her strength and displaying a magnificent unwillingness to fail, she grasped the teats hard, pulled down, and squirted me full in the face.

"Oh, I'm sorry!" she cried.

I began to laugh and wiped the milk from my face. She fell to laughing as well. We soon enjoyed that milk in our coffee and breakfast porridge.

• • •

My illness had put me far behind in my chores, and in that first week, as the last leaves fell from the trees and the ocean took on its steely winter-gray coloring, we worked many long hours in silence. By day we put up the fruit, carted corn to the mill, lugged apples off to the cider house, and carded the fluffy clouds of wool that had gathered dust in baskets since the summer before. Then, as the light waned, we sat in silence by the fire, spinning, boiling, and peeling until our hands were as stiff and red as those of scullery maids.

The silence was not uncomfortable to me; indeed, I have observed that companionship does not rely upon words so much as it does a person's inner state. Martha's soul was patient and deep. She asked for nothing, expected nothing.

One day, as we sat working by the fire, my thoughts drifted to the question of how Martha had known the Quincys. I knew her family had been their neighbor in Boston, but little else.

"Know you my landlord the colonel?" I asked.

"Colonel Quincy, you mean?"

"Yes."

"Oh, I saw him often when he resided in Boston. He and his former wife were friends with my parents, until the beginning of the Troubles."

"And does your brother remain in Boston?"

"Oh, yes." She smiled.

"And have you sold the ancestral house?" I inquired.

"No—that is, our former home is occupied by the Continental Army. Thomas keeps rooms by Rowe's Wharf. He does the occasional errand—for General Howe."

"General Howe!" I exclaimed. While I knew that Martha had come from a background quite similar to my own—Royalists for whom life in the colonies had already become increasingly dangerous—I had no idea that her brother was actually working for the British Army. This was bad news indeed. General Howe had commanded the forces at Bunker Hill. A boy of Howe's army had killed my Jeb.

I had hoped to invite Martha's brother to visit. Now, that was out of the question. I could hardly introduce him to Abigail, or to Susanna Brown, whose husband even now remained with Colonel Prescott.

As if reading my thoughts, Martha said, "I will go to him for Christmas. It is all arranged."

I did not ask Martha what she thought of the Cause, nor did I offer my opinion. But the divisive issue of loyalties remained unspoken between us.

The following Tuesday I was called upon by William Glover, whose mother was thought to be expiring. Martha came with me. It was her first expedition. It had snowed the night before, and our breath made fog in the frigid air. Our toes froze as we scuffled through the unshoveled snow up to the road.

As we neared the Glover house, I proceeded to discuss proper comportment in the chamber of one who was expiring or who would soon expire. I had seen many deaths, but poor Martha had not. She lost color at the sight of the unconscious woman, but she refused to sit when I proffered her a chair. I felt the pulse; it was quite slow and faint. I knew the end to be near. William sat sobbing, and I comforted him as best I could, knowing I could not do as much for his mother.

When I found no pulse half an hour later, I showed Martha how to close the eyes. I gently asked the son to leave us so that we could wash the body and dress it in what clothing the family had prepared. It was customary to have one's death garments woven well ahead of time, sometimes years ahead, so as not to be caught without them when the time came.

Martha shuddered at this idea. "I do not like to think of my raiments being in a drawer, waiting for me."

"No, but it is practical."

"Have you yours?" she asked, rubbing the rose oil I had given her into Mary Glover's feet.

"No, but God grant I have *some* time yet." I smiled. I would turn twenty-one on the twenty-third of December.

•   •   •

As we made our way home late that night, Martha asked, "Is the transition between life and death always so seamless, then? I saw no change in Mrs. Glover."

I grasped Martha's hand in mine, for clearly the sight of this, her first death, had unnerved her.

"Not always. But I have learned to be grateful when it is."

"I should not like to just . . . drift away like that."

"Shall I throw you a parting ball?"

She glanced at me warily in the cold moonlight. "No, but something. Some awareness, at least."

"Awareness that one shall soon be eternally unaware is not a state favored by mankind."

At this bit of philosophy, Martha fell gratefully silent on the topic.

•   •   •

Two days later Martha attended her first birth. As bad luck would have it, it was a complicated one.

The Holbrooks' house stood on the main road, just beyond the parish center. Smaller than my own cottage, it was attached to a small smithy next door. Within, it was dark, and the ceilings were so low I felt in danger of bumping my head. I saw no maid, and two older children chased each other throughout the close rooms in a noisy game of tag. I shushed them sharply and bade them go to their chamber. My tone must have frightened them, for off they went!

Martha silently cast her eyes about her, but I could tell she was appalled at the close conditions. In the great room—a misnomer, in this case—Beth Holbrook lay, quite unwell, insensible of her children running wild. I moved to examine her. Martha stood off a ways, wordless, but I bade her approach. Beth looked up from her bed, relieved that I had arrived.

I proceeded to touch the mother. Martha stood by my side, positively agape. To me, the place Martha now gaped at in amazement had become little more than a gateway to me for the living

JODI DAYNARD

creature within. Sometimes the gate would not open as it should. At other times, the child's head would lodge beneath the *os pubis* and I would have to reach in, simultaneously lifting the head and turning the body to dislodge it, then quickly pulling the babe out before it could get stuck again.

Such was the case with poor Beth Holbrook. The woman screamed as if I were murdering her. Martha now looked as though she might faint.

"It is painful, but causes no harm," I reassured her.

She looked horrified but said nothing, and within five minutes the child was born. The babe, a fine girl no worse for having been stuck, cried lustily. I cut the umbilicus, cleaned the child, tied its belly-band, and put it to the mother's breast. It took to sucking immediately. The sight brought tears to my eyes, which Martha did not fail to notice.

I instructed her to massage Beth's belly. Martha did so without flinching, and soon the placenta was delivered.

Beth looked at me gratefully.

"Bless you," she said, and began to cry out of sheer relief.

"The worst is over. You're very brave," I said.

"Have you children of your own?" she inquired.

"Oh, no," I said mildly. "I was wed but a few months before my Jeb died at Breed's Hill." I wrapped her stomach and placed a cotton cloth between her legs and fresh sheets beneath and above her.

I was amazed at how much easier my story had become, as if, told often enough, even the worst events could be told calmly.

"I'm so sorry," she said.

We spoke some more as I showed Martha how to place the pillows and to massage the mother's hands, one by one, as the baby sucked. I have found massaging the hands affords great pleasure and relaxes the mother so her milk will come in. Throughout her lesson, Martha continued to look at me with mute amazement.

84

Soon Beth lay back against the pillows and shut her eyes. She and the baby dozed contentedly. It was now past two in the morning, and by the time we finally returned home, it was past three. Neither of us could sleep. I got a fire going, boiled water, and made us some chamomile tea.

Martha had not said a word. It seemed she had not yet recovered from the shock of seeing her first birth. But the birth was not what Martha had on her mind at all, for suddenly she blurted out, "How can you continue to do that which causes you such suffering?"

Her question startled me, for I had never given voice to this obvious truth. I was unable to reply at once. Gathering myself, I said, "I have been trained to midwifery and healing from an early age. My poor dear mother trained me. It appears that God did not fashion me to have my own children, so I must be content with helping others bring theirs into this world. Indeed, I am highly gratified by it."

My tone brooked no opposition. Surely, had I spoken one more sentence, I would have burst into tears. Martha acknowledged my speech with a nod, and we moved on to speak a little of Mrs. Holbrook's travail.

"And now, I think it wise we get our sleep, as the animals are hungry at four, whether we sleep or no."

And so we both slept like the dead. I awoke an hour and a half later, grieving in my heart for all I had lost and all I would never have. I went to wake Martha but took pity on her when I saw how pale she looked. I let her sleep and went to do the chores myself.

Martha descended an hour after I had risen.

"You shouldn't have let me sleep," she said with annoyance.

"It's all right, Martha." I offered her a mug of coffee. "Perhaps after another bad night, you shall do the same for me."

"Indeed, I shall. You've been very good to me, Lizzie."

I noted with silent pleasure that Martha had finally used my Christian name.

•　　•　　•

Before we knew it, Christmas was upon us; a carriage arrived for Martha—presumably from her brother, Thomas. By this time I had grown attached to Martha and did not want her to leave me.

I told her to be careful; indeed, I was greatly worried. Rumors that Washington planned to attack the Regulars—even now, in winter, across the frozen Charles River—had our parish in a panic. The idea that the British commanders certainly knew of these rumors, if not of more concrete information, made me shake with fear at the thought of their attacking us first.

"I'll take care, I promise," she said as I wrapped a woolen scarf around her neck, patted her bonnet down, and kissed her. She laughed then, in good spirits to be on her way finally, to a most beloved brother.

I waved good-bye until I could no longer see the carriage. Then I returned to the house. I felt restless and did some chores, baking bread and spinning several skeins of wool. But when I paused for a moment, my fingers burning with the effort, the silence rang in my ears. I set aside my work and tried to read my beloved Shakespeare sonnets, but it was of no use. With Martha gone, the house felt too empty. After pacing a while, I gave up in disgust and decided to visit Abigail.

Although the sun shone, it was very cold that day. I had Thaxter saddle Star for me. As the afternoon light grew dimmer, the horse seemed grateful for the work and trotted energetically down the lane. Only the crows made any noise, cawing disapprovingly at us from their perches on neighboring fences.

My excitement at seeing my dear friend grew as I approached her house. I could not wait to tell her all about my new charge and share with her those things women shared with one another. I was ready to speak of my lost family, my hotheaded brother, and my dreams for the future. Despite the cold and the war and my loneliness, I had begun, in the past few days, to hope that someday I might feel love again.

I arrived before the Adams house to find it all lit up. I was ready to dismount when a certain vision made me pause.

Within, a family sat around a blazing fire. John Adams, our celebrated delegate to the Continental Congress, sat in the great chair with little Tommy on his knee. He was reading the child a book with colorful pictures in it, and the boy clung to his neck. Abigail was winding yarn upon a clock reel, which popped at regular intervals. Nabby wrote a number down in a little book each time it did so, keeping track of its length for her mother. Charlie and Johnny played chess on the table behind them.

Star scuffled his hooves impatiently, no doubt wishing me to make up my mind whether to descend or no. Abigail paused in her work and looked toward the window—a look, if not precisely of alarm, then of readiness. She knew from hard experience it could be anyone, friend or foe: a beggar, a drunk work hand, prisoners entreating a meal, officers needing a place to sleep out of the cold. That it was merely I she would not have guessed. She stood as if to move closer to the window, but I suddenly decided that I would not disturb her long-deserved idyll. I nudged Star with my heels and we returned back down the road, I having discovered a new level of loneliness, and Abigail having discovered nothing but a slight gust of winter wind.

14

THE IMAGE OF ABIGAIL SITTING BY THE fire with John and her children brought me quite low. While I loved Abigail and rejoiced for her, reunited after nearly a year with her beloved John, the image of that family around the blazing hearth put me in a self-pitying frame of mind.

I could not bear going up to my cold chamber, whose fire had gone out, and so pulled a pallet by the kitchen hearth. I removed my bodice, petticoat, and stays, and lay in my shift to burn on one side and freeze on the other. I turned myself periodically, like a roast upon the spit.

From my shelf I took my volume of Shakespeare's Tragedies— the third volume from Pope's six-volume set—and began to read. The light was dim, and my eyes soon closed. I fell asleep, King Lear raging between my ears.

When I awoke, alone in my kitchen at dawn, it was Christmas morning, 1775. I rubbed the glass and gazed beyond my heat-fogged window. The fields shone with brilliant, blinding whiteness. It had snowed.

I lifted myself up with a heavy spirit. It was freezing cold, and I had not slept well. (It is not good to begin a winter's day exhausted, as Nature takes no measure of one's readiness before demanding

Her tasks.) I moved to boil water for my coffee and spoke to myself with a firm tone. I told myself that I must stop sighing the lack of many a thing I sought. By many measures, I was a rich woman. I had sixty acres, a loom, a horse, two cows, and a servant. I had wood for fires, sheep's wool for hats and mitts, milk for butter, porridge, and cheese.

Indeed, all about me were signs of my industry. Health and youth were mine as well. "The worst is not, so long as we can say, 'This is the worst.' " Why, then, did these thoughts not console me? What was this heavy dolor that could not be consoled?

The image of Abigail and her family—I did not have *that*. Nor would I ever, I believed.

It was in a feverish state of self-consolation that I did my chores that morning, and when I finally was able to make myself some porridge, I considered my relation to the parish women. They had been slow to call upon me—and why not? Could they not feel my self-pity? Could they not sense how I begrudged them their healthy babes? Henceforth, I resolved, I would endeavor to love my neighbor, not envy her. I had the gift of healing, and heal I would.

It was soon midday, and I had fallen asleep after taking a small meal of bread, butter, and ham. The stomp of boots by my door woke me. I had lain down in my petticoat and bodice with no stays. My hair was loose, and I hurried to wash my mouth with some saltwater and put my fingers through my hair. I greeted Abigail at the door with a crooked smile.

"Come in," I offered. "It is very cold today."

"It is." She nodded. She did not take her eyes off me as I led her into my warm kitchen.

I took her muff and bonnet and cloak and set them on a chair where they would stay warm for her ride home.

Abigail frowned. "You look strange this morning, Lizzie."

"Why, thank you," I said wryly. "Care for some real English tea? It was a gift of my horrid sister-in-law."

"Oh, I would! So long as John is not about." She cast a quick glance around, as if I might actually be hiding him behind a door.

"Fear not. If ever he honors me by a visit, I shall serve him good patriotic blackberry tea."

She sat at the table, noticing the pallet by the fire and the Tragedies open facedown upon the floor. Her warm, brown eyes noticed everything—quickly, too.

I served the tea with some Indian-meal cakes on a china plate, a beloved treasure of my mother's.

"And you have been looking very carefully at me," I said. "You see, I am astute enough to perceive your observance of me. What do you find, may I ask?"

She placed a hand on mine. "I find you alarming. Like those people left in forests to be raised by wolves."

At this, I let out a decidedly unlady-like snort. "No, indeed. Though I lay awake half the night, it's true."

"Thinking what thoughts, may I ask?"

"That I must stop my self-pity and get on with the godly task of helping others."

She smiled enigmatically. "That is indeed a Christian thought on this holy morning. But so hard to live up to in practice, I find. I often resolve to stop pitying myself, but am rarely successful."

"In any case, I hope to try—" I faltered, not wishing my hard-won resolve to crumble.

"Oh"—she reached out to me—"I have given offense. I'm sorry. Don't let my old bruised heart keep you one minute from a true heroine's mission."

"You laugh at me now."

"Indeed, I do not." But her lips tightened as if she would laugh at any moment.

I went to the fire to fetch more hot water. "The thing is, philosophical consolation is all I have. I can't change my state. I can only change my relation to it." I did not say, "loveless, lonely, barren state," but it is what I thought.

"And you must *keep* that philosophy, Lizzie. But sprinkle upon it the flavor of the everyday. I mean only to warn you that it is human to feel lonely and sad and to pity oneself."

We were silent for a while then, each lost in our own thoughts. Abigail was no doubt thinking of John's imminent departure. In eleven years of marriage, they had lived together but half that time. Finally, she asked, "It was you last night outside my window, wasn't it?"

"Yes," I admitted, ashamed.

"And why did you not stay? We would have welcomed you, Lizzie."

"I didn't wish to intrude. You looked . . . happy."

"One is most inclined to generosity when one is happy, is one not?"

I felt her mild rebuke. "Well—" I began.

"Well, nothing." She stood. "I must go. But I—we—would like it very much if you joined us for Christmas dinner. My father will be with us, and the Cranches."

It was an offer too tempting to refuse.

•   •   •

Oh, the memory of that dinner has lasted me many years: children ran everywhere, and Richard and John, still young and hale, carried on a most fascinating conversation about what kind of government we should have in the event of Independency.

"We *shall* have it!" Adams shouted, tongue loose with cider—or so I thought. When I knew him better, I would know he always spoke loudly and with great passion. They spoke of bicameral and unicameral systems. Adams argued most vehemently that no branch of government should have overweening power over another and that, at all costs, one must have a separate judiciary to balance the executive—or was it the other way around?

We were all so merry, and with the din of children all around us, we women listened to this most historic of discussions with scant attention, for children were asking for meat to be cut and drink to be passed. A servant-girl passed a savory tart, and by the fire in that tiny room it became so stiflingly hot that Abigail was finally prompted to open a window, letting in freezing air but stopping the conversation between John and Richard only momentarily. What a scene!

When I had kissed Abigail good-bye and shaken John Adams's hand, knowing it was futile to refuse the offer of Mr. Cranch's chaise, I departed, feeling as happy and full of life, friendship, and hope as I had felt lifeless, alone, and hopeless the night before.

15

MARTHA RETURNED FROM TOWN THE FOLLOWING WEEK light-hearted and at ease. She had seen her brother. Despite the fact that he was a Tory, he must somehow have been a decent human being to be so beloved by his sister.

Her first gift to me upon entering my warm little cottage was a frown and, removing her cloak, the words, "This house is not nearly so clean as I should like."

"Well, get going then," I retorted. I had taken to sleeping by the kitchen hearth in her absence and was embarrassed by the arrangement now, for it spoke not only of my powerlessness but also of my loneliness.

"Give me some of that good British tea of yours first, and I shall."

Saying nothing about my pallet by the fire or about the books and teacups scattered about me, she removed to her room, presumably to tidy herself and take off her wet boots. I was left to boil water and marvel at how glad I was of her return.

Martha had arrived just in time to help me with two births, both uneventful. We left the women cleverly and were compensated a few days later by a packet of pins for one baby and some fine linen for the other. Fewer and fewer people could pay us with actual money.

"At this rate," Martha mused, placing the linen on a table in the parlor, "we will soon be able to open a store."

"Yes, we'll call it The Midwives' Bounty."

We laughed, ignorant of the prescience of her words. Within a year, we would be compelled to sell all our goods for cash to buy the necessities of survival.

But for now we were comfortable, and as the weather warmed, leaving the bitterest cold behind, we grew ever more content. There were three more babies that February—three more gifts, we joked, for "the store." These babes all arrived on the Sabbath, to the great dismay of Parson Wibird.

There came disease, too. Canker rash, pleurisy, and the throat distemper all arrived that spring of '76, followed hard upon by mumps. Parents and children died. I tended to many, and while I could do little more than Dr. Phipps, the simple people of our parish had, at long last, begun to trust me. They liked my gentle ways, my slow, soft, comforting presence. Since Christmas, I had made every effort to hide my envy of the healthy babes and their mothers. Hiding it did not extirpate this envy from my soul, but at least I was no longer weeping at every birth.

But the biggest event that spring was the departure of the British Army from Boston. Oh, happy day!

All winter we had awaited some dreadful event, an aggression from one side or the other. Then, on Sunday, March 3, we all heard the roar of twenty-four-pounders from the north. I saddled Star and, with Martha behind me—she was a slip of a girl, her weight hardly more than that of a good winter cloak—we cantered off to Penn's Hill.

We ignored the rude stares of the townspeople—they should have known by now that we had neither means nor the inclination for a lady's saddle!—and arrived within a quarter of an hour.

Once more was I moved by a wild desire to don a man's costume. Oh, the freedom such costume might afford! In truth, I found my onlookers' disapprobation both shaming and distracting. To remove these painful emotions from my sensibilities would grant me leave to accomplish my tasks unimpeded. I even went so far as to imagine wearing something of Jeb's, for while he was broader than I, he had not been much taller.

We alit from Star, whereupon Abigail came to greet us. Shivering at the din and rattle of the windowpanes around us, we three ascended Penn's Hill together.

What we saw while upon that hill can hardly be described: our cannonballs sailed through the air, and then fell directly down upon the enemy's encampment in town! At first, Abigail could not understand why we should defend such an inconsequential little hill, but I contradicted her.

"No, you're mistaken, Abigail. This is a war of the mind as well as the sword. Our enemy will no longer feel so safe as they have done. Nor will they look upon us with such contempt as before. We are a force to contend with," I said exultantly.

"I hope you're right," she replied cautiously.

My words proved somewhat prophetic when, on the seventeenth of March, from atop Penn's Hill, we saw the entire British fleet readying to depart our shores. It was the largest fleet of ships anyone had ever seen in our waters.

"They look like a forest," Abigail said. Then, as they began to move, almost in unison, she cried. "Look, oh, look, Lizzie!"

Abigail and I hugged each other at this happy event. I cannot adequately describe the relief we felt. The oppressive fear of attack, the daily doubt, the diseases the soldiers had spread—pitiable soldiers, on both sides—they were truly gone from our midst. Gone to New York, we soon heard, where disaster lay in wait for our men.

But in Braintree we rejoiced and welcomed a much-needed spring.

16

SPRING, 1776. IT HAD NOW BEEN ONE full year since my beloved Jeb had been killed. And, while I knew I should never forget him and doubted whether I should ever discover a man I liked half so well, I had in that time healed my heart sufficiently to be grateful for my lot. I was at ease in my soul and had won over enough families to find a means of support for myself, without which I don't know how we should have survived the war.

In July, Abigail and her children removed to Boston to take the smallpox inoculation. She would not return to Braintree until September. What with her children's illnesses, she was much occupied and wrote us infrequently. Left to ourselves, Martha and I did our best to farm the land, dry the herbs, and pick the flax. We worked quietly and companionably, avoiding the increasingly urgent questions of the day or any talk of her brother.

Then, that same month, a most exciting event occurred: news reached us of a Declaration of Independency. Parson Wibird read out the broadside at meeting, but when we heard that this declaration would be read from the Town House, I told Martha I would go. *That* I would not miss, not for anything in the world!

What's more, the time had come to affect my long-dreamed-of plan. I would go, but not as myself. I would go in relative safety—as a man.

After hearing my intentions, Martha said, "You can't be serious."

"But I'm perfectly serious."

I thought she'd objected out of a sense of decorum. In those early days, before I truly knew Martha, I believed that I was the more radical. And, for the longest time, she let me think so. I thought her indifferent to the Cause at best, and that idea made me more obstinate.

Still muttering her disapprobation, Martha helped me place a crate board across my breasts and wind a cloth about me. Among Jeb's clothing beneath my bed, I found breeches, stockings, a vest, and a cap. The cap still smelled of my Jeb's hair, bringing to me a stabbing pain as fresh as it had been one year earlier.

When I was dressed, stifling the tears his scent had brought, I looked at myself in my small looking glass, the one with the painted edging that had been my mother's. I could not help but smile: I looked quite like a boy.

"My hair is a bit long. Help me cut it, Martha."

Martha rolled her eyes but found a knife.

"Not too much," I said. "Enough to make three tolerable passes of the plait."

She cut about four inches, which made me sad. But having tied it with a fine piece of linen, it looked correct.

"You make a handsome lad." She smirked. "Though you do realize that when you return, I will send for the men from the madhouse."

"You may do so, Martha," I concurred, "once I've heard the Declaration with my own ears."

● ● ●

My experience will be hard to fathom for ladies who have not had the sensation of riding a horse in leather breeches rather than petticoats. Suffice it to say it is a most pleasant experience. The legs are warm and protected, the seat is comfortable, and one is not obliged to be forever rearranging one's skirts for modesty's sake. It was to be my first such disguised outing, but by no means my last.

At Boston Neck I suffered a moment of panic when the guards required me to show them a pock scar, and it was only at the last moment that I recalled a tiny one at the nape of my neck. I lifted up my braid to show them and remembered to keep my voice low. I was waved through at last, to my great relief.

When I arrived at the Town House, there was such a crowd that I thought it safer to remain on Star. This position afforded me a good view of women with their babes, and soldiers, guards, and officers of the Continental Army standing with their muskets. They looked disciplined, not like the boys who had questioned me in Roxbury one year earlier. Their costumes were bright blue and neat, if not entirely clean, and their arms were at the ready. I kept a healthy distance from them, for while I did not believe they would ever fire upon us, it was easy enough to imagine the crowd becoming rowdy or even violent at the reading of this document.

At last, Colonel Crafts emerged on the balcony holding a broadside. The crowd quieted at once. Only the cry of babies and the scuffling of horses' hooves intruded upon the expectant silence.

Looking to my left, I saw a small woman and her four children and someone who looked like Richard Cranch. It *was* Mr. Cranch! With him were Mary and Will, Abigail, Nabby, Charlie, Tommy, and Johnny. Abigail's face revealed little as she waited for the momentous words to be read. Few knew that this little woman, dwarfed in the crowd, was the wife of the man who, along with Mr. Jefferson, had created this Declaration.

The solemn reading began. Abigail scanned the crowd, looked up and saw me with no recognition upon her countenance. She looked away, but suddenly her head swiveled back toward me and she stared—quite rudely, it would have been, had I in fact been a boy. With a mixture of embarrassment, surprise, and joy, she smiled her recognition. There were tears in her eyes, as there were in mine.

I raised my cap to salute her. She nodded, and then turned toward Colonel Crafts.

The words of our Declaration are commonplace now. Were you not there to hear them, you can have little notion of the effect of these ringing words, so true, so longed for. I repeat the first few here so that you might endeavor to hear them as we did, proclaimed from the Town House. Oh, what poetry to our ears!

When in the Course of human events, it becomes necessary for one people to dissolve the political bands which have connected them with another, and to assume among the powers of the earth, the separate and equal station to which the Laws of Nature and of Nature's God entitle them, a decent respect to the opinions of mankind requires that they should declare the causes which impel them to the separation.

We hold these truths to be self-evident, that all men are created equal, that they are endowed by their Creator with certain unalienable Rights, that among these are Life, Liberty and the pursuit of Happiness.

Not a sound was uttered. Not a wheel turned.

"God save our Colonies!" Colonel Crafts finally cried. Three cheers went up, followed by a din of ringing bells, shouts, and cannons firing from land and sea. The king's arms were lifted off the Town House, torn apart, thrown in a pile, and lit on fire in the middle of the crowd.

Seeing the wild crowd and fearing an imminent auto-da-fé, I left at a canter and did not stop until I reached the Bull & Horn tavern in Milton. There I watered and oated Star and was obliged to use the men's necessary, terrified at every moment lest some man with too much wine in him should discover me squatting upon the bowl. Oh, the mortal terror of that moment!

I was suddenly quite ravenously hungry, for in my excitement I had set off without a morsel that morning. In the tavern, filled with the smoke of pipes and the smell of stale cider and rummy breath, I ordered myself a cider and a plate of ham and biscuits. I was dining happily when I found myself stared at by a young, pretty girl sitting with her family at a table across from mine.

I smiled at her, and she blushed.

Oh, this would not do! I paid quickly and left, and was soon glad to be back in my soft woman's body without the tight wrappings and heavy breeches.

That is a faithful account of my first hours as a man—which ruse I would have need of in the years to come, for a darker and more serious purpose.

17

IN MY MIND, I SHALL ALWAYS LINK together the day I first rode out as a man and the day I heard the Declaration from the Town House. It was a day of exultant hope for the future and for freedom, both personal and communal. This hope would have to serve as our food in the long months ahead.

By August, the price of goods had doubled yet again, and I knew Martha and I would have to be quite disciplined if we were to survive the winter. We got to work on the farm picking flax, making cheese, gathering fruit, storing wood, cleaning the stables and the necessary, gathering wool, mending fences and windows with the help of Thaxter—the list went on and on. My muscles grew so hard that I begged Martha to feel them: Were they not like those of a man?

To look at us working side by side in the blistering heat of an August afternoon, you'd think we were both indentured servants, not highborn ladies. Even the Quincys up the hill were obliged to practice frugality. They had far fewer dinner parties than before and parted tearfully with two very dear servants. Still, Mrs. Quincy continued to leave the occasional basket of provisions upon my stoop, for which I could repay her only in the occasional jar of preserves or basket of flowers.

Looking from a perch of relative security now, I find there to be a certain absolute beauty in the closeness that comes with shared suffering. Such beauty could not be spoken of, and was hardly perceived. But it was certainly felt among us in the North Parish. We looked upon one another with a kind of true and open love and gratitude that is hard to imagine in peacetime. This exquisite state of our souls disappeared after the war's end, to be replaced by more comfortable, if more attenuated, emotions.

At the end of August, all of Braintree was abuzz with a horrible rumor that John Adams had been poisoned in New York. When I overheard this news at meeting, so great was my alarm that I immediately sent a message to Abigail in Boston. I was greatly relieved to receive a reply from her the next day:

The rumor is nonsense. I have heard from the victim himself, and apart from a slight indigestion due to overindulgence, he is alive and well in Philadelphia.

Soon after the Adamses and Cranches returned from Boston, we received crushing news that was no rumor: Washington had suffered a terrible defeat in New York. To make matters worse, the patriotic fever that had run through our boys in the beginning had, by the summer of '76, died out. In its place came opportunism and greed. We now had an army of men who had been bribed by the offer of forty shillings a day.

As autumn harvest turned to winter, our spirits sank as low as they had been exalted at the reading of the Declaration. Men who had not enlisted for the ready cash had gone off privateering, leaving us a parish of women and old men. It had now been two years since I had seen my brother off for parts unknown. I was certain Harry was dead, for I had received not a single letter from him in all that time.

I did receive a perfunctory letter from Mr. Boylston, however, to inform me that they were well, under the circumstances, and installed in Portsmouth at the house of Mrs. Boylston's brother, Robert Chase. Mr. Boylston inquired after my health. He said nothing about Star, nor did he renew that invitation to join them that had been so repulsive to me.

I tore up the letter in disgust. And while I had not the luxury of tearing up the five-pound note—it was by then worth two days' hired labor—I would have heartily liked to.

"Oh, those people!" I fretted aloud.

Martha, who had been spinning on the little flax wheel by the fire, stopped her work. "Who was it?" she inquired gently, not wishing to intrude.

"Mr. Boylston. It is not a Christian sentiment, but I should like to think that those who hold themselves superior get their come-uppance sooner rather than later."

"No doubt they will," Martha replied calmly, returning to her spinning, a mysterious smile playing across her face. Of all our chores, Martha liked spinning best. It seemed to calm her, to set her mind free to wander. At such times, she reminded me of Klotho, the old woman of Greek lore, spinning fate.

"You believe in an eye for an eye, Martha?" I asked uneasily.

She answered, "I believe that we are called upon to do things in this life that we would not do in an ideal life. I believe that to reach that ideal, one must be prepared to sacrifice."

"So, in essence, you are saying that the end justifies the means."

"Yes. Not in every age, but in some. In ours."

"Well, then, you would make a very bad"—I paused, then added—"Quaker."

We both smiled. I would have liked to discuss the issue further, for we had scrupulously avoided the topic of the war and politics. I now found myself wanting to sound Martha out, to know her true thoughts. What particular ends did she have in mind? I believed that to sin for good and to sin for evil were equal in God's eyes. By what means could I support this Cause, in which men on both sides died every day? And if war itself were sinful, Jeb would have died committing a sin. He would have died for nothing—worse than nothing. Here, my thoughts came to an impasse.

Martha suddenly stopped her spinning and said, "I'm hungry. Have we any of that pie left from yesterday?" *So much for philosophy*, I thought.

* * *

Soon winter was upon us, and a very hard one it was. It was so cold on certain nights that we were even obliged to bring the chickens and hogs indoors. My poor, clean kitchen became a menagerie. One night we awoke to a horrible, almost human-sounding cry. We rushed down to find that a hog had licked the door frame and gotten its tongue stuck—it was frozen to the frame! We raced for water in order to unfreeze him, but by the time we had filled the pitcher, he had pulled himself loose, leaving part of his bloodied tongue on the door.

It was so cold I actually feared for Star, and one night I gave in to my fears and brought him clomping into the kitchen. Normally horses are creatures of habit; they do not relish going where they have never been before. But such was Star's trust in me that he stepped inside my side door almost daintily, with no prodding on my part. He took a cheese for his troubles during the night, and I did not begrudge him.

On Christmas Eve I rode out to the Adamses, but this time I knew I would not enter. Standing before that house once more and seeing it lit from within, I found myself suddenly understanding that I was not alone in wanting things beyond my reach. Perhaps the pain of wanting what I could never have held a lesson for me: Was it not human to suffer so? What is nobler, in the end, than to tilt at windmills? What more hopeful than to believe that the two parallel lines of desire and its fulfillment will eventually meet in one moment of pure joy?

It was with such hope in my heart that I returned home that night unseen by Abigail, who was much preoccupied with her beautiful family. Instead of pitying myself, I pitied the poor chicken whose neck I broke the next morning and served for Christmas dinner—stuffed, roasted, and delicious, with a glass of wine for my dear Martha and me.

18

IN THE EARLY DAYS OF 1777, ABIGAIL and I finally set about being of some use to Washington's army. In January, we took up a collection for spare blankets and men's shirts, and our efforts were rewarded with the receipt of some hundred blankets and near two hundred shirts.

"Being of some use" defined our lives that year. It became increasingly necessary to use one's energy and wits to find clever ways to subsist when provisions could not be had. Sugar, flour, and labor were now entirely out of reach. Abigail set about selling lace and pins. I was obliged to sell Bertha, one of my milk cows, and also some of the fine linen we had woven that winter. We began knitting and weaving small items, those we could create in a spare moment, for sale in town. In exchange for our muffatees, tippets, gloves, and socks, we received such items and provisions as we had most urgent need of.

John Adams left home for Philadelphia once more on a cold Thursday morning. I was present to witness his departure, for Martha and I had arrived at Abigail's very early that morning to help her fold shirts for Washington's package. As John performed a hasty, last-minute search for some forgotten item, Abigail affected great preoccupation with her gathering and folding of the shirts. I thought her stoicism admirable and infuriating in equal measure. We averted our eyes as John embraced her before venturing out of doors to his waiting horse and companion.

Abigail glanced up and smiled at him with a self-possession that tried my worn patience to breaking.

"Abigail! For goodness' sake, throw your work down and run to him!"

She stared at me, taken aback; and then, sure enough, she did.

"Oh, my love," I heard him say as he embraced her one final time.

She waved until he and his traveling companion, Mr. Bass, were out of sight. Then she collapsed into my arms and wept long and hard. She had good reason to weep, for she knew something John did not: she was with child.

•　　•　　•

In April, the Episcopal Church closed its doors. Abigail and I bade good riddance to a number of Tories among us. Abigail wished aloud that all such families as the Millers, Vezeys, and Cleverlys might be "extirpated from our midst" and "shipped back to England." But, suddenly recalling that my own dear father had been "shipped back" in this manner and that I had never laid eyes upon him again, she put her hand on mine and said, "I'm sorry, Lizzie. I forget that Tories are still human beings, with fathers and mothers—and daughters—quite like ourselves."

"My father was no Tory. I do believe that, had he been forced to choose, he would have chosen our side." I smiled, for she had not offended me.

The churches may have closed their doors, but that did not prevent the Tories from designing to foil the revolt in secret.

In May of that year, her body visibly heavier with child, Abigail appeared at my door looking very agitated. I was planting my medicinal seedlings in the kitchen garden when she alighted from her chaise waving a large five-pound note.

"I've been duped!" she cried angrily. "Monsters!"

She asked for tea, and, as I prepared it, she recounted a dastardly plot to which she had just fallen victim. Apparently, a certain Mr. Holland, of Londonderry, New Hampshire, had left his home and gone into hiding, where he was attempting to destabilize our faltering economy by introducing counterfeit currency. He had been a tavern keeper and prominent citizen but had disappeared just before the scandal broke. Abigail had been handed one of Mr. Holland's false notes somewhere in Boston. She looked livid.

"Calm yourself," I said, bidding her to enter.

"I will not be calm. I'm furious!"

She then proceeded to tell us the news she had in heated tones.

Martha, who had listened to Abigail's rant in silence, suddenly offered, "Perhaps he is here among us."

"What a terrible thought, Martha." I shuddered. But Martha, usually sensitive, ignored my peremptory tone.

"You must admit it is possible that is how Abigail got her false note," she persisted.

"No, I agree," Abigail said, looking quizzically at the girl. "It's entirely possible that the fellow hides in Boston."

"Or in our very own parish."

I stood, angry now. Why had Martha not taken my hint to be silent on the matter?

"Martha, that's quite enough. Would you have us not sleep at night? Are things not bad enough that you must frighten us out of our wits?"

"Lizzie," Abigail objected, placing her hand on mine, "consider that perhaps I have come here and frightened *her*, not the other way around. For which I am sorry, Martha."

"Oh, don't be sorry," said Martha. "I, for one, am not afraid. And for another, I think it wise that we prepare ourselves for such an occurrence. As you yourself have said, Abigail, designing Tories are everywhere."

With that dark thought, we were all now silent, and a deep gloom settled upon us. Had I heard irony in Martha's voice when she had said, "Designing Tories are everywhere"? I knew not. Nonetheless, when Abigail had left, I soundly scolded Martha. She said merely, "Forgive me. But is it not better that she, of all people, remain on her guard?"

"Perhaps," I admitted. "But keep in mind her state. I fear for her, Martha. I have a very bad feeling about this baby and have had these several months. Indeed, I can't shake it." Martha looked at me askance. "Isn't that just the sort of superstitious nonsense you loathe hearing from the mouths of ignorant midwives?"

"True."

Just as I moved to return to the garden, I caught her looking up at Jeb's musket on the wall. I walked out of doors into the sunshine and heard her say, "We should learn to use that."

"An excellent idea," I replied.

We did learn to use that musket, Martha and I. It was a simple, if not a very accurate, mechanism. We got Thaxter to show us how. You had to pour a small amount of the powder into the pan of the lock, close the pan, and then drop the cartridge, powder first, into the barrel. Ram it home, cock the lock, look down the barrel—and pray. There were no sights to aim by.

We shot crows from the sky, a plague of them that blackened our fair spring and stole our food besides. The crows kept coming back. We made a scarecrow, arguing about whose face we should give it. I said Eliza; she said King George. So as we had the need, we made two of them. Eliza stood in the pumpkin patch; King George watched over the vegetables and herbs.

Martha frowned as we stuck George in between the rows of beans. "Is he guarding his troops, and are our legumes now Loyalists? In that case, I shouldn't like to eat them."

I hesitated to reply. Was Martha telling me that she was on the Rebel side? I fervently wished to ask but feared her answer. Instead, I replied merely, "It's best not to stretch our minds too far on the scarecrows' allegorical significance. It will suffice if they serve to keep the crows away."

In fact, they did do their job well—especially as Martha and I often could not resist taking a small stone and throwing it at one of the faces as we passed by, laughing.

"It's very un-Christian, what we do," I said one time.

"Indeed. But if we succeed in scaring the crows and thus subsist another year, is that not a virtue?"

We were back to our old argument of whether ends justified means, for which I still had no answer.

All that spring and into summer, I kept a watchful eye on my dear Abigail. I simply could not shake the feeling that something was amiss. I don't know why I felt this way—call it an intuition. But I didn't like her fatigued look or her pallor. Her back gave her a great deal of pain as well, and through the month of June I visited her near every day on some pretext or other.

One day I came bearing a newfangled instrument, called a London Dome, by which I believed we would be able to hear Abigail's babe *in utero*. I had received this instrument from an odd source: a servant of a doctor from Milton had come up to me after meeting. She asked would I like a few of the "good doctor's" things. Apparently, this doctor, of unpopular sympathies, had returned in haste to England, leaving both his wife and much of his equipment behind. I inquired of the servant what the instrument was for, but she said she didn't rightly know. As soon as she pulled it from the back of her missus's carriage, however, I saw at once what it was. I had only read about such things; they were quite rare in our parts.

On this day I had brought the Dome with me. In my naive excitement, though, I had not thought through the possible consequences of using such a device.

I had Abigail lie back on her bed and then placed the large trumpetlike end on her belly, where I felt the fetus. I could then hear, to my great delight, a muffled but distinct heartbeat. So fast it beat, like that of a little bird! I let Abigail listen, and, at the sound of her child's heart, she burst into tears.

Then, on a hot morning in July, when Martha and I were going full tilt at weeding one of our gardens, a boy came from Mrs. Adams, who bade me come at once.

"Oh, Martha, I'm afraid," I said as I ran to saddle Star.

I was soaked through by the time I reached Abigail's, having been obliged to turn around at the meetinghouse when I realized I had forgotten my sack, which included the London Dome.

I had expected to find Abigail in bed and in distress. But she was not. She was sitting upright on a stool in the kitchen, working dough for bread. Lacking wheat flour or leavening, it was stiff and heavy and hard to knead. The doors and windows banged on their hinges to receive what scant breeze saw fit to blow across her sweaty brow.

Seeing her up and seemingly well, I sighed with relief.

"What is it, Abigail?" I asked, setting my bag down. "Have you news from John?"

I took the dough from her and forced her to rest. Still, she said nothing, but she wiped her brow with a cloth. Normally her keen brown eyes held mine; today they would not meet mine at all.

"I have," she said, and once more my relief was palpable. God forgive me for saying so, but at that moment I would rather have lost the Revolution than Abigail and John's baby.

"The news is bad. We have lost Fort Ticonderoga."

"That is bad news." I made a fist and continued pounding the dough.

"You will make it stiff as wood like that, you know."

"Oh, sorry." I ceased my pounding and used my fingers instead. "Well, what is the strategy? What does John say?"

Once again she was silent. After a pause, she said, "There is more." She looked at me at last. Seeing her eyes, I actually felt a pain in my groin. "I believe my baby is dead."

I stared at her. "But you are two weeks away. Nay, not two."

"Even so."

"What makes you say this? Come and sit by me. No, better—lie yourself down, and I will listen." I proffered the Dome.

"No." She put her hand out in defense, as if my fancy London Dome were a weapon.

"But it may yet be alive," I protested.

"Which would be even worse, to know it to be alive yet in distress."

It had begun to occur to me that perhaps I had been mistaken in my quest for more "modern" tools such as the London Dome. What good was knowing something without the means of changing the malady? Cassandra knew the torment of such knowledge all too well.

"All right, don't fear. Come lie you down and tell me what has happened."

I lifted her to her feet and laid her in the bed in the parlor, for her own chamber was far too hot to suffer in these summer months.

"Last night," she began, "I was given to a fit of violent shakes."

"But you're not shaking now," I observed.

"No, it passed after an hour's duration. But I've felt no movement since that time."

"Lie quietly and let me feel you, at least," I said. I helped her unfasten her petticoats—stays had been absolutely forbidden by me after the fifth month, despite the custom to wear them throughout one's pregnancy. I thought such a practice nonsensical in the extreme. A mother passing out every half hour because she is unable to breathe cannot be good for the child inside her.

I placed my hands on her belly and felt the baby's position. It was head down, not entirely engaged, and I could perceive no movement whatsoever. The Dome would have told the tale, but I would not press the point. Knowledge where there is no possibility of action, as Abigail correctly noted, can only cause suffering.

I removed my hands. "Truthfully, Abby, I do not know whether your baby lives. But I do know that you have done nothing to cause it harm. Nothing at all—" I grew angry then and knew not why. Tears sprang to my eyes as I slapped my hand on the bedstead.

"Nor you," she said. I then realized I blamed myself with thoughts of that unsavory Dome. As if reading my thoughts, Abigail smiled wearily and said, "I'm glad I heard her heartbeat. She was mine for a little while, at least."

Oh, God! These generous words tore at me the way cool ones would not have.

I stood, seeking to steady my emotions with those prescribed procedures all medical people rely on.

"Abigail," I said, "whether it lives or no, I believe it best to make the quickest possible delivery. If it be alive, it will have its best chance this way. If it be . . . gone, 'tis best for you as well we not tarry."

"What do you propose?" she said wryly. "Have you a stork in that sack of yours?"

"No, indeed," I replied. "I have something far better than a stork." I went to my bag and removed a vial of white powder.

"What is that?"

"Our ancestors used it to make their eyes beautiful."

Still, she did not guess.

"Belladonna," I said. "The ladies placed drops of it in their eyes to dilate their pupils. It was quite the fashion at one point."

Abigail sighed. "I sometimes have the distinct impression that our forebears were deranged. Anyway, what do you propose to do with it? The baby can hardly come out my pupils. Though I wish it could."

"No. Listen." I explained to her how, in extreme cases, I coated the opening of the *os* with powdered belladonna to help dilate the cervix without the swelling that often occurs with manual attempts.

I proposed we try the belladonna if she were not in travail by Friday. It was now Tuesday. She agreed to the plan, and I left her half an hour later, lighter in spirit than I had found her.

But this poor child was not to be. Early Saturday morning I was called once more to her home, where I delivered my poor friend of a stillborn girl, whom she named Elizabeth and cradled in her arms.

Sad as this sight was—Elizabeth was a perfect, beautiful baby— it was also a relief, for the cause of death was readily apparent: the baby had been strangled on its own cord, which I found wrapped tightly 'round its little neck.

19

ABIGAIL WAS SLOW TO RECOVER HER SPIRITS, and a low mood in one so bent toward optimism set Martha and me low as well. There was now little to be had of any goods at any price—not lead, nor powder, nor coffee, nor tea. Our mills were obliged to make molasses from cornstalks. We worked our fingers so hard making knickknacks that they grew swollen and numb. At times we felt as if God had abandoned us.

News from beyond our town was bad as well. The British Army had captured Philadelphia, and Congress was forced to move out for its members' safety, first to Lancaster and then to York. For several days before she received word, Abigail anguished that the Regulars had captured John.

Martha and I continued to deliver babes, though how these women became with child we knew not, since the men were all gone. We hid these activities as best we could from Abigail. Indeed, I did not see a great deal of her that autumn. No doubt we were both greatly occupied. In addition to making goods and delivering children, Martha and I had our usual weekly chores such as boiling the clothing, hanging it to dry on the line, and ironing. For the harvest we also needed to card the flax, slice and string the apples and pumpkins, set the corn to dry, and make our jams and jellies.

At day's end, we flopped down on our beds, breathless with fatigue. Only an unwillingness to waste our candles forced us to sleep at all.

At long last, late that October, we finally received news to lift our spirits. Martha and I were lugging bushels of apples down the steep cellar stairs when we heard a chaise pull up by our door. It was now quite unseasonably cold. The following day it would snow.

"He has surrendered! He has surrendered!" we heard the voice of our beloved friend. We knew Abigail meant General Burgoyne. He and his near six thousand soldiers had given themselves over to General Gates at Saratoga.

Martha was so astonished that she dropped her end of the basket, and the apples went tumbling down the stairs.

I made us chamomile tea as Abigail recounted everything she had heard.

"There is to be a great celebration in town tomorrow, and you must come."

"I should like that," I said.

"Oh, no, there is far too much to do," said Martha regretfully.

"But think, Martha. You might see your brother," I said. "Thomas."

She sighed wistfully. "Yes. Perhaps."

"But is he not in the South now?" Abigail asked, puzzled. General Howe was at that time in Germantown, Pennsylvania. I had forgotten about Mr. Miller's connection to Howe, no doubt because I had wished to.

"No, he stayed behind."

At the mention of Martha's brother, we fell silent, each no doubt thinking our own thoughts. *Why had he remained in Boston?* I wondered but did not ask. Possibly to guard the few British holdings left at the wharf or perhaps to monitor Rebel activity.

In private, Abigail and I had discussed the possibility of Thomas Miller's being a spy for the enemy.

"If he is, he's very obvious about it. Besides, everyone's a spy these days for one side or another," she'd said bitterly. "John dares not send me information of any great import, for fear of it. But I hear a great deal about what he ate for dinner."

"How vexing," I'd replied.

Catching my serious look, Abigail laughed.

•　•　•

We come now to a part in my narrative that I do not like to tell. Soon after we heard the news of Burgoyne's surrender, I became suspicious of my own dear Martha. My thoughts began to run away with me immediately after I heard that Thomas Miller had stayed behind in Boston rather than leave with Howe's army.

On the day after we heard the good news, we rode in Colonel Quincy's fine carriage to Boston. Abigail sat by my side, and Martha was seated across from us. I looked at her and could not rid myself of the thought that she was a spy sent by her brother to oversee pesky Rebels in the North Parish, with a particular interest in the tiny lady who sat by my side.

In my own defense, and for the sake of Truth, I must reveal certain facts that I have thus far omitted from my tale. Since earlier that spring, I had caught Martha reading or writing letters, which she did not offer to share with me. Passing by her chamber one evening, I happened to notice several drafts of a letter made out to her brother in which General Howe was mentioned.

But what of that? Was the poor girl not entitled to communicate with her one living relation on earth? But the mind must have the story and, missing the truth, will piece together a fiction from ragged scraps. Thus, as we drove to Boston, my concern grew feverish in my brain until I had worked myself into a genuine panic.

We stayed at the house of Abigail's uncle, Isaac Smith, where Abigail occupied her favorite room—a closet of her very own. It had a pretty little writing desk by a window. Abigail pronounced it a very great luxury to be without her children for a full day. She said she would use the time to write John a letter. Martha and I were quite comfortably installed down the hall, where we shared a bed.

I watched Martha undress for bed. To say I observed her might be more accurate, for in my overwrought state I fancied she would at any moment betray herself in word or deed. I don't know precisely what I expected. Would she mutter "Long live King George!" in her sleep?

"You stare at me quite profoundly," she said mildly. "One would think you'd never seen a naked woman before."

I caught the irony in her tone, as we both knew I'd seen women in every naked particular. Indeed, Martha's slender little body was quite worth looking at. She had the kind of body clothing hides rather than complements. Her full breasts, slender, curving hips, and long, well-turned legs would have smitten any man who gazed upon them.

"I'm thinking you are very attractive without your clothing."

She raised her eyebrows and placed her shift before her, suddenly as self-conscious as Eve after biting the apple.

"Well, you parade about in manly garb astride a horse. Why then can't I be like Guinevere and fly naked through the streets? Oh, Lizzie"—her tone became cheerful—"I'm vastly contented! For tomorrow I see my beloved brother. It has been too long."

It was arranged that we would take the colonel's carriage the following day, and that Mr. Miller would meet us at the wharf. We set off in some trepidation, for while few Tories remained in town, it was not unknown for sudden personal conflagrations to occur. More than one man had been caught in a crossfire of muskets.

At the wharf the celebration of Burgoyne's surrender was in full swing, with fire displays and loud demonstrations. We stood observing a band of jokesters burning the king in effigy when a fine carriage pulled up beside us and a servant descended, then helped a tall young man to alight from the carriage.

"Thomas!" Martha cried. She went running toward him. It was Mr. Thomas Miller, the notorious and beloved brother.

"Oh, sweet sister!"

He lifted her off the ground and hugged her fiercely. There were tears of joy on the poor girl's face. When her brother finally released her, Martha saw fit to introduce us. Another young, quite dandified man alit from the carriage behind Thomas and bowed, though I doubted he knew to whom he was bowing.

Mr. Miller introduced his friend, whose name I now forget. But he was the owner of the carriage and no doubt from a family of considerable wealth. Thomas's friend soon mounted the carriage and waited there, not wishing to intrude upon the family scene.

Martha then said formally, "Abigail Adams, this is my dear brother, Thomas Miller. Thomas, Abigail."

Abigail allowed him to kiss her hand. She bowed slightly, but not without casting me a fleeting sideways glance. I gave him my hand limply, with obvious reluctance. To his credit, Thomas Miller bowed deeply and appeared not to notice my slight. He then gazed across the crowded wharf. "Quite a celebration, isn't it?"

"We've all been in ecstasies since we heard the news," I said.

Mr. Miller's was not a countenance one could exactly call handsome. He had a large, straight nose; big, wide-set eyes of an astonishing amber color; and a full mouth. His hair, like his sister's, was a rich auburn brown.

Mr. Miller looked entreatingly at Martha, who saw her cue to end the awkward scene by mounting the carriage. He took her hand and helped her up. From her perch, she cast me a regretful look. As they pulled away, Thomas Miller glanced down at me briefly, then nodded respectfully to Abigail as he bade the horses go.

"Regards to your husband." He tipped his hat to her. "General Howe is a very great admirer, as am I."

Abigail and I looked at each other without a word. We both knew that, while General Howe might admire John Adams, he would not be distraught by the appearance of a noose around his neck.

"Insufferable platitudes!" I cried once brother and sister were gone.

But Abigail replied, "I thought his manner quite pleasant and sincere."

"Then you have been too much out of company to recall the meaning of *pleasant* or *sincere*," I replied sullenly. I was angry with Mr. Miller, not her. But she took the offense, and rightly so.

"And you must take care not to judge men too hastily, for grave mistakes have been made by those more perceptive than you."

Here, she turned her back on me.

·   ·   ·

This was the closest Abigail and I ever came to having an argument. She was older than I by eight years, and I had been insufferably rude to her.

We sat across from each other in silence on the journey back to her uncle's house that afternoon. I had regretted my words moments after uttering them. Who was I to tell Mrs. John Adams that she had been so much out of company that she did not know *pleasant* or *sincere*—she who had dined with Dr. Franklin and John Hancock, and even His Excellency and Martha Washington?

I felt miserably ashamed of myself. And yet, so much had my obsessive thoughts taken hold of me that, by the time we approached the house late that afternoon, I could not prevent myself from saying, "It would do well, I think, to take care what you say in Martha's presence."

I had said it to puff up my own flagging sense of importance and perhaps to regain some of my lost esteem in her eyes. It was an egregious error. For what had we, in those days, if not our loyalty to one another?

The effect of these words was fat upon the fire.

Abigail pulled herself up and faced me squarely. Though she was tiny, I felt she towered above me. "And how do I know that you yourself are not a spy?" she said. "You, of all people, have my ear and my trust. You are privy to my most private correspondence with John. You profess to be my friend and Martha's. Perhaps *you* are not who you profess to be!"

Reader, if you had any idea how these words cut me, you would pity me. I watched her stride into the house, saw her aunt's servant racing after her most officiously, leaving me alone and utterly bewildered on the road.

Moments later I was able to compose myself sufficiently to move toward the house. I dropped my bonnet, cloak, mitts, and scarf on a chair, crossed into the hallway, and followed her upstairs. I found her sitting with her back to me by the window, staring out at the steely-gray autumn sky.

"Abigail, forgive me," I said. "I can't live knowing I have fallen in your esteem."

"There are many things we say we cannot bear, and yet we do," she said calmly.

"No, truly, I *cannot* bear it. I will die." And with these words I fell by her feet, took her hands, and lay my head pitifully in her lap. "You are my only friend. Without you, I am alone in the world."

I thought she would say that Martha was my friend, too, and that I had grossly wronged her. Instead, she said, "You must learn to love yourself and your own company. As for others, there is no guarantee. You have only yourself for certain, until the last breath."

"What a lonely thought!" I cried. "A most terrible, lonely thought."

My misery and distraught tears pricked her maternal sensibilities at last. She placed a hand on my head and caressed me, and the touch of her hand made me sob like a child. I threw my arms around her calves and hugged her tight.

Finally she said, "All right. Enough. Ready yourself for bed, dearest. You will weep yourself into a terrible cold, and then you will give it to the rest of us."

I smiled, though my face must have been frightful.

"Dr. Franklin believes we must sleep with an open window." I sniffed.

"Then we must do as Dr. Franklin says."

She nodded toward the window, bidding me open it slightly. Then she patted the edge of her bed to let me know that I might stay the night if I chose.

And, with this brief exchange, our trust was reestablished. I forsook Martha that night, and Abigail and I slept soundly, snuggled against each other, until late the next morning.

•   •   •

I wish I could say that the painful argument with Abigail spelled the end of my suspicions about Martha, but it did not. However, I am of such a nature that, once an idea enters my head, it is like a tapeworm—no amount of pinkroot will rid me of it.

Martha stayed on several days with her brother, and when she finally returned to snowy Braintree, she looked refreshed in spirit. My jealous love of Abigail had, if anything, grown since I'd quit Boston. I asked, "How was your visit?"

"Oh, wonderful. Lizzie, if only . . ." Here, she gave an enthusiastic rendering of that happy reunion, about which I asked not a single question, and she soon fell silent. While at first Martha might have ascribed my coolness to indifference toward her brother, she quickly sensed my coolness toward her person, as well. The house felt cold and lonely, though we both were at home.

• • •

We had been back in Braintree but a few days when Abigail called upon us to say that she had, that same morning, received a letter from her husband with both the most excellent and the most bitter news.

"Well, don't stand there—tell us," I said, ushering her in from the freezing cold. It had begun to snow, and I had tarried nearly all night delivering a woman of her first child.

Martha, who had tarried all night with me, stood by the fire. She was making bread, and it was nearly done. But she had hardly slept, and twice already that morning she had burned herself in the task of retrieving the loaves from the back of the oven. It was one of those blasted old fireplaces that often consumed its poor housewife in flames. Martha seemed to have grown particularly careless with herself; her right forearm oozed two nasty open blisters.

When she saw Abigail, though, her wan face lit with joy.

She wiped her hands on her apron and went to greet her.

Having set her cloak and hat over the back of my tall chair, Abigail began, "Well, the good news is that John shall be home early this year. In a fortnight!"

"That's wonderful," I agreed, smiling. "And what is the bad news?"

I set before us three bowls of a hearty ham-and-bean soup with Martha's warm rye bread, upon which we greedily lathered sweet butter.

"The bad news is that he has just received word that he's to leave again in February. For France."

"France!" I stared at her. "You've agreed to this?"

"Do I have a choice?" She smiled. "It's a mission of the utmost significance."

"What is in France that could be of such importance?" I asked in ignorance. Abigail looked at me, aghast.

"What is in France? Why, France is in France, Lizzie," she said. "John will be instrumental in—"

"Abigail!" I stood, rudely interrupting her and making Martha jump. Martha spilled her spoonful of soup and burned herself for the third time that day.

"Abigail," I said again, more softly this time, "I have full forgotten the cider. How stupid of me. Martha, would you kindly fetch some cider from the cellar?" I handed her a pitcher for the task.

Though exhausted to the point of faintness, Martha complied without complaint. "Of course," she said. "I'm thirsty as well."

Once she was gone, Abigail hissed, "Lizzie, what is the matter with you? Have you gone mad?"

"Indeed, I'm not mad. But don't you think it unwise—terribly unwise—to reveal something of such patriotic import, some fact upon which our very success or failure depends, to the beloved sister of a man in General Howe's employ?"

She moved close to me. "Lizzie, you're incorrigible. Surely we have enough problems without suspecting each other at every turn. This has got to stop before—"

Suddenly we both perceived Martha standing before us, holding a pitcher in her hand. The cellar door was open; apparently she had never descended. She set the pitcher on the table. Her hand hovered there for a moment, shaking, as if unsure of its purpose. A bread knife sat upon the table. She took it up and held it in one fist. Her face was white when she turned to us, taking us both in. Slowly, her eyes focused on me. Neither Abigail nor I uttered one syllable.

"You think I'm a traitor, don't you?" she asked me.

"I—"

"Say it. You think my brother a spy and I his willing accomplice. Since you hardly know your own brother, you cannot conceive that I might love mine without the least regard to his politics. Perhaps you cannot imagine it. Imagine laughing with one's brother about silly things, old memories, distant hopes. Such lack of understanding I can bear, as it stems from ignorance. But what I cannot bear is the thought that you"—she stared at me—"and even you"—she turned to Abigail—"believe me capable of being disingenuous with my friends. My *sisters*. Did I not weep for you, Lizzie, when first you told me about Jeb? Did we not cry together upon hearing of the terrible retreat at New York? Did we not laugh together with joy at the news from Saratoga? You think me capable of such crocodile tears of joy and grief? What a monster I must seem to you."

"We think no such thing," Abigail said gently.

"You may not," she conceded, tears of misery flowing now, "but what of *her*? And to think of the bed I've shared with you, and the night upon night I've tarried by your side. Not for gain— God knows, there's been none of that—but because I so admired you . . ."

"Martha," I began, but she interrupted me.

"What will it take to convince you? Must I suffer a deep wound for the Cause, as you both have? Will you believe me true then? So be it."

Before we could move to stop her, Martha thrust her left hand out and sliced across her palm as a butcher cleaves a fillet. And though the pain must have been extreme, she neither flinched nor cried out, but merely took a single sharp inhale of breath before dropping the knife and collapsing to the floor.

I ran to her, Abigail close behind. There was no time for reproach. Blood flowed everywhere. I grabbed my sack and pulled out a dry cloth to press to the wound. Blood seeped through it at once, and I knew she had cut very deep.

Martha nearly fainted as I removed the bloody cloth and pressed another to the wound. After this had been accomplished, we led her toward the bed in the parlor, though she muttered it was a scratch of no consequence. Abigail eased Martha's stays and bodice as I transferred some hot coals from one fire to another, soon warming up the room.

Martha's eyes were open and blank as I applied a cool cloth to her face. Looking at her full on in this objective manner, like a patient, I recalled how young she was—not seventeen—and how I, although quite young myself, was the world to her: mother, sister, and friend. In my suspicion, I had robbed her of all three at once.

"Rest awhile," said Abigail. "I'll watch her."

"I cannot rest," I replied quickly. Having ascertained that the bleeding had fully stopped and that there was as yet no redness or swelling at the site of the gash, I put on my cloak and took up my bonnet and mitts. Turning to Abigail, I smiled weakly and said, "I must walk. I won't be long."

As I left the house, the cold wind off the sea assaulted me. I wished to see no one and headed down the dunes, making my way toward the open, iron-gray winter sky above the water. The snow was thick in places, covered by a dense, slippery crust made by a brief rain the day before. I slipped; the jagged ice scratched my calves. But my legs were numb, and I felt not the tearing of flesh. I walked across the snow toward the sea, letting the wind and the salt air slash my face. Ice froze between my wet eyelashes and nostrils and lodged in my throat and lungs with every breath; still, I did not stop.

I reflected upon my ignoble suspicions of Martha. I knew them to be ignoble, and yet I was still not convinced that she had told me all there was to tell. Some important detail was missing. Perhaps I would never know it. Was it my right to know her secrets? Martha owed me nothing. She did not owe me—nor did I merit—her most profound confidences.

I reached the town landing. It was desolate save for two old men hoisting a coffin-size crate from a dory. They grunted with the effort and soon succeeded in tying a rope twice around the heavy load and dragging it toward a waiting cart and horse. The horse's breath made clouds in the frigid air; it stomped its foot impatiently and shivered, gazing myopically at me with big brown eyes.

I wondered what was in the crate, hoping it was sacks of flour, but doubting of it. Finally curiosity got the better of me. I inquired what lay within.

"Oh, a body, miss. That of a boy died at Freeman's Farm, what's family wanted him buried here."

Freeman's Farm had been one of the battle sites in New York a few weeks earlier. I apologized and thanked them for telling me, then turned away. It seemed an ill omen.

I held my cloak around myself as I gazed out at the black sea and black sky. The sun retreated. Men, women, animals—even the sun seemed to shrink from my company. I thought perhaps I was unfit to live. Over there, across the water, lay England, where my father had died. In that water, in its cold deep, my brother floated, whether beneath the waves or upon a ship's deck I did not dare to guess.

As I stood at the water's edge, a thought occurred to me: Could I envy Martha? Like myself, she was an orphan with neither money nor connections. Yet there was a difference. She had a living brother.

There is no more despicable emotion on earth than envy, yet none so common to the human heart. Could it be? Could envy have poisoned my heart so? This thought had the ring of truth in my ears.

I needed to repent my sin and beg forgiveness at once, and I returned to my cottage. I banged through the door, threw down my cloak and bonnet, placed my boots by the fire, and announced, "Martha, I'm heartily ashamed of myself. I've searched my soul and do believe I've found the source of the poison in my breast: envy! You have a brother to love, and I know not what has become of mine."

Martha closed her eyes and nodded.

Abigail merely observed, "Your leg is bleeding."

I looked down and, sure enough, bright-red blood spread along the edge of my petticoat.

"Come, let me stanch that before you track blood all over the house."

•   •   •

After Abigail had bandaged my ankle, neither of us spoke much. And while Martha stared at the ceiling in a rigid state of hurt, I divulged that secret I had dared not say before: "Well, I suppose if John is to risk his life to make a treaty with the French, the least we ladies can do is make some good blankets for him for the crossing."

I saw Martha blink, but she said nothing. Abigail, however, had a slight, satisfied smile at the corner of her lips.

Abigail and I began dyeing wool the next day—a smelly, messy task best done in warmer months. In a few days' time, though her left hand was still bandaged, Martha joined us. She had few words for me at first. It was her turn to judge me, and I let her. She had great powers of observation, and I prayed humbly that she would merely dislike me from then on and not loathe me enough to leave.

Martha let me flap in the breeze a good while—several weeks, in fact—before letting me know, as we read companionably by the kitchen hearth of an evening, that she had forgiven me. She let me know not by words but by leaving off work a moment and placing her hand on mine. So forcefully did I feel her touch, bereft of it as I had been, that I wept.

"Oh, Martha, you don't hate me, then?"

She sighed. "I tried, but could not. For, were the situation reversed, I should feel just as you have felt."

I hugged her to me then, grateful I had not destroyed our friendship.

That same day, Abigail, Martha, and I hung the dripping skeins upon the warping board. We dressed the loom and tied the heddles to make a nice warm overshot weave. And with this wool, we wove two blankets, one for John and the other for John Quincy. One was red and white, the other blue and white. They each had thirteen stars and were signed: *M. M., A. A., and E. B., November 24, 1777.*

20

FEBRUARY 1778. I COME AT LAST TO the heart of my narrative: that period of time, lasting roughly eighteen months, during which John was in France and we found ourselves entirely alone in a hostile environment.

We lived on dreams. Indeed, our conversation those dark weeks, as we sipped our Liberty tea, often went something like this:

"Oh, to have a cake of jam and butter frosting . . . light as air."

"For toast with fresh butter," Abigail added.

"What would you give for it, Abigail?" I asked.

"For a large, moist, fluffy sponge cake with good tart jam and butter?" Abigail considered, shutting her eyes for a moment. "Mr. Adams, I believe, would be a fair trade."

As it happens, the day John Adams left, Mr. Brown, Susanna's husband, a handsome, good-natured lad, came by with an apple pie to "pay us" for another daughter we had birthed the week before. We were all smiles, but could not wait for him to leave. The moment he did so, we raced for spoons. But then I stopped and said, "Martha, we must bring this to Abigail. Tonight John and John Quincy leave for France."

You could see her shoulders sink at this, for the pie was nearly on her tongue.

"Yes, you're right."

We both stared sadly down at our pie.

That evening we were nearly frozen solid by the time we reached Abigail's. The walk took us an hour. We saw her through the window before she spied us with our gift, which I hid behind my back, the better to surprise her. I couldn't feel my hands or my feet, however, and so I hoped she would hurry to the door.

Abigail was lost in a letter she had obviously just received. Tears glistened on her face as she sat before the fire, her children around her. Mr. Thaxter, the tutor—not to be confused with my Thaxter, the profligate—and Mr. Rice, Mr. Adams's law clerk, stood listening with grave faces.

I rapped gently on the window. She started, smiled, and came swiftly to the door.

"Oh, I'm glad to see you!" she cried. "I have had a letter. John has not yet sailed but writes from the ship in Boston Harbor. Listen." She read:

On Board the Frigate Boston *5 O'clock in the Afternoon Feb. 13, 1778*

Dearest of Friends,

I am favoured with an unexpected Opportunity, by Mr. Woodward the lame Man who once lived at Mr. Belchers, and who promises in a very kind manner to take great Care of the Letter, to inform you of our Safe Passage from the Moon Head, on Board the ship.—the seas ran very high, and the Spray of the seas would have wet Us, but Captn. Tucker kindly brought great Coats on Purpose with which he covered Up me and John so that We came very dry.— Tomorrow Morning We sail.—God bless you, and your my Nabby, my Charley, my Tommy and all my Friends.

Yours, ever, ever, ever yours, John Adams

When she had finished, Abigail grew so pale I thought she would faint. I motioned to Martha to put the kettle on and knelt by Abigail's side, resting the pie on the floor.

"I can't bear it," she wept, signaling Mr. Thaxter to remove the children, which he did with great celerity. "Lizzie, terror and self-pity overcome me in equal measure."

"Now, now," I said, taking her hand, "you *will* bear it. You know you will, because you *must*."

She quieted, then laughed shortly. "You've stolen my own words to use against me."

"Not against. Never against. For what choice have you, dearest?"

"He left in such haste, he forgot our blankets," she replied sadly. I smiled. "They will keep till he returns."

But Abigail continued upon her other train of thought. "I have thought many times of the possibility that I might lose John. But Johnny, the thought of Johnny—"

"Abigail, listen." I took her hands. "Johnny is at this moment more wildly happy than he has been in his life. Think of the adventure! The learning! The exposure to a new language, new ideas. He's ready—you know he is, being far in advance of the other boys his age both in learning and sensibility. He'll be a great man someday, in part because his mother let him go to France for the Cause."

My words seemed to fortify her; she breathed easier.

"Now look here," I continued. "I have brought something to sweeten your anguish. And, as it is a very great sacrifice for me and Martha"—here, Martha and I exchanged nods—"I'll thank you to enjoy it as greatly as possible."

"What have you here?" she asked in a small voice, looking at the cloth that covered a rounded shape. I thought I saw her nostrils flare at the smell of the pie beneath. Her eyes widened. "It's not—"

"It is," I insisted, unveiling the treasure.

"A pie! Oh, a pie! You're an angel!"

We removed to the kitchen, and the children were called, and for a while all thoughts of the treacherous sea crossing and the forgotten blankets were abandoned to the heavenly sensation of real wheat crust and fruit. Thus, in a sense, Abigail had indeed exchanged Mr. Adams for a dessert. Heavenly Maker, forgive us!

·　·　·

John Adams was gone, and not just him, but any semblance of safety we might have derived from his presence. For in dependence is safety, or at least the illusion of it. This is the lesson we all learned from the Revolution.

I wish I could say my suspicions of Martha disappeared. However, they did not. Reader, I had the good sense to say nothing and to behave in no way that might expose my deepest feelings. I knew her too well by then, as we all came to know one another. We could read a single facial muscle, the minute adjustment of a shoulder blade. No doubt she read my continued doubts as well, but she, too, thought it best to pretend as if she did not.

Around this time I began to dream of my ancestral home on Brattle Street. I dreamed of it all that February, not once but near a dozen times. I had heard it had been taken over by one of Washington's officers after the evacuation of March 1776. The dreams were dark and persistent. In them, others occupied the house, but I nonetheless returned by the front door and slept in my own room, only to be discovered the following morning. In one dream, I was found by a haughty captain; in another, a filthy crowd of militia entered my chamber.

So vivid was this recurring dream that in it I recalled furniture—tables, dressers, Turkey carpets, china cabinets, and even storage chests—I had long since forgotten about. Upon waking, such grief would overcome me that I could hardly bear it, and the sensation that I had left unfinished business there did not leave me for many hours.

I had no notion what the dreams signified. I supposed that to depart from one's home in such haste had inflicted a wound of some kind. Yet, even were I to return, I felt certain that destruction within—tables used for firewood, spoons and window muntins used for bullets—would wound me doubly.

· · ·

Spring unfolded itself gradually. Purple crocuses emerged, the sight of them lifting my heart. April was still cold, the ground hard. People long indoors began to walk abroad, no longer hunched against the cutting winds. It was at the end of April, or perhaps the first week of May, that I happened upon Mary Cranch as she walked home from the cobbler's. Seeing me, she approached with great excitement and proceeded to tell me that they were expecting some very interesting boarders, men who counted themselves among the very highest echelons of our patriots.

"One, I hear, Lizzie, is quite renowned for his good looks," she added archly.

"Well, then, you must certainly have us 'round to meet him." I spoke in jest, of course: I had no expectations of meeting a man, not then or ever. But I was of a mind to enjoy a dinner at which I could speak about *Hamlet* with Richard Cranch.

"His name's Mr. Cleverly," she added.

"He is not related to our Cleverlys?" I asked, alarmed, for the Braintree Cleverlys were prominent Tories.

"Oh, no."

"Cleverly," I mused. "A good name for a handsome man. Though I do think it would be more equitable for an ugly man to receive the wits, don't you? Let the handsome man content himself with winning the ladies."

"Well, I think it is auspicious," Mary slyly replied. "But you have no need to wait for our invitation, Lizzie. The colonel has plans to invite us all to dinner."

"I look forward to it."

But two other pieces of news soon made me forget about the men who were expected at the Cranches' home. The following week, a terrible rumor caught fire in our parish that Benjamin Franklin had been assassinated in Paris. For several weeks, we lived in abject terror of its being true. I watched Martha's face for signs that she had intelligence from her brother, but could discern none. Abigail was nearly dead with worry for her "men," whom she could not reach. She would not hear from John until October, and only a report in the British newspaper, brought by some traveler to our village, assured her that he had arrived safely in Bordeaux.

The second piece of news, about the repossession of Tory houses by their owners, would have more direct bearing upon me.

One week after I met Mary on the road, we went to dine at the colonel's. The day of the much-awaited dinner party was unseasonably warm, and Martha and I chose to walk through the fields rather than take the long way around by the road. We had just emerged upon the path leading to the house when we came upon a large party that seemed to be headed the same way. When I saw who was among them—Abigail, Charles, Thomas, and Nabby—I clapped my hands in delight. I had not seen the children in a long while; they were beautiful in my eyes, both for their origins and for themselves.

Charles was nearly eight and full of mischief—he ran ahead of everyone, playing some game or other; Tommy, six, followed him like a shadow. Nabby, now a prim girl of near thirteen, exhorted the boys to slow down.

As we mounted the steps, I embraced Abigail.

"Your children have grown."

"Yes. Nabby is now just taller than I."

I observed the girl admiringly; she looked a great deal like her mother, though softer and rounder in her features. Then I looked about us and asked, "But where is your sister?"

"Oh, I believe they're already within."

"What hear you about their esteemed guests?" I whispered.

"Not much," she admitted. "But I'm greatly looking forward to meeting them. Mary tells me that one of them, a Dr. Flynt, hails from Philadelphia."

"He must know John then."

"Indeed." She smiled broadly at the mention of her husband.

The butler opened the door, bowed, and brought us inside. The children were sent off to the kitchen, presumably to join their cousins. We found ourselves before the colonel himself. Standing just behind him were Richard and Mary Cranch and three strangers.

Upon first seeing these men, the idea of Goldilocks and her three bears came to me: one was very tall, one was very short, and one was neither too tall nor too short but just right. I knew not why, upon first sight, I found these men faintly ridiculous, but the sensation was alarming.

Seeing us enter the parlor, all three men bowed.

Abigail, Martha, and I curtsied.

Dr. Flynt, the stout one, had graying hair and spectacles perched at the end of a bulbous nose. When he bowed to us, a piece of hair flipped to the side, revealing a sweaty bald spot. I had a terrible, sudden urge to laugh and grasped Abigail's wrist.

Pushing back against me to forestall laughter, Abigail inquired, "I have heard tell, Dr. Flynt, that you come to us from Philadelphia. You must have met my husband, then, for he has resided there these past three years."

"I have not had that great pleasure, ma'am." He proceeded to bow once more, so deeply that his spectacles actually fell off his face, and I feared all was lost. I glanced quickly at a portrait upon the wall as he scrambled to retrieve his spectacles from the Turkey carpet. "But upon my return, I most assuredly shall seek him out."

"You shan't find him in Philadelphia, for, as everyone knows, he is in Paris now," I said tartly.

Abigail shot me a look, but Dr. Flynt's manner had annoyed me almost from the moment I set eyes upon him. It is an unfortunate part of our nature that we judge others quickly—and often incorrectly.

The tall one, Mr. Thayer, reminded me of portraits I had seen of Judge Thomas Sewall, our Puritan forefather who had sent the Salem ladies to the ropes. Hollow-cheeked, with a tall forehead and a firmly set, grim mouth, he said he hailed from Exeter, New Hampshire, and was a surveyor by trade.

"Then you must certainly know my sister Betsy, who has lately moved there with her husband, the Reverend Stephen Peabody," said Abigail.

"Indeed, I have had the pleasure," he said unsmilingly, but nothing more could be gotten from him on the subject.

Martha nudged me and whispered, "It seems we are to have an exceedingly dull evening."

I nudged her back, shushing her.

Meanwhile, Abigail addressed Mr. Thayer, "Would you be kind enough to take a note to my dear Betsy for me when you return?"

"I would, most gladly, Mrs. Adams." Mr. Thayer raised his eyes slightly. "But, unfortunately, I have no thoughts of returning there at the moment."

"It is not illness in the village that prevents you?" Abigail asked, growing alarmed by his grave manner.

"No, no. Business matters, business matters."

"I'm very sorry for it. I hear it's a lovely little village. My sons have been, but I've not yet had that pleasure."

"Indeed, it is a pretty village."

"Full of Tories, is what I hear!" declared Josiah Quincy, who had come up to us. "All those little backwater villages— lousy with 'em."

"My dear uncle, one might say *we* live in such a backwater village," Richard countered tactfully.

"Touché!" Josiah cried, nearly spilling his cordial.

The third man, who called himself Cleverly, sat in one of the colonel's high-backed chairs with his pipe and cordial, looking the very picture of an easy country gentleman. Unlike the two other men, who were past their prime by several decades, Mr. Cleverly was quite young, and his blue eyes brimmed with a sort of amused mischievousness. He had a fair complexion and wavy blond hair.

Mr. Cleverly also struck me as someone made of a different fabric from the other two—richer and more refined. He could have been a neighbor in Cambridge, or a cousin of my mother's. And Mary was right: he was alarmingly good-looking. But I was not so shallow as to be won over by looks alone.

I turned to him. "And you there," I said. "While we're raking everyone over the coals, we may as well not spare you."

"By all means, do not." He smiled easily. "You must be Mrs. Boylston. Elizabeth, if I may. The Cranches have praised you to the skies. I'm nearly ready to propose marriage, if you will have me."

I was quite taken aback by his open humor, but took no offense. Indeed, it was a breath of fresh air, especially after meeting the other two men. He continued, "Mr. Cranch tells me you are a great reader of Shakespeare."

"Oh, not a *great* reader," I replied. "I haven't a great deal of time for reading."

"Nor do I. And I confess to preferring the sciences to literature. But if it should please you, I shall be happy to speak of Shakespeare."

"And where do you hail from, Mr. Cleverly?" I asked, ignoring the invitation to discuss Shakespeare. I would save that pleasure for Richard and Abigail.

"New Hampshire. Near Stonington," Cleverly replied. "But I find Shakespeare a far more interesting topic."

"Indeed," said Richard, who had come forward to embrace me. "Hello, Lizzie. I seem to recall promising you and Abigail a conversation about him the last time we met."

The colonel, apparently hearing the word *Stonington*, bellowed forth, "Stonington! A hotbed of Toryism."

"Josiah, *please*," Ann begged. "You'll scare our esteemed guests away."

"Your husband is correct, madam." Mr. Cleverly stood and bowed. He then began to walk about the parlor. "It was our own scurrilous merchant Mr. Holland, who was charged with that notorious counterfeit scheme. He has not yet been apprehended."

"I myself was a victim of that cruel scheme," Abigail said. "I received a five-pound note in town that served me ill indeed. I was obliged to burn it."

"A scoundrel." Mr. Cleverly frowned. "Conniving men like him may do more harm than an entire regiment."

"Hear, hear," agreed the colonel enthusiastically, raising his cordial.

Dr. Flynt and Mr. Thayer both gravely nodded assent.

The conversation might have continued in this vein had not a servant announced that dinner was ready. As the party walked toward the dining room, Mr. Cleverly took the opportunity to engage me in conversation.

"I must be honest with you, Mrs. Boylston. You defy my expectations." His voice was appropriately low, so that others could not overhear. I found his intimate tone presumptuous. "Is Braintree truly your birthplace?"

"You think it impossible that a woman such as myself should spring from such base soil?" I smirked.

"Yes, rather," he admitted, looking about him, since I had not lowered my voice as he had. I would have nothing to hide from my friends. "But I admit I had had a telltale clue: your hands are not so rough as they might be. I will hazard that you were not born here. You have been among this village's fine citizens a year. Perhaps two."

"Four," I admitted. "But you are quite astute, Mr. Cleverly. I'm a recent import. Brattle Street in Cambridge is my birthplace. My father was a judge."

"And what brought you to Braintree?" His manner was light, pleasant, and slightly ironical, as if any reply at all would be amusing.

"My husband and I were given a small farm, which we vastly preferred to a cowardly retreat to Halifax."

"I see." He nodded thoughtfully. "It all comes clear. But you must miss Cambridge and all its great advantages?"

"Indeed I do not," I said warmly, "for you'll find no greater advantage than counting oneself among the Cranches and Adamses of this world."

Upon hearing their names, Richard, Mary, and Abigail turned to me with questioning looks.

"She pays you a compliment," Mr. Cleverly assured them, which I thought rude in the extreme.

We had by now reached the dining room and were standing at our appointed places. As ill luck would have it, Mrs. Quincy had placed me directly opposite Mr. Cleverly.

"Mrs. Boylston, I fear I have offended you," Mr. Cleverly said once we had been seated. "Please accept my apologies. I meant no offense."

"Oh, none taken," I said lightly. Meanwhile, everyone had fallen silent to hear our conversation. "In any case, the provincialism of such villages as Braintree is a common misapprehension. I have every expectation that history will place our parish in its correctly illustrious light."

"I fervently wish it so." Cleverly bowed his head.

The room in which we dined was not large, but cozy and opulent. Two pyramids of sugared fruits sat upon china plates. These were flanked by silver candelabra, each holding six burning candles. Behind us a fire blazed, surrounded by fine Dutch tiles. Beneath the shining mahogany table lay a thick Turkey carpet, so soft I had a desire to remove my shoes and caress it with my stockinged feet. I feel certain the colonel would not have cared had I done so. Indeed, it would not surprise me to learn he had removed his own shoes, so little did he heed the conventions of the time.

Dinner began with a *sole meunière*. It being a formal dinner, and the company being mixed and unknown to one another, we kept to safe topics such as the weather, our hopes for that year's crops, the wheat shortage, and the mounting inflation. Politics were assiduously avoided by all but the colonel, who kept getting interrupted by the genteel pressure of his wife's foot upon his own. Each time, the colonel was uncouth enough to utter, "Hang it, woman, why do you keep stepping on my foot?"

We were next served a glazed ham with buttery biscuits and garden beans. Throughout the dinner, I could not help noticing Mr. Cleverly. I would look up between courses to find him staring at me so boldly that I was afraid something in my appearance was amiss.

I was discomfited for my own private reasons as well: I could not look in his direction without blushing. His eyes were so clear, so astute. He seemed to take in the scene as I did: with a wry sense of the ridiculous. His fair, wavy hair was neatly plaited. His chin was prominent, with a faint dimple.

Let it be said that I dislike such involuntary attraction enormously. Relying little upon Reason, it makes a mockery of one's native intelligence. What's more, I felt certain everyone at the table noticed my frequent change of color.

For dessert we had minted berries, and when dinner had ended, the women repaired to one room and the men another. Taking a seat next to Abigail, the first thing I did was ask, "Did you notice how Mr. Cleverly looked at me all throughout the meal?"

"Yes, Lizzie, I saw."

"What do you think he was staring at?"

"You, of course."

"But what *for*? I did nothing to encourage his attention."

"It would seem he is smitten. It would not be the first time in history a man fancied a woman without her provocation, you know. Though it may seem that way to you."

I nudged her in the ribs, and she glared at me to stop at once. I knew her well enough to know she was highly ticklish.

Martha and Mary were deeply engaged in a discussion about oat flour, so Abigail and I were able to continue our conversation.

"Really, Lizzie, you should be flattered. My sister has told me he's a great patriot, in our parish on some secret business. Apparently it's to do with that scurrilous Mr. Holland, of whom he spoke earlier."

My eyes widened. "Why? Does he believe Mr. Holland to be somewhere in our midst?"

"I know not. But hush," said Abigail. "Here comes the colonel. His line is not straight, but it is certain."

Indeed, I then perceived the colonel, slightly the worse for rum, tottering across the hall toward me. Cleverly kept a steadier pace by his side. The colonel then held his hand out as if I would rise and join him.

"Mrs. Boylston, will you do me the honor of a word in my study?"

At this, I became quite alarmed. I thought at once of my brother, and my heart began to pound. I asked, "Is it not something my friends might hear? For these ladies surrounding me are all my dearest friends."

"Very well. I had wished to spare you embarrassment, but if you prefer it . . ."

"Embarrassment? Is it *bad* news you have to offer?"

"No, indeed. Not at all." He came closer and placed his hand on my shoulder. "Allow me to sit down and I will tell you, for I have news that will affect you directly."

He pulled up a chair across from me. The other ladies pretended not to listen, but spoke such trivialities amongst themselves as would not impede their comprehension of the colonel's words. Martha, however, made no such pretense. She turned to look at us.

"We have received word of a new law, effective immediately, by which homes confiscated before the Troubles shall be reinstated to their families."

I glanced at Martha.

"And," he continued, "since your brother has not been heard from in these three years and is presumed—"

"Dead," I finished for him.

"Yes, unfortunately. Since he is missing and presumed dead, I have been instructed to inform you that the house . . ."

The colonel paused, reached for his spectacles, retrieved a crumpled letter from his waistcoat pocket, and announced, "That the house at 178 Brattle Street is hereby reinstated to your family, this deed being made out in your name and presented to you on this day, the fourteenth of May 1778."

I must have faltered, because the colonel offered me his glass of rum, imploring me to drink. I heard Abigail say, "Lizzie, dearest."

"I am well," I insisted, drinking off the rum in a single draught.

Mr. Cleverly offered me his arm. "Are you unwell?" he asked. "Shall I escort you home?"

"It is but two rods from this very spot. Martha shall accompany me." I smiled.

"I daresay you'll be wanting to set off. Let me then say what a pleasure it was to meet you. To meet all of you." He bowed to Martha, who curtsied politely.

"You are very kind," I insisted. "Now I must return home to gather my things. And my wits." I laughed suddenly, placing a hand to my dizzy head.

I had not grown faint from having had my ancestral home returned to me, but because I had dreamt of it so unremittingly. Could one rely upon primitive intuitions and instincts, after all? I had sensed something wrong with Abigail's babe, and it had died. I had dreamed of my ancestral home, and now it had come into my possession. I knew not whether this was a good or a bad thing. I prayed only that the house was not inhabited, as it was in my dreams.

21

AS IN MY DREAMS, I STOOD UPON the stone stoop and knocked with the old brass knocker. But no dream predicted who was to greet me at the door: not Rebels, nor a British captain, but our old Negro caretaker, Giles. I had believed him to have long since quitted Cambridge.

"Giles!" I cried.

"Miss Elizabeth," he said, bowing.

"Mrs. Boylston, now, Giles," I said. A deep tenderness for my father's old servant, my grandfather's slave, rose within me. He must have been in his seventies by then, but looked younger. He had been a favorite of my father's when my father was a boy.

"Oh, yes. Forgive me," he said, thinking I was scolding him. And so he was greatly surprised when I threw my arms around his neck and kissed his warm, dry cheek.

Embarrassed, he bade me come inside. It was then that Bessie, my mother's maid, came racing up to me. Had she been here, too, this whole time?

She was younger than Giles by perhaps twenty years, but grown quite gray. She and Giles made an odd-looking pair, for he was very tall and very black, where Bessie was white and shaped like a sugarplum. Bessie had a judgmental air, too, and when I was a child she had frightened me. But while she could take one to task rather sharply, her verbal darts never pierced very deep.

"Oh, Bessie, you are a sight for sore eyes," I said, embracing her. "I thought you long gone."

"Oh, no, miss. Miss, you look well. Very well indeed," she said, looking over me admiringly. Neither she nor Giles had seen me in four years' time.

"But how did you get here? Where's yer carriage?"

"Carriage? Oh, no. I—rode."

"Rode what?"

"My horse. Star."

"Nay."

I laughed. "If you don't believe me, go check on the road. He's tied there. I hope there's still hay in the barn."

After some further reassurances that I had not been mortally wounded on my journey, and having ascertained that there was indeed some straw in the barn, Bessie said, "But I just can't believe it's you, miss."

"Yes, I am all grown, and too tan for a proper lady," I confessed. "But you, Bessie . . ." I looked around me, as if to shake myself awake from this dream. "Excuse me for asking, but is there no one else about? Have you been here alone all this time?"

She frowned, turning to point to the empty rooms. "Who would you be expectin', ma'am? All but us 'as been let go ages since."

"But why did you not write me?"

"Oh, miss," she began, clearly dismayed, "we didn't wish to bother you, newly gone to housekeeping as you were."

"But surely you heard about my Jeb? Surely you were told about the funeral?"

Bessie hung her head. "In August that year we heard. August of '75—" Bessie sent me an apologetic glance, for the very mention of that year, she knew, gave me a deep pain. She then turned to Giles. "Was it August or September we heard, Giles?"

"August, miss," Giles assented, his hands clasped behind his back.

"So the Boylstons did not tell you? When you were not at his funeral, I felt certain you were gone. Oh, those wretched, wretched Boylstons!"

"We were sorry for Mr. Boylston. Very sorry."

I thought Bessie would begin to bawl if I did not reassure her. "Oh, I know you must have grieved." I hugged her to me. "All the more cruel that they did not let you come grieve with me."

At this point, Bessie seemed to recall my long journey and my need of sustenance, for she said, "Come, miss, there's a chair in here, in the dining room."

Two lonely chairs now stood in a dining room that had once been filled with a dozen English mahogany chairs and a fine table. Still, I was grateful for them and sat myself down on one. I felt faint and craved a cup of tea.

"Bessie, is Cook around?"

"Cook? Oh, no, ma'am. Cook left with Washington's army. They was pleased by her roasts."

"Indeed," I said. Cook, I recalled, was an old crone who didn't much like people, but who turned out the most gorgeous roasts stuffed with oysters and clams. She made excellent meat pies, too. My mouth watered at the thought of her cooking.

I forced my thoughts back to the present. "Bessie, I need something to eat, for I feel a bit faint. I shall follow you to the kitchen."

"Of course, ma'am. Ors you can set here, and I'll bring it to you."

"No, no. I wish to talk."

And so I shadowed Bessie through the dusty rooms. Peering into the parlor, I was surprised to find the portrait of my mother still there, on the wall above the mantel. Tears sprang to my eyes, not just from a sense of loss (that would never leave me, not until I was in my own grave), but from gratitude that whatever army last was here did not see fit to take it, or burn it for warmth.

"Where has all the furniture gone to, Bessie?"

She pulled a chair up by the kitchen fireplace for me. "Scoundrels, all of 'em!" she hissed as she put the kettle on. I soon had a hot dish of real tea—Bessie had carefully hoarded it for just such an occasion—and a fine rye toast with a good tart marmalade. It began to revive me.

"First it were our 'ospital—a terrible sight that was. Then it were our officers' lodgings. They're the ones what chopped up the furniture for firewood. And just now Burgoyne's men—a filthy lot. Oh, it broke my heart. But no good tellin' you, ma'am. There was nothin' Giles and I could do but watch. We were greatly afeared, we were."

"Of course you were, Bessie," I said consolingly, as the poor woman looked quite ashamed. "You're a strong, good woman, but you can hardly fight a whole company of vandals."

"And how they drank!" She rolled her eyes, now feeling free to tell all. "They drank every last bottle of rum, every cask of cider, every bottle of good wine of your father's—till there was none left and they bade me find more! But that I wouldn'a do. I said they could take my life if they wished, but finding rum so's to see them destroy the master's house—that I couldn'a do."

"Good girl." I smiled and touched my hand on her old, rough one. "They got it elsewhere, I'm sure."

"You did not make it easy for them."

"No, that I didn'."

Fortunately, they had left the heavy bedsteads. After undressing, I fell gratefully into bed, though it was not yet six in the evening. I slept through till morning and did not remember my dreams upon waking.

• • •

I had planned to stay but a day or two, just long enough to decide my course of action regarding the house and its contents. But the following morning, as we were all breakfasting cozily in the kitchen, I turned to Giles and Bessie and asked, "How have you managed to stay on here? How is it you have the means? I hope it is not indelicate of me to ask."

They looked at each other.

"Means, ma'am? Oh, we have no *means* to speak of. We been given as much so's to keep life and limb together, if that's what you mean. A man named Steadman comes reg'lar each month."

"Who is this Steadman?" I asked, surprised.

"I know not, ma'am. An acquaintance, so he says, of your brother's."

"My brother? Is he alive, then?" I stood up.

Bessie sought to quell any false hope in me. "We don't know naught but what the man gives us, and it comes reg'lar as rain."

"That it does," Giles agreed.

Now I desperately wished to speak to this fellow Steadman. Bessie told me that the fellow came on the first Monday of every month. Therein lay the dilemma: I could not possibly stop that long in Cambridge. In May, one had to plough the fields and sow the corn, and much else besides. Oh, but to hear news of my brother, my Harry—I might almost have forsaken my farm.

"Bessie, I must return home. I cannot wait for this Steadman. But I shall come back, rest assured, and find out what's going on."

"Oh, miss, but you just got here!"

"I know; I'm sorry. It can't be helped."

Seeing her dejection—the poor woman had known no society in several years and was loath to see me go—I agreed to stop the night, at which news she revived. We then toured the house and wandered the sad grounds. My father's once-pristine orchards were now all overgrown, attacked by disease. Squirrels and crows had taken up residence with their extended families and had already harvested our fruit trees, berry patches, and vegetables. It was a sorry state of affairs, impossible for one old caretaker and a lady's maid to manage.

Everywhere I turned, reminders of my old life assaulted me: a dark rectangle of wood where a carpet had been, or the smell of lilies in the garden. Harry and I had played tag on that carpet, with our mother entreating us to stop. And I had smelled the lilacs in the spring from my chamber above them.

The kitchen garden was well tended, and it reminded me of the happy years before my mother died. But I knew this was my home no longer. I could not live in it without pining for Braintree.

That afternoon I sent a message to Martha that I would return the following day. In the evening, having dined on a good roast chicken cooked by Giles and drunk half a bottle of his home-made wine, I read in my father's library until I felt quite sleepy and retired.

The following morning I was up early and had decided to leave directly when Bessie came running with a message. "You've a letter from Miss Miller!" she breathed.

"A letter? I am hardly arrived myself." I moved off a ways for privacy, opened the letter, and read:

> *Lizzie, I send you tidings that should gladden you. This morning, Gaius Harrison came to offer his services for having safe delivered his wife Sarah of a healthy babe last month. He says he'll fix our broken fence and tend our crops in your absence. Oh, happy event! On a lesser note, I have heard from my brother, and, Lizzie, the die is cast: he intends to visit you in Cambridge and will not be gainsaid. Kiss him for me, ha ha.*
> *Love, Martha*

"Bessie!" I called, but as it turned out I had no reason to shout, for, as I had read my letter, Bessie had inched so close that she now stood directly beside me.

"Yes, miss?"

"Well," I said, "you will be glad to know that I have no urgent need to return to Braintree. I shall stop a few days. Oh, I'm glad to see you, Bessie!" And I sealed my words with a hug, which Bessie, though surprised, accepted.

• • •

The following day, I answered the door expecting it to be Martha's brother. But instead, it was a messenger with a vexatious letter from Abigail:

Dearest Lizzie,

The women of our parish miss you greatly. Since you left us, there have been two births, one in the north and another in the south parish. Dr. Wales safe delivered them, but I saw fit to visit these women and heard in no uncertain terms how little they liked the Dr.'s anxious manner and his rough touching. The child in the south parish he nearly tore apart with his forceps. It was a miracle the poor babe kept its arms and legs.

Abigail went on to mention that Dr. Wales had made no soothing tea for them, nor bandaged their stomachs, nor put fresh linen on their beds, but had left all for the women and the after-nurse. And for that he charged thirty shillings! She further recounted how he kept a persnickety ledger for debts owed. No, there would be no apple pies for Dr. Wales. She concluded:

Yes, Lizzie, I fear you will be run off your feet when you return, for our women will themselves to hold out for you.

This letter made my heart heavy with longing to be home. However, there was nothing to be done, as I had determined to wait for Steadman.

.   .   .

Toward the end of that first week in Cambridge, another messenger arrived. It was a local boy bringing news that quite shocked me: the Boylstons, Mr., Mrs., and Miss Eliza, had returned from exile in New Hampshire and wished a visit from me as soon as was convenient. He stood there patiently and awaited my reply.

How had they known I was in Cambridge? They must have inquired first of Martha.

"If they wish to see me, why do they not visit *me*?" I fumed to Bessie.

"Perh'ps one of them's ill," she proffered.

"Oh, I hadn't thought of that." I placed a hand on Bessie's shoulder. While unschooled and in some ways blunt to the point of coarseness, Bessie had a sharp mind.

I did not tell Bessie that after Jeb died, I had lived in mortal terror of the Boylstons' kidnapping me and removing me from my rightful home. Then there had been the threat of their kidnapping Star. All that was long past now, however, and I chose the more generous path.

"You are quite right, Bessie," I said. Then, turning to the boy, I said, "Please let the Boylstons know that I shall visit them this afternoon, if that is convenient."

.   .   .

It was a pleasant, fair day. I easily strolled the half mile up Brattle Street, looking quite the Tory lady in my pale-green silk gown. Apparently the various armies that had passed through my house had seen fit to leave me my old garments. While they were several seasons out of date and somewhat loose (I had grown strong and lean in the intervening years), few ladies these days could afford to wear silk at any price, and thus I cut a handsome, if outmoded, figure. Upon gazing in a looking glass before departing, I was happy to note that my tan had faded somewhat as well.

At the Boylston home, a Negro servant greeted me. This, I believe, was Cassie, the family's cook. She bade me wait and scurried off.

While I waited, I looked around me. The home had suffered since I was last there. Some of the large pieces of furniture were missing, along with the gilt mirrors and several Turkey carpets. The parlor floor was bare, though clean. I saw no servants save Cassie. Signs of distress were everywhere, and I nearly forgave the Boylstons then for trying to steal Star from me.

The biggest change, though, was in the noise—or lack thereof. Though there were just me, Bessie, and Giles in my home, with little material wealth besides, at least our moving about made a happy clamor. Here, I heard nothing at all, not even the bustle of family.

In a few minutes Mrs. Boylston appeared. The woman had lost a great deal of flesh, and her hair had turned entirely white since I had seen her last. Though not yet fifty years of age, her posture was that of a much older woman.

Most surprising of all, however, was that she seemed genuinely glad to see me.

"Oh, Lizzie, it's good to lay eyes on a friend, for we have gone without society these three years together."

I might have quibbled over the importance of going "without society" at such a time as ours, but I had not the heart for unkindness, even for one who had been so unkind to me.

Madam Boylston asked Cassie to bring us "some refreshment." I gathered by the euphemism that it would not be real tea and sighed. If one could not get a good dish of tea at the Boylstons', one could not get it anywhere. At my own house, we had long since run out.

"You look well, Lizzie," she said as we waited together for our tea.

"And you," I replied with the required lie.

"Oh, no. I fear our troubles have aged all of us greatly. And Mr. Boylston is not at all well."

"Not well?" I repeated, for though I was no great admirer of Mr. Boylston, he was the father of my beloved Jeb, and in a time requiring less sacrifice, he might have been a good enough man. I certainly wished him no ill, though he had caused me much pain. "What ails him?" I asked. "Has he had a doctor?"

Cassie arrived with our "refreshment" of hyssop tea and some very nice cakes. I ate one greedily. One can only imagine how rare food was if I can recall the passage of time by my repasts!

"Certainly. It is the consumption undoubtedly."

"Oh. I'm truly sorry."

"Dr. Bullfinch has bled him almost daily and applied leeches. All to no avail."

I hid an involuntary grimace. I believed these treatments to be of little use and some genuine harm. "Does he wish to see me?" I asked. I had medicines that might ease his chest greatly, though I knew of no cure on earth. With such a disease, only our Maker can enact a miracle.

"Indeed he does. That is why"—she paused, sensing her own indelicacy in phrasing it so—"that is *one* reason we called upon you."

"I shall see him now, if that's agreeable to him. And how fares Eliza?" I asked, for not a word had been mentioned of their daughter.

At the mention of Eliza, Mrs. Boylston's face grew pinched. A cloud literally seemed to pass over her, though the rest of the room was still quite bright with late-afternoon light. "She is well enough, I suppose," she said tersely. "My husband shall discuss her presently. I will inquire as to his current state."

And with that she left the room, leaving me alone for several minutes. As I walked about, I noticed a collection of miniature portraits above a mahogany chest of drawers. Among them, quite shockingly, was a portrait of Jeb. I reached out—hesitated—then, as a hard lump of indignation filled me, I snatched it from the wall. At its back, I found a braided lock of his hair beneath a small convex glass. Oh, my sweet boy's hair! And to think I'd found that prancing Mr. Cleverly attractive!

I felt fresh rage at this family, rage at the fact that they had had such a portrait and never offered it to me. It would have been such a comfort to me in my cold nights on the farm. But these people were of such a bent as to hoard memory itself.

Mrs. Boylston reentered the room to find me holding the portrait. I said nothing but cast her a hard glance.

"It is a good likeness, is it not?"

"Very good," I said. "When was it made? It seems drawn from life."

"I should have shown it to you sooner. We added the . . . the lock after his funeral. But as we were obliged to leave in great haste and have just this weekend returned, there was little opportunity. You understand."

"I understand perfectly." I turned my back on her to gaze once more at the portrait.

Mrs. Boylston could not have guessed my thoughts then, that God had seen fit to place two kinds of people on this earth: those who, though they had nothing, would give you half of that nothing; and those who would give nothing, though they had all the riches in the world. And while it is blasphemy to say, I believe that no amount of piety or churchgoing changed one kind of human being into the other.

"He will see you," she said, leaving aside the topic of the portrait as I set it back on its nail.

"Very well."

I thought it odd indeed that Eliza had still not presented herself. For while there was no love between us, common civility would require that she greet her dead brother's wife. Now, however, I took this behavior not so much as a rejection of myself but as proof of their pitiable isolation from humankind.

I found Mr. Boylston ill indeed. He was sitting up in bed in a quilted bed jacket and cap, his face quite drawn. He had greatly changed in the three years since I had last seen him, so much so that I should hardly have recognized him. His eyes were unnaturally bright, and his face, which bore a pale-ochre hue, was flushed with fever.

"Lizzie!" He smiled, genuinely overjoyed to see me. "Come here, child." Mr. Boylston motioned me to his bed, whereupon he gave me a hearty embrace. I actually thought I saw tears in his eyes when I finally pulled away. I sat by the bed and held his hand.

"Mrs. Boylston tells me you are not so well as one could wish."

" 'Not so well as one could wish.' Ha! She has always been a liar. All smiles and lies. Lizzie, I'm one foot in the grave, and I know it. I have little time to suffer fools. And the truth is, the fresh sight of you gladdens my heart."

"Then I'm glad, too," I said, squeezing his hand. "What does Dr. Bullfinch say?"

"Oh, never mind what the doctor says." He waved the question away as if it were of no importance. "Doctors speak all kinds of nonsense."

"I have some very fine plaisters and teas that will ease your chest a great deal, if you will let me help."

He tried to laugh, but it came out as a terrible, hollow-sounding cough. "Oh, poke and plaister me as you like. I am indifferent."

I stared at my ailing father-in-law with new respect; not everyone faced death with such equanimity. He seemed nearly disdainful of it, like a greedy creditor.

"Then I shall poke and plaister you, as you say, by and by."

I would have to send for my things, which I had left in Braintree. Were I to send a note that afternoon, I could have my medical sack by the morrow. "I'll come tomorrow and shall turn you into a fine pincushion, if that is agreeable."

"It is," he said. "But listen"—he grabbed my arm with such force as I had not thought possible in a man as weak as he—"I have matters to discuss with you, and you must help me. In a moment I shall be too tired to speak."

"I shall listen, then," I replied.

"We have done you an ill turn, Lizzie," he began. "Very ill. I see it now as I had not seen it before. I cannot sleep for thinking how we treated you, and my lapse in judgment regarding . . . er . . . the gift we, at one point, had wished to retrieve."

By this, I knew he meant my most beloved Star. "You must have felt in desperate straits to ask for such a thing," I said.

"Exactly, Lizzie. Desperate straits such as I have never in my life known, nor has my wife. As for Eliza . . . well, her entire world came to an end when we fled Cambridge."

Her world, I thought mordantly. As if her world should by rights continue when all fell in flames about her!

"In any case, I have a little set by, and I mean to leave you something when I die. To provide for you as I should have done from the beginning."

"It's not necessary," I began. "My farm in Braintree is doing well." That was not entirely true. I had but two pounds in all the world.

"It is my wish!" he said. "But now, I must ask you to help me."

"How can I aid you, sir?" And so at last he came to the point of my visit.

"It is Eliza," he said. His breath was failing him. He paused, and the feeling grew upon me that the mystery of her absence was about to be revealed. "Eliza is with child."

"With child!" I could not believe it. "Whom has she married?"

"No one. That is the point. She is unmarried still and refuses to tell us who the father is."

Eliza, with child? I could not imagine her smiling at a man, embracing a man, much less . . . But it would not bear thinking about.

"How far along is she?"

"I know not. It is not the province of a father, you understand. I bid you find it out and . . . take care of her."

Now at last the reason for my being summoned became clear to me.

I smiled. Mr. Boylston's low estimation of the human race—the notion that barter was required for all exchanges—was more in keeping with my understanding of him, and thus in a way more comforting, than the heavenly largess of his initial greeting.

"I will help Eliza," I replied, "but not because of any promise from you of a legacy. I will help her, if she will have it—and I'm not sure she will, mind you—because it is in my power to do so and because it is the Christian thing to do."

"Suit yourself," Mr. Boylston said, now clearly exhausted. "I care little for your motivations, so long as the thing is done."

"Fair enough." I kissed him on his temple, smoothed his sweaty, thinning hair, and departed his chamber.

Mrs. Boylston awaited me in the hallway, and I was ushered into Eliza's chamber. I found her standing by a window, in silhouette, great with child. When Eliza heard me, she turned, her pale eyes lighting upon me.

"You have grown tan, Lizzie," she said without approaching to embrace me.

I could have said, "And you have grown fat," but I did not. I smiled. "Oh, I was far worse a few weeks ago. In summer, one might well mistake me for a mulatto, I am so many hours at my work in the garden. Or upon Star," I could not help but add.

At my joke, Eliza turned cold. "Mama insisted that I see you, though I can't see what for. I am quite well."

"Indeed, you look well. You are with child."

"How astute." Her eyes stayed on me resolutely and did not gaze down at her own roundness.

"Shall we sit?" I asked, trying to maintain my composure. What did I care of Eliza or her problems? She could not harm me, and it is more honorable to be kind even if one is not repaid with kindness. She grudgingly sat across from me on her bed.

Someone knocked—the girl again. The poor thing: she worked hard, endeavoring to be everywhere at once. My guess was that only two or three servants remained from a former dozen. Now Cassie set down the dishes of tea and cakes for us.

Eliza massaged her back with one hand. "I have not been as unwell as some I've heard tell of, but my back aches terribly," she could not help but remark.

I pitied her then. Whom did she have to talk to? What friends did she have? Not a one. There was no one in the world with whom she could discuss her present situation.

"That's the baby's head growing against your spine. You ought to have a servant massage you each day and place hot chamomile cloths upon it. That will greatly relieve you."

"Oh, it's not so severe as all that," she said dismissively, "but I thank you for the suggestion."

"And the father? Is he unwilling to marry?"

I had been careful about broaching the subject of the father, but that seemed Eliza's clearest solution—to marry now, as soon as possible.

"He is"—she turned away from me—"he is dead," she pronounced.

"Dead?" I did not believe her for a moment.

She would say no more upon the subject of the father, and I thought it wise to let it go for now. "Is there no one else—?"

"To marry, you mean?" she asked, a half smile playing across her face. "No one I wish to marry. Or wish to trick into marriage."

"I wasn't speaking of trickery. Some men, when they love, are capable of great forgiveness."

"I know of no such men," she said pointedly, with a slight shake of her blonde curls. Not being a clever manipulator of others, I am slow to recognize manipulation when I am the victim of it. But I confess that it was only then I understood why I had been called upon. In my discretion and my skills lay the solution to Eliza's problem.

"Eliza, there is another way. How many weeks, to the best of your understanding, since you conceived?"

She looked around the empty room as if someone might overhear our terrible words. "Twenty," she replied, and, without the least warning, she burst into tears.

I was moved by her tears, but it is a well-known fact that women are often quite wrong about their dates. And so I pursued gently, "Might I lay my hands upon you to ascertain for myself?"

"Certainly not!" She dabbed her eyes with a handkerchief that she'd pulled out of a small silk bag.

"Oh, come now, Eliza. If I am to deliver this babe, I will be obliged to touch more than your belly."

"Disgusting!" She turned away from me again.

I laughed heartily. "You must take your quarrel up with our Maker. Woman is His design, not mine. Come now, allow me."

I helped her back on the bed.

"These stays are far too tight. I'm loosing them. You'll harm your child and yourself to wear them so. You shouldn't wear them at all—or very loosely, at the least." I placed my hands on her belly. It was warm, pale, and quite beautiful. If only her character were as lovely! My hands told me the babe was indeed about five months.

"I'm finished," I said. "As close as I can tell, you are due in middle to late October. Let us talk about it."

What I recommended to Eliza was that in her last month, sometime in early October but well before it would be unsafe for her to travel, she come to stay with me and Martha in Braintree. This move would have the double advantage of discretion for her and convenience for me, as it was the busiest time of year on a farm. I could not possibly leave Martha alone.

She glanced only very briefly across at me. "I will consider it. Thank you."

As we parted, I could not help but say, "Come what may, Eliza, let no ignorant, backward woman, nor no cocky, inexperienced physician, deliver you. It would spell death."

"Thank you," she said again, proud as ever. I soon left her and a house from which no one bade me so much as a good day.

22

AS I WALKED DOWN THE ROAD TOWARD my ancestral home, I felt lucky to be free from such grievous encumbrances as Eliza now had, and I pitied her. And while I entirely doubted her story of the dead father, the man must have been a rogue or an idiot not to marry her—she of a good family, a dying father, and a large home and furnishings. Then a terrible thought occurred to me, and I regretted not having asked: perhaps she had been ravished. I had heard numerous stories of soldiers and their rude, violent ways. I prayed for her that it was not so. But the more I thought on it, the more likely it seemed.

I was home before the sun had fully declined. Crickets chirped, and the spring evening light cast a glow over the old manse and orchards. I sat out back on the brick patio with a glass of Giles's bilberry wine, feeling suddenly whole and strangely happy. Giles approached so quietly that I started at his cough.

"Madam, you had a visitor."

"When?"

"While you were abroad."

"Who was this visitor, pray?"

"A Mr. Miller, he said his name was. He said he would return tomorrow morning."

"Oh, thank you, Giles."

For some vexing reason, neither Giles nor Bessie was to be found the following morning when Mr. Miller rang. And though our small number could hardly be disguised, it was quite mortifying to have no doorman. Instead, I had to suffer the humiliation of hearing Mr. Miller shout as he stuck his head partway through the unlocked door, "Hallo! Anyone home?"

I was then in the kitchen, where Bessie and I had, half an hour earlier, taken our mid-morning tea, having been up and working already for many hours.

Bessie finally emerged, cobwebs on her head from the cellar.

I sighed. "Bessie, would you kindly see our visitor in? Giles seems to have disappeared."

"Certainly, Mrs. Boylston," she said with mock formality. "Giles is tinkering in the cellar."

"What could he be about in the cellar?" I asked.

"His experiments. You know."

"Ah, yes—I forgot."

I recalled now that Giles fashioned himself somewhat of an inventor. And it's a testament to my family's faith in him that they allowed the old slave free use of a musket, when he once informed them that he wished to improve the lock mechanism.

I smiled at the memory. It's a wonder Giles didn't manage to shoot himself. I swept the cobwebs off Bessie's gray head as she passed me, for Mr. Miller was still waiting. She scurried out to him, took his hat and walking stick, and brought him into the empty parlor with its two sad chairs. Earlier that morning, we had found a table in an upstairs chamber and brought it down, completing the pathetic semblance of a formal seating arrangement.

"Miss Elizabeth," he greeted me, bowing briefly before sitting down, "you look well. Er, what's her name? The plump one there," he whispered, leaning in to me just as I sat down.

"Bessie, you mean?" I asked.

"Yes. Bessie!" he called, and she turned, having no doubt heard his epithet. She scowled at him.

"Bessie, have you some cider?" Mr. Miller fanned at his neck. "I'm positively parched. Not ten and already quite a hot day. They say we shall have a drought this season."

I rolled my eyes at Bessie. "Yes, Bessie, some cider, please. And our best cakes."

We had but one type of cake, which we ourselves had eaten for breakfast, and a tiny smile sprang up at the corner of her mouth.

"Yes, madam," she said in a fine English such as she never used with me.

"Oh, madam, of course," he echoed. "Madam Boylston. I do apologize."

And with that he stretched himself out in the too-small chair. His legs were long, and as he stretched back and suddenly yawned, I worried lest he tip over and fall backward upon his head.

"You're smiling," he said after he had finished his stretch. "Why so?" He looked at me over his elbow. His wide amber eyes glittered bemusedly, and his dark plait, hastily tied, had come partly out of its ribbon. I had an odd urge to retie it.

"I was just thinking what a funny sight it would be were you to fall backward in that chair, as you are very like to do in another moment."

"Oh, sorry." He laughed, sitting back up. In this posture he was equally risible, however, as his knees were now nearly at his neck.

Our cider came, and a plate of corn cakes. Bessie curtsied officiously.

Mr. Miller took a big bite of a cake and washed it down with his cider, which was nice and cool.

"Now that you are in possession of your house once more, what do you plan to do with it?" he asked directly, looking around.

"I await further news of my brother."

"So, you have a brother?" He looked surprised and somewhat pleased. "I thought you all alone in the world. Is he younger or older?"

Mr. Miller shifted uncomfortably in his chair. His waistcoat and breeches, I noted, were finely made, though somewhat rumpled. All in all, he had the air of someone who had come from wealth but cared little for worldly possessions himself. "Two years younger. But I know not whether he's alive or dead—it is this I wish to determine before I decide about the house."

"Oh, I see," he replied in an altogether different tone. His voice was now somber, and I could not tell if he were in earnest. "Tell me about him, if you would."

"Well," I began, "his name is Henry—we call him Harry. He went off on a privateer ship, the *Cantabrigian*, near four years ago this autumn, when he was but sixteen years of age. I've not heard a word from him since, except—"

"Except?"

"Someone has been paying the servants all this time. I had thought them long gone."

"Then he must be alive!" Thomas slapped his leg. "Hang me if he isn't, the rogue!"

I smiled at his familiarity. I was not so sanguine, but merely said, "I pray you're correct, Mr. Miller. But in any case, it will do no good to conjecture. Either he is or is not. At the next post, I will inquire of the messenger."

I thought it was time to change the subject. "Have you heard from Martha?"

"Of course." He sat up and took a sip of cider, but his eyes remained steadily upon me. "That's how I knew to find you here."

"Were you looking for me, then?" I could not help but tease him. For something in Mr. Miller's bearing, some faintly ridiculous insouciance as he sat so uncomfortably in that too-small chair, made him an alluring target. Part of me, I admit, wished also to break through his unflappable good cheer.

But Mr. Miller merely set his mug down. "Why do you ask?"

"I meant merely to point out that 'to find' something implies that one was looking for it." I stared back.

"Not at all," he contradicted easily. "I find many things quite by accident. This ring, for example." He turned a ruby ring around the long, slender pinky of his left hand, then held it forth for me to examine. "I found this quite by accident along the pier at Rowe's Wharf. Quite a 'find,' I'd say."

I knew he was teasing me, but I would not be made fun of so easily. "You are very good at avoiding questions, Mr. Miller. You have not as yet answered me."

"As to whether I was looking for you, do you mean?"

"The same."

"Indeed I was, as a matter of fact," he admitted. "I wished to thank you for taking in my wayward little sister and teaching her something useful. Of course, she would never have needed to be useful, had our parents not—" A certain raw emotion seemed to break through his glib ease.

"—left you." I finished for him.

"I was going to say, got themselves trapped like so many frightened sheep."

One would think the death of parents would invoke more pity than anger. But I understood Mr. Miller's anger. For a long time I was angry with my father for dying—he was supposed to return to me, as were Thomas and Martha's parents. But Thomas Miller seemed to hold their very flight against them as well.

"Yes, Martha has done well. Learned a great deal—she is a very able girl."

He looked at me questioningly. "And you, Mrs. Boylston, are good at staying the course," he concluded, his large amber eyes continuing to watch me.

"The course? Of what, pray?"

"Of the conversation. You insist upon steering me back to safer channels."

Now it was my turn to smile. "I suppose it's what I'm used to doing. Keeping others focused on the safer channels."

"And must I now give birth to something?" he asked in mock horror. "What a half-human monster that might be!"

"Oh, don't joke about such a thing, Mr. Miller," I said, but I myself was smiling. Never in my life had I engaged in such free conversation with a man. I had not known many men, it is true. But never had I known one so willing to stray quite so far from convention. There seemed no art whatsoever to Thomas Miller. Artless as a child, I thought.

The idea that Martha and he were involved in anything politically important now struck me as ludicrous. Were I General Howe, I would not trust this Mr. Miller with anything more than shining my shoes. Indeed, he had already made a bad impression on Bessie, it seemed. She lingered among us, casting him baleful looks as she pretended to dust the empty bookshelves. I was about to change the subject when he stood, pulled a gold pocket watch from his vest pocket, and stared at it with some surprise.

"Nearly eleven!" he exclaimed. "I have an engagement in town at noon which I've nearly forgotten."

He then extended his hand and shook mine heartily, as if I were a man. He said his good-byes to Bessie and was already half-way out the door when he poked his head back in and said, "I shall call on you again, if the idea is not too repulsive, while you're in town."

I merely curtsied.

Once we'd heard his carriage grow fainter, Bessie turned to me with one hand on her hip. "What kind of hot wind just blew in here?"

"A sirocco, I think."

Our eyes met, and we laughed quite heartily at the puzzling individual who had announced his intention of calling upon us again.

Only well after he'd gone did I realize that Mr. Miller afforded me no opportunity to ask him about himself. I knew not where he lived, nor whether he had a profession or survived on more than words and good cheer. Martha had insisted that, apart from doing certain "errands," he was "indifferent to politics." In these times, to profess oneself indifferent to politics was the same as professing oneself indifferent to air.

I could not but wonder whether, like Shakespeare's Mercutio, Thomas Miller was indifferent to love as well. Looking at him now, I thought him not so wholly unattractive as I had previously done, though he had not the classical beauty of Mr. Cleverly. His features were too big and bold, his face too animated. And, though tall, he had not the gentle elegance of some but rather seemed quite the proverbial bull in a china shop. He was young and eligible at a time when men were few, yet Martha had mentioned nothing of his being attached to anyone.

No, Mr. Miller's pieces did not fit, I pondered disagreeably after he had left, and there could only be one reason for it: I did not have all of them in my possession.

·   ·   ·

One week had now gone by without my hearing from Martha. I wrote her every day, though some days I had little to recount. Worried, I wrote to Abigail inquiring as to whether she had been to the farm. The following day, I was greatly relieved by my prompt correspondent. Martha was quite well, Abigail reported, as was the farm. She went on to say that it was exceedingly hot for June. They were predicting a scorching drought, and Martha had been kept busy by her chores. The colonel had twice that week invited Martha to dine at his home.

I felt a flash of envy, followed immediately by a stroke of shame. Surely I could not begrudge Martha a night or two of gaiety?

Whether it was this envy that propelled me I know not, but I resolved to return to Braintree the following Wednesday, the tenth of June. It was now Thursday, and Steadman was three days late. Bessie was mystified.

"And you say he's never been late before?"

"Never. Not even when the Reg'lars were here."

"He has been detained, then," I said with a certainty I did not feel. "He's sure to arrive next Monday."

He did not arrive the following Monday, but another letter from Abigail did, with news that the distemper had arrived once more in our parish.

I worried for Martha, for she had not yet had the illness. I knew I had to write and press upon her the need for immediate inoculation. I was certain she could take the inoculation in town and hurried to send word to Dr. Bullfinch.

The following day I heard from Martha at long last:

Dear Lizzie—

I hear through our mutual Friend that you are afraid for me, but do not be. I am much engaged at the moment and could not possibly "take the cure" in town, tho I thank you heartily for your kind offer. In any case, I believe I may already have "taken the cure" by way of the Cranches and their friends, for I dined with them all the other night and Billy is now quite ill, as is Dr. Flynt. I do what I can to ease their suffering, as you taught me. Billy has many eruptions, but Dr. Flynt, tho I can find but one, fares far worse.

Rest assured I am well and remain, etc. etc.

Remain, etc. etc.?!

I rose from my seat in the kitchen. "I must leave as soon as possible."

"What's that you say?" Bessie asked. I believe she had grown mildly deaf, for I found myself often shouting at her.

"I must go. There is illness in the parish. I'm greatly afraid for Martha."

"There is no one to take you now, ma'am," she said, confused.

I resolved to send a message to the Boylstons, for I had clothing and linen I would take to Braintree. But just as I was about to send word to the Boylstons requesting their help, Mr. Miller pulled up in his chaise. It was a sunny morning with a perfect blue sky over the Charles. People strolled or rode down Brattle Street just as if there were no war, as if rumors did not whisper of the imminent destruction of Boston.

Mr. Miller alit from his chaise with a bright step. He bounded up toward me.

"I have resolved it!" he said by way of greeting. "We must extract you from this tomb. I have a burning desire to take you to the public garden for a walk. The cherry trees are simply—"

But when he saw my face, all comedy ceased. He reached for me and, quite unconsciously, placed his hand gently on my arm. "What is it?" he asked. "What's wrong?"

"The distemper. It's in my parish. I've had a letter from Martha and—foolish girl!—she has been among the sick, as heedless as you please. Mr. Sharp is perfectly clear on the matter of visiting those sick with distemper."

"Who is that you speak of?"

I had been referring to one of my most useful medical texts, Samuel Sharp's *Surgery*. I could not expect anyone else to know of it. I said, "Never mind. I must go at once. I await only a word from the Boylstons as to whether they can lend me a chaise."

"Hang the Boylstons," said Mr. Miller. "I'll take you home. Is not my chaise as good as the Boylstons'?"

"Indeed, it seems excellent. But there is the matter of my horse," I replied.

"Hm. Well, he shall have to trot alongside, for I have not a double harness."

"That shall do very well. I thank you," I said, grateful that he should have come at such an auspicious time, sorry only that now I would miss Steadman by a mere day or two and would not be able to interrogate him. I had, however, prepared a letter for my brother, which I had written in haste the night before and thankfully now remembered to give to Bessie.

Giles made his appearance with the trunk I had packed. He looked at Mr. Miller's chaise and at me and rolled his eyes. Apparently he was excellent at geometry as well as chemistry, for he had quickly determined that either a trunk or I might go with Mr. Miller, but not both.

"What shall I do with this, ma'am?"

"See if the Boylstons will allow their carriage to be used for the delivery of my things. It needn't be today. And Bessie—" I turned to her, for suddenly I felt sorry to leave her alone. She had been my companion these past weeks, and I hers. But I was going toward friends, and she would be left with no one.

"Bessie," I repeated. "You'll not forget to give Mr. Steadman my letter?"

"I won't, ma'am."

"Good."

She curtsied and then, seeing that I was soon to depart, came toward me and threw her heavy arms about my neck. Giles brought my beloved Star and attached him by means of a rope to the side of the chaise. Star kept butting his head upon my hand, as if asking why it was he was not being put to better use.

"Oh, Star, we're heading home. You shall get a carrot for your patience," I told him, rubbing his forehead, which he liked.

Once we had taken off down Brattle Street, I was silent, and soon became lost in thought. Mr. Miller sat calmly by my side, looking out at the day, also quiet. I was thinking at that moment about the letter I had written to my brother. I used to write him with such feeling, such love and longing, as would make my bodice wet with tears. But last night I had resolved to write in as mechanical a fashion as possible to save myself that grief. Yet, try as I might, I did not succeed at my task of remaining unmoved.

Suddenly, Mr. Miller turned slightly, but as we were quite close it was enough for me to startle at the sight of his amber eyes. He turned forward quickly and said, "You're smiling. I'm glad you've thought of something to smile about at last."

"Oh, I was merely thinking how immutable are certain impressions and feelings. When one remembers the dead—really remembers, in every detail of voice and manner—they seem so fully alive. Have you not found that so?"

He frowned. "I don't know. I try not to think of the past."

"Not to think of the past? Is that possible?" Though but twenty-three, I felt that a great deal of my life was already behind me.

"I said I tried, not that I always succeeded."

"But if you forget," I said heatedly, "then they are *truly* gone."

Mr. Miller's face clouded over, but he said nothing.

"Forgive me, Mr. Miller," I said. "It is my own anxiety for your sister that makes me heedless of the feelings of others."

"It matters not." He shrugged in a way that made me feel even worse. "You meant no harm. I did love my parents, you know."

"I'm very sorry," I repeated, and indeed I had a lump in my throat for Mr. Miller.

"Really, you needn't be. It matters not."

"But it *does*, if it gives you pain," I insisted.

We were past Roxbury now, and I heard the gulls overhead and saw boats drifting up and down the coast. The scene was so charming, so calm, it served almost to mock us.

"Look you how beautiful the sea is today," he remarked.

"Yes."

And then, apparently, we neither of us dared say another word and were silent all the way to Braintree.

23

WHAT TRANSPIRED THE MOMENT I SET FOOT in my parish prevented me from taking further notice of Thomas Miller, who in any case became swept up in the arms and attention of his agitated sister.

The farm was far worse than Abigail had indicated. The earth was parched, and a dozen hale men would not have sufficed to carry the necessary water from the well. With labor now at twelve pounds a month, our case was hopeless. How we would survive the winter without our crops I knew not.

Martha and her brother went off together. I saw them down the road a piece. They were taking a walk, and I could see only Martha's back, which shook as if in mirth or grief. But I knew it could not have been mirth. About what did my dear Martha have to grieve? Mr. Miller flung an arm protectively about her shoulders.

I was not home fifteen minutes before I received an urgent message from Thornton, a servant of the Cranches, that Dr. Flynt had taken a turn for the worse and could I come immediately. He had run down through the dunes and was covered in sweat.

"Thaxter!" I called. "Saddle Star at once."

He hesitated, unused to taking my orders. I felt that I had grown older during my Cambridge stay and now clearly saw that Thaxter considered himself his own master. He had treated me without proper respect since Jeb's death, and I had let him. I resolved to be his master from that day forth.

I was soon trotting past Martha and her brother, who looked up at me as if from a very great distance.

"My carriage—" Mr. Miller offered, reaching out to stop me.

"Not necessary!" I called, then left them behind.

I arrived at the Cranches' farm drenched in perspiration. Mary came to the door, embraced me, and pointed upstairs.

"He's in the second chamber on the right."

I ascended and soon saw for myself that Dr. Flynt was quite dead. He lay on his back, his belly making a hill of the bolster, his powdered wig protruding up off his bald pate on one side, his eyes staring up at the ceiling. A teacup lay spilled on the floor, miraculously unbroken. A young servant, weeping in a chair in the corner of the room, told me the gentleman had died not half an hour earlier.

"Thank God you are come," said Mary. She embraced me tightly.

"Please go, Mary," I told her, nearly pushing her out of the room.

"But I have had the distemper," she said.

"I've not yet ascertained what ailment he suffered from."

She deferred and left me. Richard Cranch soon made his appearance, but I asked the same of him: to allow me to examine the deceased.

"Perhaps you might locate his family," I said, as he seemed quite eager to be of some use.

"I have set Mr. Cleverly to the task. He says he knows the whereabouts of a sister in Philadelphia, though the parents are dead."

"Philadelphia? He must be buried before her arrival, then," I said, referring as delicately as I could to our scorching heat.

"Of course. I shall call upon the parson."

"Yes," I said, adding, "though it is my recommendation you remain vague as to his illness. We mustn't alarm the entire parish."

Richard thought this very wise. Once he had left, I invited the maid to bring me towels, warm water, and a slab of soap. When she had done as I asked, I shut the door and carefully undressed Dr. Flynt.

It took only moments to notice two remarkable things about the deceased: the first being that he had *not* had the distemper, though I noticed upon his face and torso old marks from a childhood case. The eruption that had been reported by Martha must have been a mistake. Perhaps she had confused his old lesions for new ones. The second thing I noticed were his eyes: they were wide open and ablaze in his round, soft face, and the pupils were unnaturally dilated. I closed his eyes gently, greatly puzzled, and finished my task of washing and dressing the body.

When I had finished and had washed myself and just emerged from his chamber, quite drenched with perspiration, I nearly ran into Mr. Cleverly. He seemed to have been pacing the hallway with some agitation—altogether natural, given that there had been a death in the very house where he was staying. The question crossed my mind as to why Mr. Cleverly tarried here in Braintree, but good manners forbade my asking. I would inquire of Richard by and by and get the answers I sought.

"Mrs. Boylston," he said, frowning. "A grievous business to come home to."

He took a step toward me. I blushed suddenly at the notion of my miserable appearance—and smell.

"Indeed it is. Have you found the sister?" I asked, backing away with mincing steps.

"I've sent word to her, yes."

"Is there no other family?"

"Not that he mentioned. He was not married, at least."

I nodded, understanding his meaning. At least there would be no wife to notify of the tragedy.

Cleverly seemed heedless of my disheveled state or the possible contagion upon me, for he leaned in so close his lips nearly touched my ear. "Did he . . . did he *suffer* very much?" he whispered.

"In truth, I don't know. I must speak with those who were with him. Had he a doctor?"

"I don't believe so. It was thought he had the distemper, since little Billy does, but he took a sudden turn this morning."

"Was he alone?" I inquired.

"That servant-girl was with him, I believe. He was at the colonel's on Sunday and looked quite well then. He had a good appetite and spoke cheerfully of his time in Philadelphia."

Cleverly bade me good-bye and retreated down the hall to his room. I would need to interview the servants and speak to Martha when I returned home. But first I needed some refreshment, as I was feeling quite overcome by my journey and now this hasty, tragic call.

"You look positively ill," said Mary, coming up before me on the stairs and taking my arm.

"No, I'm well. Just tired and weak. I haven't yet eaten today."

"Haven't yet eaten? It is after four in the afternoon!" Indeed, the timepiece on the parlor mantel downstairs, made by Mr. Cranch himself, confirmed it. Mary sat me down and had her maid bring me a plate of cheese and ham with butter and a fresh slice of rye bread. I ate and soon felt well enough to speak.

She sat across from me, and Richard, returned from Parson Wibird's, soon joined us. Both waited quietly for me to finish my meal. I espied Mr. Cleverly pacing in the hall. He popped his fair head in now and again, but as no one invited him to join us, he soon disappeared. I felt for him. His friend lost, his lodgings violated by sickness both known and unknown. How dreadful!

When I had finished my meal and was gratefully sipping the last of my dish of tea, Richard said, "We are grieved to impose upon you like this, Lizzie, and you not an hour returned from town, but we had no one else to turn to."

"I've prepared him for burial," I said matter-of-factly, hiding my fatigue as best I could. "And the sister has been sent for. Have you spoken with the parson?"

Richard replied that he had.

"Then it is all we can do. The rest is up to our Maker."

They bowed their heads at my mention of the Lord, in whose hands the soul of foolish Dr. Flynt now rested.

Finally Mary raised her head and whispered, "But it wasn't the distemper, as we thought?"

I shook my head. "I do not believe so. Dr. Flynt apparently had the pox as a child. And his eyes—"

"What of his eyes?" asked Richard with alarm. I was about to tell them about Dr. Flynt's dilated eyes, but at the last moment thought better of it.

"It is nothing. I misspoke; forgive me."

Mary had begun to tremble, and I took her hand consolingly. "I do not believe his illness to have been of an infectious nature. That is the good news. You and your guests have nothing to fear. For it was certainly not the yellow fever or the throat distemper."

My gentle friend's relief was palpable. Of course, she was thinking of her children, especially little Billy, who, though mending, was confined to his bed.

Mary said, "Do not take this amiss, Lizzie, but it would relieve me were you not to visit Billy today. I checked upon him myself half an hour ago, and he's well. He is bored and asking for a deck of cards."

I smiled. "Boredom is an excellent sign in a patient."

She returned my smile weakly.

"I won't visit him today, then. But by all means take him his cards, for if you do not, he may decide to fetch them himself."

"Oh, you are right!" Mary stood up, excused herself, and went to fetch a deck for her convalescing son.

I understood Mary's concern, though convinced within myself that whatever Dr. Flynt had died of was no common malady.

Richard stood as well. "Thank you, Lizzie," he said, taking my hand. "I can only hope we shall see better days than this. Days of good conversation." He smiled, though behind his eyes I saw a great deal of concern.

I soon took my leave of the Cranches, there being nothing I could do either for them or for Dr. Flynt. By the time I returned home that day, aching and exhausted, Mr. Miller and his chaise were gone.

Martha was in the kitchen mending a petticoat. "My brother was sorry not to have the opportunity to say good-bye to you."

"I had a great deal to do. The Cranches, as you can imagine, are in a state of upheaval. I did my best to quell rumors of a plague."

I stared at Martha, who sat quietly, then said, "It was not the distemper, Martha."

She stopped her sewing. "It was not? What else could it have been?"

"He had no eruptions upon him. I looked at him *cap-à-pie*. Only old marks."

I waited for her to say something.

"I knew him to be feverish and assumed he had the same as Billy," she said thoughtfully.

"I saw no sign of fever," I said. I then added, "One must never assume."

"But I left him cleverly last night," she insisted.

"Dr. Tufts was not called, then?"

"No, indeed! He is much occupied in Weymouth at the moment."

"Well, do not blame yourself." I recalled that serious illness was beyond my fledgling assistant's realm of expertise. It was my fault for being in town instead of at home, helping her. Sometimes a patient may look quite recovered but then take a sudden turn with no warning. It was natural enough for Martha to assume the distemper, but I thought it a sufficient lesson for the day to remind her never to assume.

Always look for evidence—this was another truism my mother had taught me.

"It has been a long day, and I am tired."

"I will tidy up," Martha offered. She set her knitting down and her voice quavered, on the verge of tears, as she asked, "You are not angry with me?"

I put my arms around her. "Of course not."

"I couldn't bear it if you were angry with me."

"No, no. Just puzzled and, as I said, quite exhausted. You are an apprentice yet, Martha, and I would do you a great wrong to expect more skill than I myself possess. In truth, I doubt whether even I could have done anything for the poor man."

"Poor man," she repeated thoughtfully.

"You think him not?"

"Oh, no," she said. "But I had opportunity to know him these few weeks. And he was—"

"Was what, Martha?"

"He was no doctor; that much I can tell you."

"How came you to learn that?" I asked, surprised.

"I questioned him. He knew nothing whatsoever of the medical arts."

"That is most strange. Why might a man pretend to be a doctor when he wasn't?"

"I don't know."

It seemed a welcome moment to change the subject, and so I said, "It was kind of your brother to take me home. Did you have a good visit?"

"Oh, yes, he's so kind," she said, smiling at the memory of her brother.

"Well, let us both to bed, Martha—washing up can wait. We've had a terrible blow. I see now that you've been overrun, though you wished to spare me the truth of it. Apparently neither Thaxter nor Gaius have been of much use."

"No," she admitted. "Though Gaius did mend the fence in the north pasture, where the sheep were forever getting into the colonel's fields."

"Fixed a fence," I harrumphed. "I could have done as much in ten days' time. Alas, I cannot possibly afford another laborer. Well, we have a great deal to do tomorrow. Let us leave that worry for another day."

"Come. You're exhausted. I'll rub your feet," Martha offered.

Oh, selfish being! The thought of that made me smile. I fairly ran to my bed and removed my shoes and stockings. And though in summer Martha usually repaired to her own chamber, she would not leave me that night—nor, in truth, did I desire her to.

24

DR. FLYNT'S SISTER NEVER DID MATERIALIZE FOR the funeral, which took place that Wednesday. In attendance were Abigail, the Cranches, and myself. I had not seen Mr. Thayer since I had arrived home, and was informed that he had left for town the day of Dr. Flynt's death. Now Cleverly had disappeared as well, leaving word that he had business in town that could not be put off. I thought it odd that the two men who had arrived with Flynt should now be absent for the poor man's funeral. While they had been strangers to one another, having arrived all in a convergence, they had been much thrown together at the Cranches' and Quincys', and by all accounts had become great friends.

When I finally was able to visit Abigail the following day, she greeted me with a storm of tears, just as if she had not seen me for a year. She gave me a detailed account of what had transpired in my absence. In particular, she spoke of that final dinner at the colonel's on Sunday. After a fine meal of roast fish and savory tart, she, Mary, Mrs. Quincy, and Martha had retired to the south parlor, the one in which Colonel Quincy himself stared down at them from a very fine likeness above the mantel. Across the hall, the men had gone on talking and drinking until late in the evening.

"I'm ashamed to say we spied on them from time to time. For how long is one expected to speak of the season's style in ladies' bonnets or the best way to mend a petticoat?"

"You ask a rhetorical question."

"Very well, Lizzie. But listen. These men discussed the British offer for a truce. For the most part, they were entirely of one mind. Although," she added thoughtfully, "there was a slight altercation over the relative merits of His Excellency. Things got rather heated." She looked at me as if there were perhaps some meaning to all of this.

"But Abby, what does it signify? Gentlemen speak such nonsense every evening of the year."

"You're right," she said. "I have no idea."

I, however, continued to wonder at whether Dr. Flynt's death might have had something to do with the altercation over His Excellency's merits. It seemed far-fetched, but not entirely so. However, I thought it prudent not to share my thoughts with Abigail just then.

.   .   .

After Dr. Flynt's burial, and with no other deaths for several days, a terrified parish began to return to its normal activities. Martha and I had a great deal to do on the farm, and for two weeks following these events we worked eighteen-hour days with scarcely a break in between.

We struggled mightily that parched summer to keep the potatoes, corn, and fruit trees sufficiently watered, but it was simply not possible. How little I desired visitors in the midst of these struggles can hardly be overstated. I was thus in a truly baleful mood when Mr. Cleverly decided to pay a call one morning.

It was a fine morning, if hot. The unseasonable heat reminded me of May of '75, when Jeb left me, never to see me more.

Cleverly was perspiring. He wore a simple white shirt and linen breeches; his fair hair was combed and handsomely tied with a bow. And, no doubt, in his heart was the hope of a dish of tea or mug of cider for his troubles.

I glanced at Martha. Seeing him, she glowered beneath her thick brown eyebrows.

"I suppose you must greet him," she said.

"I can think of nothing else, except to pretend I have not seen him."

I began to dust off my pinafore when Cleverly leapt into our potato patch.

"Good day," he said, bowing to us both. "Nothing I like better than the sight of women working."

"Nothing I dislike more than the sight of an able-bodied man *not* working," Martha replied.

"Come, come, we each work in our own ways."

"And what might you be working at?" she asked with rude bluntness, looking over her shoulder at him but not ceasing her arduous labors.

"If you make me a dish of tea, Miss Miller, I will tell you." Cleverly smiled winningly.

"It grows hot. Martha"—I glared at her, setting my basket down—"come."

She knew what I wanted: a civil tongue. Cleverly, amused, followed us into the house. I bade him sit in the parlor, but he had no wish to sit. Rather, he walked about, poking into everything as we put the kettle on.

"Or would you rather a glass of cider?" I suddenly inquired. It was a hot day, and I was not heartless enough to make a man suffer, even an arrogant one. I myself was already drenched and had no great desire to find myself before the fire.

"Oh, *je l'ignore*. I am indifferent—yes, cider, I think. Thank you."

Martha removed the kettle, scattered the gathered coals, wiped her brow, and went to the cellar to fetch a pitcher of cider.

The cider was cool, and we drank it gratefully, especially knowing as we did that we would likely not get a new batch that year.

Cleverly sipped his drink, sighed, and sat back in the chair as if he might just stay all day. He looked about him, and his eyes came to rest on Jeb's musket, which hung on the wall.

"A fine musket, Miss Boylston. It is yours?"

I might have corrected him on his address, but I merely replied, "It was my husband Jeb's. He died on Breed's Hill."

Cleverly paused a moment. "Yes, I have heard. I am sorry for your loss. You know how to use it?"

"Indeed I do. I have improved my aim by practicing on crows. You know, our town now pays us to get rid of them."

"I didn't know. A handy sport. I myself do not know how to use one. Perhaps you might show me some time."

Martha had taken up her mending, not wishing to waste our precious daylight. She glanced up momentarily at the sound of my nervous laughter.

"And what would someone like yourself want with a musket?" I inquired, unable to keep the derision from my voice.

"Do you mock me? I detect a distinct note of mockery."

Mr. Cleverly crossed his muscular legs, rubbed his hands together, and cocked a pretty smile at me.

"No, not at all," I said. Then I could not help it—I burst into laughter again. Oh, it felt good to laugh. The Devil knows his work!

"Go ahead, laugh all you like," Mr. Cleverly said affably, waving at me. "But you're right; the work I do requires more brain than brawn. And why should I be ashamed of that?"

"What work is that, Mr. Cleverly?" Martha asked, not looking up from her sewing.

At this, Mr. Cleverly leaned forward, as if he had been waiting for the question. "I promised to let you in on the secret. Well, the colonel could have told you, had you asked him. Or Mr. Cranch. For they are by now both well acquainted with me. I am unfortunately not at liberty to speak of it beyond telling you what is common knowledge: I work for General Sullivan."

"General Sullivan?" I could not help exclaiming. "Is he not at this moment in Newport?"

"Ah, I remind you that I can say no more. But you shall see me come and go."

"A spy, then." I smiled, secretly gratified. I fervently wished to tell him my suspicions regarding the death of Dr. Flynt, but held my tongue.

"It is said the Devil can be many places at once," Martha muttered.

"Martha!"

"I'll say nothing more." He tightened his lips and glanced back at the musket.

Martha did not seem too impressed. She merely scowled while I marveled at the power a grudge had over my little friend.

"Well, if you're a spy, you had best be careful, for Braintree is a hotbed of Toryism. Indeed, your namesakes were most vocal in that regard."

"Yes, I have heard of the Braintree Cleverlys from Mr. Cranch. They are thankfully no relation of mine."

"I suppose our policy of live and let live is the Christian one, though it grows more and more difficult for them to remain. Were Abigail to have her way, she would round up all the Vezeys and Cleverlys and put them on the next ship bound for England."

Cleverly smiled genially, then looked at Martha. "You are very busy today, Miss Martha," he observed, ready for some playful banter.

Martha scowled. "There is a great deal of work to do. No time for palaver."

And with this, she bent so low over her sewing that her nose nearly touched the needle.

I was ready to scold her, but Cleverly suddenly tossed his fair ponytail, slapped his thigh, and exclaimed, "Ladies, I'd nearly forgotten the reason for my visit."

"We thought it a social call," I said. "Or perhaps to condole with us the loss of your friend."

"It is, it is." He frowned, but in fact it was as if he had forgotten all about Dr. Flynt's recent death.

Cleverly continued, "You may recall from our first meeting that I am a dabbler in science and inventions. And there is one invention of mine I thought might do you a service."

"And what is that?" I inquired suspiciously. "No elixir that contains the key to eternal life, I hope."

"No, no," he said, his blue eyes glittering with flirtatious mischief.

"Then what?" I asked again, curious in spite of myself.

He stood and peered out of my kitchen window upon the dunes. I could not help noticing his strong jaw, his cleft chin, his fine brow.

Mr. Cleverly turned 'round. "If you were to save one crop this summer, ladies, which would it be?"

Martha looked up from her work. We exchanged glances, then said in unison, "Corn."

"Corn. Yes, yes, I suppose you must have corn. But that is so— prosaic. I shall see what can be done about your apples as well. That way, come fall, you will have no objections if I stop by for a slice of pie."

Martha glowered at him from beneath her dark brow.

"What do you plan to do?" I inquired uneasily.

"Water them. Nothing more, Mrs. Boylston, I assure you. Water them."

"With what shall you water them? Is there a source I know not of?" I asked, all astonishment, with hope rising in my breast. My baleful mood vanished beneath the stubborn good nature—and even better physiognomy—of dear Mr. Cleverly.

His secret made his blue eyes brighten. "You shall see by and by. I must leave you now, but will return. Might I return tomorrow?"

"If you can save our crops, of course."

"Then return I shall. Good day to you both!" And off he went.

"I dislike him," Martha pronounced when he had gone.

I sighed. "Oh, Martha, he seems quite amiable. Indeed, he seems quite truly patriotic."

"Nay, madam, I know not 'seems,' " she said, quoting *Hamlet*, of which we knew every word, having often read it aloud to each other.

I tried another tack. "Well, just think of it: he wishes to try out his invention on our orchards—it is diverting, is it not? Perhaps he may turn out to be a useful sort of man after all."

"Doubtful," Martha muttered.

"Oh, Martha. You are turning into a regular old grouse."

"Call me what you like," she said indifferently and, with a final sip of her cider, stepped outside, banging the door behind her.

25

LATE THAT SAME AFTERNOON, WHEN THE HOT sun was thankfully low in the sky, we made ourselves a simple supper of soft cheese and turnip greens. I had just glanced across at Martha, thinking she looked particularly pale and drained, when a carrot-topped boy I did not recognize rode up to our house and alit, a message in his hand. It was from Bessie.

"Oh, Bessie!" I cried happily. I thanked the messenger and offered him a glass of cider, which he accepted gratefully. As he eyed our supper, I offered him some of that as well, which he also accepted.

"Did you see her?" I asked the boy.

"I did, ma'am," he said, his mouth full of food.

"And is she well?"

"She seemed so, ma'am."

With relief, I sat waiting for him to finish his meal and be gone so I could read my letter in peace.

He seemed disinclined to get back on his mare and was no doubt hoping to stop the night, but Martha and I did not encourage him. He soon left, wiping his mouth with the back of his sleeve and thanking us for the refreshment.

Once he was gone, Martha sighed and said she would lie down; she was all done in.

"Are you unwell?" I asked.

"Oh, no. Nothing a few moments' rest won't cure."

She unloosed her bodice, undid her thick brown hair from its knot, removed her shoes, and lay down on the bed. The evening was warm, but I noticed her pull the bolster over her.

I went to read my letter. "Dearest Miss," it began in a very poor hand.

I have news as must gladdin your heart. Forgiv my hastey pen, but Master Jon Steadman stands here awaitin' to be off.

I have made the inquerees you instructed and have just now heard from Mr. Steadman that, accordin' to his Contact, there is, alive as of this writing, one Henry Lee on the frigate Canta— Canta whachamacaulit as whats been these three years in the West Indies and other distant Ports. I know naught else, but Mr. Steadman says your letter this time should find its way through to him, and you can expect a reply come autumn.

"My brother lives!"

As for other news—

"What other news could I possibly wish to hear?" I exclaimed, yet read on.

Giles is well and will soon grow rich enough to buy your estate and kick us both off 'v it. Mr. Boylston, I have heard, does poorly, but no worse than when you were here. And I have heard reports of Mr. Miller at the house from Cassie as says he has been calling upon Miss Eliza. There is whispers among them as he has an idea to save her from her circumstances. What circumstances could they mean, d'you think?

I had little knowledge of Thomas Miller, but I thought it low indeed to trick a young man, however reckless, into marriage. Unless she had told him, and he accepted her dire circumstances?

But my mind returned to the first part of Bessie's letter. My brother! My dearest, sweet, rash, impetuous Harry. Alive!

I moved to wake Martha, for it was not the kind of news one can long keep to oneself.

"Martha," I said, shaking her. "Martha, my brother lives!"

She groaned but did not otherwise wake. Finding her hot to the touch, I thought to open her bodice and was horrified to discover no less than two dozen angry eruptions covering her torso. She had the distemper, and a serious case.

•   •   •

For two weeks, I thought I would lose her. Such diseases are often stronger for the delay. Had she had the illness ten years earlier, it would not have been nearly so grave. I spent my hours keeping her fever down by applying wet cloths to her entire body. The cool cloths, plus the willow bark tea, kept her this side of life. But she could keep nothing down and at times did not seem to know where she was. The pustules by now were everywhere—beneath her eyelids, in her mouth, on her groin, between her toes. They were eating her alive.

I slept but little, watching her writhe and moan, doing what I could.

"Really, it is hardly necessary," she would whisper as I ministered to her.

"It is necessary, Miss Miller, if you wish to stay this side of the grave."

"No, please. I cannot, I cannot," she would repeat, for she was in such distress of body and spirit there were times it seemed death might have been preferable to her.

One night I felt certain that Martha was expiring. I sent word to Abigail and to Dr. Tufts in Weymouth. I had not the arrogance to assume I knew everything and did not want it upon my conscience were she to die.

I could not keep her fever down. She shook, she trembled, and her teeth clacked together. Her eyes rolled up in her head, and by the time Dr. Tufts and Abigail arrived, they found us both so ill they could not at first tell who was the patient.

Dr. Tufts asked us to excuse him for a moment, and Abigail sat quietly, bonnet in hand, in my parlor.

"You are ill yourself, Lizzie. Why have you not called upon me?"

"I didn't wish to bother you. You have your own affairs."

"In time of need, you know that your affairs are mine." Even Abigail could see I was too beaten down for her to scold me as she might usually have done.

"I know."

"Though I could do nothing more for her, there are always those willing to help you."

"I know," I said again, ashamed, because had things been reversed, I would certainly expect Abigail to call on me. Indeed, I would have been hurt had she not.

"I am used to handling things alone."

"Too much so, I'm afraid." She sighed.

I'd written to Thomas Miller several days earlier, but apparently my message had gone astray, as it was only that day that he received news of his sister's illness. Just as Dr. Tufts was examining her, Mr. Miller's large form came crashing through the door, the larger, it seemed, for its passionate haste.

"Where is my sister? Is she gone? Am I too late?"

He was dressed in a pale-blue silk costume. Apparently he had been on his way to a formal event. But his eyes and hair were wild, and he had forgotten to button his shirt. I caught a glimpse of a hairless chest glistening with perspiration.

"No, no, no. Calm yourself." I stood. "The doctor is with her."

"Oh, thank goodness." He sank into a chair, noticing as he did so the unbuttoned shirt. After he had buttoned it, his eyes looked imploringly at me, but I had nothing to tell him.

Dr. Tufts came out of the kitchen then, quietly shutting the door behind him.

"She sleeps," he said.

Thomas looked at me in astonishment. "Has she not had a doctor before now?"

Abigail and I looked at each other. I suddenly felt stricken: perhaps I had left her in my own care too long.

Intervention from these thoughts came from Dr. Tufts himself: "Mrs. Boylston has done as much as I could have, maybe more. I believe she has saved your sister's life. But now only time will tell."

"May I see her?" Thomas begged. "I had the distemper as a child. There is no danger."

"Wait until she wakes. Sleep is beneficial. I made to bleed her, but she pushed my arm away and would not have it."

I smiled to myself. Martha and I had spent many an hour discussing what I believed to be the utter uselessness of that popular cure. More often than not, I told her, it meant the end of the poor body being bled.

Dr. Tufts left with Abigail, saying he would stop at her house until the patient was fully out of danger. I thanked him. Abigail cast me a warning look not to leave her in any further ignorance.

Their departure left me alone with Thomas Miller. For some reason, it was an awkward moment. He had untied his cravat. Having formalized one thing, he now unraveled another. The heedless effect was not greatly changed.

"Were you on your way to some event?"

"I was. A show at Faneuil Hall. It is of no importance."

We were both quiet. Words failed me. Thomas rubbed his hands together and looked at me with his amber eyes. The jocular, teasing manner I had beheld in Cambridge was gone. His heavy dark hair had come undone, and he pushed it out of his face almost violently.

"You look worn, Lizzie," he said.

"I was about to say the same of you. It is nothing. I'll have time to rest when she's well. It is the woman's way."

"And the man's, at times," he muttered. "But to take care of others and refuse all help yourself? It is not *every* woman's way."

"Know you a great deal about women's ways?" I asked. "Oh, but Martha has told me you were once a great favorite among the Cambridge ladies."

"My sister exaggerates." He fell silent. This was not the easy banter we had enjoyed previously.

"Anyway," I continued, "I hear that there is one Cambridge lady in particular to whom you grow much attached at present."

I regretted my words at once, but it was too late. I saw him knot his fists and started back. Good breeding stopped him from violence, of course, either physical or verbal. But I felt the slap in his eyes when he flashed them at me.

"Shame on you, Elizabeth Boylston," he whispered, not wishing to raise his voice. "To speak ill of one who is most vulnerable and can never walk among society again. To show no *pity*."

"Forgive me," I muttered quickly, turning away from him, cut to the heart by his words, yet knowing I deserved them.

But he persisted, "And should you feel the need to warn me that the Boylstons are setting a trap, I've been fully apprised of her condition."

"Does she say whether she plans to keep the child?"

"It seems so." He glanced very briefly up at me, not wanting to meet my eyes. Gentlewomen never spoke of such things with a gentleman. But here I finally felt myself on some firm ground.

"I'm glad," I said. "It's always best for a child born out of wed-lock to remain with its natural mother, if possible."

Suddenly we heard a weak voice calling from within. "Thomas? Thomas? Is that you I hear?"

Mr. Miller stood so quickly from the chair that he knocked it over. "Oh, forgive me!" he said, righting it and flying to Martha. "It is I. Dearest, it is no dream!"

•   •   •

Thomas's visit marked a turning point for Martha, even though it spelled a week of sleepless nights for me. We parted quite formally. He bowed and thanked me for everything, neither smiling nor frowning, as neutral as the cloudless summer sky.

After he left, I could not stop berating myself for having sunk so low. I had been jealous and spiteful. And though I did not like Eliza, it had been cruel to begrudge goodwill to one so vulnerable and utterly alone. I recalled that the same blood that flowed through my Jeb flowed in her veins as well. He, certainly, had loved her and wished for me to treat her well. My nights were painful with thinking of it; my days, hardly less so. I burned with shame. Nor could I cease to think of Mr. Miller's remarks about my always being the healer, never the one in need of healing. Did I use my gift to remain invulnerable? Perhaps I did.

Meanwhile, when news had spread that Martha would live, Mr. Cleverly renewed his visits. At first I shooed him away, but on his third visit, he refused to go.

"Please, let me in," he entreated. I opened the door for him, and he took my hand at once. The touch of his hand was electrifying, especially to one who had not held the hand of a man in near four years. We soon walked together into the garden. He had just turned to me and was about to say something when I heard a groan from within and went running back.

"What is it?" I bent at once beside Martha. I thought she was in further distress and readied myself to call for Dr. Tufts.

"I would not accept his proposal of marriage if I were you," she said, her breath exhausted by the long phrase.

I smiled, greatly relieved. "On the mend and meddling once again, are you? I'm delighted to see it."

But whatever Cleverly was going to say to me that afternoon in the garden, the moment had fled. When I returned, I found him over by the well, staring at it with some intention in mind, the nature of which I could not guess.

After that day, he came and went only to tend to his invention. I saw him linger in the gardens, walking to and from the well and altogether appearing quite occupied. I paid him little mind. Martha had suffered a setback, and I was greatly occupied with her for another two weeks.

It was only after these trying weeks had passed and Martha's fever was gone and she was out of danger that I was able to walk abroad. One morning Martha and I walked together behind the stables toward the orchards. It was a fine July day, slightly cooler than it had been. I had brought a carrot for Star. Martha kept picking at her many scabs, and I had to grasp her hand and say, "You must resist that temptation. Who will want you all pocked, then?"

"I care nothing for men." She sniffed.

"You may not now, but you will later. Pocks last a lifetime."

Glancing about me, I noticed as if for the first time the farm's devastation. All was now dead and dry. The few surviving tomatoes had burst their skin with thirst. The peaches were blighted, food now only for the animals and the greedy crows.

"I'm sorry, Lizzie," Martha said, depressed. "This devastation is my fault."

"Don't be an idiot. I'd rather have one live Martha than all the tomatoes in the world."

She smirked. "Fulsome praise."

We were passing behind the stables when we came upon a sight that made us gasp: between two rows of thriving corn, a soft mist of water magically sprinkled a golden spray. The stalks were vigorous and healthy. On every one, small juicy cobs looked ready to burst from their silken sheaths. Corn was difficult to grow in the best conditions; this to us seemed a genuine miracle.

"What can this be?" Martha asked, astonished.

"The work of Mr. Cleverly, no doubt," I replied, although I was as astonished as she.

Soon Martha confessed that she was tired. I brought her back inside. I then went abroad once more and found Mr. Cleverly at the well. He was adjusting a metal lever at the terminus of a long waxed cloth tube. He was drenched in perspiration from his efforts. I had the impulse to lean across and wipe the wet lock of his blond hair from his forehead.

"What have you done here?"

He glanced up. "My invention works, you see." He was wrestling with something that appeared to be stuck and did not stand to greet me.

"This is your invention? This tube?"

"The same. It's really rather simpleminded. Is your patient better?"

"Oh, much. She's out of danger. But you look parched. Come in for some refreshment, at least. The noon sun scorches."

His bright eyes met mine with unabashed interest. "An excellent idea."

And with that he stood. I helped him with a hand, as one of his legs had painfully fallen asleep in his long crouch. I blushed at touching his hand again.

"It is a watering system," he said. By his smile, I knew he had seen my blush. "Quite simple in concept. It involves pricking the hose with even rows of holes, then channeling the water under pressure of a pump. I'm certain it's been done before, though perhaps not in these parts."

Cleverly's system looked to be working brilliantly, and I was exceedingly grateful. But I kept wondering: *Why did he take an interest in me and Martha?* What could I, a penniless midwife and widow, have to offer such a distinguished gentleman, scholar, and inventor—one who had the ear of our esteemed General Sullivan?

·   ·   ·

Abigail was not lacking an opinion upon the subject, which I heard later that same day as we sat having tea at my kitchen table.

"You see thyself in the most abject of lights. You have a great many skills, forty acres of land, a horse, several sheep, and two cows."

"One cow," I corrected sadly. "I was obliged to sell Bertha, if you recall."

She continued, "You're of noble lineage, though that may count against you these days. You're not entirely unattractive, though a little tall. And, apart from certain eccentricities, you've quite a pleasant, if slightly headstrong, personality."

"A ringing endorsement, indeed." I smirked. "Besides, who is calling the kettle black?"

"You forget I'm already happily married. Presumably, John married me despite my many flaws."

"You concealed them well," I muttered.

"Hardly." She laughed. "About as well as you, I should say. Anyway, if Cleverly likes what he sees, what harm is there in getting to know him? He comes recommended by Richard Cranch himself. One can hardly do better than that."

"No, indeed," I mused. "Yet I know him so little. He says he is on business with General Sullivan."

"If that is true, he must be very highly regarded. Not just by Sullivan, but by General Washington as well."

"He is wonderfully clever," I said.

"And far more handsome than a man has a right to be," she replied from across the kitchen table.

I blushed. "Yes. But you must come and see how he saved my corn and apples. Perhaps he could fashion something similar for you."

After we had finished our tea, I took her to see the watering system.

"Oh, goodness!" she exclaimed at once. We stood between two rows of healthy corn.

Abigail turned to me. "It was exceedingly kind of him to help you, Lizzie."

"It was. And yet, Martha doesn't like him."

"Then Martha doesn't have to marry him."

Martha appeared as though summoned by these words. She stood in the dooryard, a quilt around her shoulders. "Whom don't I have to marry?" she asked. She looked pale, and it was obvious to Abigail and myself how much flesh she had lost. The chickens pecked at her thin hands as she fed them.

"What are you doing out here in this unhealthy air?" I asked.

"Oh, I grew so bored with that hideous old kitchen. I'll go mad if I spend one more minute in there."

●　　●　　●

Martha gained her strength back and was soon sneering at Mr. Cleverly again. He came every day, ostensibly to check on his "system." Soon, however, he would abandon this pretense.

Eventually even Martha had to admit it was a relief to have a man about. Clearly, Mr. Cleverly had never done a day's farming in his life, but he made a good effort at it now. Martha and I often fell to laughing as we watched him clumsily mount a ladder or squish about in the chicken coop with his fancy boots. He particularly enjoyed grooming Star and was amazed to discover that I rode him astride, like a man.

"Shall I see you ride?" he asked me one day.

"Indeed you shall not." I frowned. "Unless there is a babe impatiently seeking entrance to this world."

"He is a beauty," he said, leaning into Star's stall and petting his nose.

"I agree. The breed is nearly extinct. He was a wedding gift from my husband's parents."

I glanced at Mr. Cleverly and blushed to find he was looking not at Star, but at me.

.　　.　　.

Cleverly often took his meals with us that summer. He did his best to engage us in our favorite subjects, such as literature and philosophy, although his natural bent tended more toward Galileo and Newton. He was an attentive listener as well, and had a lovely way of falling silent mid-sentence, as if he found everything we said most fascinating.

"Oh, how exceptional. You must show me how to work this," he said one time about our loom. And when he saw my medicines, he was struck positively speechless. Holding a pouch of snakeweed, he looked at me as if I were Hippocrates incarnate. "And when, precisely, does one use this?" he asked. In short, he was every bit as gentlemanly as Abigail had insisted he was. Even Martha grew to tolerate Cleverly.

.　　.　　.

In late August of 1778, the drought was at its worst, and there was little to be done for it. Most people had given up all hope of having corn, potatoes, or fruit that year. My flourishing apple orchard was the talk of the parish. I had to shoo the neighbors' boys away from my apples, though they were not yet ripe.

Meanwhile, the Battle of Newport raged. We heard bad reports, which grew ever more distressing until news of a decisive defeat finally reached us. All of this was offset by wild, reckless hope, fostered by news that France had declared war against Britain. *Surely we must beat the British now!* we all thought. Yet there were no signs of it.

Abigail brought news. Apparently she had met two travelers from England who had told her that her husband and child were alive and well. Though she would not hear from them directly for another month.

"I shall roundly scold them as soon as may be."

"Capital idea. Then John shall write you less than ever." But at this joke, tears sprang to Abigail's eyes.

"Oh, dearest, I meant no harm," I said.

"I know. But Lizzie, he doesn't write me as he should." She wiped her tears. "I have written a dozen letters and received nothing in return."

"Abigail, I'm certain that is because his letters are intercepted. Read the London papers, and you shall no doubt find his letters printed there."

She smiled briefly and nodded, glad of the condolence. But I told myself to take care with my words next time. We were all rather fragile inside, despite our intrepid appearances.

•　•　•

When Martha was quite well, we received an invitation to dinner from the Quincys. We arrived at the great house on a hot August evening looking like ladies of the Orient: in her convalescence, Martha had fashioned fans from reeds, and we used them now to combat the heat. When we knocked at the door, the colonel himself opened it. It made us wonder whether he'd been obliged to let his butler go.

"Lizzie, we're overjoyed to see you!" exclaimed Ann from behind him.

"As are we," I said, kissing her.

Mary, Richard, and Billy were there, as were Mr. Cleverly and Mr. Thayer, who apparently had just returned from his trip. He was as stooped and sullen as ever and offered no details about either his absence from or his return to Braintree.

The Cranches greeted us with delight. "Are you ready to discuss Hamlet's madness?" Richard asked good-naturedly.

Overhearing Richard Cranch, Mr. Cleverly frowned. Perhaps he had not counted on having competition for my attentions that evening. He moved to a corner of the parlor and spoke quietly with Mr. Thayer. A few moments later, Cleverly greeted both me and Martha with a perfunctory nod. He proceeded to glance periodically in Richard's direction, however, with a displeased expression.

"And do you not believe that Hamlet came to his madness honestly?" Richard was asking. "I, too, should go mad were I to see a ghost."

"Hamlet is as sane as you or I," I replied.

"Indeed," Abigail agreed. "He merely dissembles in order to get close to the king. How else can one get close to those in power?"

"You may both be right," Richard conceded amicably. "And yet I do believe it would unhinge one to get a glimpse of the afterlife. It would put all our assumptions into question, would it not?"

I glanced at Mr. Cleverly, who now conversed with Colonel Quincy. It seemed as if he would ignore us all evening. After dinner, the entire party retired to one room. At this point, I felt free to tell the colonel the excellent news about my brother. "But I cannot imagine why he never wrote to me before," I said. "It was so cruel of him to leave me wondering whether he was dead or alive."

"My dear girl," replied the colonel, blowing on his cigar, "many of our ships find it disadvantageous to have their persons and whereabouts known."

"*Our* ships?"

"I have heard tell of the *Cantabrigian*. It is an important supplier to Washington's army. Did you not know?"

"Not at all! I thought him pirating hapless merchants in the West Indies."

"West Indies—is that what he told you?" the colonel guffawed. "Mind you, it's not all altruism what those fellows do. I'd say rather about half and half."

"Half and half?" I inquired.

"Half the stuff goes in their own pockets. The other half goes to Washington. Or perhaps a little less."

"You mustn't be so fastidious, dear," added Ann, who had been following our conversation in silence. "I seem to recall your ancestors pocketing all of their haul."

He waved her way and bellowed, "A different time, that was. Entirely different!" Ann referred to the fact that the Quincy wealth stemmed in great part from the colonel's father, John Quincy, who acquired a fortune on a privateering vessel back in the 1740s.

Suddenly, Mr. Thayer shuffled toward us.

"A bad wind blows our direction," whispered Martha.

Thayer was upon us, bowing before the diminutive Abigail. "Excuse the interruption, ladies, but I merely wished to inquire of Mrs. Adams whether she has heard yet from her husband. Mr. Cleverly and I were just discussing the topic."

Abigail smiled. "Do you know Mr. Adams?"

"Only by reputation, madam, of course. No, we simply wish him well and wish him a safe and productive journey."

During this stiff speech, Mr. Thayer did not smile. His face had an altogether alarming look—so much so that I could see he made Abigail anxious. I decided then that people who are unable to smile really should not place themselves in society. At least, not in the company of women. Let their own sex be importuned by them!

"I have not heard from him directly, but I have heard from someone who chanced to meet with John and John Quincy and pronounced them well. Why, do you know anything to contradict this report?"

I knew her well enough to hear her heart race with anxiety, and I secretly cursed Mr. Thayer.

"No, indeed. Certainly not. We are glad to hear of it. Very glad. Who was it you said saw him?"

One more question and I would punch him with my own fist.

"I didn't say, sir." She smiled.

"Oh, leave the poor woman be," interjected Mr. Cleverly, who until this point had said not a word to any of us. He then returned to the other end of the parlor, casting me a backward glance. Abigail and I merely shrugged at each other, and a certain look in her eye made it difficult for me to keep from giggling.

Apparently Richard then felt the need to apologize for Abigail, for he said, "I'm afraid, Thayer, that our womenfolk have grown as tough as shoe leather."

"Richard!" cried Mary, appalled, certain her husband had offended the esteemed Mrs. Adams.

"Fear not, Mary." Abigail smiled again, understanding, as I did, that Richard's refusal to defer to her was, in fact, a sign of his love and respect. "Richard is right. Still, I trust no one these days, I'm afraid. Especially not where it concerns my husband."

"You are prudent, dear," said Colonel Quincy, and we then passed on to other topics.

26

"YOU TRUST NO ONE, BUT I AM to trust this man Cleverly, about whom I know hardly more than you know of Mr. Thayer?" I scolded Abigail the next day as we pulled my flax—what patches had not already died.

There was a breeze off the ocean, and the gulls squawked. Martha was well, and my brother was alive. I thanked my Maker for having precious little to complain of, though in the back of my mind Dr. Flynt's death still nagged at me.

"I did not say trust him," she mused. "I merely think you must begin at least to consider marriage. You cannot go on as you are forever. With the summer we have had, I fear for you this winter."

"And you think Cleverly is the right sort of man for me? He is handsome, I admit."

Abigail smiled. "He is that, but he also has a brilliant mind. You need someone who is your equal intellectually. A woman needs a true partner, not just a keeper, if she is to be truly happy."

"It seems he has not read *Hamlet*," I said. "He was silent and sulking while Richard and I conversed, as if I belonged to him and none other."

"Yes, Lizzie. I noticed. But you cannot expect even the most educated of men to have your precise interests."

"But not to know *Hamlet*?"

"Do *listen*, Lizzie. I have made inquiries into the Cleverly family of Stonington, New Hampshire, and they are of a very high and unimpeachable patriotic rank."

"How did you make these inquiries?" I asked, grasping one of her tiny wrists.

"I have friends." She smiled.

I would not have been surprised had Abigail sent a letter of inquiry. Abigail loved me, and she no doubt wished to see me married off before my youth and prospects faded.

Abigail said it seemed likely that Cleverly would propose to me. "If he does, what will you answer?" she asked.

"I know not. Truly I don't. I hear and believe what you say. But Abigail, I cannot say that I love him. I feel I hardly know him."

However, it had been a detestably hot summer, and I was ready to give myself up to the Devil himself if he offered relief from my chores. Furthermore, I now believe that loneliness of an intimate nature warps the mind and has us seeing phantom qualities in a man, not the truth about him.

Such was my state of mind the following afternoon when Cleverly came riding up on a fine horse. It was still miserably humid, but a breeze off the ocean whispered of cooling relief to come.

Cleverly dismounted, tied his horse to my post, and in no time at all stood stiffly, like a knight errant, in my parlor. Martha had just returned from some chore, and I was relieved not to be alone with him. But then she left me to go into the kitchen, where I heard her clumping noisily down the cellar stairs, presumably to fetch us all some cider. Cleverly took my hand and looked beseechingly at me.

"Elizabeth, shall we walk in your garden of Eden?"

"So long as you don't expect me to share an apple with you."

I glanced at him: he wore a clean linen shirt, and his fair hair seemed freshly washed. His face was clean-shaven and he held his chin high, as if someone were taking his measure. *What was Cleverly's true measure?* I wondered. More to the point, could I see myself waking up beside this man?

"Believe me to be in earnest," Cleverly began when we had moved far enough from the cottage, "when I say I didn't come to Braintree to find a wife. But I did find you, Lizzie. I have never met such a one as you in my life. A woman so lively of mind, and so very able—"

He looked directly into my eyes. I said nothing, as no words came to mind. I could not put aside the question of Cleverly as bedfellow. Could I imagine it? I tried . . . and yet, I felt no warmth, no tenderness.

I was just wondering whether my lack of feeling was due to some numbness of my soul, one that might thaw with use, when fate intervened. Galloping down the lane toward us was Richard Cranch. He looked gravely disturbed.

I removed my hands from Cleverly's and ran to him. "Richard, what is wrong?"

"It's Mr. Thayer. He did not come to breakfast. I told a servant to rouse him." He came close to me and said quietly, "She found him lying in his room—stone dead."

Martha had just come up from the cellar and was carrying two stoneware mugs of cider into the parlor. Overhearing Richard, she dropped them with a crash to the floor. Cleverly leapt to her aid.

"Dead?" she asked. "But we saw him last night. He seemed perfectly well!"

"He *was* well," blurted Mr. Cleverly from where he crouched to pick up the broken pottery. "Deuced well enough to importune Mrs. Adams."

I recalled how the unsmiling Mr. Thayer had inquired about John Adams's whereabouts and whether he'd reached his destination. Had that conversation been significant?

"Please come, Lizzie. We must have answers. But *quietly*. We mustn't alarm the parish."

"I'll get my sack. I'm sorry, John." Cleverly's Christian name was John, but as I had never once used it, it sounded quite strange now. I glanced at him with what I hoped was a regretful expression.

"Of course." He bowed.

I quickly saddled Star and followed behind Richard toward his home.

●　　●　　●

The Cranch household was in a state of turmoil. News had already spread among the servants. Poor Mary was racing about the servants' quarters, endeavoring to stop the panicked rumors from reaching her children or beyond the house. This time, however, unlike with Dr. Flynt, I sensed that the news could not be kept quiet.

"Show me to him, if you please," I said to Richard at once, for I had no wish to be detained by anyone.

Richard led the way up the stairs. Mr. Thayer's chamber was on the second floor, in the back. Mr. Thayer was right where they had left him: he lay upon the bed fully clothed, as if resting. He could not have long been dead. Feeling him, he was still warm, his muscles still supple. His eyes stared straight up at the ceiling.

"Would you give me a few moments?" I said to Richard, who leaned upon the doorframe looking very grim.

"Of course," he said. "Should I send for Dr. Tufts? Or Constable Vesey?"

"Let me examine him first," I replied, and, in a glance, Richard understood how loath I was to set the town in a panic.

He left me then, and I took a breath, composing myself for the examination I needed to perform.

I removed Mr. Thayer's clothing and observed him, this time writing everything down. I began with the color of his face (bluish white), lips (blue, deepening to a plummy purple at the edges), and eyes (pupils greatly dilated). I moved down to describe his torso, assessed his body temperature (eighty-nine degrees Fahrenheit), and so on, until I reached his feet.

After finishing my exam, rather than endeavoring to turn him (for now he was becoming more difficult to move), I partially covered him with a bolster that lay folded at the foot of the bed.

I took a moment to compose myself before calling Richard. I looked one last time at Mr. Thayer before covering his face: though I had never liked the man and found him humorless and ill-mannered, I pitied him now. Mr. Thayer had died of no natural illness.

It is our limitation as a species that we are often blind to that which we do not expect to see. I knew this had been the case with me. I now saw clearly what I had not seen before. Mr. Thayer had been poisoned. Like Dr. Flynt, he had been murdered. Once the notion of poison arrived in my head, it lit easily upon a drug with which I was quite familiar. I owned a vial of it myself, and it had served me well for stubborn cervixes. Now it all seemed quite obvious: the bluish tint, the dilated eyes.

Dr. Flynt and Mr. Thayer had been poisoned with belladonna.

The question now became whom one could trust to tell. The decision could no longer rest with me alone. I decided to tell Richard my conclusion and hoped I would not find myself in trouble with the local constable. Why had I not come forth with Dr. Flynt's death, had I suspected foul play? he might ask. I had to steel myself for that interrogation.

But the first thing I needed to do was to tell Abigail, for I now believed her to be in very grave danger.

27

SO BEGAN OUR SEASON OF TERROR. THE moment I had determined that both Dr. Flynt and Mr. Thayer had been murdered, there was no rest from fear—not for myself or for those I loved: Martha, the Cranches, the Quincys, and, most particularly, Abigail and her family.

I had little doubt that it was a plot, for no other explanation served to illuminate why the lives of two patriots in the household of a known patriot would be extinguished. Further, I reasoned, of all the places in all the colonies for murder to take place, the North Parish of Braintree could signify only one certain target: John Adams and his family. But why kill Flynt and Thayer? I had not been impressed by their characters. Surely they could not have played a very large role in our struggle.

I considered other possible targets besides the Adamses. Since the early years of the war, John Hancock had been chiefly absent from town, and his wife and family were with him in Philadelphia. An assassination plot on them would have been hatched in those parts, not ours. Washington was by then deep in the South, so surely he was not the target. As I raced toward my beloved Abigail that morning, I endeavored to piece together a plot whose clues were not all present and accounted for. I believed that someone, or some group, wished to threaten John Adams's family in order to force John home.

I had implored Richard to do nothing and notify no one until my return. I was exceedingly glad of my foresight now, for by the time I reached Abigail's farm, I had become convinced that the news should not go beyond our circle and that reporting to the constable would do far more harm than good.

I found her hauling a bundle of dried flax into the house. She had opened the door and was holding it ajar with her rear parts as she backed into the entryway. When she saw me approach, she set the bundle down and came to embrace me. Her body felt tiny in my arms, and she was covered in a fine salt sweat.

"I'm heartily glad to see you, Lizzie. What brings you? Is there something wrong?"

She had quickly caught my bearing. I could not hide it, nor did I wish to.

"Abigail," I said, taking her hands, "let us sit."

"Are Mary and the children well?" she asked, her voice thin and fragile.

"They are all well," I quickly reassured her. "None we could count among our friends are ill. Yet the news is still bad."

"Then tell me." She pushed aside a basket of pocky apples rescued from her ailing trees, finding room by the table for us to sit.

"Millie, could you bring us some cider from the cellar?" she said to her servant-girl. She was someone new, a day laborer I'd not seen before.

The girl did as Abigail instructed. Then little Tommy came running in, followed by Charles, whom he was shooting noisily with a popgun.

"Boys, kindly go out of doors. Mrs. Boylston and I wish to hear ourselves speak."

"Yes, ma'am," said Thomas.

Once they had gone, I said, "Mr. Thayer is dead."

"Mr. Thayer—Mary and Richard's guest? But we saw him just last night. He seemed perfectly well!"

Just then, Millie came back with two mugs of cider. We fell silent until she had put them down, curtsied, and left the room.

Abigail whispered, "Was it the bloody flux? That scourge is among us again—but," here, her expression grew dubious, "I've never known that dolor to carry one off quite so—suddenly."

"No. Listen, Abigail. It was nothing natural—he was perfectly well. I believe him to have been murdered—poisoned. My suspicion is that he was poisoned with belladonna. He had all the signs."

She looked at me as if I'd gone mad. "You must be mistaken."

Abigail glanced down at our mugs of cider, and the same thought occurred to both of us: we pushed our mugs away.

"I'm not mistaken. And I have even worse news."

When I was certain Millie could not hear us, I said, "Abigail, I now believe Dr. Flynt to have been poisoned, too. In my heart I suspected as much, but could not say with any certainty. I convinced myself it wasn't so and kept silent. Now I deeply regret that silence. Perhaps, had I said something then, Mr. Thayer would still be alive."

I was in an agony of remorse when Abigail took hold of my arm.

"You did what you thought best at the time. It is very easy to judge a thing from hindsight, when the larger truth is known. Except"—she released me, then sought my eyes—"do you know what that larger truth *is*, Lizzie?"

"What I suspect is that you're in grave danger. There are traitors among us, those who are no lovers of the Cause." Then, motivated to disclose all so as to lighten my heavy conscience, I added, "I have no proof, but I suspect a plot to force John home for some sinister purpose."

There. The worst had been told. Rather than react with astonishment, Abigail was moved to smile.

"He and I have spoken of it in our most private moments. I have daily feared it."

"But Abigail, we must thank God that between intention and act there is yet a broad chasm." I looked at her carefully. She met my eye without flinching. "Here is my question to you: Do we tell or not? We must think through this action very carefully. Further evil that we cannot foresee may ensue."

In asking Abigail this question, I harkened back to my conversations with Martha: How can one know good and evil when events nest themselves one within the other, like hollow wooden dolls?

Abigail was silent a full minute before she carefully began asking me questions. "Where lies Mr. Thayer?"

"In his chamber at the back of the second story."

"And who knows of his death?"

"The servant-girl was there when I arrived."

"Which means all the servants know."

"And the Cranches."

"And Martha, and Mr. Cleverly, and no doubt the children. What did you tell people about his death?"

"I made no pronouncement. The servant found him there this morning. He took a late supper of biscuits and cheese with Mr. Cleverly and the Cranches at around eleven, then retired to his room. No one saw him after that. Perhaps they assume he suffered a heart attack."

"Has he family?"

"I know not. Mr. Cleverly might know more. I recall he came from New Hampshire."

I could see her fine mind working by the intense movement of her eyes. She sat perfectly quiet for some moments.

We could both hear the pop-pop of Thomas's gun and the shrieks of the children playing in the garden.

"It is not for us to judge alone," she said finally. "What we decide upon must be decided as a group, composed of our most trusted circle."

"Richard Cranch," I said.

"And my sister," Abigail added.

"The colonel," I continued.

"Of course."

"Ann and Martha?" I hazarded.

Abigail shook her head. "No. I wish for people of weight and standing in our community. Whatever decision we come to, we must be beyond reproach. We may not be right, necessarily—for we have already seen how right so often becomes its opposite in hindsight—but we must be judged to have made a unified and rational decision based upon honorable motives."

I stared at her in astonishment. "And you think Martha and Ann unworthy?"

"They are women of lesser standing in our community. It pains me to say so, but there it is. I have uttered that which must never be said again to anyone."

I was silent. I knew she was right. "You have the mind of a statesman, Abby. John would be proud."

"Let us pray," she said with grim determination, "that John will never know of what he has to be proud."

With that, we reached for our cider and, sniffing well aforehand, drank of it.

Half an hour later, we returned to the Cranches' in Abigail's carriage. Meanwhile, Richard had sent word for the colonel. Soon, we—myself, Abigail, Richard, Mary, and the colonel—were gathered in the parlor. It was dark and close within, as we had shut the doors and windows to prying ears on this mid-September afternoon. Mary instructed the servants not to disturb us.

Just before we took our places on the sofas, Richard informed me of another shocking fact: while I had been at Abigail's, Mr. Cleverly had departed, with no immediate plans to return.

"He told us he had a dreadful fear of contagion, said he had family as depended upon him for their sustenance. There was also some mention of urgent business . . . I'm truly sorry, Lizzie," Richard added. "He wished to take his leave of you, but we urged him on. Were we wrong to do so?" Richard looked miserably at me.

"No, no," I hastily replied. "But where did he go? Is there no note?"

"It appears he had no time." Richard looked down. "In any case, we thought it best that he keep his destination to himself. New Hampshire, I imagine." Then Richard said gently, "This tragedy affects us all, but you most personally, Lizzie. I am profoundly sorry."

I merely nodded. I should have felt grieved, but what I recall feeling most of all was—relief! All question of love or affection put aside, I was by no means ready to change my life, my calling. I would not have given up my farm. Could I see Mr. Cleverly mending fences, cleaning cow dung? I could not.

I smiled involuntarily. "Thank you for your kindness, Richard. But I have not been unduly harmed by Cleverly's departure. He will be safe this way."

I believe everyone in the room then cast me a glance, endeavoring to glean my true feelings. Some of those present might even have presumed Cleverly to have already proposed to me. While modesty would have prevented me from divulging such business, these were my dearest friends—indeed, my family. And so I put them out of their misery at once.

"He did not propose to me, and there was no understanding between us."

"Well, that at least is some good news." Richard smiled kindly.

With this confession providing relief, we now turned to our business. Richard Cranch began, "First, let me begin this gathering by saying how grieved I am by yet another death in my house. Any death in our parish is a grievous event when it occurs. But when visitors are harmed, patriots in my own house . . . And now to find that the cause of their deaths may not have been natural, these are grave circumstances indeed. I think I may say that we are of one mind—to do what we can to maintain both the honor of these men and the welfare of our community. Are we not?"

"We are," everyone replied.

"Good. Then let us proceed in an orderly fashion."

He looked at me and was clearly going to question me first when I interrupted him. "Sir, I think we should bring in the servant-girl to hear her precise recollections of last night. I shall serve as secretary, if you like."

"I agree." Richard summoned the girl, Susan, a tall, skinny creature with bad teeth.

She gave her trembling account of the previous night and early morning. "I found him, eyes staring black and ominous-like. I knew at once he were dead."

She curtsied, and was about to make her exit when Richard stopped her.

"A moment more, Susan, if you can bear it. Did you tend to Mr. Thayer during the night?"

"He asked for tea to be brought up at about eleven thirty, sir. Said he couldn't sleep, so I brought it to him straightaway."

"And was it you yourself who made the tea?"

"It was."

"And before that?"

"Before that?" she asked. "Oh, well, he didn't ring for one of us, if that's what you mean, sir. It were just that one time."

"Thank you, Susan. You may go," said Mary. "It has been a trying day. You may take the rest of the day off."

"Oh, thank you, ma'am. I am a bit . . . Well, we're all very upset."

"Do all the servants know of our troubles?"

She nodded. "I believe so, ma'am. Hard to keep somethin' like this a secret." But before she had entirely left the room, she stopped and turned to Richard. "What did he die of, sir? The servants are all terrible worried." Everyone's eyes rolled to me.

"We're trying to determine that now, Susan," I replied. "But my best guess is a heart attack."

"Oh!" she said, placing a hand to her mouth. I believe it was to cover a smile of relief as well as her bad teeth. No one could rightly catch a failing heart. Susan left.

The meeting then began in earnest. I told the group that I could find no evidence of organic illness despite a thorough examination of the body. I told them that his pupils had been unnaturally dilated. His lips had been slightly blue, his larynx swollen closed—all the signs of either a severe allergic reaction or belladonna poisoning. I had never seen either before, but had read about them in medical books.

"Still, I am certain it was either one or the other," I said.

"But as for an allergy—he ate nothing but tea and biscuits."

"Yes." I nodded. "Such an allergy usually follows hard upon ingestion of the substance, which is why I'm afraid I must seriously weigh the latter explanation."

"Poisoning, you mean."

"Yes."

"Thank you, Lizzie," said Richard.

We then proceeded to conjecture for a few moments as to why someone might have wanted to murder Mr. Thayer and Dr. Flynt.

"But Lizzie," Richard interrupted, "are you absolutely certain Dr. Flynt died of unnatural causes as well?"

"I am now. I was not so then because there was illness in the parish, and because—well, I'd been told he had the distemper, and so my judgment was clouded. For prior suggestion often removes the spectrum of possibilities from the mind until later information opens it up again."

Richard looked at me then with some admiration and asked, "Who told you he had the distemper?"

"Why, Martha. She tended your Billy in my absence in Cambridge and looked in on Dr. Flynt."

"Why did she believe Dr. Flynt to have had the distemper?"

I grew uncomfortable. "I cannot account for it," I said. "She said she saw one or two eruptions. She thought it a mild case, as he had a fever. All I saw upon examination were old scars from a childhood illness. She must have been mistaken, through inexperience. And as you know, she had a nearly fatal case herself soon after."

He nodded thoughtfully.

The question of motive could not be solved, though our consensus was that two willful acts of murder had occurred, probably a Tory plot. We passed on, finally, to the subject of what to do.

Here, unfortunately, there was sufficient disagreement, particularly between Richard and the colonel, to involve us in nearly two hours of debate. We took no refreshment in that time, not wanting to alarm the servants, which made it doubly tiring.

Richard believed—vehemently—that we needed to notify the constable and coroner immediately, followed forthwith by an inquest. He thought that this was certainly the most direct route to the truth, and that knowing the truth of the matter was the only way to proclaim ourselves safe from further attacks.

The colonel, also a believer in the truth, disagreed about the means by which we should discover it. Older and more experienced, he had little regard for the judicial system. Indeed, he called our judges "His Royal Incompetencies." (I did not remind him that my own father had been among their numbers.) Furthermore, such public proceedings would have the effect of terrorizing the town and alerting the criminals.

"By your means," the colonel said to Richard, "we embrace a false sense of security by sharing knowledge of these heinous acts, having been committed, while allowing the perpetrators this same knowledge. Perhaps we even aid those who shelter them."

In the end, I had to concur with Colonel Quincy. However unfortunate it might be, our government was in a state of anarchy and corruption.

"Not to mention," I pointed out, "that even if exposed, the perpetrators, if found to have just political cause, might suffer no penalty at all but merely find themselves shipped back to England."

It was then resolved, with even Richard acquiescing, to call Parson Wibird and the undertaker and say that the unfortunate Mr. Thayer had felt unwell at dinner and apparently suffered an apoplectic fit during the night.

Richard would write to his brother-in-law, Parson Peabody, in an attempt to locate a wife and children or other immediate family of Mr. Thayer.

Abigail promised to call upon me in the next few days.

"A moment, Abigail," I said before she departed.

"Yes, Lizzie?"

"Perhaps you should—go away. Perhaps you should return to Betsy's home, in Exeter."

"Betsy's, in Exeter?" Abigail looked as if I would send her to the moon. "I dislike her husband, Parson Peabody. What's more, I have a farm to tend. And who knows that these killers—whoever they are—seek to harm me? It is most doubtful."

"Rest not uneasy, ladies," said Mr. Cranch. "The colonel and I shall do everything in our power to ensure your safety."

I bowed, thinking, *And how, pray, will you do that?* I said nothing further, however, and went home exhausted, depressed, and shaken. The day had begun with such promise and had ended thusly, mired in fear, tragedy, and loss.

It would be a comfort to tell everything to Martha, good Martha, whom I imagined would still be working in the fields as I had left her. I would tell her everything. Together we might even draw up a list of suspects.

· · ·

As was so often the case, how I imagined finding Martha that day was quite different from how I actually found her.

She was bent over the cornflowers, having a puke.

"Martha, dearest, are you ill? Not again!"

She looked up at me when she was able to, wiped her mouth with her sleeve, and then put an arm on her stomach. "I have been most violently ill. But it is nothing serious. A bad egg, perhaps. Poor cornflower," she said, attempting to smile.

"Come, let me make you something, for indeed you are white as flax. Nay, whiter. I will make you a dish of chamomile tea and tell you the news. Come, dearest."

Martha lay down on her bed in the kitchen, which we pushed over nearer the dairy, as it was cooler there.

"I hate this room," she said peevishly, looking around.

"You shan't be here long if you are ill from an egg. But I don't like you being ill again so soon after the other. You are very weak still and must take care."

"I will kill the chicken what gave me her bad egg!" She smiled, then grasped her stomach and hunched herself into a fetal position.

I made a sudden, unwelcome connection between Mr. Thayer's death and Martha. I asked, my heart suddenly racing, "You did not eat anything at Colonel Quincy's last night, did you?"

"What mean you?" she inquired, looking at me oddly. "I ate the same as everyone else. It was all quite delicious."

"I mean, nothing else? No tea or coffee?"

"Again, only what everyone had. Why?"

"It is not the cause of your illness, then. Thank goodness." I sat beside her. "Shall I tell you, dearest, what transpired, or is it better to wait?"

"I should like that tea," she said weakly.

"Of course," I said, having forgotten my offer. I hurried to make her a good hot dish of tea. When I handed it to her a few minutes later, she sat up, sipped at its consoling warmth, then lay back down.

"I think I shall sleep. But when I wake, tell me all about it."

She let me unloose her bodice as I pulled off all but her thin shift.

Martha did not wake up that day but slept until late the next morning. I tested her pulse every hour and remained awake all that night, so anxious was I. At a certain point, I thought to check my own store of belladonna. I crept into the dairy with my candle, careful not to wake Martha. The vial was as I had left it; the amount looked unchanged. I breathed a sigh of relief that at least I had not been the unwitting vehicle of evil. I was left to wonder only from whence the poison had come.

When Martha woke later the next morning, she seemed almost entirely recovered. She made to get up, but I would not let her accompany me to the fields.

"Have you fed the animals?" she asked.

"Rest assured, it is all done."

I had risen early, as usual, and had taken consolation in nature. Several of our maple trees had just begun to turn, their leaves tinctured here and there with golden yellow. A breeze from the ocean was soft and caressing, and the air smelled sweet from the red, ripe apples. Nature was so good. What made us, her children, less so?

I said merely, "I believe it is entirely possible you gave yourself a sunstroke. For now, let us spare the life of the poor maligned chicken."

As if on a playwright's cue, one hen strutted nervously through our back door, which we had left open to circulate the air.

"There she is!" Martha cried. She spoke to the hen: "If you wish to avoid a bath of plum sauce, be gone! Shoo!"

The hen ran back outside, leaving a small agitated parcel as its parting gift.

"Now you may tell me everything," Martha said. "And when you are done, I shall write to my brother."

"When I'm done, you may wish to leave the parish forever and live with your brother."

"Indeed, I am not so cowardly!"

"It would not be cowardice, dear Martha, but prudence."

"Tell me what you know and be quick about it."

Our decision had been to exclude Martha from our reckoning, but I had not that talent of lying by omission. Not, at least, to Martha. And so I told her everything about my determination of foul play by poisoning. I further told her that inquiries were underway to locate Mr. Thayer's family. Finally, I told her of our decision, after much debate, not to reveal to the authorities what we knew. I gave her some of our reasoning behind this decision.

"It was the right decision, Lizzie," she asserted, "as best as one can judge."

"I hope so. While I am no lover of the Tories of this town, I believe history will look favorably upon our tolerance of them. To persecute civilians would be to commit the very sins of which we accuse our enemy."

"Although perhaps sin is sometimes necessary." Martha stood shakily from her bed and looked out the window upon the shimmering dunes.

"Oh, Martha, I have no wish for a philosophical discussion right now. And you cannot have the strength for one. Let us leave off for another time."

Turning toward me with real entreaty in her voice, she replied, "But I do *fear* these men, Lizzie. I fear they're plotting more mischief. Mr. Cleverly must be careful. You should warn him." She gave me a hard look I could not read, for I knew her to be no lover of Mr. Cleverly.

"Mr. Cleverly!" I started up. "Oh, Martha—I omitted him in my account. But perhaps the news will lift your spirits. Apparently you won't be getting rid of me after all. For he is gone from our midst. He has fled for his life. It's now fairly certain I will die in bed by your side, an old maid."

Martha grew thoughtful. "I do confess it: I am glad. Not because I disliked Cleverly—though I did, but because it should crush me to part from you. It is selfish, I know."

We hugged each other then and sipped our tea like the little spinsters we felt certain to become.

28

LATE AUTUMN, 1778. AS AUTUMN DESCENDED ON Braintree, everyone feared to leave their homes, even for meeting. Despite all our attempts to instill the idea that Mr. Thayer had died of a heart attack, rumors flew regarding the deaths at the Cranches', making our poor parish believe, and rightly so, that the war had come home to roost. And yet, within several weeks, even the fear instilled by these deaths could not compare with the greater terror of illness, drought, and starvation.

Indeed, there were some among us who might have preferred poison. Our parish had gathered barely enough harvest to survive the winter. Prices were such that currency was useless. No one could afford the least item, not even the Quincys. Not pins, not meat, not rum. There was no grain to be had, and many lived on old moldy stores of oats and Indian meal, with no meat at all, save the occasional sacrifice of a chicken.

We harvested the corn and the apples, but they gave us no joy, knowing as we did that our friends went without. I had not quite forgiven Cleverly for leaving without so much as a letter to me. Surely that would have involved little risk to his person. He could not have loved me very much, I decided. Thus, the apples no longer seemed quite so tempting as they once had, and only the thought of sharing our bounty eased our spirits. We would have wonderful gifts for all our friends that fall.

I had been four years in Braintree by this time, and from those early days of loneliness when I was shunned and looked upon with suspicion, I had reached a position of respect. The less educated no doubt still whispered behind closed doors that I was a witch, a mistress of alchemical arts. But even they sought me out when the sickness was upon them.

By the fall of 1778, I had delivered near two hundred babes. Each one occasioned a pie, or a bottle of spirits, or service of some kind. Susanna Brown, the woman who had foolishly chased her husband out to Grape Island in the summer of 1775, became a particular friend, and I safe delivered her of another child that autumn, a boy this time.

*　　*　　*

In October, Martha received a long letter from her brother with the news that he would shortly be arriving with Miss Eliza. In the midst of our turmoil, I'd forgotten all about her! Eliza's presence in my home was the very last thing I wanted.

But I had promised. And as the unfortunate woman had nowhere else to turn, I made preparations for her arrival, readying my own chamber upstairs until I changed my mind and prepared the bed in the parlor.

I also learned, much to my great dismay, that Martha had told her brother about Mr. Thayer's murder.

"Martha, how could you? I told you we had resolved to tell no one. I assumed you understood."

"I just had to tell him, Lizzie, for I did not feel safe otherwise."

"And how can your brother, of all people, keep you safe?" I blurted, my manner making my opinion perfectly clear: I thought

Mr. Miller was as like to warn the Tory perpetrators as bring them to justice.

"Oh, no, not my Thomas," Martha objected to my silent accusation with a gentle smile.

"And why not 'your Thomas'?" I asked. "Is he not sympathetic to the Tories?"

"Perhaps. But he would never do anything to endanger me. Or you. Besides, I swore him to secrecy, and he has sworn. Look—" She handed me his letter. It was written in a beautiful hand and filled with tender concern for his sister. Oddly, I thought, it did not suggest she return to Boston, where he could better protect her. But he had stern advice for both of us: to avoid the houses of the Cranches, the colonel, and the Adamses, for the present.

"What advice can this be?" I said. "To avoid our most dear friends?"

"The advice is sound, Lizzie. For surely if the danger is anywhere, it is there in those homes. And while we may fall inadvertent victims ourselves, he can do nothing to protect them."

"I will not cease calling on my friends, if invited, Martha. I cannot. Do you think Abigail would shun us, were the situation reversed?"

She smiled ruefully. "Certainly not."

"You see."

"But we must take great care. Perhaps we could bring our poor hen and have her taste the food and drink before we do."

We met each other's eyes and laughed. It was but a momentary relief of tension.

That same week, Richard received a letter from Parson Peabody in New Hampshire, Abigail's brother-in-law. But the news was not what any of us had expected. According to the parson, no Ebenezer Thayer existed—or at least, he had not heard of any such Thayer in his or any nearby parishes.

That was shocking news, and quite dismaying. Surely someone must live to grieve for the man, we reasoned. Since his death, no letters had come for him. If he had received any letters prior to his death, there were none among his effects. We thought that very strange as well. Had Cleverly been misinformed? Colonel Quincy was disturbed to hear the news. "They must have been using pseudonyms," he said.

"They must have been important to the Cause to have need of pseudonyms," I offered.

"It would appear," mused the colonel. "Yet they came out of nowhere and disappeared into nowhere as well. It is quite distressing."

This news merely served to fuel my desire to learn more about these men and their killers. For while our group had made a pact of silence, I had little doubt that servants would talk. The Cranch servants had already spoken to others. And while people always gossiped and rumors always flew about that were subsequently repudiated, such as John Adams and John Hancock having jumped a British ship or the assassination of Benjamin Franklin in Paris, *this* rumor had a heat and urgency that would not be extinguished.

The town continued to whisper, and I thought it was only a matter of time before whispering would turn to accusation, accusation to condemnation. Now our townspeople were whispering in meeting that poor Mr. Brackett, the innkeeper, had been heard to be critical of His Excellency. The tanner had been abroad for nearly a week. Perhaps he was meeting in secret in town and plotting mischief! As the Salem of our forefathers had taught us well, once such panic takes hold, there is hardly a fact on earth that can serve to dislodge it from the minds of men.

Thus, it was imperative—a Christian duty—that we find the perpetrators and bring them to justice, not in the eyes of the royal court, upon whom we could not depend, but to Washington himself, who would not spare the rope for enemies. Death by hanging for traitors was His Excellency's one borrowing from British rule.

Though these events be many years in the past now, and memory, my faithful companion, grows old like myself, I believe it was at this moment that I began to envision a plan of action. I had grown impatient of ignorance. Why could I not know, why could I not seek answers as a man would? What did I lack? The will, I decided. One could learn what one willed oneself to learn.

The plan would have to wait several weeks, however. For, on Saturday the tenth of October, Thomas Miller arrived with a very large, very fretful Eliza Boylston.

29

MARTHA RAN TO THOMAS, AND SO GREAT was her relief at seeing him that she wept in his arms. I saw him obliquely, since I occupied myself with Eliza, for whom the long carriage ride had caused great discomfort. But though I made no outward notice of the reunited pair, I did notice one thing: the eyes of Thomas Miller. As he held Martha, he glanced at me briefly. It was not the jovial face I knew. Tears had pooled beneath his amber irises and threatened to career down his face. For whom or what did he grieve? Catching me looking at him, he attempted to smile, as if to say, "All is well, truly." I was moved but showed it not, and went inside with Eliza.

The weather was growing cool, especially at night, and I was glad I thought to give Eliza the parlor bed. In the parlor, one could easily start a fire with coals from the kitchen, and, when her sickness was upon her, I could watch her progress while continuing my work.

Eliza set her bags down; Thomas still had the trunk in the carriage. My house was cozy, with signs of industry everywhere. It was not entirely tidy, but it was clean. Not like Abigail's house; there, if someone filched a pin in the night, she'd know it come morning.

No, my house had herbs and fruit strung up here, sewing there, and the loom and its accoutrements taking up the entire "good" parlor, along with chairs and strings set up for candle-making. In that room, the floors were never entirely clean—keeping them so would have been a livelihood unto itself.

I expected Eliza to make a cutting remark about her new abode, but she merely sat herself down on my one fine chair and said, "Thank you, Lizzie. I don't know what I should have done had you not allowed me to come here. I think I should have died. That infernal house! I have paced its halls these many months till I thought I should go mad!"

Just then Martha and her brother banged through the front door with Eliza's trunk.

"You may leave it here—by the bed. And Martha, could you make some tea? Hello, Thomas," I said, for I had not yet had the opportunity to greet him.

It would be woman's work in my home soon, and for that I would need to send Mr. Miller packing. But as he had just arrived, I thought it only good breeding to ask him to stay for tea. He accepted with alacrity, and we were soon sitting comfortably by Eliza's side. Any dark fantasy I had had concerning Eliza's love for Mr. Miller or his for her quickly vanished the moment I saw them together. He acted as a kindly brother to her—nothing more. When she smiled at him, it was a smile of gratitude, not love. But the real question was, What difference could that possibly make to *me*?

Martha brought us cheese and oatcakes and the one remaining jar of last year's raspberry jam. There would be no more once it was gone.

Eliza dug in hungrily but pronounced herself full after a minute, holding a hand to her breastbone. Conversation between the four of us was awkward. All our minds save one were upon the dreadful murders, but it was knowledge I had no intention of sharing with Eliza. Martha and her brother implicitly agreed, I could tell, because when something is on one's mind of which one cannot speak, those thoughts tend to halt speech altogether. Therefore none of us had much of anything to say.

Of course, I had a great deal to discuss with Eliza, but her forthcoming pains were nothing I cared to mention with Thomas present. Finally, looking around for some conversation, Eliza said, "You have a great number of apples. And yet, I have heard talk of a terrible drought this year."

Here again, Martha and I looked at each other.

"A happy fluke," I said, "and one that you shall certainly enjoy while you're here."

"We have had terrible shortages," Eliza complained. "I haven't had so much as a teaspoon of sugar these six months."

I merely smiled. There seemed so much we could not say to one another.

Mr. Miller said, "I doubt very much if these ladies have had a slice of bread in six months, much less sugar."

"Oh. Indeed. I am sorry. It is always more difficult in the country. But in truth, though there be goods in town, we have no money for them and must barter for everything. My dowry is gone—"

Eliza looked quite downcast for a moment, but only a moment. Then she did the most extraordinary thing: she burst out laughing. "My dowry! Imagine!"

She kept laughing and could not stop. She laughed so hard I thought she would bring on her travail, and I stood up to take charge of her.

"Martha, lie her down just there, will you? I'll walk Thomas to his carriage."

At first surprised by my abrupt halting of the tea, Martha caught my intentions at last. She hugged her brother good-bye for a long minute.

Eliza called out after Thomas, "Thank you, Tom! I am more grateful than I can say." She wiped the tears of mirthful release from her eyes.

"And I wish you a—er, safe—" Thomas backed out awkwardly, bowing, his sentence left unfinished.

I followed him into the yard, as there were things I would talk to him about alone.

"She may be weak, but she is not without courage," Mr. Miller said as he waited for his horses to be hitched to the carriage. Without, it was a crisp fall afternoon. The surface of the ocean, black and inscrutable in its depths, reflected the brilliant gold of dune grass. *It was a dark-gold color not unlike Thomas Miller's eyes*, I thought.

"Yes," I answered. "She complains not at all for herself. I have always believed that hardship brings out one's true nature. It appears she is less spoiled than I thought."

"Perhaps, in her circumstances, she merely played a part because it was expected of her."

"Perhaps," I replied. I looked toward the sea. Great gray herons had not yet seen fit to leave us for the winter, and they blended with the dune grass like tall shadows. Beyond the dunes, the old maples and oaks of town glowed in vivid reds and oranges. I then sought to meet Thomas's eyes, but now he, too, was looking in the direction of the sea.

"How fares her father?" I asked.

"Very ill. Mrs. Boylston—" he began, turning toward me at last, and my heart thumped an extra beat in anticipation of what he would say. But just at that moment, Thaxter came round with the horse, which he had fed and groomed and hitched to the carriage.

Mr. Miller did not continue his sentence, and I said, "You have heard about our town treachery? I had no wish for Martha to tell anyone else, least of all—"

"A sympathizer," he finished my sentence with an ironic twist of his mouth.

"They'll be found and brought to justice, despite your sympathies," I said.

He leaned up against the carriage as Thaxter waited. Then, without any warning, he grasped my hand in his and held it close. "You must be very careful, Lizzie. There are dangers. Think of me what you will, but know that whatever I may be, whatever my unfortunate circumstances, I would do nothing to harm you or those you love. It is my solemn promise."

I felt a wrench in my heart then, I knew not why. His voice . . . his voice held such a different tone from the mocking one I'd heard in Cambridge! His eyes were quite level and quite grave. And his hands were warm, engulfing, and firm.

"Mr. Miller."

He looked at me intently for a moment, then stepped into Thaxter's waiting hands and soon disappeared up the path to the road. I stood there looking after him, puzzled at my own feelings. It was as if we had glimpsed something in each other that belied appearances. I shivered in the breeze and looked away. Then I returned to my warm house and, with some effort, turned my attention to Eliza.

As my first task, I endeavored to put aside my feelings for this woman who had once disapproved of my marriage to her brother and then treated me so poorly after his death. Her behavior was unforgivable, and yet I found it easy enough to leave the question of forgiveness for another time.

I was a practiced and knowledgeable midwife, and that is what I resolved to do: practice. To that end, I steered my patient clear of all discussion of our common family, connections, or our history. I set Martha the task of weaving a dozen clouts, which took her the better part of that day and the next.

On that first day and the ones following, I strove to improve Eliza's state of mind. It is my experience from the many births I have attended that the outcome of a woman's travails depends upon her mind's preparedness.

I had not been sanguine about Eliza's laughter. No, in it, I saw the telltale signs of hopelessness that often lie behind such outbreaks. In such a case, I did not think it prudent to be too subtle. Nor had we the time for subtleties, judging by her false pains that came and went all the day she arrived and into the next. I judged her to be but a week or two away, for the babe was fully engaged in the pelvis now.

I asked her directly, "Eliza, do you wish to live to care for your baby, should the Lord grant it come into the world in health?" It appeared that I startled her with my brusqueness.

"I wish for the child to live," she replied sincerely. "I care little for myself."

I shook my head and glanced knowingly at Martha, who had left off her weaving for a few moments and now sat with me in the parlor. Eliza lay propped in bed, her yellow hair loose and hanging in cascades to her waist, her full breasts and belly showing pink through the parting of her shift.

An emotional change had taken place along with Eliza's physical transformation. That she was despairing, I had no doubt; but this despair was real—and in its authenticity, I saw a glimmer of hope for her.

"The child cannot have a good chance if you have not the will to live. While I don't wish to frighten you, I've heard tell of many a mother expiring before her child was ever born. It is the saddest case of all, for she takes the healthy child with her."

"Have you seen that happen?" she asked.

"No. But it is a frequent enough occurrence. You may choose to die some other time, if you wish, but not before the babe is in my arms."

She sighed. "I'm not sure why it is, Lizzie, but I trust you. I promise I'll not wish to die until—another time, as you say."

She stretched herself and groaned on the bed, her lower back quite sore.

"Good girl. Now we have the best possible outcome to look forward to. I am very pleased. Indeed, I am." I stood from my chair and approached the bed. "As a reward, I will now massage your aching back. Martha, help Miss Boylston turn on her knees."

I massaged her lower back, relieving her greatly. And so we both put things aside: she, her wish to die, and I, my forgiveness of her.

It was not until her third day with us that I asked her whether the father knew of the child about to be born. We were taking our scant breakfast, Martha and I eating but half a biscuit each, while placing a morsel of cheese and two biscuits before Eliza, which we endeavored not to glance at hungrily. Eliza answered in the affirmative, letting go the old lie of his death, which I had never believed anyway.

"And was he not free to marry?" Martha inquired.

Eliza shook her head, smiling wistfully, letting me understand by her smile that it had not been a case of ravishment.

"He has no wife, if that's what you mean."

"Do you love this man?" I finally asked. "And does he love you?"

"Oh, yes," she said, tears starting instantly to her eyes, "but I beg you, ask me no more questions, for I can say nothing else at present."

Here, I ceased my interrogation, for I thought it prudent not to upset her further.

The day was quite fair for mid-October. Martha and I ventured into the fields to gather our pompions. Remarkably, they had survived the drought, though they were smaller than usual. It was in the midst of this activity that we heard a cry and rose to our feet:

Eliza stood by the kitchen door in her shift. Her waters ran down her leg, forming a pool on the ground.

"Don't be frightened," I said. "The baby is coming."

"But I feel no pain," she replied, confused. "If this is the extent of a woman's pain, then we are a miserably weak lot."

Martha and I shared a knowing glance.

"It will come on gradually," I said.

We then left our pompions and the golden glory of the fields surrounding us to bring another poor innocent creature into the world.

·   ·   ·

To recount the following dozen or so hours is almost beyond my narrative talents. It was a hard back labor, but Eliza bore it as I have only rarely seen among her class. She breathed with me, she rid herself of all encumbrances of shame or modesty. She ground her teeth, slammed her hand on a table—enough to bruise it quite blue—and altogether reverted to the animal that God or Nature intended us to become at these times. Those women who endeavor to remain genteel or composed have a much harder time of it, driving the pain farther inward.

No, Eliza was like a splendid madwoman—she raged, she shouted, she even cursed. Martha and I encouraged her to such an extent that anyone overhearing us might have thought we performed an exorcism.

In those days, the height of her pains would have been the traditional moment for asking the name of the father, for it was thought no woman in travail could tell a lie. But there was no lawyer present, nor did I see fit to call one. She did feel moved to utter words, however, and what she said came as a surprise. I had just told her she could push at the next pain when Eliza blurted out, "I am sorry I did not love you as I should have. I was wrong. It wasn't you. I couldn't bear to lose—to be left alone—" Her pains came again, and she grimaced, just managing to say, "Can you forgive me and be my sister?"

I have never had the hardness of heart to bear a grudge when a soul asks my forgiveness. And, if one is to believe the old wives' tale, Eliza was telling the truth. I forgave her and became her sister then.

In another two minutes, a healthy boy slipped into my hands. He was black as night.

30

THE BLACKNESS OF WHICH I SPEAK LAY more in my mind's eye than in the babe itself. For though I knew him to be a Negro (mulatto) child at once, the color of his skin was actually quite fair, almost akin to an almond.

"It's a boy!" I cried.

He was large and lusty and cried at once. I cleaned him quickly and gave him directly to his mother. He found her breast and began to suck. I delivered her placenta, checked its wholeness, and sewed up her slight tear. Martha moved as my third and fourth hands. We shared one mind at such times, and I had no need for words as she did those tasks that were quickly needed, one upon the other.

"Shall it live?" Eliza asked me.

"That's in our Maker's hands," I replied. "But a healthier newborn I have never laid eyes upon."

"Then I shall name him now. John, after his father. He is a well-loved man." At these words, she wept.

Think not that I was so advanced of my day and age as not to be shocked by little John's entry into the world. I was—thoroughly. But as his conception was an accomplished fact, and, as the mother clearly knew her own child's origins, there was little need for me to utter such inanities as, "By God, it's a Negro!" That would have been tactless indeed. I held my tongue, as did Martha, knowing Eliza would tell all in her own time.

Martha and I gave Eliza fresh linens and made her comfortable. I felt a pang of regret that she had no women around her. Usually I had to swat them away like flies. But Eliza had only the two of us.

"Is there anyone you wish me to send for? Your mother, perhaps?" I asked, though I knew the answer.

She smiled. "My mother has no wish to see us."

"Perhaps her feelings will change in time, for he is her grandson, bar all else. Do you have a friend you might call upon?"

"All my so-called friends left my side long ago. Only Thomas Miller remains. He is so good." She smiled up at me, and I thought it a kindness to say nothing, for I knew not a single man or woman to call a Tory "good," except another one.

"Well, then, you have three friends."

"And my slaves, of course," Eliza added thoughtfully.

"Cassie, you mean?"

"Oh, no. The others. The Whipple slaves. They're not *my* slaves—I mean they're my *friends*. They are most dear to me. Most good."

I knew not to whom or what Eliza referred; her words made little sense to me.

"Speak no more now," I said. "You must rest."

I took the babe, who was sleeping, from his mother. His little hands started out as I lifted him. We had carried a drawer from my chest of drawers down the narrow stairs. Martha swathed him in soft cotton, and we put him in there, warm and cozy.

Once mother and child were safely asleep, I washed myself and collapsed in my own bed, where Martha soon lay as well. It was now nearly three o'clock in the morning, and we were both delirious with exhaustion. We would need to be up in an hour's time.

"What think you of it, honestly?" Martha whispered to me.

"I cannot think. Tomorrow she will tell us. Or we can bribe it out of her, if necessary."

"I wonder what will become of the poor little fellow. Will she keep him, do you think?"

"I know not. My eyes close, Martha . . ."

Martha fell silent at last, and I fell asleep.

• • •

We woke to the beautiful sound of a baby crying. But upon descending the stairs, I was horrified to discover Eliza out of bed and reaching to pick up her child.

"Back in bed at once!" I commanded. She did as she was told, but not without her baby. She clutched him to her breast even as she nearly fell back upon the bed.

I watched my charges carefully for the next few days. Making as if to sew or card, I counted Eliza's breaths, watched the rise and fall of her chest. At one point, I thought her cheeks looked flushed, and I moved to feel her forehead with my own face. But it was flushed from the fire, not fever. Twice a day, I checked Johnny, too—I could not relax until a week had passed and all remained well. In the week since his birth, Johnny had darkened in color to that of a roasted chestnut, though there were bits of gold in his thick head of hair.

"You watch me carefully, Lizzie," Eliza said, suckling Johnny one afternoon.

"You've noticed," I replied.

"It is very obvious."

Martha added, "She thinks she is so sly, but one reads her easily, I find. Does one not?"

"Indeed one does." Eliza smiled.

"I'm glad to provide amusement for you both."

The two women laughed amiably at me.

Abigail called that same afternoon to find a most shocking scene. I had not told her about Eliza, and so she was to come upon a messy home with a woman and babe in the parlor bed, surrounded by linen, cloths, and powder! Eliza was out of danger now and was sitting up when Martha and I greeted Abigail at the door.

"Good God!" Abigail cried. "It's more close and crowded in here than Dr. Wales's pox hospital. And the two of you look bruised about the eyes." She turned to me and whispered, "Who is that?"

"My sister-in-law, Eliza Boylston. I safe delivered her of a little boy one week ago tomorrow. The child . . ." I took my friend out of doors into the chilly autumn air and finished in a low voice, "The child has no father. Or none she will as yet willingly name."

"Poor thing," Abigail said.

"The news is worse," I whispered. "For the child is of mixed race."

"A Negro?"

"Indeed."

"Was it a case of ravishment?"

"No. She loved him—still does, I believe. The situation could hardly be worse. Her father is dying."

Abigail passed a hand wearily across her head. "And I came to tell you of pleasant, easy news. So pleasant and easy, it allowed me to forget, for a few hours, what impossible, treacherous times we live in."

"It is good to forget once in a while, if you can. I don't begrudge you your good news."

At that moment, I think I actually would have fallen face forward in my dooryard had Abigail not steadied me and led me inside.

As I leaned on her, Abigail scolded, "You deliver others safely but will have no man of your own. You look down your nose at the feminine badinage of our quilting ladies, though it would save you many hours' work. And who, Mrs. Boylston, do you allow to care for you? No one. You are most irksome."

"You care for me," I objected. But I found my strength had entirely left me, even that with which to defend myself against her.

When I had eaten something, my limbs grew heavy, and I fell asleep in the good parlor chair. I awoke an indeterminate time later to find Abigail next to me, holding little John.

Eliza was still in bed but looked animated and happy, a happiness doubled by Abigail's loving treatment of Johnny.

"There. You needed that rest, Lizzie. You must take care not to let yourself sink so low."

"It's my fault," Eliza added. "Lizzie has been an angel. She and Martha, I mean." Eliza glanced at the girl, who stood in the kitchen door, having deftly allowed Eliza and Abigail their private conversation.

"No, you're mistaken. They're no angels. That one"—Abigail glanced my way—"is a thorn in my side. And the little one"—she glanced at Martha—"well, still waters run deep. She could perform a successful amputation upon you, though she appears hardly strong enough to carry a bucket."

At this, Martha's eyes flashed at Abigail.

"No," Abigail concluded, snuggling the babe and smiling at him, "this is the angel. Such a gentle, good soul I have never encountered in a babe, and I have had five. Five born alive," she corrected herself.

"Yes. That's his father in him," Eliza said.

We all nearly cried then. The truth was, we had, in a week's time, fallen in love with Johnny. His mother had little to give, yet he complained so little and suckled so well, we thought him blessed. Indeed, we had gone so far, late in our sleepless nights, to resolve to keep him should the mother die.

"Excuse me a moment, Miss Boylston, for it was on some business that I came, and I must now address Lizzie before returning to my own children. My Nabby is gone, and the boys are no doubt getting into mischief." She stood and gently handed the babe to Eliza.

I stood, too, a bit dizzy, and accompanied Abigail into the yard to bid her good-bye. There was no carriage, and I soon realized she'd come the near two miles on foot.

"It grows cold," I said. "Do you wish to take Star?"

"What, and sit astride like you? Heavens, no."

"It's a good deal more comfortable that way," I offered.

"We women were not made for comfort," Abigail said with asperity. "But to the matter at hand. As you may know, the French fleet has been in town these few weeks, and I have had the honor to meet and dine with Admiral d'Estaing aboard *La Sensible*."

Abigail gazed out toward the iron-gray sky over the ocean.

I looked beyond the dunes to where Abigail was gazing and saw a large, elegant schooner. In my preoccupation with Eliza, I had not noticed it before.

"What polite and sober men." She smiled at the recollection. "Lizzie, if you could see them, it would lift you up. How far our own lawless, greedy citizens have sunk by comparison! These French seamen are the noblest men I ever beheld."

I waited silently for her to come to her point, for to hear about noble men after the week we had passed was like hearing about men on Mars.

It was growing cool. The wind was picking up, and I wished to return to my patient.

"But then, you must wonder why I prattle on. I come to the point: Wednesday next, I'm invited to dine with the Admiral d'Estaing at the colonel's. I want you to come with me."

"Abigail, by all means I will accompany you if all be well with Eliza. But I am greatly afraid, for I was cautioned by one who counts himself a friend of the enemy."

"You speak of Martha's brother, no doubt. Thomas Miller." Her eyes were bright and unreadable. "Yes, he's a well-known sympathizer."

"A sympathizer, perhaps, but he loves his sister, and he has come to have a true regard, I believe, for us."

"For *you*, you mean," she said.

I blushed, ashamed of my feelings, especially before the wife of our great patriot. "My point is this," I said with an effort. "He has most emphatically warned against assembly at the colonel's. He says it is a danger to all involved, including the colonel himself."

Abigail was silent, and I thought she was considering the import of my words, but she took my hands and said, "Think of it, Lizzie. What victory for them if we allowed them to instill such fear in us that we cease all assembly with one another! If they wish to divide and conquer, they shall not do it on Braintree soil. No"—she shook her head—"I may lose my life, but I won't have the history books say that the wife of John Adams, who daily risked life and limb, cowered in her boots."

And that was all that she ever said upon the matter. Then she placed a little hand on my arm. "But, Lizzie, you may make free to decline the offer if you wish. I speak only for myself."

"And I speak for myself when I say I would as soon let you go alone as walk a favorite lamb into a lion's den. No, I shall go, too."

Abigail embraced me warmly in the chilly air. She felt tiny and insubstantial in my arms. I marveled at how such an indomitable spirit could live within so childlike a body. She began to walk down the path, then turned suddenly. "Oh, but Lizzie! I have entirely forgotten! Eliza told me all about the father of little John."

She began to walk away, but I ran after her. "She told you?"

"Oh, yes. She spoke quite freely about him." Abigail gave me a small, wicked smile.

Oh, she knew full well my tendency toward envy! Abigail had achieved in one hour what I had failed to accomplish in a week's time.

"Who is it?"

"You must ask her yourself. She will tell you now, I am certain."

"But how did you wrest it from her?"

"I needed not *wrest* anything," she objected. "To gain a confidence, one must simply give one."

She left me to ponder that simple equation, and I went inside to warm myself and to discover who had fathered little John.

31

WE HAD WAITED UNTIL THAT WEEK TO make a true fire, scraping by with bits of coal and ash. But it had grown so chill that I feared for mother and child. It was now cozy within; at what cost to us later I neither knew nor fully cared. I sat myself in the kitchen with the strong intent of doing nothing for five minutes together. Watching Eliza nurse John, I wondered what confidence Abigail had shared to get her to name a man she had kept silent about for nine months or more.

When Eliza had finished nursing, she passed the besotted infant to Martha. Eliza had a devilish look on her face as she now reached into her pocket.

"What have you there?" I asked her.

"It's a gift. I waited to see if I liked you well enough to give it to you."

"And?"

"And it seems I do, for it is yours."

She handed me the small object. It was smooth and round. I opened my fingers and looked down. It was the portrait of Jeb.

"Oh, Eliza."

"It is yours, Lizzie. It always has been. My mother—but let's not even discuss it."

"No, let us not. Martha, look! Come look at my Jeb!"

Martha came by and peered over my shoulder at the portrait. Being nearsighted, she grabbed my hand and pushed it to her nose. I felt such emotion being able to show a likeness of my husband to Martha. Oh, Lord forgive me, the *pride* I felt! I had been so long without a man's company and had so envied Martha that to claim this handsome lad as mine, once—

"He is handsome indeed, Lizzie. I see now how very poor a replacement I am."

"Nonsense," I said, my moment of pride instantly vanishing. "Where shall I put it? Oh, in my chamber, of course." I raced upstairs to safely store my treasure.

I had forgiven Eliza upon the birth of her son and can date the growth of my affection from her apology. But the gift of the portrait began our true friendship. We held hands, laughed, and passed Johnny around. Some time later that afternoon, Eliza told us all about her man—as dead to her, she believed, as Jeb was to me.

His name was John Watkins. He was a slave owned by her uncle Robert Chase, a wealthy merchant in Portsmouth, New Hampshire, to whom they had fled at the start of the Troubles. Apparently, this uncle had twice refused Watkins's appeal for freedom, although, by this time, many other slaveholders in Portsmouth had liberated their slaves, or allowed them to purchase their freedom.

Robert Chase, however, made good money off of Watkins, who worked as a shipwright building our warships for a man named Colonel John Langdon. Mr. Chase had no motive to liberate Watkins.

"Does he know of his son?" I asked.

"Oh, yes. We are able to write letters through—others."

Eliza further told me that Watkins's own father was the former royal governor Benning Wentworth, uncle of the governor who fled Portsmouth in 1775.

"He's uncommonly handsome," Eliza shared, blushing. "He has light-brown skin, blue-green eyes, and wavy, dark-brown hair. But it is his character that continues to move me."

I had thought Eliza a spoiled, resentful creature. But, hearing her stories, I began to wonder whether I had been somewhat mistaken. Eliza went on to tell us of the ships Watkins had built for a war he himself was not allowed to fight. And she told us of the boar he had caught for them, only to be whipped in the square for his efforts.

"Yes," Eliza concluded sadly. "I know God loves us all, but I believe John to be a favorite son."

Favorite son? Were Watkins such a favorite of God, why did God see fit to perpetrate his misery? Why did he remain a slave? I listened to Eliza's description of John Watkins with growing rage.

"But surely something can be done?" I inquired.

"Lizzie, you are such an idealist, despite all that has happened to you. I have no such illusion."

"I shall think upon it when I am not so distracted by—by other events."

Eliza smiled at this. "Think upon it all you like," she said. "If you could let my parents know I have survived, it would be gift enough. To me, if not to them."

Indeed, I had heard nothing in reply to the message I had sent to her mother the previous week, that her daughter had been delivered of a healthy boy. If it had been my own dear mother, I knew that no illegitimate child—however green, black, or yellow—would have kept her from my side. In my heart, I condemned that mother who had not the courage to love her own daughter despite the pain or loss of status it might cause herself.

Had Mr. Boylston not been so ill, I knew he would have risen from his bed to see his daughter.

The following day, however, we received the very sad news that Mr. Boylston had departed this life.

Eliza was deeply grieved, though not shocked. "I am alone in the world now," she said. "Except for him." She nodded to the boy, who lay sleeping in his drawer, blissfully unaware of our troubles.

"It is grievous indeed you could not be with him at the end," said Martha.

Getting up as if to dress herself, Eliza replied, "I shall be with him now, however. My stays, Martha."

"Your stays? Are you joking? Surely you have no idea of going abroad?"

"I have every idea of attending my father's funeral, and you won't prevent me."

She looked at me with that imperious noblewoman stare, and I saw the old Eliza I had once vowed never to forgive.

"Well, then, go if we absolutely cannot stop you. But I beg you, don't take the child, for Boston is filled with disease and every other hazard just now."

She considered my words. "Yes, I shall leave him. Only I hope my leaving him does not interfere with your dinner with Admiral d'Estaing."

"Oh, I shall be glad to watch him while you go," Martha replied. "I have no stomach for society just now."

Martha helped Eliza with her stays and hair. We generally wore our hair in simple buns, like farm women, but that would not do for Eliza on this occasion. Suddenly, as if awakening from a dream, Eliza cried, "But I've nothing to wear!"

Martha offered that she had a mourning dress—the one she had arrived in, but Eliza doubted that it would fit her.

"I'll inquire of Ann," I said. "I'm certain she has something appropriate."

"Oh, no," Eliza replied. "I wouldn't have them know my sad business. It would mortify me."

"Trust me," I said.

An hour later, the Quincys appeared, and the moment they espied Johnny, they made quick work of us adults and fairly wrestled each other for Johnny. When they left, Eliza found a black gown upon her bed.

•　•　•

Before Eliza departed, we wrapped her well in blankets, having instructed her at length concerning what she must do to ensure her supply of milk remain intact. This regimen I made her promise to follow strictly. Were she to let nature take its course, the babe would starve upon her return. And we had made sure she had left us her milk as well . . . but perhaps such details are unsavory to my reader. I know not. A woman's milk, however, is a fact of life. And facts of life cannot, or should not, cause very great offense.

When Eliza had gone, I turned my attention to preparing for the dinner the following night. I felt growing trepidation, and it helped little that Martha reiterated how I must take great care and remain vigilant to all those present, including any unfamiliar servants. However, I could not deceive myself: Abigail was an easy target, should anyone wish to harm her.

As she gave her warning, Martha was dancing around the kitchen with a crying Johnny, who had a touch of colic and no doubt sensed his mother's absence.

I replied, "You've been abroad even less than I these two weeks, but you speak as if you have intelligence."

"I've had a letter." Martha shrugged, continuing to dance with the baby. I knew at once she meant from Thomas, and I felt a swift pang of envy. But try as I might, I could get nothing more from her, and I went to dress.

•　•　•

Dinner with Admiral d'Estaing was far from being the fretful occasion I imagined. It was, in fact, a pleasurable respite from those terrors and doubts that had plagued us that fall, an intimate affair, with just the Quincys, the Cranches, myself, and Abigail. Mrs. Quincy served only the best for the admiral and his company, though I suspect she had to let a servant go in order to pay for it. There was fresh bread and flounder and genuine tea, all things we had not eaten in months and months.

But to describe the man himself. His name alone, Charles-Henri Théodat d'Estaing, bespoke his noble lineage. The admiral was dressed in a blue silk jacket with a red vest matching his sleeves. His face was long and slender, his brow tall and fine, bespeaking intelligence mixed with forbearance. He was not very tall, but he cut a fine figure. Unlike his king, whom most suspected of mere political goals, the admiral aided us out of belief in the virtue of the Cause. To us, he was a great hero. Alas, to his own ailing country, he would be counted a traitor and beheaded a decade later.

The admiral bent gravely before me and brushed his lips against my hand.

"Madam Elizabeth Lee Boylston," said Colonel Quincy.

"The Boylston family is quite famous, is it not?" the admiral asked me.

"Indeed." I smiled. "They are among Boston's most prominent citizens. They were obliged to leave town for several years"—here he caught my drift at once—"but my husband and I did not go. My husband died at Breed's Hill."

"A great patriot, then. I am truly sorry." He bowed.

The admiral's English was correct, though heavily accented. He was curious about everything we told him of our ways and manners. I spoke to his aides as well, half a dozen delightful French officers, each one handsomer and more polite than the next, in their bright-blue uniforms and stiff white gauntlets.

After two glasses of wine, I tried out my bookish French—d'Estaing and his aides were delighted! We spoke together in his native tongue for only a few minutes, however, not wishing to cause discomfort to our friends.

It was all just as Abigail had described: we had not seen such gentlemanly behavior, or such exalted ideals, in a very long time. I had the opportunity to discuss these opinions after dinner when Mrs. Quincy led the women into a separate parlor, leaving the men to their pipes and port. "Why is there such a difference, Abigail, between these men and ours? These men positively shine from within."

"I have thought hard upon it, Lizzie, and I believe it may have to do with their relative innocence. They've not lived here, among us." Her lace-covered arm then swept toward the window, whether gesturing to Paris or Boston I could not tell. "They've not yet fought or suffered our winters or been beaten down by our reality. For them, everything is still a great idea. Oh, make no mistake," she added wistfully, "there are those among us who continue to think of the great ideas as well."

I knew then that she was speaking of her faraway husband and said, "Yes, it would seem that all *our* good men are in *France*, just as theirs are here."

We were laughing at my remark when Ann Quincy leaned toward us from across the parlor and asked, "What do you laugh about? I long to laugh." She sighed wistfully and played with a handkerchief in her lap.

"Oh, a trifle," replied Abigail.

We blushed with shame, for we had both been very malign. It was poor etiquette to break from the group under such circumstances. We ought to have spoken about the day's fashions, the newest bonnets, ways to make biscuits without wheat. But even this benign custom Abigail and I could no longer countenance. As if bonnets and gloves held the least importance when the war was at a stalemate and our citizens were being poisoned!

Though I am loath to mar the memory of this excellent evening with darker thoughts, I must be truthful and say that I watched every morsel we placed to our lips.

It is difficult to describe the terror I felt. Perhaps Abigail felt it, too, but we did not discuss it. We had to put our trust in the colonel and his servants. But that did not prevent me from allowing every beverage, every sauce, a moment on my tongue to taste for any unnatural bitterness before swallowing it. And while I never told Abigail this, I endeavored to keep her talking so that I could taste everything before she did.

Reader, I tasted no poison. But at this dinner I had my first taste of the rebel spirit within myself. It was a tincture that galvanized my soul. As I found myself tasting food for my beloved Abigail, I knew I was then prepared to stake my life for her. And not just for her, but for John, their children, and the Cause, for which the esteemed Admiral d'Estaing and his men did battle.

Unlike Abigail, who helped her husband with her marvelous words, I had no one I could influence in that way. Indeed, I had no husband and no child to whom my existence mattered. While I mattered to myself, I understood then that beyond me, things far more significant than I hung in the balance.

Manly thoughts in a manly time!

It grew late, and Abigail and I soon took our leave. I paused by the men's parlor to thank the colonel and the admiral, catching them in passionate private conversation. The aides spoke among each other, also in French. I caught the admiral's fervently whispered words to the colonel, "C'est la Rose en ville où on droit faire la reconnaissance scrupuleuse."

When the men saw us, they abruptly ceased their conversation, and an awkward silence followed.

I said, "Excuse us. We merely wish to take our leave, as it is quite late."

They all rose to bid us good-bye. Admiral d'Estaing bowed, brushed his lips across my hand, and said, "It has been a great pleasure."

His blue eyes searched mine, or so I imagined. He then turned to Abigail, bowed, kissed her hand, and said, "I hope to have the pleasure of seeing you again. If you write to your husband, please give him my very best wishes."

Abigail curtsied, and we exited the house somewhat tipsily. The admiral's phrase had meant nothing to any of the others. Indeed, Abigail had heard it not. I, however, had not only heard, but knew its meaning.

In her carriage, Abigail regarded her hand and announced, "I shall never wash this hand again." Then she giggled like a schoolgirl and departed.

I had laughed with her, but as I walked through the dunes my soul was on fire. For, hearing the admiral's words, I had finally determined upon a course of action.

32

I SLEPT VERY ILL THAT NIGHT. IN the morning, Martha complained that my tossing and turning had kept her awake. She then proceeded to torment me until I confessed to her what I had heard. I translated the words for her. Though she had learned some French from a nanny, she had retained almost none of it.

Alone, *C'est la Rose* meant nothing. However, there was a well-known tavern, the Rose and Crown, on Rowe's Wharf, which even I knew to be a Loyalist meeting place. It was this tavern that Admiral d'Estaing, intimate friend of George Washington, suggested needed "scrupulous watching."

What I had resolved during that sleepless night was to return to my house in Cambridge and take up residence at this same Rose and Crown tavern. Not as a woman, naturally—for such a creature would instantly be suspected as either a spy or a whore—but as a messenger boy. The freedom I felt astride Star, and my earlier, unbidden wish that I could don a disguise and rise free and unobserved, now seemed destined for this one purpose.

It may be difficult to fathom how a young, well-bred woman such as I became a spy. But one need only remember how desperate we women were. We wished to be of some use. When there was little to grow and even less to buy, what we were left with were our wits. As for myself, so little did I feel like a woman in those days that I could have spoken as Hamlet did: "What have I to fear? I do not set my life at a pin's fee!"

Martha was dead set against it. I would be gone too long and too frequently, and she would be kept in a state of constant anxiety. "You know not what you do!" She turned to me angrily.

"We're none of us born heroes," I replied. "Our heroism or ignominy must come from the choices we make. You yourself have argued that, in certain times, the ends justify the means."

"Yes, but I had no idea of you going so far beyond the bounds of—"

"Propriety? Indeed. However, recall that it is only a mask, as many of us apparently see fit to wear these days. Beneath the board you place upon my breast, beneath my trousers, I assure you I am as much a woman as I ever was."

"You're incorrigible is what you are." She turned away, upset and no doubt afraid for me.

I moved to face her. "A fork in the road has presented itself to me, Martha. I have no one to support, no children or husband. Oh—don't object. I say this not to gain your pity, or to pity myself, but because I'm in the right. I know I am, and so do you. I'm resolved."

I continued. "Luckily, we have finished the heaviest of chores, so I hope to burden you but little with my absence."

We had already dried and milled our scant corn, pressed our cider, carded our tow, and killed a young hog, which had been given us for the birth of twins. We saltpetered it and hung its parts to dry.

Martha looked at me gravely. "If you are resolved, then there is nothing I can do," she said. "But know that if you fail in your disguise, it will prove fatal to you and perhaps to others as well."

Her argument sent chills through my body, but I merely nodded.

Martha had nothing more to say. She ignored me the rest of the day, took her supper alone, and retired to the second chamber, without giving me her usual embrace.

"What is all the fuss I heard?" Eliza asked upon my descent into the parlor, where she sat giving little Johnny to suck. She had been oddly subdued since her return from her father's funeral the previous evening. "Have you had words with Martha?"

"Oh, it is nothing," I said, not very convincingly.

I knew she did not believe me, but she continued to nurse her babe contentedly.

•   •   •

History would not write about me, nor judge me as it would my friend Abigail. But each man or woman must judge himself on this earth, and, like Abigail, I wished not to look back years hence and find myself lacking.

In general, I was not a good sleeper. But the night before my first foray as "Johnny Tucker," I had a great deal of difficulty. I had not the warmth of another soul beside me, and in the absence of the noise and clutter of the day, my thoughts swooped down upon me like dark, noisy vultures, creating a cacophony of regret and reproach. On this night, I was afraid of discovery and of discovering equally. I was afraid for Abigail and for Martha. And yet, how quickly heroism can seem like self-importance! I, like Sancho Panza upon his donkey! The vultures cried until dawn broke and at last I was able to rise.

It was frightfully cold that morning. The sky was dark. Steel-gray ocean waves crashed pitilessly upon the shore; my breath enshrouded me.

I dressed slowly and carefully, finding the buttons of Jeb's breeches difficult to fasten; a slight trace of his smell in his shirt made me catch my breath and doubt my mission, but only momentarily.

I finally descended the stairs when, halfway down them, I bumped into Eliza. Seeing me, she shrieked, "Help! Someone, help!"

"Shh!" I grasped her arm. "It is I, Lizzie!"

"Lizzie? What on earth are you about?"

I descended the stairs and Eliza followed me into the kitchen.

Martha, who was already within, replied, "She goes to get her neck broken by the enemy." Martha had just set three porridge bowls down on the table. She now picked something up and came toward me with a hairy black thing.

"What do you have there?" I asked warily, stepping back.

"It is a mustache."

"A mustache? Whose?"

I suddenly had the impish image of Martha, Queen Mab–like, removing a mustache from someone's face in the night. Knowing Martha as I did, it would not have been entirely out of the question.

"Yours," she said gravely. "For if you're to do something, you must do it correctly. Not like that farce that had Mrs. Adams recognizing you from across a crowd."

"Oh, Martha." I went quickly to embrace her. "You don't hate me."

"Not entirely," she said, her coldness finally wearing thin.

And what of Eliza? Did she remain in the dark? Our home was small. Secrets were a luxury that could be kept about as long as toast with jam.

"Would you kindly tell me what is going on?" she asked.

Martha and I exchanged glances.

"Eliza, sit yourself down a moment and I shall tell you," I said.

We then recounted the horrifying story of the murders. While Eliza listened, Martha endeavored to attach the mustache to my upper lip. I finally bade her leave off until I had finished my story.

I was loath to tell Eliza the truth for many reasons. Mainly I still believed her to be indifferent to the Cause and loyal to her family, her upbringing, and all she'd known.

As I spoke, Eliza took up the activity before her: powdering my medicinal herbs, which we had set to dry weeks earlier. She did so carefully and methodically, using a clean surface. I had taught her to be scrupulous around my medicines.

First I told her about Dr. Flynt and Mr. Thayer and something of their characters—one as affable as the other was taciturn. I told her of their dilated eyes and blue lips, and that all of us who knew of the deaths presumed a plot to unhinge the Cause. I told her about Mr. Cleverly, who'd saved our crops and nearly proposed marriage to me, but who had fled the scene after Mr. Thayer's death. Finally, I told her what I went to do that day: become a Rebel spy.

I waited for her reaction, my heart beating in my throat and my eyes close to tears for fear of reprobation.

But Eliza merely looked up from her work, sighed, and said, "How I admire you, Lizzie, you cannot know." She smiled sweetly, yet forlornly, too.

"Then you do not wish to leave?"

"Not at all. Why would I? I'm happy here."

"So you approve my course of action?"

She smiled again without looking up from her work.

"It's not for me to approve. History and God alone will know whether you're in the right. But to follow your conscience: that is your great gift. Yes, the courage to follow your conscience . . ."

"Will you help me, then?"

Eliza sighed. "I feel so weak, Lizzie. So useless. In my life I had everything. All the comforts and luxuries, society, and admiration. But freedom to exercise my will, my *conscience*, I never had. I hardly know what freedom is. But I am willing to learn."

My heart reached out to her then. "Oh, Eliza, you're a *brave* girl!" I embraced her, tears in my eyes, for I could feel her suffering.

She smiled. "Hardly. But I have borne it, haven't I?" She looked at me inquiringly.

"You have borne it like a soldier," I said. "Your brother would be proud."

Finally Martha interceded with an impatient air. "Enough chat. We must continue Lizzie's transformation if she's to have any chance of fooling even the most foolish of men."

Eliza did indeed blanch at the notion of my becoming a man. That was a frontier that nothing in her breeding or sensibility would allow her to cross. She could accept treachery, war, even death. But riding astride a horse in breeches with a musket across my back, my breasts tied flat with board and cloth? Oh, no, *that* she objected to most strenuously.

Her refusal on this, the easiest point of necessity, had Martha and me laughing and near prostrate on the floor. Unlike Eliza, whose womanhood was in full effulgence, ours slept within us, hibernating like bears. What was it to me to bind my breasts? I hardly knew what they were *for*, except upon other women's bodies.

•   •   •

After we had washed our cups and dishes, I went about creating a parcel. Little Johnny Tucker, messenger boy from Weymouth, would need one. I found a scrap of paper and twine and wrapped an old box with it. I then wrote a direction very ill upon its front. Thus, the address was visible, but not the name. I could say I received this parcel from someone in town, but the name had become smudged in transit. The parcel was for someone thought to be passing through Rowe's Wharf.

At long last, I was ready to set off astride Star. Thaxter had given him a good, long grooming, and I had told Martha to go out to retrieve the animal on some pretext so that the man would not wonder at my strange person.

Martha brought him up to the front door. His dark chestnut coat fairly shone in the wintery sun, which was already high in the sky when I mounted him. It was only slightly unsettling that he whinnied immediately upon seeing me, unfooled by my disguise, and I fervently hoped that man had not half the wits in these matters as a Narragansett pacer.

At the last moment, Martha came running out with a blanket. "Here. You will be cold."

"No, I need it not. It is but extra weight, and too womanly, besides, to place it upon my lap."

Martha turned to move inside, but something about Star caught her attention.

"He is too good," she said.

"Star?" I looked at the noble beast and realized the truth of Martha's words. He was something an officer might ride upon, not an errand boy. "Martha, what do you suggest?" I felt my plan about to unravel.

But Martha considered the problem for a moment and said, "Alight from him before you arrive at the wharf. When you give him to the stable hand, say it is your master's."

"That is good; that will do," I said, relieved. Martha eyed me once more as I used a stool to mount my horse. She then moved back inside. Heading down the road, I looked back at my beloved cottage one final time. I felt a clutch in my breast as I saw my friends wave at me from the parlor window. Soon their warm breath obliterated them to my eyes.

We took the path to the road. It was slick with ice and, unprepared, Star skidded, nearly sending me flying over his withers. I slowed our pace. The fields of grain to either side of the road were now utterly desolate, covered with a light dusting of snow. There was no bird in the sky, no sound whatsoever save the eerie scrape of frozen leaves in the wind and the distant, lonely clink of the blacksmith at his lap stone.

I was cold almost at once and regretted not accepting the extra blanket Martha had begged me to take. Within my house, I had felt the cold but not the wind. I frowned at the thought that one's imagination is never strong enough to plan as well as one ought. I felt the wind keenly now and urged Star to a trot. He sensed my excitement and advanced swiftly. I had to hold him back to keep him from breaking into a canter across the hill, for, with the unpredictable patches of ice, we surely would fall and break our necks. We settled on a trot through Milton, which kept the blood flowing in my poor limbs.

By the time I reached Roxbury and Boston Neck, my feet were numb. But I thought it prudent not to stop until I reached the wharf. I kept feeling for the false little mustache about my lip to ensure it was there. The board, shifting upon my chest as I trotted, dug into my clavicle, no doubt forming a welt there.

I arrived at Rowe's Wharf and descended immediately. Leading Star by his harness, I followed my nose to the smoke and fermented-apple smell of the tavern. I hitched Star, who was frothing at the mouth and in dire need of water, to the post outside the tavern. A boy—looking much as I must have done—rushed to care for the horse in fullest expectation of a penny or two for his troubles.

Money! The sudden, terrible truth struck me then: I had forgotten all about money, and so had Martha. It had been so long since we had used—or seen—any that it had simply slipped our minds. I stuck my hands in Jeb's breeches, finding a penny for the stable boy's troubles, but no more.

The thought of turning back brought tears to my eyes. No, no. That was too much to bear! I could not. I was numb with cold, tired, and hungry. I had to stop, come what may. I would think of something.

Luckily, the tavern was crowded, and I easily blended in. Though it was still relatively early, many men had already gathered there. I thought it possible that some had never left from the previous night. These specimens swayed to and fro in their seats as if on a ship in rough waters.

As I walked in, I kept my gaze down. My cap hid my face, but I was able to survey the scene once my eyes had adjusted to the dark. In one corner, by a round table, four men smoked and played cards. Near the back, by the barrels of rum, stood a few rough sailors and fishermen. A deep cloud from pipes hung chokingly in the air, and altogether I received the shocking impression that this tavern was quite a low place. It was like nothing I had pictured in my mind. Here there were no gentlefolk. I heard no tinkle of feminine laughter. No, there were only men, and rough ones.

The owner, one Mr. Smythe, a balding man of about forty, was rushing to satisfy his many customers. When he caught me in his shrewd gaze, he knew at once I was a stranger. I looked about me as if for a place to sit, tired of my long journey. I remembered my story: Johnny Tucker from Weymouth (who *wasn't* named Tucker from Weymouth?) with a package for someone not from this town, whose name had unfortunately become obscured.

As the hurried little man finally saw fit to approach, having delivered his other orders, I panicked and thought, *Sit you down and order a drink, nothing more.* I thus held my tongue and kept my eyes down when he nodded in the direction of a free table. It stood in a far corner, beneath a beaded Indian cloak that hung upon the wall. It must have held some particular significance for the owner, but I thought it prudent not to ask.

"Punch, please," I said huskily, still not knowing how I was to pay for the drink.

He nodded again and went off. I exulted in my ruse's success thus far, tempered only by the sinking feeling that my journey had been a waste of time and effort. Any notion I might have cherished of coming upon a group of whispering Tories, full of intrigue and intelligence, had already been sadly disappointed. But I was there and in need of refreshment, so I was obliged to go through with the charade. Mr. Smythe returned with my punch and announced, "That'll be two pence, please."

I foraged in my sack, knowing the search to be useless. My only consolation as I did so was that I must've presented a convincing portrait of an idiot.

Mr. Smythe then did something unexpected: he smiled, twisted his mouth in pity, and announced, "That's all right. It's on me. First time visitor, like."

"Oh, I'm much obliged," I mumbled somewhat too politely. "I can pay you on my next stop here, for I left Weymouth in haste, I'm afraid. But I am good for it."

Mr. Smythe nodded. "Oh, that's all right. Do a good turn, it comes back to you, like. Or that's what they tell us in meetin', right?" He winked at me as he turned to answer another customer who was calling to him.

"Hang on there, fella!" he called back.

I was touched and surprised by Mr. Smythe's kindness, whatever his political views might have been.

His behavior served to remind me, once again, how very unclear right could sometimes be from wrong.

"And you are—?" he inquired, extending his rough callused hand.

"Tucker, sir." I was going to proceed with a Christian name, but he seemed satisfied with that, so I offered none.

"Well, Tucker, what's your business here, if you don't mind me asking? I've not seen you before, have I?"

"No, sir," I replied, abashed. "I'm afraid I've made a bungle of things. I've been sent with a package for a man what's supposed to be at Rowe's Wharf. But look at the direction. The ink's all blurred . . ."

I took my dirty parcel from the bag and thrust it at him, suddenly aware of my small hands. Mr. Smythe didn't seem to notice them. He took the parcel and turned it over.

"You've abused this parcel very ill, lad," he said, and I hung my head as if in shame. Then, Lord forgive me, the spirit of invention o'ertook me:

"It's my first assignment, sir. I thought to help the family, what." I stifled a smile of self-approbation. I'd improvised quite nicely!

But Smythe said, "Only take care so's folks'll hire you. It won't do to leave directions to get washed off in the snow."

Now, having soundly scolded me like a disappointed father would his own son, Mr. Smythe took up the package once more and asked, "You said you'd be wanting a stranger, like?"

"Yes, sir."

"Well, there be but one stranger arrived this week, far as I know."

"One man, you say?" I replied, certain I had already made great strides for the Cause.

"Indeed. And it's your luck he's sittin' right over there."

Mr. Smythe turned and pointed to a far, smoky corner of the tavern. I squinted and inhaled, and then all my limbs froze. There in the corner, nearly obscured by the smoke that rose above his head, sat Mr. Cleverly.

33

HE MUST HAVE FELT OUR STARES, FOR he lifted his head and stared straight back at us. His eyes soon focused on me, and I detected both suspicion and hostility. Unlike everyone else in the tavern—rough wharf men, for the most part—Mr. Cleverly was dressed the part of the upper-class Tory I had envisioned when Admiral d'Estaing had first mentioned this tavern. He wore a pale-blue silk costume and powdered wig. He had been speaking to a man across the table from himself. The question was: What on earth was he doing here? I had—we all had—thought him long since gone from our midst.

"That's Mr. Cleverly of New Hampshire. He would be the man of your parcel."

"Mr. Cleverly?" I repeated.

Hearing his name across the room, Mr. Cleverly stood. "Oh, no! That is not my man," I said quickly. I panicked to think of handing my parcel—a box of cornhusks, as it happened—to Mr. Cleverly.

Oh, this would never do! Another step closer, and he would surely recognize me. I unconsciously put a hand up to feel the soft strip of fur that Martha had secured above my lip. Thank goodness it was still there.

I continued, "No, my man's name began with a—with a *W*."

"A *W*, did you say? There's no man here, no stranger, by the name of *W* that I know of."

"Oh, no. I have mistaken the wharf entirely." I slapped my head, stepping backward. "It is Long Wharf I seek, not Rowe's."

As I rushed away, Mr. Smythe rolled his eyes and smirked. Clearly he thought me the stupidest lad he'd ever seen.

"You'd best stick to a laboring job, Tucker," he called after me helpfully. "In the barn, with the animals, like!"

I felt a deep shame that I'd duped this kind man. I unhitched Star and, once beyond the wharf, set off with great celerity for the safety of home.

●　　●　　●

"Mr. Cleverly?" Martha asked as she faced me by the fire, slowly picking my mustache off my face. I winced in pain, for the glue had penetrated my skin and threatened to pull it clear off. "What's that ass still doing in town? I thought he'd long since evaporated."

"Apparently not. And you should have seen him in all his pompous finery. He wore a silk costume!"

"Silk?"

"Yes, and a powdered wig!"

"In a tavern such as that?" Martha sounded incredulous.

"You've been there?" I asked, surprised.

"Oh, no. Well, in passing. It is quite near my brother's lodgings."

"I had not the time to finish my drink," I said sadly, as I had been looking forward to enjoying my first rum punch. Jeb had often enjoyed this drink.

"A good thing, too, or you might have frozen in a ditch in the road."

Having finally succeeded in removing my whiskers, Martha asked, "What now?"

"Well, I suppose I must ask Richard whether he knows Cleverly is still about, and to what purpose. Could he be on the trail of our criminals?"

"It is not my job to concern myself with such things," Martha said pointedly.

"Oh?" I queried, somewhat offended by her disinterest. "And what is your 'job,' as you call it?"

"To see that you don't get up to too much foolishness. Come, I'll boil you a bath. You smell."

I grinned maliciously, pressing my odiferous body toward her as she fled in the other direction, holding her nose.

•   •   •

Two days later, I left for Cambridge once more, this time having been kindly loaned a small chaise and coachman by Colonel Quincy. I insisted upon taking Star, however, and so the coachman hitched him and a pretty little mare of the colonel's to a double harness. Before leaving, I heard from this same coachman that the Cranches had gone to town. I was delighted to hear it, as I would thus be able to discuss the presence of Mr. Cleverly with them later in the week.

Poor Star! He was unaccustomed to being used in such a manner. Pulling a chaise was neither fish nor fowl: he had neither the freedom to move as he chose, nor the welcome human weight upon his back. Indeed, he disliked his new job intensely and kept curling his head around to chew on the pesky harness.

By the time I arrived at my house in Cambridge, Star was frothed at the mouth and I was frozen solid, much colder than I would have been had I simply ridden on Star. I vowed never to put horse or rider through such torment again.

Bessie greeted me with a cry of alarm and brought me into the parlor to thaw. The coachman, bidding me a good stay, took himself off to a nearby tavern. Once in the parlor, I discerned a more hopeful aspect to the old manse, though I knew not whence it came—there was no more furniture than previously, nor art, nor Turkey carpets. But apparently Bessie and Giles had been cleaning and maintaining the house in the hopes that it would be used again someday.

Soon I understood that this hopeful spirit came from Bessie herself. She had been unable to suppress a guilty smile, and no sooner had I sat down and asked for a dish of tea than Bessie said, "A letter come for you yesterday, miss. As I knew to expect you, I thought I'd best not forward it."

"You did well, Bessie," I said. "From whom is the letter?"

But she had already left the room to fetch it, leaving a half-eaten corn cake. She soon returned with the letter for my perusal. Its seal was broken; it had clearly been opened.

"Bessie. This letter has been opened, yet it is addressed to me."

Bessie looked down. "Forgive me, miss! I couldn'a help it! I had to know—I just had to!"

I began to scold her, until I saw what had brought Bessie to such a pitch. Could I forget my own dear brother's hand?

Dearest Lizzie,

If you are reading this, it is because at long last a Letter has succeeded in getting through to you. Truth be told, I have not had many Opportunities to write, being not only much engaged but cautioned to conceal our Whereabouts.

I have received three of your Letters, the last being dated this May past. Suffice to say I was exceeding glad to know you are well. Though it is near four Years since he gave his Life, your dear Jeb is never far from my Thoughts. I have taken special care to stay above the Earth myself, knowing I am your last Relation upon it. If I could speak of the Things I have seen . . .

But never mind. For now, I have but one true message, which is that I am very like to see Boston this year. I cannot say when. Rest easy, dearest Lizzie, that my first act upon dry land will be to fly to you, my most beloved sister . . .

By the time I had finished reading, tears ran down my face and bodice. Bessie fetched a cloth for me so I would not drown in them.

Mine were tears of joy, but joy that is not without pain, like a sleeping limb that tingles to life. Harry was alive, and I would, God willing, see him that very year! I cried and cried, till Bessie said I must leave off crying or make myself sick.

The idea that Harry was alive nearly made me abandon my resolve. Thrice that week I attempted to return to the tavern, and thrice was I obliged to turn around in fear. There had been a kind of freedom in the belief that I would not be greatly missed were the worst to befall me.

This would not do! On the day of my fourth attempt, I arose and sought help from those close to me.

"I can keep my secret from you no longer," I announced to Giles and Bessie that evening. "You must either help or denounce me."

"Denounce you, miss?" asked Bessie, confused.

I looked up at my two servants and nearly laughed. So unaccustomed was Giles to being asked his advice that his face assumed the gravest air imaginable, as if the weight of the world were now upon him.

I quickly told them my plan. Bessie fell to shrieking, saying I'd get myself killed in no time flat. Giles was silent and left the room. I thought he considered me a lunatic beyond redemption, but he returned in a few moments carrying a filthy leather vest.

Let me not mince words: it stank.

"What do you propose I do with this?" I asked him.

"If I may, ma'am."

"Make free to tell me and be quick about it, Giles!"

"Ma'am, if you are to convince anyone of your new identity, you must—pardon me, it is indelicate—you must smell a little worse."

I looked at Giles in astonishment. My smell was something I had not once considered. I practiced good hygiene as unconsciously as I breathed the air. But of course he was entirely correct. A messenger boy would not adhere to my standards of cleanliness.

Then I did something that no doubt made Giles blush, had his skin not been too dark to show it: I kissed him on the cheek.

"Thank you for your invaluable contribution to the Cause, Giles."

Giles shuffled out, one leathery hand pressed to the spot where I had kissed him.

I had been given my servants' "slow leave" at last. But, around noon the following day, after I had set off, it was my own trepidation that had me nearly turning back several times.

What's more, the weather made for treacherous traveling. I had not gone half an hour on Star before I felt I could go no farther. My feet were icy, my lungs ready to explode. My hands became vices about the reins. With difficulty, I pushed my shawl across my mouth to keep the air from singeing my lungs. The ties about my breast felt like the straps of an iron maiden, but I continued apace until the latter part of the afternoon, when I finally arrived at the Rose and Crown.

Before entering, I looked briefly around at my whereabouts, though I dared not remain long out of doors. Even with the frigid air, the wharf stank of manure and urine, rotting fish, and unwashed men.

I dismounted and asked the stable boy to oat my horse. I kept my eyes down and mumbled my order. The boy nodded, and I went in. This time, I had remembered to bring some coins, which

I had had to borrow of Eliza. Looking about me, I was relieved to find no sign of Cleverly. There was no sign of Mr. Smythe, either.

The sweet smell of tobacco filled the air. Soon a practiced young server came by to hear my order. Hot rum punch was my request. I hoped that I would not become so drunk as to fall off my horse and be found frozen in the gutter. But drink I must. Drink, and keep my eyes and ears open.

The server returned with my rum and asked me was there anything else I required. He said they had a ham just out of the roaster. I told him I'd have a ration of that with some buttered bread, for eating might help my head from growing dizzy.

The ham came on a wooden trencher. It was a thick, large slab, smoky and delicious. A chunk of real bread accompanied it. The sight and smell of it nearly made me swoon. Gradually, as I satisfied my hunger and thirst, my ears opened to the conversation around me. Some men playing at cards were speaking about Washington's latest defeat. At a table to my right, four men were discussing their recent distemper inoculations, sharing in disgusting detail the happy eruptions upon their various relations or themselves.

At one point, I got up to warm myself by the massive fire burning in the tavern's great room. At the fire, I picked up one interesting conversation about the current whereabouts of Mr. Stephen Holland, the traitor behind the counterfeit money plot, who had thus far eluded capture. Some men were saying in hushed tones, "They say he stopped right here!"

"No."

"Indeed. They say he's been spotted out at Isaac Jones's place."

"Go on!"

My ears perked up. Jones's place was a notorious Tory gathering place in Weston.

I had begun thinking once more about that five-pound note Abigail was obliged to burn when I felt a pair of eyes staring at me from across the room.

I bent my head and shuffled back to my seat. When I thought it was safe to do so, I turned my eyes up in the direction of the stranger, who continued to stare directly at me.

It was Thomas Miller.

He was at a table with several other gentlemen, and, after a brief moment, he ceased to look at me. I sighed with relief. He went back to his conversation and paid me no heed. They all spoke earnestly, quietly. Indeed, their subdued behavior made them stand out. The men accompanying Mr. Miller seemed a cut above the tavern's coarse clientele, though they were not dressed formally. I ordered another rum punch. But, Reader, my heart pounded so in my chest, and my hands shook so violently I could hardly drink it!

Was it fear of discovery that had me shaking? I would be less than honest if I said this were my sole concern. I had little fear of this. My disguise was excellent: my own mother would not have known me. My emotions then can be summed up in one word: *longing.* Oh, to unmask myself and throw my poor benumbed body into the arms of a tender protector! I knew this to be the fantasy of a love-starved widow. And yet, oh, if only I could forget about my mission and the war and the necessary taking of sides! Were we not all Colonials? Were our parents not all friends, even relations? Which part of my warring self was I to trust—head or heart? Surely both could not be right.

Thomas Miller had gone back to his conversation, and I drank a third rum. Head and heart were both on fire half an hour later when I paid my bill, donned my cap and coat, and endeavored to walk a straight line out the tavern door toward my horse.

I never drank strong drink. I disliked the dizziness it produced, just as I disliked the rocking of a boat. Now, with three drinks in my burning belly, I found myself quite drunk.

The wharf was dark save for the firelight that spun about me as I mounted Star. Firelight from homes and other establishments swirled together, creating flitting butterflies of light in the blackness above. The white smoke of my own breath and this swirling light spun about me as I set off for Cambridge. Luckily, Star's footing was much firmer than my own.

I was oddly exultant, heedless of my own perilous swaying. The world spun about me, and twice I nearly slid off Star's back. My stomach burned from the drink, and I felt not the cold in my extremities. I shook my limbs as I rode and was much occupied with this task when I heard a horse's hooves galloping toward me from the rear. Suddenly hands were upon my reins, startling Star and myself equally.

"Lizzie, stop!" a hushed, intense voice whispered. Hands stopped my horse and pulled me off into a side street. Had I not heard my own name, I would have thought I was done for. Roadway robbers and worse were quite common at this lawless time.

"Oh, Lizzie, are you *mad*? Raving, raving mad?"

I felt a hand grope blindly across my head, and my cap fell to the ground, pulling the bit of string from my plait as well. My hair fell about my shoulders. I knew the voice, knew the hands that grasped both sides of my head in the dark and pulled me into an embrace far more filled with terror than desire.

34

NOWADAYS IT IS COMMON TO EXAGGERATE THE virtue of our "women of the revolution," of which I was one. Each year broadsides marking the anniversary of our victory, replete with caricatured renderings, make us out to have been stone statues of righteousness.

But I am here to say that it was not the case. We were flesh and blood. We suffered great loneliness and loss. We felt the spectrum of contradictory desires, intensified by starvation of body and spirit. We felt drawn to unsuitable men. The temptations of improper conduct warred with parental whispers and exhortations. But it was not merely our virtue at stake. It was our place in history. We did not work for such a place, but we were uplifted by the notion. We hoped our stories would not go entirely unnoticed.

But I have left my poor reader at a critical moment: myself, drunk, in an alleyway with Mr. Miller! My eyes closed as Thomas leaned in to kiss me. I was still wearing Martha's mustache and Giles's smelly jacket. At the touch of his lips on mine, I felt all my hours and years of strength dissolve. I felt my coldness and loneliness begin to burn, my womanhood begin to escape from my costumed manhood like a genie released from a bottle.

Thomas pulled away, looked at me, and laughed sheepishly at having kissed what any passerby would have believed to be a boy.

"You are very convincing in your repulsiveness," he said. "And you are also dangerously drunk." Then he muttered to himself, "My fear for you shall be my undoing." Addressing me once more, he said, "Promise me you will not entertain such a foolhardy pursuit again."

"I cannot promise that," I said defiantly, yet slurring the *s* in the word *promise*.

"Truly, Lizzie. You must cease this foolhardiness." He pulled Star deeper into the alleyway, his voice hushed but intense.

"Why must I, if I find out the truth? Already I have heard such things as lead me to suppose . . ."

"Lizzie, by God. Will you not listen to reason? It is dangerous. There are those among us who wish you ill."

"Me?" I laughed. "Why would anyone care about me? I am of no importance."

"You are among a handful who know those men were killed. Do you think that such men as are willing to assassinate John Adams or Abigail and her children would have any compunction about ridding the world of a snooping midwife?"

"Assassinate John or Abigail?" Then my worst conjecture was true. "How come you to know these things?"

Thomas was silent. I stared at him, fury growing out of me at the thought of harm coming to Abigail. Star must have sensed my tension, for he lurched forward toward the road. Mr. Miller hung on to my cape.

"You must be close to these scoundrels. Indeed, you must—I *loathe* you," I said, wresting myself from his grip. "Leave me be. You cannot stop me."

"Lizzie, don't!" He reached out in the darkness, getting my cape, but no more.

"Leave me be," I said again, weeping now, for what I wanted and needed I could never have. Tears of confusion and self-pity flooded my eyes. But it was with renewed commitment that I rode off toward Cambridge, leaving Mr. Miller alone in the alleyway with my cape for consolation.

•   •   •

The following morning, I woke with a massive headache. I lay in bed most of the day with the curtains drawn. Bessie buzzed about me like a wasp, condemning my behavior of the previous evening.

"Bessie, please. This hardly helps."

"I dare say it doesn't." She removed a cloth from my head and slapped a cool one on to replace it.

"Ow!" I cried, putting a hand to my head.

Bessie would not let me leave the house for the next several days, and in truth I had not the energy to do so. What's more, I feared another encounter with Mr. Miller.

Did I think of him as I lay in bed? Did I recall that kiss over and over in my mind? Though mortified, did I believe myself to be in love with him?

I knew it as the most hopeless fact of my existence. Worse, I could not blame it entirely on the drink. Should Mr. Miller have approached me stone sober, I might have behaved just the same. He was not a handsome man, as Cleverly was. His bearing was dignified, but his person was rather unkempt. What, then, had undone me? In two words: his eyes. Not their color, which was beautiful, nor their clarity, nor their occasional warmth, nor even their mocking intelligence. No, it was the way they looked at me. It was as if his eyes saw me as I was. They saw everything true and little else, much the way Star knew me though I was in disguise. Like my beloved Star, he had an instinct for me.

But youth is resilient, and by the end of that second week in Cambridge, I had recovered sufficiently to rise from my sickbed and return to the tavern. I was surprised that Mr. Miller had not visited me, then hurt. Finally I put all thought of him aside and made my way to the tavern.

What passed by my ears in the next several days was enough to set a Rebel's hair on end. Mr. Holland and one other associate, whose name I did not glean, were most assuredly in town. They continued to plot ways to bring down our forces.

As I listened to the tavern gossip, I became confused by the fact that not one but several plots were in the works. The worst, and most fearsome, involved the deaths of our great leaders. Another involved a counterfeit money scheme. Yet a third involved a surprise attack on Boston. If I had imagined that our war took place through official channels only, I was soon disabused. My time at the tavern taught me that our enemies were everywhere. They were very close. I could only pray that so, too, were our friends.

After several days of such bombardment on my ears and dispirit of my soul, I decided to visit the Golden Ball. I would go in the comfort of a coach, dressed as a woman, if not entirely as myself. It was Bessie's idea, actually. She said there was a coach "as left at noon reg'lar" every day from the Common, returning at seven the same evening. For the Golden Ball, I would go as my former self: a Cambridge lady. Mr. Isaac Jones, the tavern's proprietor, would be alert to strangers, but I would give him no cause to question me.

"Bessie, you come with me," I said one evening after we had taken our supper in the parlor.

"What need have you for my poor body?"

"Well, I can't very well go alone, can I?"

"You go alone astride that pacer of yours in the freezin' cold and in a rough part o' town, but you wiln'a take a coach to an elegant country tavern?"

"Of course not. In the former scenario, I am a man. It won't do at all to be a woman traveling alone."

Bessie wasn't convinced.

"Well, you'll be needin' to think o' yer options then, as wild horses won't be draggin' *me* on such a journey."

She turned her back on me, then pivoted around again as poor Giles made an entrance.

"Giles!" She grinned wolfishly at him.

Bessie accompanied him toward me. Reader, I have told you previously that my old servant was quite clever. Indeed, it had not taken her five seconds before she lit upon my solution. "The missus has a plan what needs your help."

"Anything, ma'am," he said, setting the tray down and bowing.

"Giles, would you have a seat?" I asked.

Giles sat, but his legs were so long, and he was so unused to sitting that his knees danced; his hands tapped the chair legs. He then ceased all activity and sat like a marble statue, only to begin dancing again a few moments later. Bessie handed him a teacup in the hopes that holding it might still him. The teacup rattled perilously.

I explained my desire to go to Weston, to the Golden Ball tavern, and my need for a companion. He listened attentively, his grizzled head bowed. When I was done, I asked him would he accompany me the following day. He nodded.

"Am I to go as your slave, then?"

"As my slave? Heavens, no."

"It would be a most convincing guise, madam."

"You're no doubt correct, Giles. However, there is only so far I am prepared to go for the Cause. That would be too far. You shall come as my—my husband's valet. My husband had been . . . in Worcester . . ."—I thought aloud—". . . and is to meet us there. However, he does not show up, and we must return home. Only if we are asked, you understand."

"I can think of worse stories," Giles muttered.

"A ringing endorsement!"

"It's good—it'll do," encouraged Bessie, glad to be well out of it herself.

"But remember, say nothing unless asked," I cautioned.

Giles replied, "Miss, I never say anything unless asked."

"Oh! My apologies." I blushed, for I had forgotten my place, and, more importantly, his.

•   •   •

The following day, we strolled to the Common. I had donned my finest gown and cloak; Giles wore a dusty black suit and held a large hat box—filled with what, I knew not. Certainly not a hat. Still, it seemed perfectly correct to both Giles and me that, as my servant and traveling companion, he would hold a large box. God help us if he were obliged to open it!

The sky above the Common was bright blue: no cloud or breeze told of the frigid temperature. I was glad of the half-dozen passengers standing there, for they lent some warmth to the air around me. I nestled in among them. Waiting for the carriage, I observed young men walking briskly in and out of the entrance to Harvard College. The college had recently opened its halls after being occupied by our army and then by Burgoyne's troops.

The ride was very slow, uneventful, and silent. I have observed that the closer in proximity one is to others, the stronger are the walls one erects to preserve one's space. At least, that is true for those of my class. I know little of how such a ride among farmers might have been—friendlier, I suspect, if perhaps more odiferous.

For two hours, we clopped slowly down the road to Weston, during which time I read upon my book (something conveniently borrowed from my house—I cannot recall its title). Giles peered out a window, taking in the view. It was almost certain he had never been anywhere beyond Cambridge and its environs. His eyes did not turn away from the snow-sprinkled, fallow fields. The landscape became wild and unspoiled once we crossed the river in Watertown; only the smell of burning wood and the occasional plume of smoke told of the human race.

At last we arrived at the Golden Ball. It was not large but was quite handsome. The front looked much like any house on Brattle Street. To the side and rear, through wavy panes of glass, I espied beautiful rooms, all large and fine. Before me lay a quaint country scene. Society came and went, laughing and cheerful with drink, heedless of the cold, seemingly heedless of the war. "Oh, but he shouldn't have!" and "Oh, but he did!" and "Wicked man!" I heard as two ladies passed me, exiting the tavern.

Giles, of course, could accompany me no farther. He went off to a back room where the Negro servants were able to take refreshment. He had gone off with my command to "give every man thine ear but few thy voice." I had turned to explain, but Giles nodded, saying he understood my meaning.

I entered.

At once I saw a large public room hosting a blazing fire. The wide floor planks glowed with recent waxing. Such a spirit of conviviality pervaded the room that I nearly forgot my mission. I sat at a table that afforded a vision of a dusky field beyond the house. A red-tailed hawk swept across my view and disappeared. I turned to find a man I believed to be Mr. Jones awaiting my request. He was stooped and flushed in the cheeks; sweat rolled down his temples as he juggled a half-dozen orders at once.

•   •   •

Mr. Jones had been a Tory sympathizer. Three years earlier, his tavern, the Golden Ball, had been broken into and vandalized by a group of violent men disguised in face paint and masked. They had smashed bottles and windows, destroyed furniture. They turned out to be Paul Revere's men. But if Mr. Jones had any political con-victions remaining to him, I neither heard nor saw a hint of them that evening.

The smell of good food and cheer surrounded me; on the day's menu was turkey. I had another rum punch as it gradually grew dark. I spent a pleasant several hours alone with my own thoughts; I cannot tell you these thoughts now but recall a feeling of hope that suffused itself with the rum. It was in such a hopeful mood that I finally broke down and ordered the turkey, giving up my last earthly sou to do so. I nearly swooned when this turkey—moist, succulent, and smothered in gravy and potatoes—arrived. Oh, it was nearly as good as love!

I grew warm within, but alas, in those hours, learned nothing save perhaps for the fact that our few remaining Tories were sitting out the war in excellent good cheer.

Giles emerged at the same time I did with a scowl upon his face. Although it had grown dark, the moon was rising bright and round. When I asked him how he had fared, he merely said, "A coarse lot, ma'am." I could see his faint distaste and smiled, recalling that Giles had no more been among "coarse" servants than I had.

"Well, but do you have news?"

"Aye," he whispered, leaning in toward me, "but none as I dare recount here."

"Shall it wait, then, till we are safely home?"

"It's in here and shall not get out." Giles raised a finger to his gray noggin.

It was seven in the evening now, and the coach stood wait-ing. Just as we were to board, I turned back to the tavern to find someone staring at me. I squinted against the darkness: was that Mr. Miller inside the doorway, standing next to an elegant young woman? Was it he? But it could not possibly be.

I looked briefly toward the carriage. The coachman had extended his hand for me. I turned back to the tavern entrance, but the man and the woman had disappeared inside.

I was shaken by this apparition, having banished Mr. Miller from my mind—or so I thought. Now, on the slow, dark ride back to Cambridge, I recalled our embrace. Had that been a dream, too?

I must have dozed off, because Giles soon nudged me awake. I had been leaning on his shoulder, drooling slightly.

"We're nearly there, Miss Elizabeth."

"Giles, I've not been *snoring*, have I?" I whispered to him and ignored his mistaken address.

"No, miss."

"That's a relief, at any rate!"

I readied myself to descend. Once on the ground, we walked quickly home, for it was now quite, quite cold.

We ran the last three blocks from the Common, Giles barely keeping up and gripping the box against his chest. Once we were inside, heaving for breath, Bessie brought us tea and got a fire started for us. When we had thawed out, Giles finally unburdened himself of his intelligence. Bessie and I leaned in, the better to hear him.

"Well," he began, "there was a great deal of nonsense at first. But I did learn two things. The first is that our Isaac Jones is a Tory no longer. It seems he takes the better bet. He now delivers supplies to the French in New York."

"Then I was entirely mistaken," I said. I felt foolish for my ignorance. "I've wasted your time, Giles."

"No, miss, wait a moment. There was a servant by the name of Billings. This Billings, of New Hampshire, began speaking to a mate about someone named Holland. This Holland, well, he'd launched a scheme with someone by the name of Benjamin Thompson. Billings had seen both men with his own two eyes, he said. In Boston. I set the conversation to memory, Miss Elizabeth, recalling as how you mentioned Mr. Holland once."

"And what were these men up to, did he say?"

"Only as they had a plan backed by 'high money.' What means that, ma'am? 'High money'?"

"Someone of position. Someone with the means to finance such a scheme. And?" I encouraged Giles to tell all he knew.

"That's all," he said, folding his hands expressively, as if closing a book.

Bessie was unimpressed. "A day orf gadding about fer *that*?" she spat. "Why, I coulda told ya as much meself."

"Be silent, Bessie," I scolded. "*You* had not the courage to go."

I turned back to Giles. "You did excellent well, Giles. Better than I. Thanks to you, we have another name: Thompson, of New Hampshire. And we know the Golden Ball to be no threat to us. That is a step forward, I should think."

A little life came back into Giles's dejected countenance. "Thank you, ma'am. Anything for the Cause," he added.

It was late, near ten o'clock. We retired soon thereafter. I resolved to take our findings to the one person I trusted most: Richard Cranch.

As it happened, Richard and Mary were staying at a friend's house in town, having been successfully inoculated against the distemper. Mary still had some eruptions and fever when I arrived at their door, but I was able to greet Richard warmly in the parlor. It was good to see my dear friends.

"Lizzie, how the sight of you gladdens me!" Richard exclaimed.

He offered me refreshment and, when I had declined, made certain that the servants had gone and that the doors to the parlor were shut. I then told my friend about Giles's findings, and also of my having seen both Mr. Cleverly and Mr. Miller at the Rose and Crown tavern.

"Mr. Miller recognized me and pursued me into an alleyway," I added.

"Into an alleyway?" Richard asked, alarmed. "Was it a threat? Goodness, Lizzie, you take your life in your hands."

I had told too much, and yet not enough. I blushed deeply, then hastened to add, "No, no. He meant to warn me, to exhort me to take care. He said a tavern was no place for a lady."

"And with that I really must, if nothing else, agree with the man."

Richard was thoughtful as I told him about Giles's findings at the Golden Ball.

"I shall make inquiries regarding this Thompson of New Hampshire," he finally said. "I must also warn Cleverly, if I can find him. I would not have his death on my conscience. Why is the fool in Boston?" Richard muttered to himself. He then glanced at me. "But perhaps I err to mention him in your presence?"

"Not at all." I smiled. While Cleverly's regard for me had turned out to be superficial, mine for him had clearly been equally so. No, I mused with an ironic smirk, I had no feelings whatsoever for our patriot, and all the feeling in the world for his enemy!

"And Lizzie," he continued, "I won't patronize you by scolding, but if you don't value your own life, think of those who do. I hesitate to tell you, but we've had deaths in your absence."

"Deaths? Not more poisonings, surely?"

"No, no. Women—"

I caught his drift at once. "Women in travail, you mean?"

"Precisely. Women and their innocent babes. There is some woman calls herself a midwife come down from Milton to profit from your absence. Of her three deliveries, two have ended in tragedy."

My heart cramped in my chest; I could say nothing.

Suddenly, Mary appeared through a crack in the parlor door. I ran to her, and she took my hand. Hers was hot with fever.

"Lizzie, what Richard says is true. You're greatly needed. Leave revolution to the men and come home."

I embraced them both and said I would think upon it. Richard said he would return the next day to Braintree. I made my way back to Cambridge, where Bessie boiled me a hot bath and later shared her supper with me in the kitchen, by the hearth.

•   •   •

To say I was torn in my desires is to discover the weakness of words. I wished to continue at the Golden Ball. I felt certain no one there suspected my identity. I wished to see Thomas again, or at least to ascertain whether it was he I had seen in the tavern doorway. But I also longed for home—my real home, on the farm, with Martha and Eliza and Johnny.

One wish, at least, was answered. The following morning, I was awakened by the sound of a ruckus at the front door.

Bessie had let me sleep unaccountably late—it was near nine in the morning! I wrapped my dressing gown about me and padded out into the hall in my bare feet.

"But the missus ain't awake yet," I heard Bessie say.

"So wake her." This was a man's voice.

"That I wil'na do—it'll be a full hour before she'll be fit to receive anyone."

The man would not be gainsaid.

"She may greet me in her shift, for all I care!"

"Oh! Scoundrel!"

I arrived just in time, it seemed, to prevent my loyal servant from coming to blows with Mr. Miller. I stared at him and clutched my dressing gown to me. My hair was in a braid down my back.

"You look like a truant schoolgirl." He smiled.

"I am risen unusually late. I must dress—" I turned as if to retreat to my chamber.

"Oh, do not bother on my account," he said, glancing with sudden modesty at the floor.

"Not on your account, Mr. Miller. On mine."

As I went to dress, I heard Bessie say, "She'll not catch her death if I can help it. She's been gallervanting about in the cold—"

"Bessie!" I interrupted. Bessie, believing me to have gone a fair distance, nearly dropped the pitcher she was holding.

"I'm sure you're right, Bessie," said Thomas Miller. He glanced at me briefly. "I myself have come upon her mid-gallervant."

To me, he said, "Dress, then, Elizabeth. I shall keep."

"Please serve the man some tea and cakes, Bessie. I shall return."

Oh, my heart, how it pounded to see him! But what could he want? On what pretext could he be wishing an audience now? I thought surely it must be to express his remorse, to apologize for his grievous lapse of judgment in the alleyway. Yes. And it was the strange truth of our times that I would gravely accept his apology for giving me one of the greatest moments of my life.

Ten minutes later, I glided into the parlor with mincing, practiced steps. Seeing me, Mr. Miller began to laugh until tears leaked from his eyes.

"Ah," he exclaimed, still laughing but trying to stop.

"What do you find so amusing, Mr. Miller?"

I sat across from him as Bessie entered with the tea. "I—" here, as Mr. Miller looked at Bessie, something in her appearance, some grave if utterly false propriety in her manner, got him roiling again. He put his hands out before him. "Forgive me," he said. He could literally speak no more, and waited until Bessie had left, though she did not do so before casting me an alarmed look, as if to ask, *Should a doctor be called?*

"It is all right, Bessie," I assured her. "You may leave us."

"I'll be in the garden, ma'am, and Giles is in the cellar. If you need us, that is," she added.

"I shan't need you. You may go."

When Bessie was gone, I was finally able to ask, "What, pray, has prompted you to such an *éclat de rire*? Or daren't I ask?"

"Forgive me, forgive me," he pleaded, looking at me through an outstretched hand. "It's just that your walk, those little steps you took just now, struck me as . . ."

I cut him off before another attack came upon him.

"Mr. Miller," I said severely, "you've awakened me and I have not yet had my tea, though granted it is unconscionably late. Pray do not judge me into the bargain."

"Oh, I do not judge *you*," he said. "Your steps were perfect."

"What do you mean?"

"Only that you could no more convince me you are a Brattle Street lady than a dirty messenger boy."

His words mortified me. I had been born and bred on Brattle Street, and my mother would have been counted a noblewoman in her native England. She had taught me perfect manners. Indeed, I had spent much of my eleventh year with a book on my head, walking from room to room until I would forget it was there.

Of course, my anger stemmed from the fact that I knew Mr. Miller to be right. "Kindly state your purpose here at this early hour, Mr. Miller. Surely you must have had some purpose, if only in your own mind."

He saw my face and reached out to me. "I've given offense. Oh, Lizzie, I had not meant to. Indeed, I—"

I looked at his eyes, at the mouth I had kissed, now pursed in dismay.

"I meant simply to ascertain whether you had . . . recovered . . . from the tavern. I thought you might have suffered some ill effects."

So, an apology for his boldness in kissing me would not be forthcoming. And while neither the gesture nor its acceptance would have been sincere, the notion that he thought me ill-bred enough to continue on without such an apology further infuriated me.

"That was full one week ago," I said. "Six days," he contradicted.

"Why seek me out now, so belatedly?"

"I wished to come the very next day," he asserted, leaning toward me.

"And why did you not?"

"I—I did not feel myself welcome."

"And do you now? Feel yourself welcome?"

Mr. Miller grasped my hand and, lowering his voice, said, "I feel I am trapped in a game, a game I do not even wish to play," he said, far from his previous nervous laughter.

"Then do not play it." I removed my hand from his and stood.

"I fear we have no choice."

"Well, then," I said softly, knowing him to be in the right, "perhaps we should change the subject."

"Yes, let's do." Mr. Miller sat back.

"I'll begin. Tell me. Was that you the other night at the Golden Ball? I thought I saw you in the doorway."

"Me? At the Golden Ball? What would I be doing there?"

"I know not."

"You would have seen me come and go. There is but one coach per day."

"How knew you that?" My eyes flashed quickly at him.

He recovered quickly. "Everyone knows," he replied.

"You might have arrived previously," I suggested.

"Which returns me to my previous question—why?"

"To spy on me, perhaps."

"But how could I have known you were there? No, fear not, Lizzie. I have better ways to occupy my time."

Yes, we played a game. A terrible game. But neither of us could quit our playing.

"The woman you were with—she was quite beautiful. A cipher, no doubt, but my brother, Harry, once told me that men do not wish their women to be overly burdened by intelligence. Is that true, Mr. Miller?"

He considered my question and then chose to ignore it. "Did it bother you to see me—or rather someone you mistook for me—with a beautiful woman?"

"Not in the least! Why should it? I merely wondered whether congratulations were in order."

Mr. Miller observed my annoyance and pursed his lips. "But we ignore the central question."

"Which is?"

"Why *you* were at the Golden Ball."

"I cannot say. Let us change the subject once more."

"By all means."

Here, there was a long pause.

Mr. Miller sipped his tea, then looked up at me. "Tell me," he asked, "for I believe it is now my turn: Why is it you became a midwife? You had no need of such a living, surely."

I was taken aback by the question. For one, it was not seemly to discuss such a thing with a man. Then I reasoned that if Mr. Miller was not put off by the topic, I would not be.

"My dear mother was quite skilled at midwifery. She used to take me with her, and while the . . . work . . . was often onerous, the rewards were very great. Not all of us women were born for leisure, Mr. Miller. Some of us wish—indeed, *need*, from the depths of our souls—to be *useful.*"

I sipped my tea, which was now quite cold. It was a gesture not unlike my mincing steps, but Mr. Miller did not laugh at it. Instead he asked, "And should you like to have your own children someday? Or are you content to be forever helping others do so?"

There was a moment when I might have given a bitter rejoinder. I said merely, "It seems the Lord has not blessed me with that particular gift."

One look at me and Thomas Miller broke off his line of questioning.

Finally I smiled. "It seems there is little we may talk about, Mr. Miller."

"Yes," he replied. "And a great deal we must not talk about."

With that, he rose. "But you must have wished me gone from here long since. I beg your pardon. Good morning. Send Martha my love, if you speak to her." Far from love, his voice was filled with anger. He then bowed and was gone from our midst.

I stood there, stunned. Why had he come? Why had he left? Why had he been angry?

"Bessie!" I called.

Bessie came running. "Miss Elizabeth! Are you well?"

"I'm perfectly well. Mr. Miller has come and gone."

"Did 'e do somethin' unseemly?"

"Not at all. Oh!" I cried, and stormed back to my chamber.

• • •

By late morning, I was easier in my mind, for, replacing sleep with reflection, I believed that I had resolved my problem quite logically: I was not in love with Mr. Miller. The very idea was absurd. Look how ill at ease we were together, how impossible for us to speak comfortably on any given subject. Words were the medium of communication, but it was precisely with words, it seemed, that we could not communicate. How else, then? No way else.

I turned my mind in the direction of home, and had begun to pack when I was interrupted by a quick succession of raps at the front door.

I called out, but neither Giles nor Bessie replied.

"Is there a Mrs. Boylston residing here?" The boy who stood before me looked a great deal like myself in disguise: pale, young, a slight fuzz above his unshaven lip. He even wore a dirty vest.

"Yes?"

"I was told to deliver this to Mrs. Boylston."

"Well, then, you have hit the mark."

The boy thrust the message at me, tipped his cap, and rode off.

I shut the heavy door against the frigid cold, white fog following me inside. I moved toward the parlor and the warmth of the fire, where I opened the letter.

One glance had me springing toward the kitchen. "Bessie! Bessie!"

Bessie came out, holding a dishrag. "What is it, ma'am? Is someone ill?"

"Bessie, kindly finish packing my things at once. And tell Giles to saddle Star. I must make for home immediately."

"But what's happened?"

"The letter is from Martha. We've been raided. Our provisions, my supplies—they have been smashed to bits."

35

IF I HAD DELUDED MYSELF PREVIOUSLY THAT the danger had
been to Abigail or other prominent figures alone, I could no longer. For this attack on my home, I saw at once, possessed a personal, vengeful quality. Our parlor window had been smashed
through. The barrels of cider in the cellar had been cleaved with
an ax. Several chickens in the yard had been beheaded, their glassy
eyes glancing wistfully toward their bodies across the way. In the
kitchen, my medical sack had been rifled through and many costly
supplies taken. Teas and powders had been removed from their
bottles and poured all in a heap.

What a waste lay before me!

Had it been thieves, I would have understood. But this act was
conceived out of sheer spite. Most alarmingly, my vial of belladonna, marked clearly with skull and crossbones, was missing. It
had not been dumped and left like the others, but removed, with
what monstrous purpose I knew not.

Martha was engaged in picking up bits of the smashed glass
from the window. Eliza had Johnny on her hip in a sling, a wool
cap upon his head. She was washing the kitchen floor and looked
done in. Within, it was freezing despite the fire in the hearth. I
could see our foggy breath.

"Take care you don't cut yourself," Martha said. "There are shards everywhere."

Clearly my friends had passed through whatever state of rage or terror now befell me. It would be many more hours before I could share their calm.

"Eliza, Martha, cease your labors a moment and sit with me. I must know the particulars of what has happened."

Eliza wearily set down her mop and approached me. Martha, who had been on hands and knees looking for the last bits of glass, stood and came forth. They both embraced me sadly.

Looking about, I saw a farm at the brink of winter: solitary, vulnerable, bereft of men. Whatever strength we'd shared had shattered and become as invisible as the shards of glass.

"Can you tell me what happened?" I asked. "Please, spare no detail."

Martha silently glanced at Eliza, and a terrible thought ripped through me. I asked at once, "He didn't harm either of you in any way?"

"Oh, no," Eliza assured me, seeing that I had misunderstood their look. "It is thanks to the Maker of all things that I had been sleeping upstairs with Martha in your absence. We kept but one fire burning that way, and it is warmer for Johnny, who was sleeping between us." She glanced at me to see if I would meet her words with reprobation. I did not. Eliza continued, "No, thank God, we were not downstairs and thus could block the door against them."

"Them?" I uttered in horror. I had imagined but a single culprit.

"Yes. There were two at least. We heard their footsteps."

"They must have heard you upstairs. Oh—heavens!" I suddenly realized the treachery they had narrowly escaped.

"Perhaps," said Eliza. "But they seemed little interested in us. They made a great ruckus destroying what they could. That seemed to be their purpose, not to harm us."

"I wonder if they knew I was in town, and you within," I mused.

When I thought of the danger and terror my friends had undergone on my account, I felt deeply ashamed. I took their hands. "This is my fault and no other's," I said. "Someone must have seen through my excellent disguise, though how that could be I know not."

Thomas Miller sprang to mind. He was the only one who knew. I did not believe Thomas would knowingly endanger his sister or me; indeed, he had sworn to it. But could he have told someone, warned someone of my knowledge? I thought it likely that he had, however inadvertently, caused this devastating occurrence.

"Who knows but that *I* may be the target and cause of this mayhem," Martha blurted suddenly.

"You?" I said. "What have you to do with anything?"

I did not mean to be dismissive. Martha had been so brave; her courage had been a key to our survival. She flinched at my words, then said, "Perhaps there are those on *our* side who wish to send my brother a message."

I shuddered. "I do not like to think those of our own side capable of harming us in this way just to get at Mr. Miller."

My friends knew me too well. The way I said his name gave me away.

"You—and Mr. Miller?" Eliza said, repeating my words, now in a wholly different sense.

"I thought so," Martha concluded. "Lizzie"—she was moved to grasp my arm—"you mustn't see him. Please listen. Perhaps when the war is concluded, one way or another. Promise me!"

"I have no need of such promises," I replied disdainfully.

"Nonetheless," Martha said, her eyes narrowed. "Swear you will not."

I had only once before seen this ferocious aspect of my dear friend, and then it had been directed at herself.

"All right, if you wish it. I will swear it. In any case," I said, hiding my hurt, "there will scarce be opportunity to see him now, for I must not go abroad while danger lurks here for you."

Martha let the matter drop at last. I donned my cloak and mitts and went outside to round up the frozen chicken carcasses; they were too valuable to waste. While there, I fed the surviving animals and hugged my Star, who whinnied with glee to see me. Still, in the way he nuzzled my face, I felt he knew something was amiss.

We all spent the rest of that awful day in silent labors. I made a stew of the chickens, and while the pot was on the fire, I righted what was left of my medicines, knowing I had not the means to replace anything that had been taken or destroyed. Apparently Thaxter had gone to find a glazier in Weymouth—though what we could trade in payment for so many panes of glass I knew not. The apples we had congratulated ourselves upon were all gone, as was the cider. But of all the destruction, the most hurtful had been Martha's look! So hard and unforgiving!

When my labors were done, it was late, and I was exhausted. Johnny developed the croup that same night and would not stop barking and crying. His unfamiliar wailing was a sound reflection of the mood that had overtaken us. I was seized with an absolute desire to lay my head upon Abigail's breast, though it was already dark.

Thaxter had not returned; presumably he had decided to stop the night in Weymouth. Thus, I saddled Star myself and fetched a stool. Without saying where I was going, I mounted Star and departed. I had meant to leave in silence, but at the last moment I could not refrain from calling out, "Eat the stew—it is ready!"

Within my house, all had felt broken and violated. But the frigid air braced me, reminded me that I and my friends were whole and unharmed. I rode straight through town and down the main road, crossing no one save a few oblivious drunks reeling numbly out of Brackett's tavern. The cold air dulled the usual acrid stench of the tannery, too, with its drying, eviscerated carcasses and vats of jellied horse bone. The church was silent and dark as well. It seemed as if Braintree's parishioners had chosen to remain by their safe hearths until the crocuses showed their purple blossoms. *None of you are safe*, I wanted to tell them. *Not even by your hearths, surrounded by your loved ones. It is all an illusion.*

Abigail must have recognized Star's stride, because I had no need to knock. She was at the door, and I was in her arms before a word was said. I cried as I had not allowed myself to cry in my own home.

It was a full five minutes before she could pry a single word from my lips. However, it became apparent that she already knew of our catastrophe through Colonel Quincy.

Abigail made me tea and insisted I drink it by the fire. She offered me cake, which I could not put to my lips.

Nabby came into the parlor and sat placidly, consolingly, with us. She was such a docile girl. I quite liked her, although around her I was always at a loss for conversation. Thomas and Charles came running in but went running back out again when they saw the tearful scene. Weeping women were not their province, though no doubt they'd seen many such tears before.

Abigail waited patiently. I knew she would wait all night if necessary. It took near half an hour before I had the strength to tell her all that had happened. Finally I recounted Martha's words, and the fresh, new grief I felt I could never repair.

She listened in utter silence. Then she replied quietly, "You must think of it in this way: she loves you enough to want to protect you, for that is what she does in speaking to you so. Martha must believe her brother to be involved in some very dangerous business."

"Or perhaps she believes I am dangerous to *him*."

"I hadn't thought of that," she said quietly. "In either case, the situation is clearly grave, and we have good reason to fear. Let us discuss what to do in the morning. Perhaps we should all repair to Weymouth—"

I looked up in alarm at this suggestion. Abandon the farm and flee to Weymouth? Why should we concede defeat when His Excellency had not done so?

"No, that you well know I cannot do."

"For now, then, hold on to this one thought, dear Lizzie: your brother lives and shall return to you."

Oh, a sweeter or more timely reminder could not have been bestowed upon me. It was true. Amid all else, my brother lived and was presumably breaking waves toward me at that very moment. Now I simply had to survive to greet him.

As I rose to leave, Abigail grasped my hands in hers and whispered, "Take heart, Lizzie. You can yet do a great deal of good, even without all your witch's potions. However, you must think no more of your snooping. Your friends need you."

Abigail went on to insist that I return later that week for a bushel of her own apples, which I reluctantly agreed to do, for the thought of going the winter without a morsel of fruit or bread made me feel heartily sorry for myself.

36

NEWS QUICKLY SPREAD OF THE ATTACK UPON my house. By the following day, we began to receive a steady stream of visitors giving what aid they could. Susanna Brown came by with pins. Gaius brought salt cod. Still others brought eggs or a chicken. I was moved by my neighbors' kindness, for they had even less than I.

Ann Quincy arrived with an entreaty to join them in the great house for the winter.

"Elizabeth," she said, as she always insisted upon using my Christian name, "you will be far safer with us. You cannot remain here, three women and one child, all alone."

Ann and Josiah Quincy had met Eliza and her child soon after the babe's entrance into the world. Eliza had been anxious and fretful, but the two old people made a mad dash for the child, falling instantly in love, and nary a word was said either about Eliza's matrimonial state or the dusky color of the child.

Eliza glanced at me with longing, but I thanked Ann warmly and declined. She left us then, but only after we had promised her that, at any further hint of danger, we would hasten to her house up the hill.

After she had gone, I heard a relieved sigh from Eliza. "Oh, Lizzie, I nearly succumbed. Just think of it: tea in a warm bed, and a *real* servant!"

At that we glanced over at Martha, who was absorbed in some sewing. She was edging some cloths we would add to our stock of trade goods. She looked up, not knowing what we had said, and Eliza smiled sheepishly. Martha and I had not spoken since the previous day.

"Far be it from me to imperil your safety." I addressed my comments to Eliza. "Indeed, I think it an excellent idea for you to repair to the house."

"And leave you here? I could not be so selfish, whatever you may think."

Later that afternoon, Eliza and I had managed to restore some order to the dairy and were resting a moment when Martha, whom we had not seen for several hours, suddenly appeared on the stairs with a small trunk in her arms.

We gaped at her.

"Hello! What do you do there?" I asked.

"I'm leaving."

"Leaving? For where? Is Thomas ill?" I must admit that my first thought was for him whom Martha had forbidden me to love.

"No, he's well. I shall go to him. It's all arranged."

I approached her, little Johnny in my arms. Seeing him, her hard face softened, and she smiled. To see her smile for him but not for me was almost beyond endurance.

"Have you sent for him?" I asked.

"No," she admitted. "I have not had the opportunity."

"Then how do you plan to go? And why?"

"I shall find a ride upon the road to Boston." I glanced entreatingly at Eliza.

"Martha, there are four feet of snow about the house. You shall be frozen through before you make the road."

"Nonetheless, I cannot remain here."

"But what has happened?" I felt the tears finally release themselves.

"I have harmed you, Lizzie. I shall continue to harm you, and perhaps Eliza and Johnny, too, if I remain here."

"But why? Because you told me what I already knew? That I must not love your brother? That in these times I must keep to my small circle? I know it all full well. You've told me nothing I have not already told myself a hundred times."

"But you sought solace at Abigail's breast for something I did, and I'm mortified. I could never meet her eyes again."

"She defended you," I said. "She said it is because you love me and wish to protect me."

"Well, that's true," she said. "Though I have no illusion that I can protect you. Or this little man," she reached out to Johnny, who himself was reaching for the glint of silver about Martha's throat. It was a locket I had not seen before, a pretty thing etched with a floral design. I presumed she wished to wear it on her person while she traveled.

I embraced her then, Johnny between us.

"Martha, don't leave. I beg you. I shall be good."

"Good? I doubt that." She looked up at me. When I saw her disbelieving eyebrow, I smiled, for I believed she might reconsider, if only to keep me from further mischief.

•   •   •

Martha did not leave us then, but so much damage had been wrought that I was obliged to sell some furniture. I parted with my mother's bedstead in the parlor. It was a family treasure that had sailed from England fifty years earlier. It brought tears to my eyes to see it disassembled and carted out through the snow by rough and careless men. But I now had eight pounds silver in my pocket, with which I was able to buy another cow and a sack of corn flour. With these things we would survive the winter, which was already ominously cold.

Our spirits grew very low. Little Johnny caught a heavy cold, and for three days we took turns standing with him over a kettle of boiling water, until we were soaked and fairly boiled ourselves.

News of the massacre at Cherry Valley sank us further. We heard of women and children scalped, and other barbarisms as well. We discussed these events among ourselves and agreed: mankind was capable of ungodly evil. Our conversations depressed us, and at one of our lowest moments, I reflected, "I wonder whether our species is worth saving. I doubt that even our liberty will change man's essentially bad nature."

At the time, my friends did not disagree.

I took to sleeping with Jeb's musket by my side. All of us slept in my chamber now, my chest of drawers pulled up against the door, so as to have a fighting chance should we come under attack again.

Babes did not cease coming into the world simply because I had lost my supplies, however. December of 1778 brought three births. Poor babes! Mothers near starved, with hardly a sniff of milk for the infants. And yet, however dire conditions might have been, the sight of a healthy baby never failed to delight its mother and bring hope into the most dejected household.

The three births brought us material sustenance as well: we received a good bottle of rum, a fine piece of linen, and, much to our delight, a jar of apricots preserved in honey.

The apricots put us all into a swoon. The night we received them, we did not taste them but simply sat by the fire and stared at each and every apricot within the jar, remarking on its fine qualities, savoring each one in our imaginations.

We were staring at this same unopened apricot jar one frigid evening in late December when we heard the roll of carriage wheels upon our little road. We were in such an excited state of imagination that at first we assumed the carriage sound to be imaginary as well.

It was not. We all ran to the window and saw a lady dressed in an admirable cloak, fur collar, and muff. She descended her carriage with the help of her coachman.

Mrs. Boylston.

Seeing her through the window, Eliza cried, "What punishment has my Redeemer in mind for me?" I do believe Eliza was more frightened by the sight of her own mother than she had been at the sound of the vandals' footsteps.

"Dearest, nothing shall happen," I said, gently leading her away from the window. "Your mother can have no power here."

Eliza's mother did look daunting, however. She was still quite beautiful and perfectly appointed, but her grim slit of a mouth told of no happy mission.

She was at the door, and I was obliged to give her entrance, as it was glacial outside. The coachman unhitched the horses. I watched Thaxter, teetering, lead them to the stable. "Unless he wishes to assist me in birthing the next babe, he had better not be dipping into *our* rum," I muttered to Martha.

"We must have a word with him by and by."

Mrs. Boylston stood in the middle of my parlor as she removed her things and set them down on a chair by the fire. Her face looked pinched. She was clearly ill at ease, but also curious, for she had never been within these walls before, not even to visit when Jeb was alive. She studied the lively industry about her with some surprise. Her daughter stood before her with little Johnny in her arms. He had grown in leaps and bounds these two months, oblivious to our own wounded universe.

"Mother." Eliza bowed her head.

Would she not embrace her own daughter? She would not. Wicked, Pharaoh-hearted woman! Martha and I involuntarily placed our hands to our hearts.

"You must be frozen." I remembered my manners. "I shall bring some tea."

"Thank you," she said. Then she offered, "You all seem quite cozy here."

"We are quite busy," I admitted, "what with one thing and another."

I brought chamomile tea and oatcakes, and we all sat about the fire in the parlor.

Mrs. Boylston sat resolutely not looking at little Johnny. The infant kept grinning at her, but each time he did so, she looked away. Oh, she was made of inhuman stuff! Forgive me, but I abhorred her then. Someone who is able to resist the love of a child must be damaged beyond God-given humanity.

She soon got to her business. "I want you to return home. I am all alone now."

"As was I," Eliza countered, "until dearest Lizzie took me in. This is my home."

"You cannot possibly wish to stay here," said Mrs. Boylston, casting about her at the many chores left undone.

Eliza smiled nervously. "It is simple and crowded, I agree. But it is more to my liking than our cold and drafty house with all its useless finery. And, as you see, Johnny thrives here."

Johnny was busy grasping his mother's pendant and putting it in his mouth. She kept gently removing it from his clutches.

"I care nothing for it," she said, meaning her grandchild.

"Care or not, 'it' is still your grandson. His name is John."

"There is an inheritance waiting for you when I die," replied Mrs. Boylston.

A resigned smirk fell across Eliza's face. Mrs. Boylston could not have known the crucible of emotions that Eliza had passed through and that had made her, at long last, indifferent to either status or money.

"Let me have it then. Or, if you are not inclined, don't!"

Then, perhaps remembering their uncertain future, she grasped the boy to herself and turned away.

I rose at once.

"Shall I call for your horses, ma'am? There can be little more for you to accomplish here."

Mrs. Boylston looked at me, her eyes glittering with some well-pondered intent. "If you would keep the bastard, I'm certain I could persuade my daughter to return home, where she belongs. I am in a position to recompense you."

"Keep Johnny?" I looked at Martha, who had remained silent during this interview. "Oh, we have not the means to keep a babe, ma'am."

"I will never part from Johnny!" Eliza glared at her mother.

"Well, perhaps a winter of *this* will alter your thinking," said Mrs. Boylston, gathering her things. She cast a withering glance about her.

"Never!" And with that, the daughter fled into the kitchen. In a few moments, after bidding good-bye and good riddance to the mother, we moved to console our friend.

37

WINTER, 1779. APART FROM THIS UNWELCOME VISIT, the end of '78 saw us in relative tranquility. We all lost flesh, except for little Johnny, but we suffered our hunger in genteel silence. We kept busy working to "turn water into wine." We wove the last bits of flax, baked the last pompions, made soup from fish bones, and fried cod in lard. We none of us went abroad, not even for meeting. We were too frightened, and besides, there was no coal to warm our little coal foot warmers.

It was after the New Year that I decided to resume my spying activities once more, to the great objection of Martha, who threatened to leave me for good should I do so. But I knew it to be an empty threat.

My modest hope was that I would stumble upon something important—perhaps some news of this Mr. Holland or Mr. Thompson. This was precisely what my friends feared. Indeed, Martha insisted that it was only because I had left off my spying that our enemies saw fit to leave us in peace. There was logic to my friend's words, but I heeded them not.

On the Saturday after New Year's, just as I had amassed my gear and donned my mustache and smelly vestments, I heard voices approaching. A loud rap on the door followed. I started up and peered through the newly glazed parlor window to find Colonel Quincy and Richard Cranch stomping the snow off their feet.

"You are in for it now." Martha smirked. I had begun to pick at my mustache when the two men fairly burst open the door. I stood.

The colonel stepped back, unsure of whom he had found sitting in Elizabeth Boylston's parlor.

"Excuse us," said the colonel, "but we were looking for Mrs. Boylston on a matter of utmost urgency."

Richard Cranch grinned. "Uncle, do you not recognize your own relation?"

But such a spectacle was beyond the old man's imaginings. "Why do you smirk, man?"

By this point, I had succeeded in peeling off the mustache. Upon seeing my gesture, the colonel actually began to sway, believing a man to have forcibly removed his own mustache.

"Martha, some whiskey at once," I called to her.

"Is this a joke, Elizabeth?" asked the colonel, now recognizing me.

"No, sir. It is no joke."

"Well, I'm certain you're up to some dangerous foolishness, but we have news that cannot wait."

"May I sit?" asked Richard, who stood in his dripping coat. In the excitement of the moment, we had all forgotten our manners.

"I'm very sorry. Yes, do," I said.

Richard wasted no time. "I have made inquiries into the name of Benjamin Thompson that your man in Cambridge learned of, and I've discovered some interesting facts. Apparently there has gone into hiding one Benjamin Thompson, age twenty-five, of Portsmouth, New Hampshire, who disappeared around the same time Mr. Holland did. He has a wife—a wealthy heiress, one Sarah Rolfe—through whose connections he was able to gain an appointment as a major in a New Hampshire militia. But he abandoned her after Rebels broke into his house last year, and he fled with Holland. This Thompson fashions himself a natural philosopher. Indeed, it seems he has even published a paper of some sort. Now it is said that these men are here in Boston."

The news sent a thrill of danger through me and, unbeknownst to my guests, made me even more eager to set off. I now believed that I would make significant discoveries at the Rose and Crown.

"All the more reason why you must entertain no wild thoughts of roaming, Elizabeth," the colonel added.

I nodded demurely. Martha looked at me askance. She knew me better. After downing their whiskey, the colonel and Mr. Cranch made to leave, but not without the colonel wagging a finger at me as he left. "Take heed of what we've said, Lizzie. A woman's place is in the home."

•   •   •

I now waited until early the following morning to set off, and during this time I came to doubt my purpose. Or, not my purpose, but the sagacity of leaving the farm. Yet I saw no other way to find the truth.

Fear for my friends held me back a moment. Yet, let it be said in my defense that I never have liked mysteries. If I do not know something, I usually wish to know it as soon as may be. I have never understood those who are content with a mere scrap of a story; no, I must know the end—and the middle as well, if possible. Furthermore, I saw no reason why this God-given curiosity should be the province of man alone. We women are just as curious; yet we are taught that curiosity is not seemly. Foh! The destruction of my home and livelihood gave legitimacy to my desire to know who lay behind it.

But I must also include a second reason for my pursuing this foolish course: the slender hope of seeing Mr. Miller again. Oh, I had no hope of anything coming of such a meeting. The sight of him alone, the thrill of looking into his eyes and fancying I saw some fleeting tenderness—this must, I knew, be the end of it. Yet even this thought of one fleeting moment gave me great pleasure. Several such moments might afford me years of memories.

Having tossed and turned for several hours, I finally rose at three to prepare my disguise, waking Martha in the process. She rose but refused to help me. "Go ahead. Get caught, land in a stinking prison, and hang by your neck until you are dead."

"Would you not care even a little?" I said, standing there in my costume, my lips moving beneath the heavy mustache.

"Not in the least."

But one glance at my face had her running into my arms.

Eliza, overhearing, rose to join us. Seeing me from the kitchen doorway, she frowned. "Oh, you're a trial. Did you not hear Colonel Quincy?"

"I heard him."

She came up to me and tenderly straightened my mustache. "Do be careful."

"I always am," I replied.

•　　•　　•

Dawn was just rising as I rode back to the Rose and Crown tavern. My mustache was somewhat the worse for wear; it now resembled a small, dead rodent. No one was abroad, and I was alone on the road; whiteness surrounded me. I saw no bird or other living thing save a snow-dusted opossum that scurried in front of Star on the icy road and nearly caused my demise. Star faltered, his front hooves rising off the frozen ground; but he recovered quickly at my soothing voice, and we soon arrived at Milton. There, a few hardy souls were about, tending to their chores.

At Roxbury, I could no longer feel my feet, and so I thought it prudent to stop at the tavern, though I did not tarry. By midday, I once more found myself at Rowe's Wharf. Unlike in the fall, the wharf was desolate. The odor, however, owing to the cold, was slightly better. Feeling little need to dissemble, I gave Star directly to the stable boy, kicked my frozen feet against the iron scraper, and entered.

Within, I took myself a seat in my usual corner so as not to be noticed. The air seemed smokier and more fetid, the men nearly paralyzed with drink, and the floors more tacky with spilled cider than I remembered. Mr. Smythe was there, looking somewhat more stooped and pale. I was glad to see him.

"Back in town with another package, eh?" he asked. "Didn't erase the directions this time?"

"No, sir," I said.

"Well, live and learn." He shrugged philosophically. "What'll you have? You fancied the punch, if I recall."

"Indeed. Kind of you to remember, sir. The same, please, sir."

I looked around me when he had gone. Through the smoke, as my eyes adjusted to the light, I saw various groups of men hunched over their mugs. Some played checkers, taking a glacially long time between moves. Others looked my way, but, finding nothing of interest, turned back to their conversations.

Someone guffawed, and I turned to see a red-faced farmer exclaim, "I'll wager you ten shillings he'll surrender before you have your corn sowed. The papers is saying he can't get men to join, not for all the money in the world."

At this proclamation, I stood. The men turned toward me, expectant. But I had not the courage to confront a drunken group of Tories. Nor did I think it would serve my purpose. I made as if to adjust my trouser leg, and when I sat once more without having said anything, I felt a presence looming behind me.

I turned to find Mr. Cleverly.

"If this be your true bent, Lizzie, it is well I did not remain in Braintree." He smiled. "May I join you?"

I was too shocked to utter a syllable.

But Cleverly continued easily, pulling a chair and crossing his legs, "This boyish garb oddly suits you, Lizzie."

"Please, Mr. Cleverly," I whispered, "keep your voice down. It is my fervent wish that no one know."

He laughed. "Doesn't everyone know? Certainly Mr. Cranch does. And besides, whom do you presume to fool? Only fools would be fooled by your costume."

"That has not been my experience."

"Oh, and so you have been at this before? I *thought* I recognized you," he exclaimed. "When was that? Let's see—September? October? One would think you'd have given up such foolishness by now. What can it serve?"

"You think women incapable of making any contribution?"

"No, indeed." Cleverly's eyes narrowed. His face came close. "I think you capable of doing a great deal of harm, all for the so-called 'good' you do."

I was about to make a bitter rejoinder when we were interrupted by the arrival of my punch. I reached into my breeches and paid Mr. Smythe what I owed him.

"Two pence, is it?" I said in a rough voice.

He nodded, casting a puzzled glance at Mr. Cleverly. When he had gone, Cleverly resumed his discourse.

As I observed him now, I saw a great deal I had not seen before. He was glib and easy, but his eyes were cool blue discs. On his left hand, which tapped out a rhythm against his thigh, I discerned a faint band of light skin around his ring finger.

• • •

Upon seeing Cleverly's pale band of skin, the mist cleared, and I finally discerned the truth. And this truth frightened me like nothing had since I woke to the cannons in Charlestown.

"Alas, these are not times for domestic pleasures," he was saying, "much as I long for them." Here he sighed deeply and added, "Love and war are an unhappy equation."

Preservation told me to flee. But I stayed. "Why do you tarry here?" I inquired pointedly. "We had all thought you returned to New Hampshire after Mr. Thayer's death."

"I might ask you the same question," he returned. "For surely you have no wish to leave your farm exposed to those who wish you ill."

The way he emphasized the words *wish you ill* made my heart pound violently. Constricted as I was by the board upon my breast, I felt that I could hardly breathe. Yet I managed to say, "Are there those who wish me ill, Mr. Cleverly?"

"It is common knowledge," he said mildly. "And I for one was very sorry to hear it."

I knew then he was lying. No one beyond our parish knew of our misfortunes. I had to leave, and now. I left my punch untouched and began backing away.

"I see you are eager to leave." He smiled. "And so must I. I underestimated you, Lizzie," he continued. "For that, too, my sincerest apologies. You are a strong, admirable woman. But I am concerned for you."

"Concerned, sir?"

"Yes, for you may find that to be too busy is some danger. By the way, was that horse I saw beyond the window yours? It is a beautiful animal."

"Yes."

"Did you ride it here?"

"Yes. Why?" I asked.

Cleverly's eyes shone with cool amusement, but he did not reply. "Give my warmest regards to Martha. I shall always remember—"

But I put out my hand involuntarily to stop him from making me sick to my very soul. Cleverly bowed stiffly and departed.

Mr. Smythe was upon me. "Is he the man you was looking for?" he asked.

"Yes," I said. "He is."

38

I GALLOPED BACK TO BRAINTREE—MY STAR PUT to the test as never before. I had made the most grievous mistake of my life. And so reckless was I in my gallop home that, upon encountering a carriage making its way up the snowy road, Star slid, and only heaven above kept me from tumbling over his withers and breaking my neck. I stopped neither at Roxbury nor at Milton but proceeded in haste to the house of Richard and Mary Cranch.

I fairly thrust poor Star, now frothing at the mouth, at the stable boy. I ran up the steps and into the house, entirely forgetting about my costume. Within—what stark contrast to the world I had just left!—the life of a judge and family man presented an ordered and comfortable reality.

A fire blazed in the parlor. Several guests were reading and dozing off. A foursome was playing at cards. Susan, the servant-girl I had interrogated that summer past, glided in on small, silent feet to deliver tea to the guests.

Upon my wild entrance, the guests looked up. One of the men playing cards frowned and said, "Mr. Cranch is in the west parlor."

I bowed and made my way to the west parlor.

"Who is it?" I heard Richard Cranch's voice.

"It is I," I whispered, entering the room. "Lizzie."

Immediately, a startled group stared up at me. Richard, Mary, and Abigail were all there; they wore grave faces. No one smiled at my disguise. Did they not know me?

Mary and Abigail stood and came toward me.

"Lizzie, has something happened?" asked Abigail. "Are you ill?"

"I believe I have placed us all in mortal danger."

"Come, let us remove your costume. Say nothing until then, for truly you look very ill."

The women excused themselves and brought me to a spare bedroom, where they stripped me down, called Susan to boil water for a bath, and left me to recover from my journey before they would brook further discussion.

Half an hour later, dressed in something of Mary's, I presented myself in the parlor, whereupon Richard said, "Lizzie, we have news of a very serious nature."

"Does it pertain to Mr. Cleverly? For that is what I came to say. I now believe this Cleverly to be a spy for the British Army. He was sarcastic and arrogant and—"

"Calm yourself, Lizzie," said Abigail, shaking her head. "We have it on greatest assurance that Cleverly is in the service of our General Sullivan. We made inquiries after you told us of meeting him in Boston. Here, see for yourself."

With this, she handed me a letter. It was in the tiny, neat handwriting of a learned and cautious man.

To the honorable JQ.

    Be it known to you that upon the question of Mr. C. about whom you have lately written to me, you have my every assurance that he is a Good and Loyal servant to our Cause. He has served in various capacities of importance to myself and others these past two years.

    Your obedient, T.S.

I can hardly describe my incredulity at reading this letter. I sank down by Abigail's side in a wing chair. I could not alter the impression so vividly and recently made on my mind regarding Mr. Cleverly.

"But are you sure?" I looked at Abigail.

"Most sure," she said. "Only imagine the care someone of General Sullivan's status would take with his closest allies."

As the relief began to quiet my pounding heart, another emotion took the place of the terror I had felt: humiliation. So humbled, so utterly foolish did I feel, that for several minutes I could say nothing. Tears pooled in my eyes and tumbled down my cheeks. When I finally found my voice, it was only to say, "I am very sorry. I am sorry for alarming you all."

"Oh, Lizzie," said Abigail, coming to embrace me. "You're a brave soul. But perhaps now you must admit that it serves no purpose to go about endangering yourself as you have."

"I was convinced of it, Abigail."

"Convinced of what, dearest?" She placed her hand on mine.

"That this man Cleverly is our Mr. Thompson."

"But you have just heard—"

"No, listen. My apple orchard. His invention—do you not recall? He has a pale line across his left ring finger. He has worn a wedding band, Abigail. And in our conversation together he said that love and war were an unhappy equation. Is that not the mind of a philosopher?"

Richard, who had been silent for some minutes, interrupted. His face was as grave and sorrowful as I've ever seen it.

"Lizzie, I have further information that belies your conviction regarding Mr. Cleverly. We have just now had a visit from the colonel with irrefutable proof."

Richard pulled his chair closer to us, the better to whisper. "The existence of a treacherous ring has been discovered. We are told that these men now plot to kill not just patriots such as Dr.

Flynt and Mr. Thayer, but our major leaders—Jefferson, Adams, and Washington himself."

I shivered. Still I could not let go of my idea. "That does not mean that Cleverly is not involved," I asserted.

Richard was silent, as was Abigail. Suddenly I realized that they were looking at me pityingly.

"Why do you stare at me so?" I cried. "Does this news have to do with me in particular?"

Glancing at our friends, Abigail spoke first. "It's best if I speak to Lizzie alone." She then took me by the arm. "Let us repair to another room."

Richard nodded. Mary kissed me tearfully and said she would call for a chaise to take me home. She would not allow me to travel again on horseback that day.

Once we were alone in the spare bedroom, Abigail sat herself down on the bed and said, "You may deceive yourself, but you do not deceive me. I know you are in love with Mr. Miller. I have no wish to break your heart, for I know you have one to break, beneath all your clever costumes. But I must tell you: Thomas Miller is involved. More than that I dare not say."

I was silent for several moments. Then I said, "I cannot believe it. To be sure, he has led a pampered, thoughtless life. He lacks true conviction, perhaps. But to plot the deaths of our great men—of John Adams? That I cannot—*will* not—believe."

I recalled my encounter with Mr. Miller in Boston on the night he kissed me. "He promised no harm would come to us. He swore it, Abigail."

"Men swear many things that they do not mean."

Abigail then fell silent, and from this silence I felt she had yet more against Thomas Miller. Exhausted and deeply shaken, I desperately wished to keep that small light of hope burning within me. For, were it to flicker out—oh, I would find myself in the most lonely, lonely darkness! Surely I could not have been so thoroughly deceived.

She waited patiently. "We have obtained this news from General Sullivan himself, Lizzie. Our Provincial Congress has sent word to the Continental Congress. They await but a signed letter from Washington sanctioning Mr. Miller's arrest. I'm most grievously sorry for you. But you *will* love one day. You will love and be loved, of that I have no doubt. For those who can love deeply always draw love to them."

Abigail placed a warm hand on my arm, but my guiding light flickered out then. I had no more strength to believe in anything. I wept before my friend. The love in my heart drained away like blood from a mortal wound. I was as Abraham before the burning bush, aware of my sacrifice. I cried and cried, for I had held back the depth of my love from everyone, even from myself.

39

HE HAD PROMISED ME, AND I HAD believed him. But then, I had nearly accepted Mr. Cleverly as well, whose devotion turned out to be as shallow as a vernal pond. In Mr. Miller, my eyes saw a rather careless man. My ears heard a very thoughtless man. But I had also thought him a man who was serious and not unkind. I felt he had a genuine regard for me.

Now I no longer trusted my own opinion. I could no longer tell right from wrong, good from evil. Perhaps I never could. Perhaps I had labored beneath a false sense of my own worth all these years. Had I not struggled to be independent, to be useful? Thank God I had not yet killed anyone, I told myself.

I said nothing to Eliza of my conversation with Abigail, but I felt it necessary to reveal the news to Martha. Perhaps she already knew that her brother might soon be arrested, and that is why she had warned me against him.

"Martha," I took her aside upon returning from Abigail's. "I know you only mean the best for me," I began.

"I do."

"And I have heard just now from Abigail that your brother— may not be safe. That he may soon . . ."

"I know."

"Well, if you know," I said, my voice rising in frustration, "why do you not run to him? Why do you not urge him to flee?"

"He does precisely what he wishes. There is nothing either you or I can do." With these hopeless words, Martha turned away from me and made as if to tend to an errand.

I had borne cold, hunger, illness, and death. But the loss of hope I could not bear. Silence grew around me. I had no words for anyone, not even for little Johnny. Martha knew my despair, yet I was far from believing that she shared it. Indeed, she seemed oddly resigned to her brother's fate.

Eliza grieved for me but dared not raise the subject. My dark, dark soul brought long shadows into our world. Soon, all three of us glided about the cottage like voiceless, unhappy spirits.

It is a known fact that parents will always try to save their help-less children. Sometimes, they succeed. But it is a lesser-known fact that children can save their parents, too. Johnny saved us then. I truly believe that, had he not been with us, we would all have succumbed to illness and never seen the warming light of spring.

Only little Johnny was oblivious to the unworthy world into which he had been born. Each morning he brought his laughter and good cheer into our dejected home. To Johnny, every object possessed fascination and delight. By March, he was sitting up, plump and jolly, his gold-brown hair forming tight curls about his head. His eyes were a warm aqua color, the color of our sky on certain summer days. When Johnny's first teeth came in, he did not cry, but merely frowned and tucked in his chin as if puzzled by the discomfort, having known so very little pain or discomfort in his life. I rubbed a numbing salve upon his gums that provided him some relief.

• • •

Eliza was justly proud of her bright child. But, though she never spoke of it, I knew well her despair of ever seeing John Watkins again. Hopeless for ourselves, Martha and I found a purpose to life in contriving a way for John Watkins to see his son.

At the end of January 1779, our selectmen finally voted to procure grain for the town, but it was to be another four months before we tasted of it. By March, butcher's meat sold for one dollar per pound. Corn was twenty-five dollars per bushel. To aid our farmers, the town now offered six shillings per old crow and two per young. I took no pleasure in the sport of killing animals, but it needed to be done.

Martha and I took turns putting the musket to use. Every time he heard a shot, Johnny's green eyes opened wide, and his mouth formed a large O. One day we heard shots and went running out to find Eliza aiming at a crow on our fence.

"You know how to use a musket?" Martha asked Eliza, disbelief plain on her face.

"Yes," she said simply. "An old Portsmouth friend taught me."

"Are you certain?" I asked. "I should not like you to shoot yourself or one of us, with that thing."

"Should we be afraid?" Martha asked.

Eliza smiled. "Only if you're a crow."

"You say you had need of it in Portsmouth?" I inquired.

"I nearly did," she replied. "There was a scoundrel who sorely needed a lesson in . . . manners."

"Did you correct his manners, then?" Martha asked as Eliza slowly moved toward the fence and took aim.

"I did, indeed," said Eliza.

We began to think perhaps we had sorely underestimated Eliza.

•   •   •

At the end of March, the last of the snow finally melted, and we began to see the stirrings of life. Upon seeing our first crocus in the dooryard, I nearly wept for joy, so bleak had been our winter.

"Martha, Eliza, come look," I said. They raced to the door and gawked at the purple flower. We couldn't have been more grateful had the ground sprouted gold.

As if to signal the new fecundity in the air, I assisted at three deliveries on three consecutive days. Martha helped me, of course. I could not have stayed awake to perform my duties otherwise. Only one father was present, the other two being off at war. We were glad to receive real coin for two of these births, and a ham for the third.

In April and May of that year, I found that there had been far too much damage done during the previous year to leave off my farming for any purpose, patriotic or otherwise. It required all three of us to work from dawn to well beyond dusk, Eliza breaking only to care for her babe. We fashioned for him a mobile crib so that he could be close to her on fair days. As long as Johnny had her within his sight, he was quite content to play alone with some spoons or banging a pot.

In addition to readying the sandy soil, hauling manure, and planting, there were candles to be made, cloth to be dyed, and babies to be brought into the world. Finally, in May, such was the rage of our poor citizens at the grain situation that the price for an old crow rose to thirty shillings. Thus, there was more shooting to do as well.

All that spring, we spoke not a word about our unhappy business of the year before, taking solace in nature and in Johnny's growth. However, I did at one point beg Abigail to write to her husband about our situation.

"Lizzie," she said firmly, "you must see that I will on no account have John return home before his work is complete, merely on my behalf. You know that is what he would do, and that is precisely what our enemies wish him to do. He has daily feared assassination. My letter could not protect him. Quite the contrary."

I knew her to be correct in her assessment. "Forgive me, Abigail. I suppose I've grown desperate."

"We have all grown desperate," she said, embracing me, "but we will bear—"

"—that which we must bear." I finished our well-worn sentence for her, and we both laughed.

By June, our flax and corn had taken fine root. Our heavenly Redeemer had seen fit to bless us with sunny days and rainy days in equal measure, and our hearts lifted. One hot morning, however, after Eliza had worked hard by our sides all week, she went to suckle John and no milk came out. We fed him a little vegetable mash, which he ate reluctantly.

I got busy with my arts: I had Eliza suckle Johnny every hour upon the hour, milk or no. She was forbidden to work in the fields with us. I gave her near all our cow's milk, and cheeses besides, till she complained that she was so bloated she would float off to sea. After a week of such rest and feeding, Eliza's milk flowed once more, and she was so grateful she wept.

40

IT WAS A HOT DAY THE FOLLOWING week when Martha and I
came from the fields to discover Eliza, doubled over in pain in the
kitchen garden. At first, I thought it to be some illness. But then I
noticed a letter upon the ground at her feet. She could not speak,
so I picked it up.

"May I?" I asked, meaning the letter.

She nodded.

The letter was from Colonel John Langdon, Watkins's over-
seer at the shipyard, and a great patriot. He wrote to inform Eliza
that her uncle Robert Chase had been forced to flee, and that
Watkins had been sold—to a most vicious man by the name of Mr.
Richards, in Kittery.

"Oh, this is terrible, indeed," I said.

"But look here. Look what he says," I pointed to a passage in
the letter, for I was certain that in her haste Eliza had not seen it:

*"But if perchance you are able to come to Portsmouth, Eliza, I
may . . . be able to arrange something. I have the means, though
it involve some danger. If you do decide to come, tell only those
you would trust with your own life, for his may be at stake . . ."*

Not seeming to hear me, Eliza said, "I knew this would happen. John warned me. I must go." She moved toward the house.

"When did John warn you? You told us nothing of it."

"When I was in Cambridge. I received a letter from him, through Colonel Langdon. I had no wish to share my misery with others. Oh, let me go!"

"A moment. A moment," I forestalled her. "Let us think."

Just then, Martha joined us from the fields, and I shared Eliza's news with her.

"At least he remains in the area and has not been shipped elsewhere," Martha said.

"Yes, thank God for that," murmured Eliza.

• • •

Eliza said she would reply to Colonel Langdon immediately, letting him know of her intended arrival in Portsmouth. I offered to accompany her.

Martha wanted to come as well, but I objected.

"We cannot both go. Someone needs to tend the farm."

"Of course," Martha said, though we could see that she was disappointed.

We prevailed upon Eliza to wait until the morning to leave, to give her letter a chance to precede her. Strange as it may seem, this same morning, Thaxter came knocking on our kitchen door with the news that he was leaving us. He looked a great deal abashed, but said he had family in New Hampshire what had procured him a good house job with a very fine family.

I had long expected his departure, but I doubted whether he had found a better situation elsewhere. More likely, he had simply tired of Braintree and its unresolved terrors.

"Whereabouts are you headed?" Eliza inquired, not looking up as she finished her packing.

"Portsmouth," Thaxter replied.

"Portsmouth!" Eliza cried. "Why, we go there this very day!"

Thaxter readily agreed to accompany us, and we were vastly contented to have a man we knew join us. We set off a few hours later.

·   ·   ·

Abigail was already sitting in her uncle's carriage when it came 'round, having decided to accompany us as far as her sister Betsy's house in Exeter.

The carriage was crowded, what with Abigail, Eliza, Johnny, myself, and Thaxter, and unfortunately required two stops, the first being at my home in Cambridge.

Eliza was loath to stop there, fearing that somehow her mother would get wind of our presence. But I assured her that I would trust Bessie and Giles with my life. Indeed, Bessie was so overjoyed to see me, to meet my friends, and to hear the sound of a babe echo through the old house once more that she rustled up a veritable feast for us.

Giles glanced at Johnny with a questioning brow now and then, but years of training kept him silent on the subject.

Bessie, on the other hand, bouncing a gleeful Johnny on her knee, blurted, "He's a dark little one, isn't he!"

"Bessie!" I exclaimed.

"Well," Bessie continued, glancing quickly about us to ascertain that Eliza was out of earshot, "it won't do for our races to be mixin' blood. That poor babe don't know he's in a heap of trouble."

Abigail and I stared mutely at each other; we neither of us were able to disagree.

The following morning, we continued our journey, and it was quite late when we arrived at Betsy and Parson Peabody's in Exeter. Betsy came running out to greet us, her candelabra trailing swathes of light in the darkness. She was in her bedclothes, and her loose, wavy hair fell all about her shoulders. I instantly liked her; she appeared warm and kind, if slightly frazzled. A keen intelligence shone from her eyes. Secretly I thought Betsy ill-suited to be a parson's wife.

After bidding Abigail good-bye, we set off, arriving at Stavers's, a Portsmouth tavern of good repute, at noon the following day. Here Thaxter took his leave of us, and we curtsied politely, though I was not distraught to see him go. He had been an indifferent field hand at best. Upon entering the tavern, Eliza and I learned that there was but one chamber available, so we agreed to share it. As soon as we reached the chamber, I undid my gown and stays and fell upon the bed. Eliza, however, could not rest. She stood and looked out the window, her heart no doubt aching.

"Lizzie," she turned to me, "would you kindly walk over to the Whipple house, to inform Dinah and Prince Whipple that I have returned? It is but three streets away. Perhaps Dinah can take word to Colonel Langdon that I am arrived."

"Of course," I said. Eliza had not mentioned these Whipple slaves previously, and I was surprised that she knew them as intimately as it now appeared.

I sat up, donned my stays and gown as Eliza explained the route, and set off. When I returned an hour later with my charges, I was obliged to rap long and loudly upon the door, for both Eliza and her babe were dead to the world.

"A moment," Eliza finally called. She opened the door. Within the chamber, it was pitch-dark. No moon shone through the window.

I, however, held a double candle, which no doubt afforded Eliza a good view of the Whipple slaves, and, to her very great surprise, Colonel Langdon himself.

Three slaves then entered the chamber and swarmed Johnny like the magi about baby Jesus. One was tall and proud-looking;

the girl, perhaps sixteen, must have been Dinah. The third was a bent old man whose age I could not guess. This was Jupiter, I later learned, Eliza's uncle's old coachman.

Sighs, exclamations, and tender clasping of hands all finally served to wake the sleeping babe, at which point the visitors took him up in their arms, each begging for a turn.

Colonel Langdon—a very tall, fair man in his mid-thirties— seemed embarrassed by this unbounded affection between Miss Boylston and the Whipple slaves.

"It's dark as a tomb in here, Eliza," I said, setting my candle down and searching for another.

Just as soon as they arrived, it seemed, the slaves tearfully departed. They said they dared not be long absent from their home, as curfew neared.

Colonel Langdon remained. Sensing that he wished to speak to Eliza alone, I turned toward the hallway. I then heard, rather than saw, all that transpired:

"Miss Boylston, I see you have earned the love and trust of those who most often find us undeserving of either."

"Yes, well. They were kind to me when my so-called equals were not," she said simply. "Do you wish to sit?"

"Nay—please. Miss Boylston, I have news as will gladden and pain you at once. Your anticipation must be very great, and so I shall be direct. Watkins—John Watkins—"

"Is he well?"

"He is better than he was."

"What mean you?"

The colonel hesitated. Then he finally said, "I'm afraid he— took a beating."

Eliza cried out and bent forward in her pain. Herein began a tale of meanness and treachery to harrow up one's soul. And yet, as I listened to the colonel, even through Eliza's sobbing, I began to discern the man's steely conviction, an intent to help Watkins despite the risk to himself and others.

"We shall find a way, Miss Boylston. Do not fear. It may take some time."

"Time," she repeated miserably.

Colonel Langdon replied, "You must feel entirely alone. But rest assured: there are others like me—even those in power." Colonel Langdon then broke off these cryptic remarks, as if he'd already said too much. "But excuse me. You must be exhausted." He then bowed and took his leave.

"An impressive man," I said once the colonel had gone.

"Yes. The best of men."

"And an impressive woman."

Eliza said nothing, but I continued. "Until this day, Eliza, I don't believe I knew you truly. Though we have been as sisters these ten months, I didn't understand your character. I'm frankly in awe. Well and truly in awe."

Eliza smiled wanly. "You didn't realize the depth of my love for . . . those you would not have expected me to love."

"No," I said. "That much I freely admit."

"Don't admire me so very greatly, Lizzie. Since I was a small child, I have lived in kitchens. My life was cold, and I sought the warmth. My life was small, and their lives bestowed upon me a depth of experience I hadn't known. What's more"—here, she stifled a smile—"I thought—I *still* think—John Watkins by far the handsomest man I ever laid eyes on."

"Well!" I replied, heartened to glean Eliza's lightened spirits, "why didn't you say so in the first place? A woman needs no further explanation."

Suddenly, Johnny, whom we had thought to be asleep, sat up with an annoyed expression. "Mama!" he cried imperiously. Eliza and I looked at each other in amazement. We had just heard the child's first word.

41

JOHNNY FELL ASLEEP FOR THE NIGHT AT around ten, as I did, though the air in the chamber was hot and close. Eliza remained awake but must have dozed off, for at some hour deep in the night, we were both awakened by a soft knock.

"Lizzie," she whispered, terrified, "that must be him. Oh, what do I do?"

"Open the door," I said, bracing her by her shoulders and giving her a push. Eliza got up and approached the door. Then she opened it.

Standing before her was a man of medium height, with a thick head of curls and stunning aqua-blue eyes. Their expression was of a tenderness that cannot be described . . .

"A moment," Eliza whispered, then turned to me. "Lizzie, this is John Watkins. My John."

I rose bashfully, as I was in my shift. I curtsied, then said, "Excuse me. I'll be just there, beyond the door. I can keep watch."

"I remain not long," Watkins replied. "The colonel waits for me below."

His voice was deep, resonant, and refined. If I had imagined he would sound in any way uncouth, I was at once sorely disabused.

I glanced at John Watkins, then turned to Eliza, eyes wide. *Yes,* my eyes said. *He is the handsomest man in the world.*

Then I noticed the dirty linen sling which held his bandaged right arm. I wondered what had happened to him but dared not ask. With his left hand, he took Eliza's hand in his. She kissed it, then moved to the bed and lifted her child in her arms.

"Your son," she said, holding Johnny out to him. "Isn't he amazing? He called me Mama today."

Watkins gazed down at his child, his eyes taking in the boy's every part. Tenderly, close to breaking, he caressed the child's head.

"Amazing, yes. Don't wake him just yet, though," he said.

"No," Eliza agreed.

I left the chamber then, and they shut the door upon me.

•　　•　　•

He left in the dead of night; I stood guard the entire time. When I finally returned to the chamber, dead on my feet, I asked Eliza no questions. They would keep till the morrow.

At breakfast we sat in one of the tavern's small public rooms, where we drank coffee and ate a fine plate of ham and eggs. After ten minutes of silence, I began to giggle. The harder I tried to squelch my laughter, the worse the urge became.

"Oh, Eliza," I blurted at last, "I must have at least some details. Do tell me something and put me out of my misery. For I'm to be an old maid and must live vicariously."

"You're a depraved being," Eliza scolded me. She gave me no prurient details, especially as we were in a public place. But she did say, "Oh, you should have seen him with Johnny. You should have seen his tenderness."

I stopped laughing, and my eyes grew tearful at the thought of John Watkins holding his son for the first time.

"It is enough. Thank you."

Eliza grasped my hand beneath the table in silent gratitude. Just as we were finishing our breakfast, a messenger approached us with a letter for me. I had been expecting no letter and felt it could only be bad news. I opened it quickly, but the messenger boy just stood there until I fished a penny from my pocket and handed it to him.

After a moment, I stood up and let out a cry of joy.

"Look, Eliza. Look!"

I proffered the letter, which was from Colonel Quincy, but gave her no time at all to peruse it.

"My Harry is in Braintree, Eliza. We must leave at once."

42

IT WILL BE APPARENT TO ANY ASTUTE reader that my joy was Eliza's misery, but she packed her things and left without a word. At least, I consoled myself, she had seen John. And she had been given every assurance by Colonel Langdon himself that help would be forthcoming. However, Eliza said nothing on the trip home, but sat gazing at some distant point beyond the road, and I did not intrude upon her private thoughts.

Our carriage was just pulling down the bumpy lane to the cottage when I beheld a tan, thin figure wave his arms at us in the summer light. He was loping down through the dunes from the great house, and at the sight of us began to run. He was tall, and as we drew closer I saw that he had a faint blond beard and sandy locks, loose and wavy as a girl's.

The carriage pulled up to our house at last. It was then I saw the man who had once been my little brother.

How often had I dreamed of him? Despaired of him? Dozens of times. And yet, no power of imagination could have aided me in guessing his fair likeness now.

I jumped down out of the carriage and went running. Harry looked puzzled. Was I so greatly altered? No, it was the light, only the bright summer light, which had cast me in silhouette.

"Harry!" I stopped short of him. Then, knowing it was I for certain, he came flying into my arms.

Oh, to feel my brother's arms around me! Flesh of my flesh, blood of my blood!

I buried my head in his shoulder, felt his thin yet strong arms. He had lost flesh and gained a foot in height since I'd seen him last. Though handsome and strong, he looked as if he had starved. I wished to feed him soon. I shut my eyes and let myself feel his breath and his heartbeat, and we stood there some minutes before I wiped my tears and said, "But it is a hot day. You must be wishing for refreshment."

Harry laughed. "Indeed, Sister, it is hot. But I am used to hotter."

I signaled to the coachman to approach the house. Once we had entered and bade the coachman follow with our trunks, I made tea. Eliza declined refreshment and went upstairs to find Martha, which left Harry and me alone together in the parlor.

Harry looked about the parlor and made an ironical face. "Poor sister. The sacrifices you have had to make."

"Tut!" I said, knowing him to be teasing me, as he always had when we were children. I found his behavior reassuring, for it told me he had not changed greatly.

"Well, you shall fare better by and by," he hinted, eyeing the rough and dirty sacks he had stashed by the door.

"What do you mean?" I asked.

"Shall I show you, then?"

"Let us rest an hour, so that we may better appreciate your gifts, if such they be."

"I'll let you judge, Sister."

"Oh, Harry! I can't believe it's you!" I rose and embraced him once more, nearly toppling us backward in the chair.

He laughed and hugged me to him.

I repaired to my chamber, where I found Eliza and Johnny asleep on my bed. Martha sat by their side, caressing Eliza's hair.

"Poor thing," Martha whispered. "I fear she is very low."

"It's my fault."

"No, Lizzie. Who could begrudge you a reunion with your brother?"

I shrugged, lay down next to Eliza and Johnny, and soon joined them both in slumber.

When I awoke, I was alone in the chamber. I washed my face, took salt to my teeth, combed my hair, and availed myself of the chamber pot, too impatient to slip out to the necessary.

Harry and Martha were below, chatting gaily, he regaling her and Eliza with his tales of the pirate's life.

"And dost thou wish to see thy bounty now?" He bowed toward me.

"Indeed I do." I laughed. "But Harry, I'm alarmed."

"Oh, don't be," he said. "We divided it all fair and square, with the lion's share sent off to His Excellency for the troops. And Sister, you mustn't call me Harry any more. I am all grown up now. My mates call me Henry."

"Pardon me," I intoned facetiously. "But I will call you Harry. I dislike the name Henry, which will suit you perfectly when you are a toothless old man."

"Let us see what you have, then, *Harry*," Martha said impatiently, for she had been waiting for hours while I slept.

"Your maid is a prickly one," he said, turning to me. Then he pivoted and bowed to her, saying, "Here we go, Your Bossiness."

Martha had already known Harry for two days, and I felt a slight envy that they had already established a teasing familiarity with one another.

Eliza smiled wanly, clutching Johnny to her. Martha merely scowled.

• • •

Can I explain the delight we felt, even Eliza, at having a man in the house? Can I describe my delight in having this dear, handsome, vigorous relation? I cannot. But perhaps I can begin to describe the almost instant camaraderie that sprang up between my fair brother and my friends:

Johnny gripped his mother's shoulder and his green eyes gazed with curiosity at Harry while I dragged the sacks from the door to the center of the parlor. Eliza caught my eye, and she smiled as best she could for my delight.

Harry now splayed himself out upon the floor, the first sack between his two long legs. He unloosed the rope about the sack's neck and began to lift the contents out. As he did so, he looked at each item, held it up, and announced its entrance into the world like a newborn babe. Out they came, to my and Martha's unending chorus of exclamations.

"Two pounds Demerara sugar," he announced, setting the paper-wrapped block aside.

"Ooh!"

"Coffee. Jamaican. Four pounds."

"Ah!"

"Bohea tea. Two pounds."

"It cannot be true!" Eliza blurted, clasping her hands together.

"Calico. Twelve yards."

"Martha, only think of it!" I said. "With such fabric we can make new frocks for all three of us."

All the while, my handsome brother continued to laugh good-naturedly at us. When he came to the bottom of the first sack, he tossed it aside and asked, "Shall I open the second sack, then?"

To cries of "Yes!" and "Don't stop now!" Harry untied the neck of the second sack and resumed his recitation.

"Ten pounds of wheat flour."

"But it can't be," I said, amazed, for not even the Quincys had such a quantity of flour. The entire North Parish had not so much.

"Yes, it can and *is*." He smiled at me. Seeing my delighted, childish face, he bent to kiss me.

The second sack included salt pork, hard cheese, a dozen oranges, raisins, and fourteen pounds sterling.

At the sight of the oranges, I rose.

"I shall give Star an orange. He will love it. I myself have not had one since our dear mother was alive."

"Oh, Sister," Harry called, glancing sideways at Martha, "when I tell you my stories you won't believe me. I shall tell of a place where oranges grow so thick on the trees you could just reach up and pick one any time you like. And lemons, too."

"Tomorrow, I'll make you an orange cake," I said exultantly, "and shall invite the Quincys. It will be a homecoming celebration."

"I accept without hesitation." He bowed facetiously, his sandy curls flopping over his face.

I smiled. "Yes, I must go to them shortly and tell them they're welcome tomorrow evening."

"They have been very kind," he agreed. "These past three nights I have enjoyed such comfort as I have not had in many years."

"Perhaps you would like to remain there?" I inquired. He might prefer having Dr. Franklin's room overlooking the dunes (so-called for it being the doctor's room when he visited) rather than the dairy overlooking the cheese.

"Oh, no," he said, seeing he had wounded me, though the wound was but a slight one. "I would rather sleep on a dirt floor and drink that hard Liberty tea of yours than be away from you now, sweet Lizzie."

"In that case, you shall be very happy here."

With that, I ran to the barn, calling, "Star! Look what I have for you!" My brother left to get his things from the great house and to invite the Quincys to dine with us on the morrow.

Before he left, I shouted to him, "Oh, Harry—kindly ask the Quincys to let Abigail know you are arrived, and that she's welcome to join us tomorrow."

"Abigail? You mean Mrs. John Adams? Why, I've already met her," he informed me, much to my surprise. "She came just yesterday, to glean news of you from Martha."

"Well, then," I amended, "if the Quincys could but extend her the invitation . . ."

He nodded his reassurance and was off.

Harry ended up staying with the Quincys for an hour or so, having entered into a conversation with Colonel Quincy about the progress of the war, while I returned to my friends.

I found only Martha. Eliza was feeding Johnny.

"How like you him?" I asked her as we worked by the small fire, preparing supper. We were used to delaying our gratification and didn't even think to avail ourselves of our treasure trove.

"He is sweet-natured and also giving, like you," she said simply.

"And quite handsome, too, don't you find?"

Martha blushed a deep crimson color. Then she sought to change the subject. "Is he much changed, Lizzie?" she asked after taking up a potato to peel.

"Oh, yes. I should not have known him. He was a boy when I said good-bye to him. And he looks poorly nourished, though none of his cheer has diminished."

"Know you how long he plans to stop?"

"Presumably some weeks, at least."

"Where shall we put him? He's tall." She spoke the words as if discussing the arrival of a new loom.

I considered. "He may have a pallet in the parlor if he wishes, but I imagine he shall prefer the dairy, as it has a door."

"Yes. I should say that's the best plan. That way, he will have protection against Johnny's crying as well."

"He's said nothing about Johnny. Do you think he noticed?"

Martha knew to what I referred.

"Certainly."

"Perhaps you're right." I nodded. Harry had seen the world now. I felt some envy. As a privateer who had traveled with a rough lot, he could not still be naive of the world's ways. He must have seen many people who looked like Johnny, especially in the West Indies.

Eliza entered then and took to helping us clear the dairy and prepare a bed for my brother. She seemed grateful for something to do.

•   •   •

The following morning, when we all awoke after a good night's sleep, I sat with my brother enjoying my first cup of real tea in some months. Eliza was off in a corner of the kitchen, feeding Johnny porridge. Martha had gone to feed the animals.

I turned to my brother and asked, "Am I much altered, Harry?"

"Indeed you are," he said. "I should not have recognized you had you not thrown your arms around me."

"Have I grown quite repulsive?"

"Repulsive? I should say not. You've grown lean. And there's a sadness I wish were not there." Harry reached his hand out for mine. "Lizzie, I'm truly sorry I was not there to condole with you at Jeb's death. By all accounts, he was a good and honorable man."

"He was a fool," I said.

Harry looked at me inquiringly. "In these times, I suppose we all must be either fools or cowards. Is there much in between?"

"Are you saying you're a fool as well, then?"

"Far bigger a fool than Jeb." He smiled.

I considered my brother's words.

"Yes, I suppose you are an even greater fool. See that you survive. For, now that I have you again, I could not bear to lose you."

"That is in our Maker's hands, but I will do my best."

"Oh, Harry." I embraced him warmly, for our banter belied my truer feelings.

●　　●　　●

I shall remember that evening as one of the finest and most joyous of the war years. For dinner we made an excellent creamed chicken stew with garden vegetables. Harry sat with his shoulders back and ate slowly, with the excellent manners my mother had taught us. But I could tell he had not eaten such a meal in many months. The glory of the evening, however, was the orange cake, with real orange juice in both cake and frosting! Mrs. Quincy greatly admired it and even asked me for the recipe. As I do believe it is one of my finer creations, I include the recipe here for the enjoyment of my reader. May it serve as a reminder that one must always endeavor to enjoy the sweet along with the bitter.

LIZZIE'S SPOILS-OF-WAR ORANGE CAKE

FOR THE CAKE: *Beat together eight soup spoons butter with one cup sugar until fluffy. Mix in two eggs and three soup spoons juice from an orange. In a small bowl, blend one and two-thirds cups flour, a teaspoon baking powder, and half a teaspoon salt. Add dry to wet mixture along with one cup buttermilk. Blend well. Stir in one cup raisins, half a cup chopped walnuts, and one soup spoon finely grated orange peel. Pour the mixture into a buttered pan and bake forty-five to fifty minutes. Cool before icing.*

FOR THE ICING: *Stir two soup spoons juice of orange and two cups powdered sugar together until the sugar dissolves completely and the icing is smooth. The icing should be thick enough to coat the back of a spoon. If it is too thick, add more liquid; if too thin, add a little sugar.*

Throughout the evening, Harry was so jolly that he set everyone else at ease. He had a great deal to discuss with Abigail, being an almost worshipful admirer of her husband.

"Quincy and I have spoken of it, and we are in total agreement." My brother called the colonel "Quincy," just as if he were a boyhood friend and not the wealthiest, most esteemed member of our community. Harry said, "While rats in Congress have crawled behind Mr. Adams's back to vilify him, who was it secured five million guilders from the parsimonious Dutch? Adams, that's who!"

At this speech, Abigail glanced at me in astonishment. My brother, with his long blond locks and brown skin, looked every bit the buccaneer. But his proud bearing and his ardent speech were those of a true gentleman and patriot. I observed other things about my brother that evening. Apart from his handsome countenance, he had our mother's gently humorous manner, her noble confidence, and that sincere curiosity about others that draws out even the most reluctant stranger. Our women were all entirely smitten.

The wine Colonel Quincy had brought did no harm by way of loosening tongues, and soon we were all laughing at one thing and another. Harry told of his travels in the West Indies and Spain. Finally, when it was very late and some of us could no longer hold our eyelids open, the Quincys took their leave. It was then near one in the morning. Harry yawned, then unceremoniously pulled off his shirt, exposing a tanned, naked chest. He undid his belt, much to our horror, and then, quite unconscious of our feelings, lay down on his bed in the dairy and began to snore, the door remaining wide open. We continued to stare at him for some time, as if a beautiful jungle animal slept in our midst!

After cleaning up, Martha and I finally collapsed together into our bed upstairs. It was one of the longest, happiest days of my life.

"I cannot move a limb." Martha giggled.

"Nor I. Shall we be better in the morning, do you think?"

"I know not. If it be not so, we shall have Johnny bring us breakfast in bed."

I slapped her for her insolence, my hand landing on her elbow in the darkness. "Johnny shall never serve, not if I have my way."

"Oh? And what is 'your way,' madam?"

"I'm fashioning a plan in my brain just now."

"Indeed," she said, "I am honored to know a woman of such great genius."

And that was the last word I heard, for after that I was fast asleep.

43

OH, THAT SUMMER OF '79, WHEN I was young and strong, and the grain grew tall and wavered in the salty ocean breeze! The sun grew hot, and gulls cawed overhead. Though Eliza's suffering was never far from my thoughts, with my brother by my side, my cup overflowed.

Each day, as Harry repaired our roof, mended our fences, and chopped and carried wood, we felt more secure, more cared for. We had been so used to doing everything for ourselves. What a luxury it seemed!

. . .

With Harry working in the fields, I felt free to take Star on a daily ride across the dunes. I could tell he looked forward to his ride, because the moment I approached his stall, he whinnied, shook his withers, and stomped his hooves. Once I had saddled and mounted him, he fairly galloped out of the yard down the path he knew and loved so well. Over the dunes we rode, rider and animal happy to be alive, to move freely in the soft, warm breeze. When I finally dismounted and led Star to his stall, he would roll his brown eyes down at me and bump my bosom with his muzzle. Oh, the joy of this mute yet unconditional love!

At night, after we had lit a good fire, Harry would tell us another story of his travels. As the darkness cooled our heated little crust of earth, we listened raptly to his tales of men as black as coal. Men with gold teeth and ear bangles large as coopers' staves. Powder a man could smoke in his pipe that would take him to heaven for days without end.

Harry told of battles, too, and dead and wounded mates. He told of His Excellency, whom he had met twice delivering goods in the South. A finer, straighter man he'd never met, he said, though he was a man of few words.

"But when did your ship fall into service?" I asked during one of these conversations.

"That first summer, July of '75. We turned around as soon as we heard the news of Washington's appointment."

While Harry spoke, little Johnny played by his feet. The child was much taken with the golden-haired sailor, and it clutched at our hearts to see him call for Harry every morning, happy to have a man about.

"Ha ha!" he called Harry. Johnny then would squirm out of his mother's arms toward my laughing brother. We began to call Johnny "Ha ha."

Martha watched Harry with increasing interest. I knew she admired my brother, but one night, when he had gone to the stables, she admitted to me, "I have never much cared for the men of my acquaintance. But he is made of different stuff. What is it, do you think, that makes him stand apart? Apart from his good looks, I mean."

"I am hardly impartial." I smiled. "But I think it is his unspoiled nature. He judges not others, but seems to find the good in everyone. You noted, no doubt, how he has not asked a single question about Eliza or Johnny?"

"Yes, I have," she said. Martha then went on to speak of other things.

•   •   •

Working out of doors each day, Harry's sandy hair grew lighter, his skin turned darker, until we hardly recognized him. More and more frequently did we find Martha stopped in mid-stride, to gaze at him, his body aglow with perspiration. And when he came in from his labor, she was the first to pour him a mug of cider and hand him a water basin and cloth. It was clear to Eliza, me, and certainly the ever-observant Abigail, that Martha had formed an attachment to my brother.

At night, after supper, when Harry told us stories of his travels, he would sometimes glance Martha's way, and we watched her fair complexion blush scarlet. But secretly I worried for Martha, convinced that her affections were in no way returned. In his travels, Harry must have had many experiences with women. He was so fair, so affable—to pluck the native beauties from each shore would have been easy enough. With what might little Martha tempt such a man of the world?

In another era, Martha might have been a very attractive girl. Her thick, dark hair was healthy. Her amber eyes, like her brother's, were large, careful in the measure they took of others, but not hard. She had a strong chin, a pale complexion, and an excellent body, which I have previously described.

But we had long since set aside our vanity. We were shrouded in plain linen caps, which had been washed till frayed and patched. Our shawls were stained yellow with Johnny's burps, which no amount of scrubbing could remove. Our hands were woefully red and callused, fingernails cracked and dirt-filled despite repeated scrubbings. No, we were scarred fruit. Unchosen.

Nevertheless, each evening, after the chores were done and the sun declined in the sky, I walked by my Harry's side along the shore. I did not ask when he would leave, nor did he mention it. Our walks, as our days, seemed to go on forever. Oftentimes, lost in conversation, we walked all the way to Milton and back.

But on one of these long walks some time in mid-July, my brother told me he would be leaving again. He knew not when but had no doubt it would be before the harvest.

"For where?" I grasped his arm.

"I cannot say."

"You know not, or you cannot say?"

"I cannot say." He turned to me entreatingly. "Dearest Lizzie, let us be grateful for what we have and not mourn what we cannot control."

"But you *can* control it!" I said, feeling spiteful and sorry for myself. I recalled how I had almost not forgiven him for being at gaming when our mother died. But the truth was, now that I had my brother back, I could not bear to give him up.

"Then I should be a coward."

"And now you're a fool!" I stormed off toward a cluster of rocks by the water.

He came up behind me. "We spoke in jest about my foolishness, but do you truly believe it, Lizzie? For that would wound my heart."

"No." I sighed. "You're no fool. I am proud of you and only ashamed of myself."

"You have borne your misfortunes like a soldier. You will be remembered for it."

"Remembered by whom?" I laughed.

"Your children. And mine. For surely you must have a goodly number of suitors?" he asked. "Indeed, I expect to find you married again, with a large brood of chicks, next time we meet."

Could Harry understand the depth of my love for Jeb? Could he understand the hardships I had suffered, which made what few men there had been in my midst largely irrelevant? Could he understand my fleeting attraction to Mr. Cleverly or my hopeless yearnings for Mr. Miller? I didn't believe so.

I said merely, "That's not possible."

"I can't believe that. Well, in any case, one day we shall look back with our families and recall these difficult times from a great distance."

"Perhaps," I conceded doubtfully.

"But Lizzie, you seem low—and not only on my account. Does something else trouble you?"

"No, no," I assured him, for I was neither willing nor able to speak of Mr. Miller with my brother.

Not one to dwell on womanly emotions, Harry said more cheerfully, "Just you wait. In five or six years' time, we shall be doddering after our many children, bemoaning the passing of these days."

"Bemoaning, indeed!"

"Mark my words," he asserted, pointing a finger at me, which I tried to grab. But his reflexes had grown too quick. He threw a hearty arm about my shoulders and we walked home in silence, the wind at our backs. It felt good to have a man's heavy arm about me.

Martha seemed even more distressed than I was about Harry's news.

"But why? Has he not done enough? He has fed Washington's army. He has fed us, though one could tell at first sight that he himself had not eaten in months. Lord, do these men not deserve a rest?"

Martha couched her distress in patriotic terms, but I saw right through her.

44

IT HAD BEEN SOME TIME SINCE WE'D seen Abigail. The July days were long and hot, and at the end of them we none of us wished to do more than wash ourselves and eat a simple supper before going to bed. Now, though, I felt inclined to visit with her, and I was just about to set off for her house when, as luck would have it, a messenger arrived with a dinner invitation from the lady herself.

The prospect of going to Abigail's to dine lifted our spirits. But, arriving at Abigail's door on the appointed evening, Abigail met us, clearly in great distress. I had baked a fragrant apple cake and brought it for her. Martha set it down on the kitchen table.

"I'm sorry, dear friends, but I have just read something most terrible—" Abigail could not finish her sentence.

"What is it?" I asked.

We followed her into the parlor, where I noticed the London broadside at once. According to this paper, a ship had been lost at sea, the result of sabotage. John Adams and John Quincy Adams were presumed to have been upon it.

I threw the paper down in disgust.

"This is rubbish," I said. "What evidence have you of its truth?"

"None," she said, wiping tears with the sleeve of her gown.

I took her hands. "You mustn't let this shake you, for I believe it signifies *good* news."

"Good news? Lizzie, I fear your words. If you love me—" She backed away without finishing her thought.

"I believe this news tells us that Mr. Adams is on a ship at this very moment, headed directly for home."

"I have received no letter about it."

"You have received no letter of any kind for six months. And yet we know him to have written. The letters do not get through. You know that far better than I, Abby."

"You're right. Oh, Lizzie, how you have calmed my quaking soul!"

She gave us all a little smile. She then took Johnny in her arms and hugged him to her as if he were the husband she had not seen in seventeen months.

"Mr. Lee, I apologize for my outburst." She turned at last to my brother, who had been standing quietly by Martha's side in the doorway.

"Don't apologize, Mrs. Adams. I admire your courage, indeed I do."

With that he bowed to her, and she, like a mother, embraced him.

Lighter in spirit, Abigail proceeded to serve us a dinner of mussel soup with a baked stuffed haddock, and she served my apple cake, made with British flour. Over dessert, Abigail, much to our surprise, suddenly bent her head and prayed.

"We thank our Redeemer for this bounty and for a safe voyage for my men." Then she added, her head still bowed, "Let us also thank Henry for the flour with which Lizzie made her cake."

"Hear, hear!" exclaimed Eliza and Martha in unison. Johnny, sensing the merriment, banged on his plate with a spoon, staring at his beloved Harry and crying, "Ha ha!" until Martha had to take the spoon from him. Thus the evening concluded in far better spirits than it had begun.

Johnny was fast asleep when we arrived home, and my brother carried him into the house; the child had grown heavy. Eliza could no longer carry him about as she used to, though he still dearly wished it.

Martha and Eliza descended carefully in the darkness, and I was about to call for Thaxter to unhitch the horses when I remembered that we'd left Thaxter in Portsmouth. Someone suddenly grasped my arm, frightening me so much that I cried out.

"Forgive me for startling you." The voice was familiar.

"Allow me to help you down, Mrs. Boylston," he said.

At the sound of Thomas Miller's voice, I cried out, "Oh! Martha! Eliza!" The fear must have sounded in my voice for Martha returned to me at once.

"What is it, Lizzie?"

"As you see," I pointed into the gloom where her brother stood. "It is your brother. What business does he have just now with us, and at this late hour?"

"I know not," Martha replied, apparently as startled as I. "But as he's here, I shall offer him tea."

"I come with no ill intent," said Mr. Miller.

Was he daft? Did the man not know he was at any moment to be arrested and perhaps hanged? "Well, why did you come, then?" I asked.

Mr. Miller smiled uncomfortably at us and asked merely, "May I come in?"

I curtsied and led him in.

Once inside, I introduced Thomas Miller to my brother, and they shook hands. There was nothing else to be done. Harry, who knew nothing about Mr. Miller or his loyalties, launched upon an amusing tale of his attempts to improve our farm. He was so affable, and so ignorant, that I cringed for him, and I imagined that Martha did so as well.

Martha went to put the kettle on, but Mr. Miller forestalled her with a hand on her arm.

"Do not trouble yourself, Sister, on my account. It is very late, and I'll stay but a moment."

"You shall not stop here, then?" she asked.

"Oh, no. I am staying at—"

Here he thought better of divulging his lodgings and turned to me. "You are very quiet tonight. Are you well?"

"Yes, very."

"Two words? Is that all you care to say?"

"I am tired."

"That is three," Mr. Miller said, a lift in his voice, but he had not the heart to joke further, as the mood around him was grave.

"You came from the direction of Mrs. Adams's," he said. "Did you dine there?"

"Why do you wish to know?"

Martha cast me a look.

"Oh, no particular reason." Suddenly, Mr. Miller grew uncomfortable. "Indeed, it is too late. I see you are eager to have me gone. I was in the village and longed to see—my sister. Forgive me. It was a selfish wish. Tomorrow is her birthday, did you know?"

"I didn't know. She never shared that with me." I turned to Martha. "Martha, is it true?"

"Oh," Martha said, looking at her feet, "I dislike a fuss."

"Well, I shall make an enormous fuss tomorrow," Mr. Miller said. "For now, I retire. Good night." Thomas Miller bowed formally and was gone the next moment. But my heart continued to pound long after he had left.

"Seems an excellent fellow," said my brother, helping himself to an oatcake in the kitchen.

"Looks can be deceiving," I whispered, for I did not wish Martha to overhear us. "More on that topic by and by. Now," I said more loudly, "you're keeping Eliza up." I gave a backward glance to poor Eliza, who was nearly falling over with fatigue. She could hardly undress before Harry retired to his chamber.

"Oh! Sorry!" My brother nodded, then made off to the dairy with a mouthful of oatcake. He returned a moment later, craving water and making choking signs at his throat.

"Go to bed already, Brother."

"I'm going! I'm going!" He trailed back with a wave of his hand. Martha's eyes smiled after him.

45

THE FOLLOWING DAY, MR. MILLER RETURNED EARLY. The very sight of him made me tremble in fear, whether of him or for him I couldn't say. For while I had no reason to think otherwise than that Abigail's information was correct, and that he would very soon be arrested, Mr. Miller's face expressed an inexplicable good cheer.

I was in the dooryard feeding my chickens when he arrived. I saw the dust lift off the path moments before his horse came into view. I held little Johnny in my arms, wanting to let his mother sleep, for Eliza had been greatly fatigued.

Thomas alit from his horse and tied him to my post. His face when he saw me was soft, his eyes tender. About his mouth was the tiniest curl of amusement. He was, once more, the insouciant Mr. Miller I had known in Cambridge, the man who made me laugh, and with whom I was entirely in love.

Seeing me with Johnny, Mr. Miller grinned. "A child becomes you, Elizabeth."

I nestled my face against Johnny's warm head. "Have you breakfasted, Mr. Miller?" I asked.

"Yes. They feed one well where I stay. Make you a preparation of any kind for my sister?"

"Indeed I do. A cake of British goods confiscated by my pirate brother. I must go make it."

I turned to go back inside, but not before glancing up the hill to ascertain whether the colonel watched our movements, for I had come to suspect that he used his spyglass for more than watching departing British ships.

"May I watch?" Mr. Miller asked.

I was surprised at this request, but could not think of a quick rejoinder. "If you like."

"I should like it very much. I enjoy the domestic arts immensely. Watching them, I mean."

"Indeed."

For some reason, I blushed at this. We entered the kitchen, whereupon he sat himself at the table, stretched his long legs out, and said, "Show me, if you will, how to make a cake."

"If you truly wish."

"I do."

"Well, one must go about it in an orderly fashion," I was moved to say, as if somehow Mr. Miller might otherwise believe me to be disorderly. "I dislike waste immensely. And chaotic habits in the kitchen breed waste."

Mr. Miller nodded gravely, and I glanced at him to know whether he mocked me. His countenance remained perfectly sober.

"Orderly, no waste. Go on."

I continued. "First, you mix the wet and the dry separately."

"Wet and dry separately."

I stopped my narrative and placed a hand on my hip. "Shall you repeat everything I say? For then this shall take twice as long, and it is a hot day, Mr. Miller."

"How else am I to remember it?" he objected petulantly, looking up at me with a disconcertingly serious expression.

I sighed and proceeded. "For this cake, I use four eggs. And a glass of milk. Excuse me."

I moved into the dairy to fetch my eggs and milk. His eyes followed my every step. Returning, I continued.

"You break the eggs thus, then beat them smooth. Should you wish for a lighter cake, you must separate the yolks from the whites and beat them separately."

"Separate whites, fluffier," this tall, serious man repeated. It might have made anyone else roil with laughter.

I kept my bearings, however, and would not be thrown off.

"Add the milk and stir. Then you add your spices."

"Spices?" he asked. "What use you for such a purpose? To add spice, I mean."

Forgive me, Reader, but I could not help but feel that every one of Mr. Miller's utterances contained a secondary meaning. But neither did I wish him to stop. No, I told him of cinnamon, and nutmeg, and baking powder. When the time finally came to mix the dry with the wet, I was scarlet in the face, and Mr. Miller stood abruptly.

"Allow me to help you. That looks demonishly difficult."

He rose to his full height and walked toward me. I remained rigidly still as he came behind me, taking the spoon from me to stir. At the same time, little Johnny crawled into the kitchen and sat by our feet. He was playing with a silver spoon. Mr. Miller pressed into me from behind, so gently one might almost call it inadvertent. But only almost.

"Like this?" he asked, beginning to stir.

I felt his breath on my neck and shivered. His arms began to fold around me, and I could feel the circular movement of his torso as he stirred the bowl.

"Yes."

Suddenly Martha appeared at the door. I blushed as if caught in some sinful act. I had thought her still asleep. She herself looked flushed and excited. Hearing her, Mr. Miller turned, spoon in hand, and Martha literally leapt into his arms.

"Birthday felicitations, Sister," he cried. "How you grow! You must be, what—forty-seven, now?"

"Nineteen, you idiot."

I looked over at Harry, who stood watching in the doorway. He leaned casually against the frame, watching Martha and her brother. Had he seen me and Mr. Miller stirring the cake? And had I seen him release Martha's hand upon entering the kitchen?

When Martha looked up and saw the red coals in the hearth, she scowled. "Are you mad, to be baking on such a day? It is not struck nine and already an inferno in here."

"It's nearly finished, and you'll be thankful and eat it without complaining, if you please."

"I have a suggestion that should please us all very well," interrupted my brother, who was in unusually high spirits. "As the cake shall keep well enough, and as it is *very* hot—"

Eliza suddenly appeared, looking agitated, in search of her missing son. When she saw him playing happily with a spoon by my feet, she sighed.

"Johnny, where did you go off to?" she cried, not expecting an answer. But to our mutual astonishment, Johnny looked up and pointed at me: "Izzzzie!"

"You went to Izzzzie?" She turned to me. "Lizzie, did you hear him?"

We were all so overjoyed at this new word that for a moment we just stood and clapped our hands together, crying, "Izzzzie! Izzzzie." Johnny clapped and shouted my name as well.

I glanced at Thomas Miller, but he merely kept his affable, unreadable smile as he stared down at Eliza's child.

"A remarkable boy."

"Yes, we love him dearly. But I must get this baking immediately."

I poured the batter into a tin and set it upon a trivet by the coals.

"I say it's too hot for baking," my brother continued, looking at me. "You shall melt away."

"Well, what have you in mind? Go on."

"I suggest we all go and jump in the colonel's pond."

Cries of both opposition and assent broke out then in my kitchen. Johnny banged the floor with the spoon.

I put my hand to my ears. "All right. Anything! But allow me twenty minutes for my cake."

And with that everyone dispersed to prepare for a swim at the colonel's pond, otherwise known as Black's Creek. Mr. Miller exited the kitchen with his sister. I lifted up little Johnny, who insisted on bringing his spoon with him.

Twenty minutes later, I had removed my cake to cool, setting it on the kitchen table by the open window. I wiped my hands and ran outside, for by this point I was drenched and could have plunged headfirst into the pond.

Dying of the heat, we all ran into the dunes, which shivered in golden, mid-summer fullness. Soon, I thought, perhaps that afternoon, we would need to begin cutting the flax. Then the corn would need harvesting, and a great deal else. But today was Martha's birthday, and a spirit of incautious joy had seized us all.

I had never had much occasion to swim and hardly knew how. I had certainly never swum in the colonel's pond. As it was salt-water, it was not a true pond. And as it was an inlet of the ocean, it was not truly the colonel's, but we called it the colonel's pond nonetheless. Once or twice, I had gathered herbs there—Seneca root and rushes for the lamps. It had never once occurred to me to throw myself into it, and I had no real intention of doing so now.

But as we approached the pond, stopping to observe the wild-flowers and other fragrant and medicinal plants that bordered it, a wild recklessness took hold of our brothers. They ripped off their shoes and began to remove their shirts, though we all called, "No, indeed! Should you wish to strip yourselves naked, go around to the other side of the rushes!"

"Other side? Bollocks!" my brother cried.

"Harry!" I said, aghast at his foul language, but everyone else merely laughed. We were so hot, the sun pounded, and the pond looked like pure ecstasy. Its surface was cool and glassy. I sat Johnny down, and he crawled to the water's edge, heedless of the rough stones and sharp shells. Then, without warning, he threw my silver spoon into the pond.

Thomas Miller glanced at my brother. The two of them took Johnny's toss as a signal of fate.

"That's it, Tom—go!" my brother cried out. "I'll race you for the spoon!"

The two men, clad now only in their breeches, ran straight into the water with pained cries of "Ah!" and "It's cold! Dear Lord!"

We looked at them disapprovingly, but only for a moment. They dove under and emerged dripping, wiping the salty water from their joyous faces. Never had I seen Thomas Miller so happy, so entirely abandoned. Compared to this, his earlier insouciance appeared studied. He tipped his face up toward the sun, let his hair fling back behind him, closed his eyes, and laughed freely. To accompany this joyous image, I had the recent memory of his body pressed against mine in the kitchen. And while he did not remove his clothing now, I could imagine full well all that lay beneath it.

I cannot recall which of us followed the men first, but within moments we had kicked off our shoes and gone running in after them, our petticoats rising up and ballooning to the water's surface.

"Ah! Ooh!" we gasped as our muscles constricted, taking our breath away. But it was too late to back down now.

"Go all the way!" cried my brother, no doubt the most used of all of us to taking a cold dip. I let myself sink down, down, into the water, before popping back up with a yelp of delight. The cold on our hot scalps was a joy unto itself. Life was good. And war? Well, as my brother had rightly exclaimed: oh, bollocks!

All but Eliza got her head under water. She did not wish to take her eyes off little John, who played so close to the water's edge. I ran, drenched and laughing, and gathered Johnny up as Martha tackled Eliza, bringing her under the now roiling surface of the pond.

"Oh! No, indeed!" Eliza cried. And then, in another moment, she was under.

"Look, Johnny, water!" I gently introduced the boy to the water as he, expressing the shock of his life, began to squeal and flail his arms and legs as naturally as if he might swim away from me. I kept a tight grip upon him.

Our cries of joy might have sounded like a sudden conflagration from afar. Soon, numb with cold, we panted toward land and fell laughingly upon the ground.

Swimming in that cold pond on that hot day, the world fell away from us. No more were we Patriots and Tories, spinsters and widows and mulatto bastards. We were young and happy to be alive on this God-given earth. We were all hopelessly in love as well, but for just this one moment it was joy merely to feel that love within us, without hope of its realization.

We lay on the ground laughing and gasping for breath for as long as we dared. The sun warmed our faces and the icy garments that clung to every bend of our limbs and torsos. Then, one by one, we gradually rose and made our way back to the house. Harry said he was ravenous and wished to sample the cake. Laughing, I told him he would need to wait until after supper, as I had not frosted it. As we neared the house, passing by Thaxter's former cabin and the barn, I thought I heard a noise and stopped. The others stopped behind me.

"What is that?" asked Martha.

"Shh," I hushed her.

It was a groaning noise, coming from the barn. The groan sounded agonized and nearly human. At that moment, Thomas Miller heard it and ordered us back with a wave of his arm. "Stay here!"

Along with my brother, he swiftly but quietly ran to the barn.

After a moment, I heard Harry exclaim, "Dear God."

"Oh, my good Lord," added Thomas Miller.

The two men then spoke to each other in tones too low for us to hear.

"Ladies, remain where you are," one of them called. "Do not approach."

But I would not remain where I was, not on anyone's orders. I ran to the barn at once just as I passed my brother running in the other direction, toward my house, with great celerity.

Inside the barn, all was dark at first. Then, as my eyes adjusted, I saw Thomas Miller bent down over a large, dark, writhing form on the ground.

It was Star. He was lying on his side, endeavoring to raise himself up. His eyes, gleaming wild and white in the darkness, soon caught mine. They were filled with agony and entreaty.

"Star!" I shrieked. I bent over him and hugged his neck as he endeavored, with all his ebbing strength, to pull himself toward me. He seemed unable to breathe. His breath came in groaning gasps. Blood leaked from his mouth. He continued to look at me imploringly with his huge brown eyes.

"Star! Star!"

Hearing my voice, his nose pressed into my neck in a loving, familiar gesture. I lay upon him; feeling me, his breathing eased. Oh, what agony for me as well as him!

"Stand away," said Thomas Miller, pushing me aside.

"I shall not," I said.

I felt his hands upon me, moving me aside by force. A powerful shot rang out, and Star fell back. His eyes rolled up, almost in relief. He was dead.

46

CLOTHING DRIPPING, I SAT FOR A MOMENT on the ground by Star's side. My beloved, my faithful companion, was now silent forever. He had been my one true companion. I could have wailed like Hecuba, made milch the burning eyes of heaven, but I did not. No, there was no time for mourning. I felt a hand on my shoulder, which I shrugged off at once. I must have appeared beaten down, at a loss for words. At a loss for life and even reason.

Far from it. It took but a few moments before I was on my feet. I looked about briefly. My brother stood there, panting and wild-eyed, Martha by his side. Eliza, having shielded Johnny's ears, had moved swiftly into the house to protect him from the horrible sight: a noble beast stilled in a posture of utter torment. Thomas Miller had set the musket down beside Star, along with its flask of powder, and disappeared. Presumably he had gone to fetch help.

I stared at the musket and reached to pick it up. I gazed about me again, hoping I might catch a clue as to the author of this evil. Nothing was out of place. I did not then see the powder residue at the bottom of his feed pail; Martha told me of it only later. But I did notice a folded paper lying upon the ground just to the side of the path that led to the colonel's. It must have fallen from Mr. Miller's pocket. It was but a small, wet rectangle, upon which brown ink had run. I at first thought little of it and stuffed it in my skirt pocket to return to its owner. Then, a moment later, curiosity got the better of me.

I picked it out of my pocket with one hand and unfolded it. I expected to find a bill of sale or an account of expenses. Instead, I saw traces of a letter in ink that had been washed away by the pond, but the telltale signature had not been entirely erased. I stared at it a moment longer before placing it back in my skirt. Slowly, I lifted the musket from the ground. Slowly, I loaded it.

"Lizzie, wait." Martha took my arm. "What is it you plan to do?"

I said nothing, only moved quickly through the garden. I met one of my new day laborers, a young man named Samuel Whitcomb. He had turned up only just the week before, seeking work. He had seemed too good to be true—a young man of few words, willing to work for nothing but a promise of future recompense. I had accepted at once. Mr. Whitcomb looked at me in silent alarm. My petticoats were dripping wet, and Medusa-like locks of hair clung to my face. In my firm grasp was a loaded musket.

"My horse is dead. Kindly call upon Mr. Billings at the tannery. He will be of assistance."

He said nothing, but merely moved carefully aside as I ran up the hill and through the dunes toward the great house. I gathered speed as I went, until once again Martha, who had been breathlessly trailing behind, took hold of me.

"Lizzie. It's not safe. Allow me to accompany you."

"No, I need no help to go a few feet up the hill. I'll return as soon as I've ascertained the truth. For I believe I now know what that truth is, though everyone sought to obscure it from my eyes. Stay with Eliza."

"Lizzie!" she called after me.

I ran the rest of the way to the colonel's, heedless of her entreaties.

Ann Quincy opened the door. She took me in all in a single glance: my wet dress and my loose, wet hair, musket at the ready. To her credit, her alarm seemed one of genuine concern for my person, not my impropriety.

"What has happened? Are you hurt?"

"I'm afraid I must see your husband on a matter of greatest urgency. It cannot wait."

She ushered me in. "Of course. But don't you wish to change first? You are dripping wet."

"No, thank you. It's only from the pond."

"The colonel is in the parlor with the others." She pointed to the right.

When my head turned in the direction of her outstretched arm, I saw Colonel Quincy, Richard Cranch, and Mr. Miller. They sat in a tight circle and were deep in discussion, which ceased the moment I entered.

When Thomas saw me, he bounded up from his chair. Like myself, he had not had time to change out of his wet clothes. Water pooled everywhere on the colonel's Turkey carpet. No one seemed to pay it the least attention.

"Mrs. Boylston."

I mastered myself, though perhaps not as well as he. "I believe you dropped this in your haste," I said. I then proffered the wet letter, but Thomas Miller didn't move to fetch it from me. He stood there as if awaiting command.

Colonel Quincy now stood to address me.

"Lizzie, my child, perhaps you'd care to change out of your wet things?"

"I would *not* care to change, thank you. I merely wish—"

Here I recalled I was still holding my musket and must have appeared to Colonel Quincy and his guests like a madwoman. But I did not relinquish the weapon. Instead, I held it tighter to me. "Allow me to know what is going on."

The musket, though not pointed at them, told them of my intent to brook no refusal.

"Please, sit," said the colonel, pointing to a chair. But I stood firm. I continued to hold the letter before me, the letter that had been all but washed away by our impetuous frolic.

"If you refuse to answer me, then I will ask him myself."

The colonel was silent.

I turned to Mr. Miller. "Why is it, Mr. Miller, that you had upon your person a letter from His Excellency, General Washington?"

Mr. Miller glanced at the colonel.

"I understand you demand an explanation, but time is of the essence," said Colonel Quincy.

Thomas nodded, then glanced up briefly at me, a look of misery upon his countenance. Yet I had no pity for him.

"Lizzie," the colonel finally began, "I'm afraid you have been deceived. But believe me when I say it could not be helped. You see—"

"What is it I see?" I cried. "That you must tell me."

"If you only calm yourself, I shall tell you."

"I'm quite calm. The fact that some evildoer poisoned my horse has made me quite, quite calm, I assure you."

Here, in a gesture of good faith, I set the musket down on the carpet.

"Well, I suppose we can keep it from you no longer," began the colonel, not looking at me. "Mr. Miller has been in my employ these three years past. I engaged him in April of '76, upon His Excellency's personal request."

All eyes were upon me, a wet, trembling, devastated creature. My silence was but momentary. "How is it I am to believe such a thing?"

"Lizzie, it is true."

The voice came from behind me. It belonged to Richard Cranch.

I turned to him. "You knew of this?"

He refused to meet my eyes. "I have known but a relatively short time, yes."

"And you, my closest friends, have knowingly deceived me? And sought to warn me against him and treat him as the lowest criminal?"

My regard for Mr. Miller was now exposed for all to see. The "him" in question remained silent while the colonel spoke. "Elizabeth, your heart is ready to serve. I have noted it with great admiration. But your skills—a successful spy must remain unknown even to his nearest and dearest. Surely you can understand that."

My head understood, Reader; but my heart—how it revolted! I could not tell my friends the true suffering I had experienced at war with myself over Mr. Miller.

"And Abigail? Does she know?"

"No, indeed," interjected Colonel Quincy. "It is she most of all we seek to protect."

"I want proof," I said finally. "I can tolerate no more doubt. Not one more moment of it." I didn't need proof, not really. What I needed was for my friends to account for themselves fully.

Perhaps I had been breathing too rapidly, for I very suddenly felt quite unwell. "I am most grievously tired," I said.

Ann came toward me. "Please. Allow Ginny to change you. I have something suitable, no doubt."

The room had begun to spin. As we moved down the hall, Thomas Miller approached to steady me.

"You look faint, Lizzie. Please—allow Mrs. Quincy to help you out of your wet clothing. When you return, you may read this." He showed me a large folded parchment.

"Is that proof of your stainless heroism?" I said mockingly. I was then overcome—by grief, fear, betrayal, and self-pity, all at once—and burst into long-delayed tears.

"Come," implored Mrs. Quincy, "I insist. The letter shall wait."

But I said suddenly, "I shall move no farther until I read what Mr. Miller has offered."

I had walked toward the stairs, where I stood waveringly. My tears had ceased as quickly as they had begun. I had reached that point of unmooring within my mind that would brook no contradiction, that cared nothing for consequences. Oh, how hard and steely this thing was! And yet, it seemed to consume my flesh as it galvanized my spirit, for I felt truly weak now and sat down upon the steps.

Mr. Miller addressed me. The awkwardness of this address I shall never forget, since all present now knew of my feelings for him, yet he did not express the slightest affection for me. Indeed, so correct was he that I entirely doubted that he shared my feelings— another grief, another mortification, to add to the rest!

"Mrs. Boylston, I understand your wish to know all, and yet you must also understand it is not safe to know everything."

"Safe?" I laughed mirthlessly. "My house has been raided. My beloved horse is dead. Think you that I have cowered in my chamber all these months? You of all people know otherwise. Give it here." I took the parchment from Thomas Miller's hand.

In faint brown script, it read:

To the honorable Jos. Q,

I was heartened to learn that the situation in Braintree has been contained and that Traitors T. and H. have been removed. But we know there to be others, both among us and among you. I have only now had a Communication from Gen'l S. that the Man who presented himself to you as his Aide Cleverly is one Benjamin Thompson of Stonington, New Hampshire. We believe him to be among the leaders of the planned attack on J.A. and J.Q.A. I have also had communication from Dr. F. in Paris, who has lately heard from his Contacts in England that this Group will stop at nothing to achieve their Aims. My profoundest Thanks to T.M. for his untiring Vigilance and strong Intelligence, particularly regarding the imminent arrival of La S. upon your shores. You must remain ever-vigilant until our great citizen is safely arrived with his most precious cargo. I know you to have spent every waking Breath to protect our Cause and our brave Citizens, and I have Faith that you shall continue to do your best in this most treacherous of Times.

Your obedient, Geo. Washington

Reading the letter, I let out a crazed laugh. So, gloomy Mr. Thayer, who had always been at his lap desk, had in fact been Mr. Stephen Holland, the counterfeiter whose whereabouts had long been sought—in our very midst. All along, in our midst! And Dr. Flynt, that paunchy, affable man who had said he was from Philadelphia, had been Holland's partner, Mr. Tufts.

As for Mr. Cleverly, that truth at least felt like some vindication. He was in fact Benjamin Thompson, the notorious scientist and wife-abandoner from Stonington. The leader of this band of traitors. About him, at least, I had been entirely correct. I had known Mr. Cleverly's treachery when General Sullivan himself had been duped.

As I sat, wet and shaking, on the back steps of the colonel's house, the final image wavering before my dizzy eyes was of Mr. Cleverly and myself, hand in hand among my fruitful orchards. I then fainted, thus mercifully closing the scene.

47

I AWOKE IN A DRY SHIFT AND a cool bed. It took me a few moments to realize that I was not at home but in the house of Colonel Quincy, in Dr. Franklin's room. I knew not how long I'd been asleep.

"Ginny!" I called at once, rising. "Ginny!" Ginny soon came running, alarmed.

"I wish to dress at once."

She nodded and soon returned with fresh stays and a fine gown of European origin. I thanked her and bade her leave. My head cleared slowly.

Thomas Miller, in the employ of Colonel Quincy these three years past. An intimate of His Excellency. My beloved Star dead, most likely poisoned by Mr. Cleverly, either out of pure spite, or as punishment for my attempts to glean information.

Unbidden, a key turned in my brain. I must have been working at the lock in my long sleep. Suddenly, I knew who had killed those men.

"God forgive her!" I moaned, sinking back onto the bed. Hearing me, Ginny and Ann came running to see what was the matter.

Mrs. Quincy sat beside me. "It is a grievous loss you suffer, Elizabeth. What a horrible, unconscionable act."

But I was not then weeping for Star. My grief was for someone else entirely.

．　　　．　　　．

She had changed out of her wet clothes and was working calmly among the rows of flax. From a distance, and through her weak eyes, I might have looked quite like Mrs. Josiah Quincy. Recognizing me at last, Martha stood as if she would run toward me. But I was a wolf in sheep's clothing. When she saw my countenance, she stopped, turned back, knelt to the ground, and resumed her work. I knelt beside her in the field and began to pull the flax with her, without a word, tying them into bundles and placing them aside to dry.

"I thought you were Mrs. Quincy," she said at last.

"No," I replied. "She lent me a change of clothing."

"That was kind of her. It's too good for flax-picking."

Martha paused, then added, "I am deeply sorry for Star." She did not look at me and continued to work.

"I know you are. You loved him near as much as I."

"I did, Lizzie!" She grasped my arm. "You must believe that. I should die if you thought otherwise."

"I know," I said again. I kissed her on the side of her head, which calmed her. Though she might soon be abandoned by all who knew her, I would not abandon her now, or ever.

"Where are the others?" I asked.

"Eliza is within, exhausted. I changed her out of her wet frock and put her to bed. Our brothers have gone to town."

"To town?" I asked. She stopped pulling flax for a moment and turned to me.

"Harry has gone for his ship. John Adams arrives tomorrow or the next day, and they shall be ready."

"Ready for what?"

"Did the colonel not say?" A thin, wry smile began to play about her lips, as if she had expected me now to know everything.

"No, indeed. They allowed me to read a letter from His Excellency, which confirmed the plot we had all suspected. Can you believe that Mr. Cleverly is not John Cleverly at all, but that famous scientist Benjamin Thompson? Or that Mr. Thayer was the counterfeiter, Mr. Stephen Holland?"

"Of course I can believe it." She took my hand. "I could not have done what I did had I not been convinced of these things. I'll admit, I did not know about Cleverly until this very moment. But Thomas and I deeply suspected it."

"And your Thomas is not what he appeared, either."

"Nor am I." She smiled, but it was no happy smile.

"Oh, Martha. I have many dozens of questions, but I lack the heart for conversation just now. Answer me just one thing: What are the enemy's intentions regarding John Adams?"

Martha looked at me gently. Or rather, this stranger I called Martha Miller, spy for General Washington, killer of two men. Men who were no patriots, but dangerous enemies to the Cause and to our most beloved friends.

"The intentions of these men from the beginning, Lizzie, have been to force Adams home and to assassinate him upon his arrival. An earlier plan had been to kidnap Abigail to force John home. I put a stop to that one. The attack scheduled for tomorrow is to be but one among numerous assassinations."

"God," I muttered.

Martha continued. "They have known about me for some months and have sought to silence me without revealing themselves. It had little to do with you or your activities. Although," she added, looking away momentarily, "your meeting Cleverly this last time, and recognizing him as you did, alarmed them enough to act swiftly against us."

"Am I responsible for Star?" I said after listening to Martha's horrifying explanation. "If so, tell me at once. I would rather at least have that upon my head than upon yours."

"I know not," she said, and I believed her. "It is possible that they were plotting retaliation for many months and your actions had nothing to do with it. However, consequence is the price of involvement. The only certainty in choosing to act is that there *will* be consequences."

Martha was right. The notion that I could do good and suffer no consequences, create no victims, was a naive and dangerous one. I felt deeply ashamed, though I knew not what I might have done differently.

"In any case," she continued, "regarding *La Sensible*, rest assured: Our men are forewarned. They shall be here tomorrow. Scores of them, along with several trusted officers of the Continental Army. We shall finally apprehend the villains."

The Martha who spoke this most privileged information was someone far tougher, far more worldly, and far more competent, than even I had known her to be.

My heart grieved for Martha and for what she had done. But part of me could not help admiring her as well. All this time, I thought she had been my apprentice; but, in some ways, I had been hers as well.

"And Abigail? Does she know John returns tomorrow? And the grave circumstances under which he does so?"

Martha reached out and grasped my arm with preternatural force. Her eyes were hard and dark. In them I now recognized the cold, knowing look that had so wounded me when she warned me away from her brother.

"For her safety and that of her husband and child, she must know nothing. Do you understand? Breathe a word, and our months of hard work shall be for naught. Promise me. *Swear* it."

I swore to it at once. "But has she really no idea he's to arrive tomorrow?"

"None, I assure you. Though you very nearly gave us away with your apt conjectures the other night."

I fell silent then, and we both gradually sank back down to the rows of flax. I could not yet make myself pass the barn and enter the house. As if reading my mind, Martha said, "Mr. Billings and two other fellows came round with a cart about an hour ago."

She gave me no further details, and I sought none, but merely replied, "Oh, that is good."

We bundled flax in silence for a while. The hot sun was finally going down beyond the hill, giving us respite. For some reason, the low sun made me think of Abigail, and I smiled.

"Why do you smile?" Martha asked.

"I was thinking how, bringing you to Abigail's the other night, I had in mind to put ideas of marriage and children in your head."

"You thought it an auspicious time to marry me off, then?"

"I'm ashamed to say I saw you in an entirely different light then, Martha. Someone who perhaps could do better than to be a poor midwife."

I thought she would object, but she seemed to have her own thoughts upon the matter. "In a sense you are right, Lizzie. I've had no thoughts for the future until now. They seemed—yet seem—an impossible luxury. Perhaps there shall be *time* enough to be happy, but where? In what place? I cannot imagine it."

I had not the lie in me to contradict her.

"I had a taste of happiness, once." I smiled wistfully. "It was very good."

We worked until we grew parched and thirsty and agreed we should go inside to check on Eliza.

As she rose, setting the last bundle wearily upon the pile, Martha said, "You must despise me now, Lizzie." She swayed in the sun, for she had stood up too quickly. Martha passed a forearm over her eyes to shade them. The hair on her brown arm was quite golden.

"I don't despise you," I said warmly. "I know not what I feel. I am still in shock, I suppose."

"One cannot love a murderess," she said simply. "I love not myself, and therefore cannot expect you, or anyone else, to love me. You recall that we once discussed whether the ends justified the means."

"I had no idea of its being of any import whatsoever. Two bored women involved in hypotheticals. But you've acted in a manner consistent with your beliefs," I said resignedly.

"I knew not then what my task would be, but I knew all too well it would be heavy. If it helps you—the knowledge affords me little comfort—we had been given orders from the highest source"—here, Martha paused so that I might follow her—"to affect a soft, secret riddance of these men. Something that might alarm their brothers in treachery but not the general public, for that would merely steer sympathy to their side and make it easier for others in the ring to hide.

"Thomas could not easily conceal himself among our parish, but I could. It was Colonel Quincy's idea, when once Abigail asked his advice about a servant for you. The deception was put into play then. The colonel was highly self-congratulatory about it."

"I knew you were hiding something from me. It drove me mad. But to think that I actually believed you a Tory spy . . ."

"Yes," she said. "Can you imagine how I felt, every moment feeling your judging eyes upon me? Believing me the enemy, a traitor to the Cause?"

I stopped in the doorway, for I had no wish to continue this conversation within.

"Impossible to bear!" I cried, grasping her hand in sympathy. "But Martha, did you take the belladonna? I searched, only to find it undisturbed. Not after—"

"Mr. Holland," she finished for me. "Yes, I took some, but such few grains you could not have noticed. The second time, I needed to avoid arousing your suspicions, for I knew you would discover the cause of death and check your stores. I thus took great pains to make some while you were in Cambridge. But I was rushed and inexperienced. It is why I was ill when you came upon me having a puke. I was not careful enough and must have swallowed a grain or two."

"Oh, Martha, you fool! You might have died! Indeed, you could easily have died."

"Lizzie, I believed my words when I spoke them those many months ago."

"And I came to agree with you, dearest. For sometimes fighting is necessary. But murder? My mind grows befuddled at how one justifies this." There. I had said it. I had said the word.

Martha nodded. "I have done it, Lizzie. I have taken life. And I am here to tell you how it feels. It is not something you can possibly know aforehand, however clever or designing you might think yourself. Having done it—twice—having taken life, I can report in no uncertain terms: it is *not* right. It can never be right. It is not what God intends, and when the war is over, I shall become a Quaker and endeavor to atone."

"You can't be serious." The words left my mouth immediately, for, with our upbringing, she might as well have said, "I shall become a man on Mars."

"Oh, I'm perfectly serious," she said. Then she added, "If I am not hanged first." She smiled ruefully, though this much I knew to be no joke.

Because I loved her, I endeavored then to shore up her spirits. I said, "If it is true that you have given up your self-love, then you have given up everything a woman can give—nay, more than is right, Martha."

"Perhaps," she considered. "Perhaps I have. What is to be done for it, I know not."

.   .   .

What did I feel? It was too soon to say. I dared not speak more then, for fear of saying something I would forever regret. But deep within my soul I rejoiced at Martha's repentance. With repentance there is hope of salvation, if not in this world, then in the next. I had only one dark, chill moment as I passed through the door: were our side to lose, Martha would be hanged. I shuddered, tightened my lips, and slipped inside, grateful for the cool darkness. None of us could eat my beautiful spice cake, and I fed it to a grateful crowd of chickens.

.   .   .

Later, after the sun had descended behind the hills, and I had bathed and changed into my own clothes and felt somewhat revived, I took a tankard of cider out with me and walked down through the dunes to the beach. I spoke little that evening to either Martha or Eliza. My experiences—of Star's agonizing death, of my new knowledge of Martha and her brother, and of the anticipation of what was soon to come—seemed to me far, far beyond words. Indeed, I felt that a year's silence would not be long enough.

As the sun set upon me, I felt consoled by the sound of the ocean waves breaking along the shore. I heard the crickets sing among the reeds and dune grass. I saw swallows dart in and out of the shadows and ghost crabs the color of the sand scuttle sideways across the beach. And I thought: *What terrible, cruel beasts we humans were.* I saw us as a species of Cyclops stalking the earth in rage and hate, unworthy of our Maker's bounty. How could I continue to live among them?

I turned my attention back to the red glow of the departed sun and the sound of the wind, water, and gulls. I shut my eyes and let the sounds and the warm sand calm me. Then, all at once, I felt gentle hands upon me.

I looked up to find Martha. She smiled tentatively. "May I sit by you?" she inquired. "I think Eliza comes as well."

"Certainly."

She sat down by my side and looked out toward the water.

"Wait you for the ship? It may be quite late when it finally arrives."

"Not particularly," I said. "I wait for peace. And wisdom. And the absence of pain."

"You may have to wait a long while yet, as will we all."

Eliza came up to us then; she told us that Johnny was asleep in the house. "I saw Martha leave and had no wish to be alone," she said. "I daren't stay long, though."

"Oh," said Martha, "I'm sorry. I didn't think—"

"I'm quite all right," Eliza assured her. "And Johnny sleeps—for the moment."

A sudden gust of wind whipped my hair across my face. I pulled it back. I had no thought of telling Eliza what I knew about Martha. I saw no point in sharing the truth with her. Of the three of us, she was the most helpless, and therefore the most vulnerable. Had she known that Martha was a target for death, she could not have remained long under our roof, for Johnny's sake if not her own. Where else had she to go?

Martha had held herself erect as a general all afternoon. Indeed, when I recall her composure, I believe it no hyperbole to say that I considered her one of the greatest women of our generation. But though she could bear danger, retribution, exposure, and even rejection, the thought of my brother's departure was too much for her.

"Oh, I cannot bear it," she said, buckling down to the sand as if seized by cramps. She curled into a ball and covered her head with her hands. "No, it is too much. I cannot bear it."

"Come now," I said, lifting her hands away from her face, "you have borne far worse. He shall return, and you shall marry and have sixteen children, and Bessie shall be run off her feet, and Giles shall have to invent a new sort of carriage to seat you all."

She grasped my hand hard as I comforted her, stroking her head until she calmed.

Finally, Martha opened her eyes and looked up at me. "I might be able to bear it, Lizzie, if—"

"If what, dearest?"

"If I knew *you* still loved me. It is a selfish, sinful wish. I know myself to be unworthy of love."

I thought about her words and everything I had discovered. I leaned my head on her shoulder and stared out to sea, my hand still clasping hers.

"Who am I to judge you, Martha? There are times in the affairs of men where right and wrong are not knowable except by our Maker. I'm grieved for Star and for you, too deeply to speak of it. But I still love you. I always shall. On some long winter night, when peace comes, we shall read the story of Moses together, for he, too, had a death upon his conscience, yet went on to achieve God's forgiveness."

Whether Eliza thought this conversation odd I know not, for she asked not a single question. Later, when we had all returned home, we would tell her near everything. For now, though, we sat in silence, the three of us staring out to sea, until a dusky darkness rolled across us.

Eliza rose to leave. Not wishing her to walk the path alone, we got up and accompanied her.

"Dear Eliza," I began. "I hope you do not think that because so much has happened here that we have forgotten your despair. I know I do not. Not for a moment."

"And it is my hope, Lizzie, that you do not think my despair forbids me to rejoice in your happiness. Indeed, only knowing of your happiness shall keep me from utter despair."

"My what?" I suddenly turned and looked at Eliza, thinking I had not heard her correctly.

"*Your* happiness, Lizzie."

"Oh." I smiled, suddenly divining her drift. "I'm not built for happiness such as you speak of."

"Are you not?" Eliza's eyes shone steadily through the shadows.

48

TIME SHALL UNFOLD WHAT PLAITED CUNNING HIDES.
—King Lear

AUGUST 2, 1779. "THE SHIP! HARRY'S SHIP has arrived!" we cried.

Worn out by the terrible events of the previous day, Eliza was dead to the world. We decided to let her sleep. We ran down the stairs, nearly tripping and falling on our heads, then out to the back of the house, from which we could easily see my brother's ship—full three masts, bowsprit and jibboom, then a scurrying of silent bodies to furl the sails. I then saw four—or was it five?—men descend upon a dinghy and make their way toward us in the low moonlight. The ship, moving very slowly, crept out of sight.

Recalling that we were still in our shifts, Martha and I ran back to the house to ready ourselves for visitors. When the men finally arrived, we were primly dressed and sitting in the kitchen with the kettle on the boil like two good little spinsters. My brother came in with four others, one of whom was Mr. Miller.

Seeing us sitting calmly in the kitchen, Harry did not know which of us to embrace first. Martha solved his dilemma by springing up from her calm pose and running headlong toward him.

"Oh, Harry!" she cried.

Coming from Martha, Harry did not seem to mind the name he had, earlier that summer, thought too childish for him. He buried his head in her breast.

Mr. Miller remained by the front door. He glanced at me, and I at him, and such was my emotion upon seeing him—the real man this time and not the poseur—that I was overcome. To my changed eyes, he now appeared tall, quite noble, and full of dangerous conviction. There was none of that levity about him that had once allowed me to dismiss him as shallow, if charming. Had he ever laughed about my mincing gait? Had he ever requested I show him how to bake a cake? Helped me stir it? Impossible.

He may yet hang, I thought. But at least it would not be on Washington's command. No, quite the opposite.

Behind our brothers stood three other men, drably dressed, their faces streaked with tar, naught but their pewter buttons shining beneath their cloaks in the wavering candlelight.

Harry introduced them. There was the *Cantabrigian*'s captain, Captain John Wiles; Colonel William Livingston of New York; and Colonel Joseph Palmer. This last I had known slightly in my early days in Braintree, before he had left for the South with his regiment. After the war, I would have occasion to get to know him better at his estate at Germantown. For now, I merely gawked at him: he was tall and looked every bit the haughty officer. Later, he revealed himself to be a tenderhearted lover of dogs and children. All of these men were high-ranking officers of the Continental Army, sent by Washington himself.

"Lizzie," began my brother, a note of apology in his voice, "we need a place to rest for what remains of this night. We dare not expose ourselves even so far as the colonel's house."

"Say no more," I replied. Martha and I busied ourselves laying pallets about. From my kitchen window, the men could take turns watching for *La Sensible*.

When our distinguished guests were crowded around the kitchen table with their tea, Colonel Palmer thought to extend to us the information the men already held:

"*La Sensible* approaches Boston," he said.

"No!" I exclaimed.

"Is it true?" Martha asked.

The colonel nodded. "It was sighted before we left, and it has been confirmed that John Adams and John Quincy are aboard."

"Dear Abigail!" I cried, involuntarily placing a hand over my mouth.

"Not a word must come from this house," Colonel Palmer warned. "A simple word or deed in the wrong ears could spell death for them, and ourselves."

"Sir, we shall not stir," Martha affirmed, looking at me.

Colonel Palmer nodded respectfully at Martha, for he must have known who and what she was.

After some silence, I rose. "We should retire. Please make free to use my home as your own. Should you need us, don't hesitate to wake us."

"Good night, dearest sister." Harry embraced me. He took Martha's hand, looked at her long and hard, and said, "Yes, you should sleep now, while you can."

Thomas Miller neither said a word nor glanced in our direction, but continued to stare out the window as he paced the room.

We excused ourselves and retired together to my chamber, where Johnny lay sprawled on his back, taking up nearly the entire bed with his long, outstretched limbs. We gently righted him and piled ourselves alongside, having given up the second chamber's bed to the men. But sleep was not to be had; I managed only to doze for a while.

"You're snoring." Martha shoved me. Eliza was asleep on the other side of her. It was close and hot.

"I certainly am not snoring," I murmured.

"You do not hear yourself when you are asleep," she said and poked me.

"*Shhh.* They will hear you," I said, eyes still closed.

"Why, is there someone you do not wish to know you snore in your sleep?"

"Martha, hush!"

Soon thereafter, I felt her sit up. "It is hopeless. I rise."

She got up, dressed, and went to feed the animals—what few were left to us after the bloodletting. Martha knew it would be some days before I could approach the barn. The poor animals were ready and waiting for her, as it was just past four and the sky over the ocean already grew light. I soon rose as well, as silently as I could, allowing Eliza to sleep.

Previously I had been too shocked to feel, but on this early morning I stifled tears at the thought of Star out there somewhere, beyond my sight, stiffening on Mr. Billings's cart. At least *he* felt no pain, I consoled myself. It was in this grieving state that I sensed someone approach from the shadows. The rustle frightened me half to death.

"Elizabeth."

I turned to find Mr. Miller. "You gave me a start," I said.

"You're up early."

From the looks of him, fully dressed, with only his face washed of its dark camouflage, I discerned that he had not slept at all.

"Martha said I was snoring."

"And were you?"

"I deny it utterly."

He smiled slightly and turned his head, gazing off into my fields, which were just beginning to lighten beneath the rising sun.

"Let us walk there"—he nodded to my garden—"for what I have to say is for your ears alone."

"If you like," I said, with some trepidation. I followed him behind the barn to where the orchard boughs hung heavy with ripening fruit. Mr. Miller stopped under one such bough and stood before me. His hands hung by his sides, his head bowed.

"There is something I cannot get out of my mind," he began. "How you have suffered—" He paused, apparently unable to continue. He pressed his fingers against a lowered forehead. "You have suffered loss, privation, hostility, and deceit. Throughout, I have observed how you have kept your head, taught another, and given shelter to a third. Unbearable has been the thought that I—"

Again, he was unable to continue.

"That you—?"

"—that I might have added to your suffering, which you've borne as few men could have." Then he said, "I beg you now forgive me."

Reader, I had already forgiven him. I found, to my surprise, that I could bear anything quite easily, so long as I did not have to suffer my previous disdain for him. Still, I could not resist saying, "And why should a woman not suffer as much as a man during these times?"

He did not come back with his usual rejoinder, and I was all too swiftly reminded that this was a new Thomas Miller, one whom I could not presume to know, one whose feelings I could not predict. I feared I had given offense.

But Mr. Miller, glancing once at me, lowered his head as if to consider my question seriously. At last he replied, "Many have done, and no doubt shall continue to do so. But not all women can bear such suffering. And it is not all women that I care about. None have borne it as you have. Oh, Lizzie!" He grasped my hands in his. "I'm glad you know the truth. You think it torture to *love* the enemy—but you cannot know the torture it was to *play* the enemy, to play the fool, knowing every moment how you despised me!"

"I *wished* to despise you, yes," I considered, allowing him to keep my hands in his, "but somehow I never could. Dare I hope that the silly boy you played was not entirely an act, and that somewhere you still harbor him? For it is a rare man that retains the freedom of the boy, however infuriating. No, while I despised your politics, I could not despise him." Here, I rolled my eyes at that ne'er-do-well who had made himself at home in my Cambridge parlor.

"If that concerns you, rest assured he still exists. But these rough times are not auspicious for him."

During this conversation, Mr. Miller had gradually, almost imperceptibly, been closing the distance between us. The hands that had taken mine were now above my elbows and fast approaching my bare shoulders.

"I'm relieved to hear it," I said. "No, I believe I suffered most when—" Now it was my turn to hesitate.

"When . . . ?"

"When for a moment I thought you loved Eliza. Oh, I despised you then."

"Jealous, eh?" He smiled. "Ah, so that was it. I recall being angry with you then for the first time. I had no thought of your being jealous, only petty and spiteful."

I shuddered. "You cannot know how I despised myself for that! Envy is the Devil himself."

"I never meant to make you feel so. But it is wonderful to hear!" He smiled openly now. "You must have loved me somewhat, even then." He moved closer to me, hopeful as he had not been before.

"Fighting myself at every turn," I said, frustrated at the memory. "Yes, I knew it as the saddest fact of my life when you ran me down outside the tavern."

"I can never forget that kiss." He laughed, pulling me closer to him. "You in your mustache and that appalling vest!"

"Oh, do not remind me of my foolishness. An auspicious beginning, indeed!"

"Never apologize for that, Lizzie. It was the most wonderful kiss from the bravest woman. And I should like to repeat it now . . ."

Here he kissed me tenderly, unencumbered by either resistance or an unsavory mustache.

We walked then through the orchards, not saying much, but every minute or so asking the remaining few questions that lingered in our minds.

"And was that you at the Golden Ball, after all?"

"It was. I felt compelled to follow you wherever you went. I knew there to be danger, though you did not."

"And the Rose and Crown? You were not there on—"

"Orders? Oh, no." He smiled. "I learned little in the taverns, though I spoke with a number of men. I made myself out to be a gambler at cards. In this noble pursuit, I lost what little family money I had inherited. We had long suspected Mr. Cleverly of his pseudonymous involvement, and others as well. I daren't say how we learned things. When we have won . . ."

"Not if?"

"No, we shall win. And when we have, I shall reveal everything to you. Oh, dearest Lizzie, how good it is to finally speak to you! *You*, as yourself, and I as myself."

"And who *are* you, Thomas Miller?" I looked up at him inquiringly. "What are your likes and dislikes? What are your particular habits? Your favorite foods? You see, I know nothing about you. I fear that if I fell in love with you as a despised Tory, I am sure to faint dead away when I learn of Thomas Miller the hero, intimate acquaintance of His Excellency himself."

" 'He was a man, take him for all in all,' " he said, his voice tinged with sadness.

I looked up at him. "You have read *Hamlet*?"

"Oh, Elizabeth." He laughed. "I am not so well read as Mr. Cranch, I admit, but I'm not an ignoramus because also a soldier. Like all good Cambridge boys, I took my degree at Harvard and planned to pursue the law before our Troubles began. Then I could not sit idly by. And when the colonel asked me on behalf of

Washington himself whether I would accept a most delicate position, I felt it my duty to accept."

"Oh, do not *mention* the colonel to me. I reserve the right to
be furious at him for some time yet. He fooled us all with his jovial
drinking and vulgar gossiping. He had us all convinced that you
were the worst of all our enemies. Even Abigail was fooled!"

Here, not wishing to join our friends just yet, we stopped by
the side of the barn. My hand was still in his.

"Every night I thought of you, knowing I could not love you,
knowing that I did. Of all the things I suffered, I should say that
was the worst. And I had no one to share my feelings with. Abigail
thought you the worst sort of traitor. Martha needed me to believe
it as well. When she warned me against you—it was with a ferocity
I had not yet seen in her. Only your sworn promise to me gave me
any hope at all. I could not entirely let go of that promise, even
when all hope had gone."

"It's over now." He pulled me close, and his hands, which had
begun in mine, made their way around me at last. "Think no more
of it, darling. All those secrets and lies are behind us. But, Lizzie"—
he pulled away from me to have a better look—"can you truly love
again? I have never loved before, but you—"

"Yes, I have loved. I loved Jeb. We were so young. He was the
best sort of man. He taught me that I could love. Without that, I
should have had no hope at all. But I'm just now thinking . . ." I
hesitated.

"What is it, dearest?"

"Well, I suppose if we are to be together, you must learn to
tolerate the language of midwifery."

"I'm not squeamish, or entirely ignorant, if that's what you
mean."

"Well, I was thinking just now that perhaps the heart is made
of the same stuff as the womb. It can stretch and may easily be
reused."

I placed a finger to my chin and must have looked like a true philosopher when, grinning involuntarily, I said, "Indeed, I find it quite a miraculous thing that I love you now quite as much as if I had never loved before."

Here I close the scene, for it is not meet that every scene be described.

•   •   •

It was a day of great joy but also of fearful waiting. Our nerves were jangled, our bodies tense, awaiting this decisive encounter. Who besides Cleverly would pop out of the gloom to harm John Adams and his son upon their homecoming? Would it be those we knew, or strangers?

The long day of waiting passed in various pursuits, and as the sun descended, the men finally took their leave of us. My eyes followed Thomas—in my mind, "Mr. Miller" had begun to disappear—as he gathered his compatriots for departure. He was focused on his task. Only once did I catch him looking in my direction. He smiled, and his amber eyes shone for a moment, but then he moved on with the business at hand.

Martha was less reserved. As my brother prepared to depart, she ran up to him and embraced him.

"May God keep you," she said.

"Let us go to the colonel's," I said to Martha. "To be among society might help us all bear up."

The men left for their ship, thanking us profusely and kissing our hands as the sky darkened over the dunes. All then grew quiet. As we made our way silently to the great house, I heard a lone dog howl.

That same afternoon, little Johnny took his first steps. Eliza was so overcome with emotion—joy at his steps, grief that his father had not been free to see them—that she seemed almost wooden, reminding me unhappily of her mother as we walked together, Johnny riding joyously on Martha's shoulders.

Arriving at the colonel's, Mrs. Quincy embraced us all and bade us enter. She had a supper prepared of tea, cod stew, and a fine apple cake. At first I felt too sick with tension to eat; we all did. Not wishing to be rude, however, we soon availed ourselves of this bounty and found it a welcome distraction.

After supper, the colonel began a game of Memory with his wife, but neither Martha nor I had the nerves to concentrate. We paced, holding on to one another. From time to time, we peered out the windows onto the descending dunes and the splendid view of the sea. From the window in the dining room, with the fine summer moon rising brightly, one could make out the contours of my barn and cottage.

When we grew tired of pacing, we stood by the window and discussed among ourselves how the ambush might occur. I burned with questions. Surely Martha, having known about the plot longer than I, had formed some opinion as to how the villains would go about it. The shore below the colonel's house and my farm was vast, stretching for miles. Tall grass wavered upon rolling dunes, and winds startled swallows and plovers from their nests in gray-white clouds. From whence would they begin this ambush?

There were several possibilities. A party could come down by boat from the north, but this would lack the element of surprise, for surely they would be seen. They could not come up from the coves at Black's Creek, since those presumably still hidden on Harry's ship would report them. That left the dunes themselves, or the very land where we now stood.

"It seems impossible to surprise anyone arriving by sea on this shore," I said, attempting to convince myself.

"It would be difficult," Martha agreed, "but hardly impossible. The men would have to lie in wait in among the dunes. They are probably there now." Whereupon she nodded toward the window, to the wavering grasses below.

"Ugh!" I shivered. "Must you say such things?"

"But you'll admit it is the most likely scenario."

Suddenly, the colonel was upon us. "What do you ladies speak of?"

"How the villains plan their attack," I said directly. "Have you any knowledge?"

The old illusion of his innocence, or ours, had been broken. We now conversed freely and nearly as equals, though I still harbored some anger against him—not so much for his deceit as for my own naïveté.

"No. I wish I did, certainly." The colonel gazed out his window, hands grasped behind his back. He scanned the waters and the dunes. "In among these trees there, probably," he concluded finally, nodding at the woodlands to the side of the very house in which we stood. We had not considered these woods, being rather far off and to the left of the beach where *La Sensible* would anchor.

"That's a very long way. Surely our men will see them descending the hill," I said.

"Indeed, indeed," said the colonel, turning away but seeming much concerned. "Yet, they may have a signal to those below. Yes, that's how I should do it."

Then, perceiving his wife approaching, he cast us a guilty look. Unlike us, Ann remained in the dark about certain particulars. It was the colonel's wish.

"What do you all discuss so earnestly?" She smiled. She held on a plate half a dozen tiny cordial glasses filled with amber liquor. The colonel reached to take one, then thought better of it and offered them to us without partaking himself.

"What do we discuss?" He turned to us, at a loss for a ready lie. He left it a question to which, awkwardly, not one of us had an answer.

"Oh, merely that it looks to be a very clear night," Martha commented ambiguously.

We sipped our sweet wine in silence. Poor Ann, apparently used to being shut out of conversations, asked nothing more.

For four years, we had lived in dread of such a night as this: war not beyond our town, but in our own yards. Citizens killing citizens—or gentle horses in their stables. *Civil* war. Neither Martha nor I could be in any doubt that the men we loved would now fight. We might now lose them. But we didn't dare utter such words aloud.

Johnny entertained us by crawling around and lurching from chair to chair like a drunken sailor. But he soon grew exhausted and began to cry, not knowing he was tired. It was Martha, needing something to do, who took him to bed in Dr. Franklin's chamber, returning half an hour later.

"He sleeps at last." She sighed. "He senses our excitement and hates to miss anything."

Midnight came and went, but no one spoke of retiring. It was a clear, fine night. A full, bright moon meant that we dared not go abroad for fear of being perceived. At one o'clock, the colonel was still playing at cards when, looking past him through the window, I spied the bow of a vessel pulling slowly, silently, sails furled, into our port.

"It's here! It's arrived! John Adams is here!"

The colonel ran for his spyglass. He looked through it. But even with the naked eye, one could see someone cast off the anchor. Then nothing. It seemed an eternity. No doubt ignorant of the ambush, the sailors on board awaited an all-clear signal from their captain before helping these two illustrious citizens ashore.

What happened next was so extraordinary that I fear I have not the talent to describe it:

In the darkness, lit only by Nature herself, a dinghy was lowered quietly into the lapping water. I took the spyglass from the colonel. By and by, I saw a man and a tall boy standing in wait for the captain's help; others shook their hands. Some even bowed before the famous Braintree patriot and his son. The captain nodded, and two sailors helped each of them into the dinghy.

We had extinguished all but one candle so as not to be seen, but we did not want the house to appear uninhabited, either. Thus, by the light of one solitary candle flickering behind us, we stood all in a row by the open veranda doors, silent as shades from another world.

Now they approached; John rowed. He spoke quietly to John Quincy. His voice carried, though we could not make out what he said.

Martha asked me to pass the spyglass. I handed it to her. When the dinghy reached the shore, John Quincy stepped out to steady the dinghy for his father. The boy had grown quite tall, the size of a man. Stout Mr. Adams, with the dinghy wobbling to and fro, stepped into water up to his knees and helped his son pull the dinghy safely ashore. They both turned and waved silently to the men on *La Sensible*.

At last they began to head up the beach toward the footpath. They had brought nothing with them—no parcels or trunks, but only what little hand luggage they could carry. No doubt their trunks would follow by the safer light of day.

None of us breathed. We saw them reach the path and disappear into the dune grass. For a long moment, I thought that perhaps my friends had been mistaken about an ambush. There was no movement, no disturbance of any kind. The likelihood of such a thing seemed, for a moment, quite far-fetched.

We heard a whistle. Then, from the leftmost point of our vision—the dense, dark brush near the house—emerged a band of men with painted faces and a single fiery torch. They were silent, organized to the very breaths they took. They raced toward the path, and I involuntarily gasped. The colonel had been right about that patch of woods.

For several seconds, I was convinced, as we all were, that our men had not left their ship in time and had bungled the rescue. Ann Quincy turned away, unable to stifle a cry. One of the bandits actually turned at the sound of this human noise above the dunes. We all believed that John Adams and his child would perish within seconds.

Eliza exclaimed, "Oh, God, I cannot watch. I can't!"

She ran to be with Mrs. Quincy when, suddenly, from the right of our vision, an overturned dinghy upon the beach came preternaturally to life. As if by levitation, it lifted itself up. Out came half a dozen men, crawling like sea creatures from a shell.

I gasped at the boldness of this plan. They must have been hiding beneath that overturned dinghy for hours. We had seen it, of course, but it was so much a part of the landscape that we had not given it a thought. Luckily, they had. They had even dug out the sand beneath the dinghy to make room for the six of them.

Two of our men instantly lit torches, while four others raised ready muskets. Then I heard one shout, "You are undone! Unmask yourselves!"

At that moment, we lost sight of the scene as the entire assemblage passed below the dunes. Three rough musket shots popped and spluttered in the night air, but we saw not from whence those shots came or whom they had found to destroy.

Martha and I shrieked and grabbed each other. For a moment I thought we would both sink to the floor. Not knowing which of our men had been hit was beyond our endurance. But we did not sink down, nor was it in our power to remain where we were. We pushed open the back door and ran, heedless of the colonel's frantic shouts.

At first, I could see nothing at all. As we approached, we heard voices, and our eyes adjusted to the dark. Then the assemblage emerged from behind the dunes. Hardly breathing, we saw our men. They were alive and had surrounded the traitorous band.

"They live. They live, Martha."

"And yet, look, oh, look!" She grasped my wrist hard and pointed.

Still holding his rifle, Thomas Miller appeared to sway unsteadily on his feet. Another moment, I feared, and he might fall down. He did not fall, however, but merely bent forward at the waist, wiping the sweat and tar from his face with the back of a sleeve.

"Oh, he is hurt! Martha!" I moved as if I would climb down the dunes to them, but Martha arrested me.

"Don't be a fool. You cannot aid him now."

She was right. There was nothing I could do but watch in agony.

The traitors stood with their hands in the air, and though their faces were painted, I could see one man unmistakably.

"Do you see him, Martha?" I cried. "Do you see Cleverly?"

"Benjamin Thompson, you mean," she replied. "And regard who stands next to him. Isn't that your man, Whitcomb?"

"Oh, Lord. It is," I said. For several weeks this boy had lived on my own property, just outside my open door. I shivered.

With wrists now roughly tied behind him, the man we had known as Mr. Cleverly stared up suspiciously into the darkness, as if somehow he knew we were there. Had I dared to move closer, I would have spat in his face.

As colonels Palmer and Livingston prepared to row the prisoners out to the *Cantabrigian*, John Adams and John Quincy Adams arrived at our door flanked by Harry and Thomas. So anxious was I over Thomas, however, that I hardly stopped to greet Mr. Adams or his son.

I ran to Thomas's side as he held himself upright in the door-frame. A manservant aided me, and together we brought him to a sofa in the parlor.

Behind me, I heard many scuffling footsteps, then shouts of joy. I turned momentarily from Thomas to look into the hall: Mr. Adams and his son had just entered and were being swarmed by an overcome Colonel Quincy and his wife.

John Quincy looked shaken. Something had just happened, but it had all transpired so quickly that he doubted his own under-standing. He turned to his father inquiringly. "Father, who were those people below? Were they bandits?"

"By and by, John," said his father, placing a hand on his son's arm. "By and by." It is entirely possible that John Adams knew not what had nearly befallen them.

I turned my attention to Thomas. Blood oozed from his waist-coat and ran onto the sofa's red damask, darkening it.

"Some cloths, please, Martha," I said. Martha reacted quickly and soon came to my side.

"You are bleeding," I told Thomas, affecting a calm demeanor.

"It is but a scratch," he replied, grimacing and holding his side.

His face was white and sweaty. I did not like his color, and my throat grew dry with fear. But I said, as if bemused, "Allow me to determine whether you speak the truth. One never knows with you."

I removed his vest and shirt and gently cleansed the area around the wound. I then dropped to my hands and knees to exam-ine the wound more closely. It looked to be the work of a knife. As gently and slowly as I could, I spread apart the wound and scoured the area with my eyes, looking for anything that might remain to fester, such as a scrap of cloth from his shirt or vest. I had to blot the blood away constantly, until one of the Quincys' servants was drenched through with running back and forth to the fire. In the end, I had gone through a dozen rags and half a dozen buckets of water.

At last, satisfied that I had cleaned out the wound as thoroughly as possible, I asked Martha to run back to our house for bandages, honey, and cider vinegar, all of which thankfully remained to us from the night of the vandalism.

Thomas had been silent during my ministrations; he seemed to take the opportunity to rest, perhaps to doze, though my gentle touch might have been painful at times. But at the application of the honey and vinegar he sniffed, opened his eyes, and said, "Are you making a salad of me?"

"Lie quietly," I commanded.

Half an hour later, cleanly bandaged and dressed in a good shirt of Colonel Quincy's, Mr. Miller attempted to stand up, but I gently pushed him back down. He took my hand and whispered, "Lizzie."

I held back my reply. No, I would not accept his tenderness on this night. On this night he was still a soldier, still in danger—as was I, of losing him.

It appeared, by Mr. Adams's exhausted countenance, that our great statesman had no wish to tarry. However, the colonel quietly asked for a word and ushered him down the hall, where they would not be overheard. I rose and followed them to the door that gave out onto the hill facing the sea. The colonel whispered something lost to my hearing, to which John Adams replied, "But how did you all know of my arrival tonight? It was a well-guarded secret."

Once again, the colonel whispered something. Then, perceiving me standing there, he turned to me. "Mr. Adams, you must know Elizabeth Lee Boylston."

I curtsied, deeply moved. I knew myself to be in the presence of a very great man. I did not believe he could know how much his wife had meant to me during all these years of his absence, how fervently I had wished him a safe return for her sake.

"Oh, yes. 'Lizzie,' Abby calls you. I've heard a good deal about you. You've been a great comfort to her in my absence. Yet your life cannot have been easy these years?"

"No," I admitted. "But then—whose has?" I attempted a smile.

There was something touching about the way he had phrased his thought as a question. Mr. Adams passed a pale hand over his face. His eyes sought out his son, and, finding him, he bade him approach.

"Would you like some refreshment, John, Master John?" Mrs. Quincy approached us and placed a kindly arm about John Quincy.

John Adams just looked up at his son and said simply, "I should like to go home now."

•   •   •

What Abigail experienced half an hour later, when she awoke to the unexpected sound of the colonel's carriage and three men at her door, can only be imagined. As we had kept her in ignorance of the grave and immediate danger of that day, so had she been in ignorance of his happy arrival. Oh, sweet reunion!

We returned to our cottage, holding Mr. Miller beneath his arms. We placed him upon the parlor bed, where he slept long and deep. Martha and Harry disappeared from sight, and I remained awake all night, watching Mr. Miller breathe, watching for signs of infection.

•   •   •

The following day, a bright sun dawned. Martha and I were in the kitchen when Mr. Miller hobbled toward us, wishing to join us for breakfast. I shooed him back to bed.

"One night with you, and she bosses you like a wife," Martha commented.

"I wouldn't throw stones if I were you," I said, just as Harry made his disheveled appearance.

"Why—we did nothing untoward!" Martha objected. "As you see, I never even undressed."

Now it was my turn to smirk.

"Many a babe has been conceived without a petticoat being removed," I said.

"Lizzie!" Martha exclaimed in horror, and swatted me.

•   •   •

We had kept our emotions in check before this bright morning, but not so now. The chains of reason had broken entirely clear of our swelling hearts. Like mothers who dare not name their children for fear of grievous disappointment, we had dared not name our love. But now they would live. Mr. Miller had no fever in his eyes, no redness around the wound. After clearing the breakfast dishes, I moved to bring Mr. Miller his breakfast in bed. I felt his pulse; it was strong and steady.

"You see, I live to vex you another day," Mr. Miller sat up to take his tea.

"It's a good thing," I said simply.

I had fervently wished to hide my long-suppressed joy but failed miserably: I burst into tears.

Thomas grasped my hand and he laughed most insolently at my tears. His laughter reminded me of the time he laughed at my mincing lady's steps in Cambridge.

"You fool no one with your cool demeanor, Lizzie. You are not at all hard. And you love me to distraction."

"I do." I laughed with him, wiping my tears. "I surrender."

Martha and Harry, still in the kitchen with Eliza, pretended not to have heard us, for in those days, privacy came not from an abundance of physical space, but from discreetly averted eyes and ears.

On this glorious day, we rested. We rejoiced. We took our men and bathed them, I most careful with my beloved's wound, which I anointed once more with my humble elixirs. Oh, we knew we could not long keep them: Harry would need to return to his ship. Mr. Miller would head north, to aid John Watkins. But we had them now, these men, and all our arts we heaped upon them. We washed their hair and massaged their callused hands and feet with warmed and fragrant fat. We were quite practiced at this caregiving, if not at love. And so we made them good for a life of peace among gentlewomen, if only for a single day.

Epilogue

I WOULD BE REMISS IF I WERE to leave off here and not tell you what followed upon the heels of these dramatic events.

The day after the foiled attack upon Mr. Adams, Eliza received a crushing letter from her mother. In it, Mrs. Boylston revealed that she would head to Portsmouth immediately, to locate the scoundrel who had ravished her daughter. Hearing this dreadful news, our friend left for Cambridge. Eliza would return about a week later, her situation greatly altered. She remained with us but two days, just long enough to scoop up her child and depart our hostile shores for distant lands, first upon Harry's ship and then upon others.

But the details of Eliza's story can be found in her own narrative of these times, and it is meet that I allow her to tell of them in her own words.

My brother and Thomas Miller left us, too. Harry's ship departed for New York, and Mr. Miller received a message from His Excellency that his presence was urgently requested by General Sullivan, then at Tioga, New York.

I knew not whether or when I would see my beloved again. Thus, the night before he left me, we whispered our eternal vows to each other before God.

It may strike my reader as precipitate that Mr. Miller and I declared ourselves, hardly knowing one another—that we loved on faith, as it were. I had known the real Thomas Miller but a day or two, and he had never quite known the real Elizabeth Lee. I had packed much of her away in camphor after Jeb's death. He had known Johnny Tucker, the revolting messenger boy from Weymouth, and Lizzie Boylston, the efficient midwife and farmeress. Soon, we would both discover Elizabeth Lee Boylston Miller, the woman.

●　　●　　●

On the last day with our men, neither Martha nor I spoke of departure. Instead, we took refuge in our usual pursuits and duties. It was in this state of quiet endeavor, pulling flax once more in the fields, that Abigail found us.

She had come on foot and was drenched in perspiration.

"Oh, Abigail!" I cried, rising to greet her. I fervently wished to hear her account of her reunion with husband and son. But she looked at us sternly and refused to smile or even embrace us.

"You cannot fool me," she said, "though you think you can."

"Fool you?" I began. "Fool you at what? We are, as you see, pulling flax. It is not entertaining, but it must be done."

She proceeded to pull us up off our haunches and march us inside. Once safely there, she accosted us.

"John spoke of a skirmish on the beach after he had mounted the hill toward Uncle's house. He wished not to speak of it before Johnny, but my child is not stupid. And I am not blind. I will not leave until you confess all."

Could you have but seen this tiny woman—a woman who had borne six children and farmed with her bare hands, a woman who'd believed herself widowed a dozen times or more, clothing dark with perspiration, her hair all out of its pins, glaring at us—you would have either laughed or cried at the sight.

It was what we felt like doing, too. Relief at the notion of our men's safety could not be suppressed. And so, God forgive us, we burst into laughter. We laughed and laughed, and only seeing Abigail near tears of frustration did we eventually grow sober, wipe our eyes, and divulge the full story that we had kept from her.

When we had finished, Abigail asked thoughtfully, "What if John or my boy had been killed? What if my ignorance had prevented my seeing them one final time? Could I have forgiven you for depriving me of those most precious moments?"

"'Tis for you alone to decide," I said gently. "But I for one am exceedingly glad that nothing of the sort came to pass."

There was a tense silence as Abigail mastered her anger. After what seemed an age, she said, "It seems I could not be a part of your Rebel circle, then." Martha replied, "We did not think so. Forgive us, dearest, if we were in error."

"You wished to spare me the personal danger, and the horror, perhaps, of seeing my men cut down before my eyes."

"'Tis true," I agreed. We hung our heads.

"It was also an order from Colonel Palmer himself," Martha added, taking what solace she could in the military chain of command.

Abigail came slowly toward us, her countenance softened. "I suppose I cannot blame you wishing to protect me. You did what I should have done in your place. You did what you had to do."

At her forgiveness, we crowded around her and wept together. Afterward, we sat together for tea. Abigail soon got up to leave, not wanting to be long from John or her son.

"Now you must promise that we shall be sisters for the rest of our lives, with no secrets between us."

"We promise," Martha and I said in unison.

Abigail returned home, and Martha and I went to find our men.

•　•　•

On the morning Harry left, *La Sensible* awaited, and the winds were fair. There was little for me to do but wake him and Martha and bid them dress.

We had said our good-byes, and my brother was about to push off with the dinghy, when suddenly he fell to his knees before Martha. She raised a hand to her heart in surprise. I watched in stunned silence as he grasped Martha's hands.

Martha gathered herself as if from within, becoming tighter and more erect as my brother spoke words I could not hear.

Eliza and I shuffled imperceptibly closer, the better to hear them. Harry stood up upon Martha's urging but then pulled her close and whispered something to her.

We heard only Martha's abrupt reply:

"Who can take such a creature for his wife?"

"Oh, I can. I can!" my brother cried, heedless now of those who overheard him. "Think you that *I* have not sinned these awful years? That I have not slashed men's throats, shot men through, strangled men with my bare hands, and all for what? What had they done to me?"

He bent down on one knee once more, in a pose of supplication. I gripped Eliza's hands, and we awaited her reply. Please, Lord, let it be the right one!

At last, she raised Harry up to face her. "I shall be your wife if you truly want me," she said, "for I am not strong enough to bear life without you."

A few minutes later, my brother, transformed by joy, helped Martha into the dinghy and bounded in after her, to be married immediately by his ship's captain. Cheerfully he called after me,

"Ready the house, Lizzie. Tell Bessie and Giles. For it seems we shall not shrink away to the land east of Eden. We are patriots, and it will be for God to judge us, not our fellow sinners."

And with that, my beloved brother was off to marry Martha. I considered fretfully that there would be no time for them to consummate their marriage, but then I smiled to myself and shrugged, for I knew they had already done so.

Martha returned to shore half an hour later and could not speak for her tears. We merely held her to us and wept with her.

Soon, after many embraces and promises to write, they were gone. It was not for many months, not until April of 1780, that Martha and I laid eyes upon Harry again.

As for Eliza and Johnny, it would be not months, but years. But see them we did, in the end. It was in July of 1794 that Eliza returned to Cambridge with Johnny, to bring him to Harvard.

Our reunion was, as you may imagine, of such joy as hardly to be borne. Johnny was by this time a noble lad, brilliant in spirit and manner alike. His skin was taupy, his dark hair curly and heavily pomaded. But he had fair green eyes, and the truth of his lineage could be left to silent conjecture, for in every respect he was a true gentleman.

We hugged and pinched him without mercy, and he took it as affably as a young lad possibly could. Sadly, he remembered nothing of us except those things his mother had told him. Eliza, Martha, and I took up our friendship as if no time had passed.

Two years after Eliza's return, our own John Adams was elected president. My dear friend Abigail became our country's first lady. John Quincy was off to Prussia. All was well: all was as it was meant to be. At some point during Mr. Adams's term, we three women got the idea to travel to Philadelphia, to visit with him and Mrs. Adams. Our joy at finding them so well, and so esteemed by all, may easily be imagined.

. . .

Several years into our marriage, as Thomas and I lay together in bed reminiscing about our early days, he turned to me and said, "You were a dreadful spy, you know."

"Indeed I was not."

"You were. You came to all the wrong conclusions, and when the truth stared you in the face, you would not believe it."

I cringed. "Oh, do not remind me of that terrible time!"

He smiled warmly and placed a large hand on my hip.

"I'll grant you that you tried. It was a brave, indeed a noble, effort. But a good spy must tear things apart, whereas your talent is to bring things to life. You are a woman in the best sense."

"Best sense!" I poked him. "Is there a worst sense?" But he did not reply to my teasing, and I sighed. "For so long I did not feel like a woman. I felt certain no one could see through my manly disguise, because I felt it not entirely a disguise. Abigail helped me in this, I believed."

"In what, dearest?"

"To feel less—freakish. Less alone in having an ... active ... mind. Oh, Thomas, I suppose I—I really am a woman, aren't I?"

My husband then shifted his hand to my belly, big with our third child.

"Incontrovertible proof would have it so."

Here, I slapped his hand and laughed.

. . .

But to end my story closer to where I began: the day before Mr. Adams was off again to write our first Massachusetts constitution—restless as Odysseus home from Troy—Martha and I received a visit from him. We were greatly surprised.

He came with a definite purpose, I was sure. It was how he did everything: no pursuit of his, even as a farmer, was ever casual. But what purpose could he have with me? I wondered.

It was, he informed me, to thank Martha and me on his behalf and that of his son. We attempted to protest, but he was quite firm with us. He was having none of our protestations. Two country midwives did not dare to contradict the great attorney and statesman John Adams!

Second, he wished to thank us for our work as patriots. He took our hands in his and told Martha she had made the ultimate sacrifice—the sacrifice of her self-love. Mr. Adams then turned to me and said, "As for you, Mrs. Boylston, I have heard from Abigail about your foolish exploits as a messenger boy. Johnny Tucker, was it?"

I blushed and had no ready rejoinder.

And so he came to his third purpose (he did itemize these said purposes, and in this very legalistic manner): to tell me that I could retire my mustache forthwith, for they had exposed all the members of that despicable, dangerous ring. Three men in New York had been hanged, including a wealthy merchant whose family had pleaded for him even as he mounted the scaffold.

I winced at this news, for I didn't like to hear of killing. Mr. Adams then recounted that, unfortunately, Mr. Cleverly— Benjamin Thompson—had managed to escape to England. He was soon to flee once more to Bavaria, where he lived as one Count Rumford.

Let it never be said that criminals cannot be charming and gifted. It is thanks to this evil plotter that we now have the Rumford stove. It is, I hear, a very great modern convenience, though I myself have certainly never thought to purchase one.

Finally, just as Mr. Adams was about to take his leave, he came to Purpose, the Fourth. He removed a letter from his waistcoat pocket.

"Mrs. Boylston, Miss Miller, you will wish to read this," he said. He bowed deeply to us, turned as if to leave, and then hastened back to kiss us both. He departed, and our hands lingered upon our cheeks where his illustrious lips had been.

Once he had left, Martha and I pounced upon the letter, breaking the large red seal at once. There, upon a piece of finest parchment, appeared before our eyes the following:

To the venerable Mrs. Elizabeth B. and Miss Martha M.

Dear Patriots,

Through Channels that shall go unmentioned here, I wish to congratulate you upon your very great and heroic Actions for the benefit of the Cause. I have known others of your sex to behave bravely and to give the Ultimate Sacrifice helping our soldiers on the Fields of Battle. But never have I heard tell of anything like the sustained Effort that you, Miss M., have made in conjunction with your Brother, Thomas M., to the great Good, both of your Community and our irreplaceable Leaders, one of whom indeed, you know more intimately than I. Mrs. B., I have been apprised of your guileful Bravery upon a most beloved Animal once belonged to your Husband, who fell fighting for our young Nation in one of our first and most important Conflagrations. It will no doubt be small Recompense to you, but it is a small Thing I can do to show my appreciation.

In fervent hopes that imminent Victory will make it unnecessary for you ever again to mount a Horse in Mustaches—I remain,

Your ever obedient, Geo. Washington

I dropped the parchment upon the table. Martha and I raced out of doors to the stable, where we found a beautiful young mare groomed and waiting. I buried my face in her neck. She rolled her eyes off to the side and snorted a greeting. And for years hence, when I rode my beautiful Victory, as I called her, I could tell myself that she was a gift to me from our great leader and first president, His Excellency, George Washington.

· · ·

From these heady days of danger, intrigue, and—yes—a bit of glory, we soon distanced ourselves. Our lives became easier. Goods and men reappeared, as did babes aplenty. Our days were far less dramatic and grew more mundane. Martha and I never spoke of her deeds again. We both knew that in opening that wound, she might bleed to death.

When Harry returned, he and Martha went to housekeeping in Cambridge, much to the delight of Bessie and Giles. I can only hope and presume they were able to console each other in privacy. I knew Martha to be too deep a soul to forget her sins, though I pray that in time she forgave them.

As for my own housekeeping, I was soon to have a partner in it, at least for a little while. Thomas Miller returned in May with a white feather in his hat, the mark of a brigadier general. I teased him that he was now too tall to fit through my cottage door. But, oh, I was proud to bursting! He would not tell me the details of his campaigns then, but waited near a year before divulging them for fear of causing me anguish.

Mr. Miller found me a great deal larger than when he had left me. Reader, do not be shocked: such was often the case in those days. We had not the luxury of ceremony. For me, this event was all the more joyous since, clearly, my doubts regarding my fertility, which I had entirely believed, had been entirely mistaken.

Thomas needed to return to the South, but before he did so, he arranged for Parson Wibird to marry us. It was a small ceremony, with only Abigail and the Quincys as witnesses. No one was under any illusion as to my altered physical state; being my dearest friends, however, they had the good decorum to pretend that it was not so.

After the ceremony, we returned to Colonel Quincy's, where we were jolly and where a toast was made to our future health and happiness. In the few weeks I lived with my new husband before he left to join General Washington, I learned many things I had not known about Thomas when I fell in love with him.

Thomas Crane Miller was a gentleman of Loyalist parents. He had studied at Harvard, near the top of his class, and had begun his legal apprenticeship in Boston when the Troubles erupted. By the time Colonel Quincy called upon him, he was ready to serve the Cause.

Although Thomas was never to practice law, he enjoyed his many conversations with John Adams regarding our new government, when Mr. Adams was in Braintree.

And yet, despite his interest in the law, like John Adams, my Tom desired first and foremost to be a good husband and farmer. Without the war, he had not that agitated ambition I had sensed earlier, and which some men possess even in peacetime. No, he loved me and the land—our land, now. He loved taking me by the hand of a morn and running out across the dunes toward the sea or toward the orchards to see how the apples fared. He loved watching me sow seeds beside him.

One day, as he was working outside, Tom came across that invention of Mr. Cleverly's, coiled serpent-like against the well.

"What is this?" he asked, picking it up by two fingers, nose wrinkled in disdain. When I told him, we agreed at once to a ritual burning, choosing to put our crops' fate in the hands of our Redeemer, unlike the man who had thought himself a god.

I returned to my midwifery, though I myself—well, very soon I would have my own babe to deliver and care for. And though I had not my beloved husband by my side when my illness came upon me that July, I had all my women friends. Susanna Brown,

Mary Cranch, and my dearest friend, Abigail, were all there to support me. Of course, I also had my midwife, Martha Miller Lee, who had, in fact, joined the Religious Society of Friends, the attendance of whose meetings were thankfully less fraught with danger than they once had been. Martha had sworn to herself and God to bring one hundred lives into the world for each of those she had taken. She has been as good as her word.

Martha safe delivered me of a boy and four other children besides. She herself went on to have six of her own, though one died soon after birth. And when, finally, John and Abigail, our president and first lady, occupied the newly built President's House on the Potomac, we visited them, and we also met His Excellency at Mount Vernon. He was a very tall, shy man of few words and great virtue. He remembered us quite well, though our actions were by then many years in the past.

As for his letter, we dared not frame it for the world to see. We kept it safe in a box, and dry, amid all our other great and good bounty in the cellar: pompions and apples, oats and corn, wool and tow, and great barrels of dried tomatoes. Occasionally, we—me, Martha, and our husbands—would take it out to gawk at it, read it again, and hug each other in gratitude that such a time had come and gone. We never did tell another soul or boast of it. It was enough for us to know it was there, in so many words.

E.L.B.M., October 19th, early morning, 1818, Peacefield. Having lovingly washed the body of Abigail Adams, as I promised her to do long ago.

Acknowledgments

A HISTORICAL NOVEL WOULD BE DIFFICULT TO write without the help of many people. First, I would like to thank Dr. Edward Fitzgerald, executive director of the Quincy Historical Society, for giving me my first tour of Quincy, Massachusetts, originally called Braintree. Also, Ms. Leah Walczak, regional site manager for Historic New England, for granting me a private tour of the Josiah Quincy house, where several important scenes of the novel take place. The Massachusetts Historical Society allowed me to see the diaries of Abigail's sister Betsy Smith, and their excellent online publication of the Adams letters and diaries was a godsend.

To create the setting of *The Midwife's Revolt*, I needed to become well versed in a number of arcane fields: cookery, soldiering, farming, horse care, weaving, herbals, and early midwifery. Old Sturbridge Village helped me visualize many of these activities. I would also like to thank the following authors for writing their inspiring histories: David McCullough for *John Adams* and *1776*; and Laurel Thatcher Ulrich for *A Midwife's Tale: The Life of Martha Ballard, Based on Her Diary, 1785–1812*.

So many people helped with the manuscript. Carol Daynard and her reading group were among the novel's first readers, as were Matthew and Nancy Daynard and her reading group. Many thanks also go to Nancy for taking a superb author photo. Marty Levy, Karen Backus, and Julie Pretzat gave me much-needed words of encouragement. My father, Harold Daynard, was my biggest fan and most astute critic. Lynne and Don Flexner have supported me in innumerable ways over the years. When I thought the novel was finished, Vivian Sinder-Brown let me know that it wasn't. Finally, to my husband, Peter, who loved me and this novel from the very beginning, and supported both of us one hundred percent.

A Note from the Author

IF A HISTORICAL NOVEL DOES ITS JOB, the reader will be hard-pressed to know where fact leaves off and fiction begins. In writing *The Midwife's Revolt*, I myself confused them after a while. But it may help those who are interested for me to reveal the process by which I wove the two together.

I began my research by taking notes on a monthly calendar. This calendar ran from June of 1775 through November of 1778. Before I even knew who my characters were, I knew their world: the children who were born, the diseases that ravaged, the snow-storms that blocked the roads, the events of the war—not merely when they happened, but when they would have reached the ears of the townspeople of Braintree and Boston. Thus, on June 17, 1775, when Lizzie eventually goes off to find Jeb, I knew it was a hot day. I knew the names of the babies she was obliged to deliver that July, even in her grief. When I learned that the selectmen of Braintree had voted to remunerate its citizens for killing the crows that were threatening their food supply, I knew Lizzie and Martha would have to learn how to shoot a musket and kill the crows, for the few schillings it would earn them. This is how the actual world shaped my story and my people, much as, I suppose, it does to us real folk.

As for John and Abigail Adams and their family, I took special care to know their whereabouts and communications throughout this time period. I knew when Abigail was in Boston taking the smallpox "cure." I knew that she had a stillborn child on the day Lizzie delivers it, although this fact was not readily available: I unearthed it among the complete papers of John Adams at the Quincy Historical Society. Finally, when I have John set sail for France on February 15, 1778, I include the brief note he actually scribbled to Abigail from the frigate *Boston*.

I took more liberties with the secondary characters Josiah Quincy, Richard Cranch, Mary Cranch, Stephen Holland, George Washington, Betsy Cranch, and Mr. Cleverly (aka Benjamin Thompson). With them, fact and fiction become harder to sort out. Still, I tried to remain true to everything I knew about them, both as personalities and as actors upon an extraordinary stage. Stephen Holland was in fact a Tory counterfeiter; he was arrested at one point but escaped to the British Army. Abigail's sister Betsy was a gifted writer; here again, this "fact" made me wonder how such a large spirit might chafe inside a conventional marriage to a country parson.

Lizzie Boylston is my own creation; she is not related to any real Boylstons of Massachusetts. Her married name conveys wealth and status to me only in the most general way. Martha and Thomas Miller, Harry Lee, Eliza Boylston, Giles and Bessie are likewise entirely fictional. The plot against the Adamses—*this* plot, at least—is a figment of my imagination.

Thus, George Washington never wrote any letters to Josiah Quincy about Thomas Miller; nor, sadly, did he ever write my heroine Lizzie Boylston to congratulate her on a job well done. Of course, I take great pleasure in his having done so within the fictional world of *The Midwife's Revolt*. It was a profoundly generous gesture, and neither Lizzie nor Martha will ever forget it.

About the Author

Jodi Daynard is a writer of fiction, essays, and criticism. Her work has appeared in numerous periodicals, including the *New York Times Book Review*, the *Village Voice*, the *Paris Review*, *AGNI*, and the *New England Review*, as well as several anthologies. She is the author of *The Place Within: Portraits of the American Landscape by 20 Contemporary Writers* and the translator and editor of Gaito Gazdanov's *An Evening with Claire*. Daynard's work has received notable mentions in *Best American Essays* as well as Pushcart Prize nominations. She has taught writing at Harvard University, at MIT, and in the MFA program at Emerson College.